'Some of the most accomplished writing and page-turning reading this side of James Lee Burke. Add a cast of characters that would make Flannery O'Connor proud, and the result is remarkable'
Delta Magazine

'I haven't read a crime thriller this memorable since Grisham's *A Time to Kill*'
JC Patterson

'Masterful . . . a terrific mystery chock full of twists, turns and red herrings'
Providence Journal

'A mystery/thriller that surpasses the humdrum and rises to serious literature'
Richmond Times-Dispatch

'On the one hand, you're afraid to turn the page, on the other, *The Last Child* is one of those rare books you wish would go on forever, such is the power and the majesty of Hart's storytelling'
Book Reporter

'*The Last Child* will earn [John Hart's] place in the ranks of America's truly great authors along with Mark Twain, Harper Lee and Tennessee Williams'
Reviewing the Evidence

PRAISE FOR *DOWN RIVER*

'The story works both as a suspenseful whodunit and as a sensitive rumination on the emotional force of family dynamics'
Washington Post

'Hart explores betrayal and forgiveness in indelible prose'
Observer

'If you value Harper Lee, James Lee Burke, Truman Capote and Michael Malone, it's time to add John Hart to your bookshelves'
New York Sun

'A novel about the power of family, how it defines and follows us, no matter how far or fast we run . . . Evocative storytelling and lush prose'
Boston Globe

'Hart spins a clever mystery and keeps skilful control of his plot'
Sunday Telegraph

'Splendid . . . a beautifully constructed story of personal redemption, family secrets and murder – a small-town epic, if there is such a thing'
Booklist (starred review)

'A taut, entertaining thriller . . . there are few books published that can legitimately be called a "must-read", but this is one of them'
Chicago Sun-Times

PRAISE FOR *THE KING OF LIES*

'*Presumed Innocent* meets *Fatal Attraction*. Hart's prose is like Raymond Chandler's, angular and hard'   *Entertainment Weekly*

'Akin to the close-range gut-roiling atmosphere summoned by the legal thrillers of Scott Turow'   *New York Times*

'Smart and swift-moving . . . Hart knows his way around the courtrooms and jailhouses . . . the way that Grisham and Turow do'   *Pat Conroy*

'Nobody does hate like Southerners, and you'll find plenty of it in the characters slithering through this well-spun murder mystery . . . a gripping performance'   *People Magazine*

'A fast-paced mystery debut'   *Wall Street Journal*

'John Hart has hit a home run with his first novel, *The King of Lies*, which has garnered universal and well-deserved rave reviews'
Deadly Pleasures

THE
LAST
CHILD

THE
LAST
CHILD
JOHN HART

JOHN MURRAY

First published in Great Britain in 2009 by John Murray (Publishers)
An Hachette UK Company

First published in paperback in 2010

3

A CIP catalogue record for this title is available from the British Library

B-format ISBN 978-0-7195-2221-5
A-format ISBN 978-1-84854-101-6

Typeset in Monotype Sabon by Servis Filmsetting Ltd, Stockport, Cheshire

Printed and bound by Clays Ltd, St Ives plc

John Murray policy is to use papers that are natural, renewable and recyclable
products and made from wood grown in sustainable forests. The logging and
manufacturing processes are expected to conform to the environmental regulations
of the country of origin.

John Murray (Publishers)
338 Euston Road
London NW1 3BH

www.johnmurray.co.uk

This book is for Nancy and Bill Stanback, Annie and John Hart,
and Kay and Norde Wilson.
Parents, friends, trusted advisors.

PROLOGUE

Asphalt cut the country like a scar, a long, hot burn of razor-black. Heat had not yet twisted the air, but the driver knew it was coming, the scorching glare, the shimmer at the far place where blue hammered down. He adjusted his sunglasses and threw a glance at the big mirror above the windshield. It showed him the length of the bus and every passenger on it. In thirty years he'd watched all kinds of people in that mirror: the pretty girls and the broken men, the drunks and the crazies, the heavy-breasted women with red, wrinkled babies. The driver could spot trouble a mile away; he could tell who was fine and who was running.

The driver looked at the boy.

The boy looked like a runner.

Skin peeled from his nose, but beneath the tan he carried the sallow kind of pale that came from sleeplessness or malnutrition or both. His cheekbones made sharp blades beneath skin stretched tight. He was young and small, ten maybe, with wild hair that rose black on his head. The cut was jagged and uneven, like something he'd done himself. Frayed cloth hung from the collar of his shirt and from the knees of his jeans. The shoes were just about worn through. On his lap, he clutched a blue backpack; and whatever it held, there wasn't much of it.

He was a good-looking kid, but what struck the driver most were the boy's eyes. Large and dark, they moved constantly, as if the boy was overly aware of the people around him, the hot press of humanity typical of a broken-down bus on a sun-blasted morning in the North Carolina sand hills: a half-dozen itinerant workers, a few busted-up brawlers that looked ex-military, a family or two, some old folks, a couple of tattooed punks that huddled in the back.

The boy's eyes most often found the man across the aisle, a slick-haired sales type in a wrinkled suit and sprung loafers. There was also a black man with a creased Bible and a soda bottle tucked between his legs; he seemed to catch the kid's eye, too. In the seat behind the boy sat an old lady in a parchment dress. When she leaned forward to ask a question, the boy shook his head in a small way and answered with care.

No, ma'am.

His words rose like smoke, and the lady settled back, blue-veined fingers on the chain that held her spectacles. She looked through the window and her lenses flashed, then went dark as the road sliced into a stand of pine with shadows that pooled green beneath the limbs. The same light filled the bus, and the driver studied the man in the wrinkled suit. He had pale skin and a hangover sweat, unusually small eyes and an edginess that scraped the driver's nerves. Every minute or two, the man shifted in his seat. He crossed his legs and uncrossed them, leaned forward, then back. His fingers drummed one knee of the ill-fitting suit and he swallowed often as his gaze drifted to the boy, then flicked away, drifted again and lingered.

The driver was a jaded man, but he ran things clean on his bus. He refused to tolerate drunkenness or debauchery or loud voices. His momma raised him that way fifty years ago and he'd found no reason to change. So he kept an eye on the boy, and on the drawn, shiny man with eager eyes. He watched him watch the boy, saw him push back against the greasy seat when the knife came out.

The boy was casual about it. He pulled it from a pocket and folded the blade out with a single thumb. He held it for a moment, visible, then took an apple from his bag and sliced it in a sharp, clean motion. The smell of it rose above the travel-stained seats and the dirt-smeared floors. Even above the diesel stink, the driver caught the sharp, sweet tang of it. The boy looked once at the man's wide eyes and slick, washed-out face, then folded the knife and put it back in his pocket.

The driver relaxed and watched the road, uninterrupted, for a few long minutes. He thought that the boy seemed familiar, but the feeling passed. Thirty years. He settled his heavy frame deeper into the seat.

He'd seen so many boys.

So many runners.

Every time the driver looked at him, the boy felt it. It was a gift he had, a skill. Even with the dark shades on the driver's eyes and the big curve in the face of the mirror, the boy could tell. This was his third trip on the bus in as many weeks. He sat in different seats and wore different clothes, but guessed that sooner or later somebody would ask him what he was doing on a cross-state bus at seven o'clock on a school day. He figured the question would come from the driver.

But it hadn't happened yet.

The boy turned to the window and angled his shoulders so that no one else would try to speak to him. He watched reflections in the glass, the movements and the faces. He thought of skyscraper trees and brown feathers tipped with snow.

The knife made a lump in his pocket.

Forty minutes later, the bus rocked to a stop at a one-room gas station depot lost in the great swath of pine and scrub and hot, sandy earth. The boy made his way down the narrow aisle and dropped off the bottom step before the driver could mention that nothing but the tow truck sat in the lot, or that no grown-up was there to take possession of him, a thirteen-year-old boy who could barely pass for ten. He kept his head turned so that the sun seared his neck. He rocked the pack onto his back, and the diesel cloud rose; then the bus jerked and was rolling south.

The gas station had two pumps, a long bench, and a skinny old man in blue clothes stained with grease. He nodded from behind smudged glass but did not come out into the heat. The drink machine in the shade of the building was so old it only asked for fifty cents. The boy dug into a pocket, fingered out five thin dimes and purchased a grape soda that came out of the chute in a cold glass bottle. He popped the top, turned in the direction from which the bus had come, and started walking down the black snake of dusty road.

Three miles and two turns later, the road diminished, asphalt gone to gravel, gravel gone thin. The sign had not changed since the last time he'd seen it. It was old and abused, feathers of paint lifting to show the wood beneath: ALLIGATOR RIVER RAPTOR PRESERVE. Above the letters, a stylized eagle soared, and on its wings, the paint feathers rose.

The boy spit chewing gum into his hand and slapped it on the sign as he passed.

It took two hours to find a nest, two hours of sweat and sticker bushes and mosquitoes that turned his skin a bright, splotchy red. He found the massive tangle of limbs in the high branches of a longleaf pine that grew straight and tall from the damp soil on the bank of the river. He circled the tree twice, but found no feathers on the ground. Sunlight pierced the forest, and the sky was so bright and blue that it hurt his eyes. The nest was a speck.

He shrugged off the pack and started climbing, bark rough

4

and raw on his sunburned skin. Wary and afraid, he looked for the eagle as he climbed. A stuffed one sat on a pedestal at the museum in Raleigh, and he remembered the fierceness of it. Its eyes were glass, but its wings spanned five feet from tip to tip, its talons as long as the boy's middle finger. The beak alone could take the ears off a grown man.

All he wanted was a feather. He'd love a clean, white tail feather, or one of the giant brown feathers from the wing; but in the end, it could be the smallest feather from the softest patch, a pin feather, maybe, or one from that downy soft place beneath the shoulder of the wing.

It didn't really matter.

Magic was magic.

The higher he climbed, the more the branches bent. Wind moved the tree and the boy with it. When it gusted, he pushed his face into the bark, heart thumping and fingers squeezed white. The pine was a king of trees, so tall that even the river shrank beneath it.

He neared the top. This close, the nest was as broad as a dining room table and probably weighed two hundred pounds. It was decades old, stinking of rot and shit and rabbit parts. The boy opened himself to the smell, to the power of it. He shifted a hand, planted one foot on a limb that was weathered gray and skinned of bark. Beneath him, pine forest marched off to distant hills. The river twisted, black and dark and shining like coal. He lifted himself above the nest and saw the chicks, two of them, pale and mottled, in the bowl of the nest. They opened splinters of beaks, begging for food, and the boy heard a sound like sheets on the line when the wind got up. He risked a glance, and the eagle dropped from a perfect sky. For an instant, the boy saw only feathers, then the wings beat down and the talons rose.

5

The bird screamed.

The boy threw up his arms as talons sank into him; then he fell, and the bird—eyes yellow bright, talons hooked in his skin and in his shirt—the bird fell with him.

At three forty-seven, a bus rolled into the parking lot of the same one-room gas station depot. Pointing north this time, it was a different bus, different driver. The door clattered open and a handful of rheumatic people shuffled out. The driver was a thin, Hispanic man, twenty-five and tired-looking. He barely looked at the scrawny boy who rose from the bench and limped to the door of the bus. He didn't notice the torn clothes or the near despair on the boy's face. And if that was blood on the hand that passed the ticket over, it seemed clear that it was not the driver's business to remark upon it.

The boy let go of the ticket. He pulled himself up the stairs and tried to hold the pieces of his shirt together. The pack he carried was heavy, stuffed near to bursting, and something red stained the seams at the bottom. There was a smell about the boy, one of mud and river and something raw; but that, too, was not the driver's business. The boy pushed deeper into the gloom of the bus. He fell once against a seat back, then moved all the way to the rear, where he sat alone in the corner. He clutched the bag to his chest and pulled his feet onto the seat. Deep holes punctured his flesh and his neck was gashed; but no one looked at him, no one cared. He clutched the bag tighter, felt the heat that remained, the broken body, like a sack of shattered twigs. He pictured the small and downy chicks, alone in the nest. Alone in the nest and starving.

The boy rocked in the dark.

He rocked in the dark and wept hot, bitter tears.

CHAPTER ONE

J ohnny learned early. If somebody asked him why he was so different, why he held himself so still and why his eyes seemed to swallow light, that's what he'd tell them. He learned early that there was no safe place, not the backyard or the playground, not the front porch or the quiet road that grazed the edge of town. No safe place, and no one to protect you.

Childhood was illusion.

He'd been up for an hour, waiting for the night sounds to fade, for the sun to slide close enough to call it morning. It was Monday, still dark, but Johnny rarely slept. He woke to patrol dark windows. He rattled the locks twice a night, watched the empty road and the dirt drive that looked like chalk when the moon rose. He checked on his mom, except when Ken was at the house. Ken had a temper and wore a large gold ring that made perfect oval bruises.

That was another lesson.

Johnny pulled on a T-shirt and frayed jeans, then walked to the bedroom door and cracked it. Light spilled down the narrow hall, and the air felt used up. He smelled cigarettes and spilled liquor that was probably bourbon. For an instant, Johnny recalled the way mornings used to smell, eggs and coffee and the sharp tang of his father's aftershave. It was a good memory, so he drove it down, crushed it. It only made things harder.

In the hall, shag carpet rose stiff under his toes. The door to his mother's room hung loose in its frame. It was hollow core and unpainted, a mismatch. The original door lay splintered in the backyard, kicked off its hinges a month back when Ken and Johnny's mother got into it after hours. She never said what the argument was about, but Johnny guessed it had something to do with him. A year ago, Ken could never have gotten close to a woman like her, and Johnny never let him forget it; but that was a year ago. A lifetime.

They'd known Ken for years, or thought they had. Johnny's dad was a contractor, and Ken built whole neighborhoods. They worked well together because Johnny's dad was fast and competent, and because Ken was smart enough to respect him. Because of that, Ken had always been pleasant and mindful, even after the kidnapping, right up until Johnny's dad decided that grief and guilt were too much to bear. But after his dad left, the respect disappeared, and Ken started coming around a lot. Now he ran things. He kept Johnny's mother dependent and alone, kept her medicated or drunk. He told her what to do and she did it. Cook a steak. Go to the bedroom. Lock the door.

Johnny took it in with those black eyes, and often found himself in the kitchen, at night, three fingers on the big knife in its wooden block, picturing the soft place above Ken's chest, thinking about it.

The man was a predator, pure and simple; and Johnny's mother had faded down to nothing. She weighed less than a hundred pounds and was as drawn as a shut-in, but Johnny saw the way men looked at her, the way Ken got possessive when she made it out of the house. Her skin, though pale, was flawless, her eyes large and deep and wounded. She was thirty-three, and looked like an angel would look if there was such a thing, dark-haired and fragile and unearthly. Men stopped what they were doing when she walked into a room. They stared as if a

8

glow came off her skin, as if she might rise from the ground at any moment.

She could not care less. Even before her daughter vanished, she'd paid little attention to the way she'd looked. Blue jeans and T-shirts. Ponytails and occasional makeup. Her world had been a small, perfect place where she'd loved her husband and her children, where she'd tended a garden, volunteered at church, and sang to herself on rainy days; but no more. Now there was silence and emptiness and pain, a flicker of the person she'd been; but the beauty lingered. Johnny saw it every day, and every day he cursed the perfection that graced her so completely. If she were ugly, Ken would have no use for her. If she'd had ugly children, his sister would still sleep in the room next to his. But she was like a doll or something not quite real, like she should be in a cabinet with a lock on it. She was the most beautiful person Johnny had ever known, and he hated that about her.

Hated it.

That's how much his life had changed.

Johnny studied the door to his mother's room. Maybe Ken was in there, maybe not. His ear pressed against the wood, and breath caught in his throat. Normally, he could tell, but sleep had dodged him for days, and when he finally crashed, he crashed hard. Black and still. Deep. When he did wake, it was with a start, like he'd heard glass break. That was at three o'clock.

He stepped back from the door, uncertain, then crept down the hall, and the bathroom light hummed when he flicked the switch. The medicine cabinet stood open and he saw the pills: Xanax, Prozac, some blue ones, some yellows. He picked up a bottle and read the label. Vicodin. That was new. The Xanax bottle was open, pills on the counter, and Johnny felt the anger

9

fill him up. The Xanax helped Ken come down after a night with the good stuff.

That was his term.

The good stuff.

Johnny closed the bottle and walked out of the bathroom.

The house was a dump, and he reminded himself that it was not really theirs. Their real house was clean and kept up. It had a new roof that he'd helped to install. He'd gone up the ladder every day of spring vacation, passed shingles to his dad, and held nails in a tool belt that had his name scratched into it. It was a good house, with stone walls and a yard that boasted more than dirt and broadleaf weed. It was only a few miles away, but felt farther, a different neighborhood with cared-for homes on big, green lots. The place was steeped in memory, but the bank owned it now. They gave his mother some papers and put a sign in the yard.

This was one of Ken's rentals. He had about a hundred, and Johnny thought this was probably the worst, a crappy dump way out on the edge of town. The kitchen was small, with green metal and scuffed linoleum that turned up in the corners. A bulb burned above the stove and Johnny turned a slow circle. The place was disgusting: butts in a saucer, empty bottles, and shot glasses. The mirror lay flat on the kitchen table and Johnny saw how white powder residue caught the light. The sight of it spread cold in his chest. A rolled-up hundred dollar bill had fallen to the floor. Johnny picked it up, smoothed it out. He'd not had a decent meal in a week and Ken was snorting coke with a hundred.

He picked up the mirror, wiped it off with a wet towel, and hung it back on the wall. His father used to look in that mirror, and Johnny could still see how he worked at his tie on Sundays, his fingers large and stiff, the tie unforgiving. He only wore his suit for church, and he'd get embarrassed when he caught his son watching. Johnny could see it: the sudden red flush and then the reckless smile. "Thank God for your mother," he'd say, and then she'd tie the knot for him.

His hands at the small of her back.

The kiss and the wink that came after.

Johnny wiped the mirror again, then straightened it, tweaked it until it hung just right.

The door to the front porch moved stiffly, and Johnny walked out into the damp, dark morning. A streetlamp flickered fifty yards down the road. Headlights crested a distant hill.

Ken's car was gone, and Johnny felt a shameful, sweet relief. Ken lived across town in a big house with perfect paint, large windows and a four-car garage. Johnny took a deep breath, thought of his mother bent over that mirror, and told himself that she was not that far gone. That was Ken's deal, not hers. He forced his hands to unclench. The air was scrubbed, so he concentrated on that instead. He told himself that it was a new day, that good things could happen; but mornings were bad for his mother. There was a moment when her eyes opened, a flash before she remembered that they'd never found her only daughter.

Johnny's sister.

His twin.

Alyssa was born three minutes after Johnny, and they'd been as similar as nonidentical twins could be. They had the same hair and face, the same laugh. She was a girl, yeah, but from twenty feet it was hard to tell them apart. They stood the same, walked the same. Most mornings, they woke at the same time, even in different rooms. Johnny's mom said they'd had their own language when they were small, but Johnny didn't remember that. He remembered that for most of his life, he'd never been alone; there was a special sense of belonging that only the two of them had ever understood. But Alyssa was gone, and everything with her. That was truth, unavoidable, and it had carved the insides out of his mother. So Johnny did what he could. He checked the locks at night and cleaned up the mess. Today it took twenty minutes; then he put on coffee and thought about the rolled-up bill.

A hundred bucks.

Food and clothing.

He made a last check of the house. Bottles, gone. Signs of drug use, gone. He opened windows to let the outside in, then checked the refrigerator. The milk carton rattled when he shook it. One egg in the carton. He opened his mother's purse. She had nine dollars and change. Johnny left the money and closed the purse. He filled a glass with water and shook two aspirin out of a bottle. He walked down the hall and opened his mother's door.

The first raw light of dawn pushed against the glass, an orange bulge beyond the black trees. His mother lay on her side, hair across her face. Magazines and books covered the bedside table. He made room for the glass and placed the aspirin on the scarred wood. For a second, he listened to her breathe, then looked at the stack of bills Ken had left by the bed. There were some twenties, a fifty. Maybe a few hundred dollars, wrinkled and smudged.

Peeled off a roll.

Discarded.

The car in the driveway was old, a station wagon that Johnny's father had bought years ago. The paint was clean and waxed, tire pressure checked every week, but that was all Johnny knew how to do. Blue smoke still belched from the pipe when he turned the key; the passenger window did not go up all the way. He waited for the smoke to turn white, then put the car in gear and rolled to the bottom of the drive. He was nowhere close to having a license, and looked carefully before edging into the road. He kept the speed down and stayed on the back roads. The nearest store was only two miles away, but it was a big one, on a major road, and Johnny knew that people there might recognize him. He added three miles to the trip and went to a small grocery store that catered to the low end of things. The gas cost money and the food was more expensive, but he didn't really have a choice. Social Services had already been to the house twice.

The car blended with those already there, most of which were old and American. A dark sedan rolled in behind him and stopped near the entrance. Sunlight mirrored the glass and a lone man sat faceless behind the wheel. He did not get out, and Johnny watched him as he walked to the store.

Johnny had a great fear of lone men in stopped cars.

The cart wobbled as he went up one aisle and down another. Just the basics, he decided: milk, juice, bacon, eggs, sandwich bread, fruit. He bought more aspirin for his mother. Tomato juice also seemed to help.

The cop stopped him at the end of aisle eight. He was tall and broad, with brown eyes that were too soft for the lines in his face, the hard angle of his jaw. He had no cart, stood with his hands in his pockets, and Johnny knew at a glance that he'd followed him inside. He had that look, a kind of resigned patience.

And Johnny wanted to run.

"Hey, Johnny," he said. "How you doing?"

His hair was longer than Johnny remembered, same brown as his eyes, shaggy and curling over the top of his collar with a bit of new silver threaded in at the sides. His face had thinned out, and some part of Johnny recognized that the year had been hard on him as well. Big as the cop was, he looked pressed

13

down, haunted, but most of the world looked like that to Johnny, so he wasn't sure. The cop's voice was deep and concerned. It brought back so many bad memories that, for an instant, Johnny could neither move nor speak. The cop stepped closer and brought with him the same thoughtful expression that Johnny had seen so often, the same look of gentle worry. Some part of Johnny wanted to like the man, to trust him; but he was still the one who let Alyssa fade away. He was still the one who lost her.

"I'm good," Johnny told him. "You know. Hanging in."

The cop looked at his watch, then at Johnny's grubby clothes and wild, black hair. It was forty minutes after six on a school day. "Any word from your father?" he asked.

"No." Johnny tried to hide the sudden shame. "No word."

"I'm sorry."

The moment stretched, but the cop did not move. The brown eyes remained steady, and up close he looked just as big and calm as the first time he'd come to Johnny's house. But that was another memory, so Johnny stared at the man's thick wrist, the clean, blunt nails. His voice cracked when he spoke. "My mother got a letter once. She said he was in Chicago, maybe going to California." A pause, eyes moving from hand to floor. "He'll come back."

Johnny said it with conviction. The cop nodded once and turned his head away. Spencer Merrimon had left two weeks after his daughter was grabbed. Too much pain. Too much guilt. His wife never let him forget that he was supposed to pick the girl up, never let him forget that she would not have been walking down the road at dusk if he'd only done what he was supposed to do.

"It wasn't his fault," Johnny said.

"I never said it was."

"He was working. He forgot the time. It wasn't his fault."

"We all make mistakes, son. Every last one of us. Your father is a good man. Don't you ever doubt that."

"I don't." Sudden resentment in Johnny's voice.

"It's okay."

"I never would." Johnny felt the color fall out of his face. He could not remember the last time he'd spoken so much to a grown-up, but there was something about the cop. He was old as hell, like forty, but he never rushed things, and there was a warmth to his face, a kindness that didn't seem fake or put on to trick a kid into trusting him. His eyes were always very still, and some part of Johnny hoped that he was a good enough cop to make things right. But it had been a year, and his sister was still gone. Johnny had to worry about the now, and in the now this cop was no friend.

There was Social Services, which was just waiting for an excuse; and then there were the things that Johnny did, the places he went when he cut school, the risks he took when he snuck out after midnight. If the cop knew what Johnny was doing, he would be forced to take action. Foster homes. The courts.

He would stop Johnny if he could.

"How's your mom?" the cop asked. His eyes were intent, hand still on the cart.

"Tired," Johnny said. "Lupus, you know. She tires easily."

The cop frowned for the first time. "Last time I found you here, you told me she had Lyme disease."

He was right. "No. I said she had lupus."

The cop's face softened and he lifted his hand from the cart. "There are people who want to help. People who understand."

Suddenly, Johnny was angry. No one understood, and no one offered to help. Not ever. "She's just under the weather. Just run down."

15

The cop looked away from the lie, but his face remained sad. Johnny watched his gaze fall to the aspirin bottle, the tomato juice. From the way his eyes lingered, it was obvious that he knew more than most about drunks and drug abusers. "You're not the only one who's hurting, Johnny. You're not alone."

"Alone enough."

The cop sighed deeply. He took a card from his shirt pocket and wrote a number on the back of it. He handed it to the boy. "If you ever need anything." He looked determined. "Day or night. I mean it."

Johnny glanced at the card, slipped it into the pocket of his jeans. "We're fine," he said, and pushed the cart around him. The cop dropped a hand on the boy's shoulder.

"If he ever hits you again . . ."

Johnny tensed.

"Or your mother . . ."

Johnny shrugged the hand off. "We're fine," he repeated. "I've got it covered."

He pushed past the cop, terrified that he would stop him, that he would ask more questions or call one of the hard-faced women from Social Services.

The cart scraped against the counter at the register, and a large woman on a worn stool dipped her nose. She was new to the store, and Johnny saw the question in her face. He was thirteen but looked years younger. He pulled the hundred from his pocket and put it faceup on the conveyor belt. "Can you hurry, please?"

She popped gum and frowned. "Easy, sugar. Here we go."

The cop lingered ten feet behind, and Johnny felt him there, eyes on his back as the fat lady rang up the groceries. Johnny forced himself to breathe, and after a minute, the cop walked past. "Keep that card," he said.

"Okay." Johnny could not bear to meet his eyes.

The cop turned, and his smile was not an easy one. "It's always good to see you, Johnny."

He left the store, visible through the broad plate glass. He walked past the station wagon, then turned and lingered for a moment. He looked through the window, then circled to check out the plate. Apparently satisfied, he approached his sedan and opened the door. Slipping into the gloom, he sat.

He waited.

Johnny tried to slow his heart, then reached for the change in the cashier's damp and meaty hand.

The cop's name was Clyde Lafayette Hunt. Detective. It said so on his card. Johnny had a collection of them tucked into his top drawer, hidden under his socks and a picture of his dad. He thought, at times, of the number on the card; but then he thought of orphanages and foster homes. He thought of his disappeared sister and of the lead pipe he kept between his bed and the wall that leaked cold air. He thought that the cop probably meant what he said. He was probably a good guy. But Johnny could never look at him without remembering Alyssa, and that kind of thinking required concentration. He had to picture her alive and smiling, not in a dirt-floored cellar or in the back of some car. She was twelve the last time he'd seen her. Twelve, with black hair, cut like a boy's. The guy who saw what happened said she walked right up to the car, smiling even as the car door opened.

Smiling right up until somebody grabbed her.

Johnny heard that word all the time. *Smiling*. Like it was stuck in his head, a one-word recording he couldn't shake. But he saw her face when he slept. He saw her looking back as the houses grew small. He saw the worry bloom, and he saw her scream.

Johnny realized that the cashier was staring, that his hand was still out, money in it, groceries bagged. She had one eyebrow up, jaw still working a wad of gum.

"You need something else, sugar?"

Johnny shied. He wadded the bills and stuffed them into his pocket. "No," he said. "I don't need anything else."

She looked past him, to the store manager who stood behind a low glass partition. He followed her gaze, then reached for the bags. She shrugged and he left, walked out under a sky that had blued out while he shopped. He kept his eyes on his mother's car and tried to ignore Detective Hunt. The bags made rasping sounds as they rubbed together. The milk sloshed, heavy on the right side. He put the bags in the backseat and hesitated. The cop was watching him from a car that angled out, less than twenty feet away. He gestured when Johnny straightened.

"I know how to drive," Johnny said.

"I don't doubt it." The answer surprised Johnny. It's like he was smiling. "I know you're tough," he said, and the smile was gone. "I know you can handle most things, but the law is the law." Johnny stood taller. "I can't let you drive."

"I can't leave the car here," Johnny said. "It's the only one we have."

"I'll take you home."

Johnny said nothing. He wondered if the house still smelled of bourbon. He wondered if he'd put all of the pill bottles away.

"I'm trying to help you, Johnny." The cop paused. "People do that, you know."

"What people?" The bitterness spilled out.

"It's okay," Detective Hunt said. "It's fine. Just tell me your address."

"You know where I live. I see you drive by sometimes, see you slow down when you do. So don't pretend like you don't know."

Hunt heard the distrust. "I'm not trying to trick you, son. I need the exact address so that I can have a patrol car meet me there. I'll need a ride back to my car."

Johnny studied the cop. "Why do you drive by so often?"

"It's like I said, Johnny. There are people who want to help."

Johnny wasn't sure that he believed him, but he recited the address and watched him radio for a patrol car to meet him at the house. "Come on." Hunt climbed out of the unmarked police car, crossed the lot to the station wagon. Johnny opened the passenger door and the cop slid behind the wheel. Johnny buckled up, then sat very still. For a long moment, neither moved. "I'm sorry about your sister," Hunt finally said. "I'm sorry that I couldn't bring her home. You know that, right?"

Johnny stared straight ahead, his hands clenched white in his lap. The sun cleared the trees and pushed heat through the glass.

"Can you say something?" Hunt asked.

Johnny turned, and his voice came, flat. "It was a year ago yesterday." He knew that he sounded small. "Are you aware of that?"

Hunt looked uneasy. "Yes," he said. "I am aware of that."

Johnny looked away. "Can you just drive? Please?"

The engine turned over, and blue smoke rolled past Johnny's window. "Okay," the cop said. "Okay, Johnny."

He put the car in gear. They rode in silence to the edge of town. No words, but Johnny smelled him. He smelled soap and gun oil, what may have been cigarette smoke on his clothes. He drove the way Johnny's dad drove, quick and sure, gaze on the road, then on the rearview mirror. His lips compressed as they neared the house, and Johnny thought, one last time, of how he'd said he'd bring Alyssa home. A year ago. He'd promised it.

A marked car was waiting in the driveway when they got there. Johnny climbed out and opened the back door for the grocery bags. "I can help with that," Hunt said.

Johnny just looked at him. What did he want? He lost her.

"I've got it," Johnny said.

Detective Hunt held Johnny's eyes until it was obvious that he had nothing to say. "Be good," he finally said, and Johnny watched him slip into the police cruiser. He held the groceries and he did not move as the car backed into the road. He did not respond to Detective Hunt's wave. He stood on the dusty drive and watched the cruiser rise on the distant hill, then fall away. He waited for his heart to slow, then took the bags inside.

The groceries looked small on the counter, but they felt like more: a victory. Johnny put them away, then started coffee and cracked a single egg into the pan. Blue flame popped in the iron ring, and he watched the egg turn white around the edges. He flipped it with care, then put it on a paper plate. The phone rang as he reached for a napkin. He recognized the number on caller ID and answered before it could ring twice. The kid on the other end had a scratchy voice. He was thirteen, too, but smoked and drank like a grown-up. "You ditching today? Let's ditch."

Johnny cut his eyes to the hall and kept his voice low. "Hello, Jack."

"I've been looking at some houses on the west side. It's a bad area. Real bad. Lot of ex-convicts over there. Makes sense when you think about it."

It was an old refrain. Jack knew what Johnny did when he cut school and snuck out after dark. He wanted to help, partly because he was a good kid, partly because he was bad.

"This is not some game," Johnny said.

"You know what they say about a gift horse, man. This is free help. Don't take it for granted."

Johnny pushed out a breath. "Sorry, Jack. It's one of those mornings."

"Your mom?"

Johnny's throat closed, so he nodded. Jack was his last friend, the only one who still treated him like he was not some kind of freak or pity case. They had some things in common, too. He was a small kid, like Johnny, and had his own share of problems. "I should probably go today."

"Our history paper is due," Jack said. "You done it?"

"I turned that in last week."

"Shit. Really? I haven't even started mine yet."

Jack was always late, and teachers always let him get away with it. Johnny's mom once called Jack a rascal, and the word fit. He stole cigarettes from the teacher's lounge and slicked his hair on Fridays. He drank more booze than any kid should and lied like a professional; but he kept secrets when he said he would and watched your back if it needed watching. He was likable, sincere if he cared to be, and for a second, Johnny felt his spirits lift; then the morning landed on him.

Detective Hunt.

The wad of greasy bills by his mother's bed.

"I gotta go," Johnny said.

"What about cutting school?"

"I gotta go." Johnny hung up the phone. His friend's feelings were hurt, but Johnny couldn't help that. He picked up the plate, sat on the porch and ate his egg with three slices of bread and a glass of milk. He was still hungry when he finished, but lunch was only four and a half hours away.

He could wait.

Pouring coffee with milk, Johnny made his way down the dim hall to his mother's room. The water was gone, so was the aspirin. Her hair was off her face, and a bar of sunlight cut across her eyes. Johnny put the mug on the table and opened a window. Cool air flowed in from the shady side of the house, and Johnny studied his mother. She looked paler, more tired, younger and lost. She would not wake for the coffee, but he wanted it there just in case. Just so she'd know.

He started to turn, but she moaned in her sleep and made a violent twitch. She mumbled something and her legs thrashed twice, then she bolted up in bed, eyes wide and terrified. "Jesus Christ!" she said. "Jesus Christ!"

Johnny stood in front of her but she did not see him. Whatever frightened her still had its grip. He leaned in, told her it was just a dream, and for that second her eyes seemed to know him. She raised a hand to his face. "Alyssa," she said, and there was a question in her voice.

Johnny felt the storm coming. "It's Johnny," he told her.

"Johnny?" Her eyes blinked, and then the day broke over her. The desperate gaze collapsed, the hand fell away, and she rolled back into the covers.

Johnny gave her a few seconds, but she did not open her eyes again. "Are you okay?" he finally asked.

"Bad dream."

"There's coffee. You want any breakfast?"

"Damn." She flung off the covers and walked out of the room. She did not look back. Johnny heard the bathroom door slam.

He went outside and sat on the porch. Five minutes later, the school bus pulled onto the dirt verge. Johnny did not get up, he did not move. Eventually, the bus rolled on.

It took most of an hour for his mother to get dressed and find

22

him on the porch. She sat beside him, draped thin arms across her knees. Her smile failed in every way, and Johnny remembered how it used to light up a room.

"I'm sorry," she said, nudging him with a shoulder. Johnny looked up the road. She nudged him again. "Sorry. You know . . . an apology."

He didn't know what to say, could not explain how it felt to know that it hurt her to look at him. He shrugged. "It's okay."

He felt her look for the right words. She failed in that, too. "You missed the bus," she said.

"It doesn't matter."

"It does to the school."

"I make perfect grades. Nobody cares if I'm there or not."

"Are you still seeing the school counselor?"

He studied her with an unforgiving eye. "Not for six months now."

"Oh."

Johnny looked back up the road and felt his mother watching him. She used to know everything. They used to talk. When she spoke, her voice had an edge. "He's not coming back."

Johnny looked at his mother. "What?"

"You keep looking up the road. You do it all the time, like you expect to see him walking over the hilltop." Johnny opened his mouth, but she spoke over him. "It's not going to happen."

"You don't know that."

"I'm just trying—"

"You don't know that!"

Johnny was on his feet with no recollection of standing. His hands were clenched for the second time that morning, and something hot pushed against the walls of his chest. His mother leaned back, arms still crossed over her knees. The light fell out of her eyes, and Johnny knew what was coming. She reached out a hand that fell short of actually touching him. "He left us, Johnny. It's not your fault."

She started to stand. Her lips softened and her face slipped into a look of pained understanding, the kind of expression grown-ups gave to kids who didn't quite get how the world worked. But Johnny understood. He knew the look and he hated it.

"You should have never said the things you said."

"Johnny . . ."

"It wasn't his fault that she got taken. You should have never told him that." She stepped toward him. Johnny ignored the gesture. "He left because of you."

She stopped midstride and ice snapped in her voice. The sympathetic twist fell from her lips. "It *was* his fault," she said. "His fault and nobody else's. Now she's gone, and I've got nothing."

Johnny felt tremors start low in the backs of his legs. In seconds, he was shaking. It was an old argument, and it was tearing them apart.

She straightened and started to turn. "You always take his side," she said, and then was gone, into the house, away from the world and her last child's place in it.

Johnny stared at the faded door and then at his hands. He watched them shake, then he swallowed the emotion. He sat back down and watched wind move dust on the roadside. He thought about his mother's words, then he looked up the hill. It was not a pretty hill. There was an edge of ragged forest dotted with small houses and dirt drives, telephone lines that curved between the poles and looked especially black against the new sky. Nothing made the hill special, but he watched it for a long time. He watched it until his neck hurt, then he went inside to check on his mom.

CHAPTER TWO

The Vicodin bottle sat open on the bathroom counter; the door to his mother's room was closed. Johnny cracked the door, saw that it was dim inside and that his mother was under the covers and still. He heard the rasp of her breath and beneath that a deep and perfect silence. He closed her door and went to his own room.

The suitcase under his bed showed cracks in the leather and a black tarnish on the hinges. One of the leather straps had broken off, but Johnny kept the piece because it once belonged to his great-great-grandfather. The case, large and square, had a faded monogram that Johnny could still see if he tilted it right. It read JPM, John Pendleton Merrimon, same name as Johnny.

He dragged the case out, got it up on the bed, and unfastened the last buckle. The top swung up clumsily and settled against the wall. On the inside curve of the lid were a dozen photographs, a collage. Most showed his sister, but two were of them together, looking very much like twins and sharing the same smile. He touched one of the pictures briefly, then looked at the other photos, those of his father. Spencer Merrimon was a big man with square teeth and an easy smile, a builder, with rough hands, quiet confidence, and a moral certainty that had always made Johnny feel lucky to be his son. He'd taught Johnny so many things: how to drive, how to keep his head up, how to make the right decisions. His father taught him how the world worked, taught him what to believe and where to place his faith: family, God, the community. Everything that Johnny had learned about what it meant to be a man, he'd learned from his father.

Right up to the end, when his father walked away.

Now Johnny had to question all of it, everything he'd been taught with such conviction. God did not care about people in pain. Not the little ones. There was no such thing as justice, retribution, or community; neighbors did not help neighbors and the meek would not inherit the earth. All of that was bullshit. The church, the cops, his mother—none of them could make it right, none of them had the power. For a year, Johnny had lived the new, brutal truth that he was on his own.

But that's the way it was. What had been concrete one day proved sand the next; strength was illusion; faith meant shit. So what? So his once-bright world had devolved to cold, wet fog. That was life, the new order. Johnny had nothing to trust but himself, so that's the way he rolled—his path, his choices, and no looking back.

He studied the pictures of his father: one behind the wheel of a pickup, sunglasses on and smiling; one standing lightly at the peak of a roof, tool belt angled low on one side. He looked strong: the jaw, the shoulders, the heavy whiskers. Johnny looked for some hint of his own features, but he was too delicate, too fair-skinned. Johnny didn't look strong, but that was just the surface.

He was strong.

He said it to himself: *I will be strong.*

The rest was harder to admit, so he did not. He ignored the small voice in the back of his mind, the child's voice. He clenched his jaw and touched the pictures one last time; then he closed his eyes, and when he opened them, the emotion was gone.

He was not lonesome.

Inside the case were all of the things Alyssa would miss the most, the things she'd want when she came home. He began lifting them out: her diary, unread; two stuffed animals she'd had forever; three photo albums; her school yearbooks; favorite CDs; a small chest of notes she'd passed in school and collected like treasure.

More than once, his mother had asked about the things in the case, but Johnny knew better than to tell her. If she mixed the wrong pills anything could happen. She'd throw things out or burn them in the yard, standing like a zombie or screaming about how much it hurt to remember. That's what happened to the other photos of his father, and to the small, sacred things that once filled his sister's room. They faded away in the night or were consumed by the storms that boiled from his mother.

On the bottom of the case was a green file folder. Inside the folder was a thin stack of maps and an eight-by-ten photo of Alyssa. Johnny laid the photo aside and spread out the maps. One was large scale and showed the county where it nestled into eastern North Carolina, not quite in the sand hills, not quite in the piedmont or the flood plains; two hours from Raleigh, maybe an hour from the coast. The northern part of the county was rough country: forest and swamp and a thirty-mile jut of granite where they used to tunnel for gold. The river came down from the north and bisected the county, passing within a few miles of town. To the west was dark soil, perfect for vineyards and farms, and to the east were the sand hills, which boasted a crescent of high-end golf courses, and, beyond that, a long string of small, poor towns that barely managed to survive. Johnny had been through some of them, and remembered weeds that grew from the gutters, shuttered plants and package stores, staved-in men who sat in the shade and drank from bottles in brown paper bags. Fifty miles past the last of the failed towns, you hit Wilmington and the Atlantic Ocean. South Carolina was a foreign country beyond the edge of the paper.

Johnny tucked the big map back into the folder. The rest of the maps detailed the streets in town. Red ink marked a number of streets, small X marks over individual addresses. Notes in his handwriting lined the margins. Some neighborhoods were still untouched; a few were crossed off completely. He looked at the western side of town, wondering what part of it Jack had been talking about. He'd have to ask him. Later.

Johnny studied the map for a few more seconds, then folded it and set it aside. Alyssa's things went back into the case and the case back under the bed. He picked up the large photo and slipped a red pen into his back pocket.

He was through the front door and about to lock it when the van turned into his driveway. Paint peeled from the hood in uneven patches; the right front fender was banged up and rusted. It slewed into the driveway with a shudder, and Johnny felt something like dismay. He turned his back, rolled up the map, and shoved it into the pocket that held the pen. He kept the photo in his hand so that it would not get wrinkled. When the van stopped, Johnny saw a flash of blue through the glass; then the window came down. The face behind it was unusually pale and bloated.

"Get in," the man said.

Johnny stepped off the stoop and crossed the small patch of grass and weed. He stopped before he got to the edge of the drive. "What are you doing here, Steve?"

"Uncle Steve."

"You're not my uncle."

The door squealed open, and the man stepped out. He wore a blue jumpsuit with a gold patch on the right shoulder. The belt was heavy and black. "I'm your father's first cousin, and that's close enough. Besides, you've called me Uncle Steve since you were three."

"Uncle means family, and that means we help each other. We haven't seen you in six weeks, and it was a month before that. Where have you been?"

Steve hooked his thumbs in the belt, making the stiff vinyl creak. "Your mom is hanging with the rich folks now, Johnny. Riding the gravy train." He waved a hand. "Free house. No need to work. Hell, son, there's nothing I can do for her that her boyfriend can't do a thousand times better. He owns the mall, the theaters. He owns half the town, for God's sake. He doesn't need people like me getting in his way."

"Getting in his way?" The disbelief came off Johnny in waves.

"That's not—"

"You're scared of him," Johnny said in disgust.

"He signs my paycheck, me and about four hundred other guys. Now if he was hurting your mom, or something like that. That'd be one thing. But he's helping her. Right? So why would I get in his way. Your dad would understand that."

Johnny looked away. "Aren't you late for your shift at the mall?"

"Yes, I am. So get in."

Johnny did not move. "What are you doing here, Uncle Steve?"

"Your mom called and asked if I could take you to school. She said you missed the bus."

"I'm not going to school."

"Yes, you are."

"No, I'm not."

"Jesus, Johnny. Why do you have to make everything so damn difficult? Just get in the van."

"Why don't you just tell her that you took me and leave it there?"

"I told her I'd take you, so I have to take you. I'm not going anywhere until you get in the van. I'll make you if I have to."

Johnny's voice dripped. "You're not a cop, Steve. You're just a security guard. You can't make me do anything."

"Screw this," Steve said. "Wait right there." He pushed past Johnny and small metal jingled on his belt. The uniform looked very crisp and made a rasping noise between his legs.

"What are you doing?"

"Talking to your mother."

"She's asleep," Johnny said.

"I'll wake her then. Don't you go anywhere. I mean it." Then he was through, into the small house that smelled of spilled booze and generic cleaner. Johnny watched the door click shut, then looked at his bike. He could be on it and gone before Uncle Steve made it back outside, but that's not what a strong person would do. So Johnny pulled the map from his pocket and smoothed it against his chest. He took a deep breath, then went inside to deal with the problem.

It was quiet in the house, the light still dim. Johnny turned into the short hall and stopped. His mother's door angled wide, and Uncle Steve stood in front of it, unmoving. Johnny watched for a second, but Steve neither moved nor spoke. As Johnny drew closer, he could see a narrow slice of his mother's room. She still slept, flat on her back, one arm thrown across her eyes. The covers had fallen to her waist, and Johnny saw that she was undressed, so still, and Uncle Steve just stood there, staring. Then Johnny understood. "What the hell?" Then louder: "What the hell, Steve?"

Uncle Steve twitched in guilt. His hands came up, fingers spread. "It's not what you think."

30

But Johnny wasn't listening. He took five quick steps and pulled his mother's door closed. She still had not moved. Johnny put his back to the door, and felt the fire come up in his eyes. "You're sick, Steve. She's my mother." Johnny looked around, as if for a stick or a bat, but there was nothing. "What's wrong with you?"

Uncle Steve's eyes showed rare desperation. "I just opened the door. I didn't mean anything by it. Swear to God, Johnny. I'm not like that. I'm not that kind of guy. I swear it. Hand to God."

A sheen of greasy sweat slicked Uncle Steve's face. He was so scared, it was pitiful. Johnny wanted to kick him in the balls. He wanted to put him on the ground, then find the pipe under his bed and beat his balls flat. But he thought of Alyssa's picture, and of the things he still needed to do. And he'd learned this year. He'd learned how to put emotion last. His voice came cold and level. He had things to do, and Steve was going to help him. "You tell her you took me to school." Johnny nodded and stepped closer. "If she asks, that's what you tell her."

"And you won't say anything?"

"Not if you do what I tell you."

"Swear?"

"Just go, Uncle Steve. Go to work."

Uncle Steve slipped past, hands still up. "I didn't mean nothing by it."

But Johnny had nothing else to say. He closed the door, then spread the map on the kitchen counter. The red pen was slick between his fingers. He smoothed his palm across the wrinkled paper, then slid a finger to the neighborhood he'd been working for the past three weeks.

He picked a street at random.

CHAPTER THREE

Detective Hunt sat at the cluttered desk in his small office. Files spilled from cabinet tops and unused chairs. Dirty coffee cups, memos he'd never read. It was 9:45. The place was a mess, but he lacked the energy to deal with it. He scrubbed his hands across his face, ground at the sockets of his eyes until he saw white streaks and sparks. His face felt rough, unshaven, and he knew that he looked every bit of his forty-one years. He'd lost so much weight that his suits hung on his frame. He'd not been to the gym or the shooting range in six months. He rarely managed more than one meal a day, but none of that seemed to matter.

In front of him, he'd spread his office copy of the Alyssa Merrimon file. A well-thumbed duplicate was locked in a desk drawer at home. He flipped pages methodically, reading every word: reports, interviews, summaries. Alyssa's face stared out at him from an enlarged copy of her school photograph. Black hair, like her brother's. Same bone structure, same dark eyes. A secret kind of smile. A lightness, like her mother had, an ethereal quality that Hunt had tried and failed to identify. The way her eyes tilted, maybe? The swept-back ears and china skin? The innocence? That's the one that Hunt came back to most often. The child looked as if she'd never had an impure thought or done an ill deed in her entire life.

And then there was her mother, her brother. They all had it, to one degree or another; but none of them like the girl.

Hunt scrubbed his face one more time.

He was too close, he knew that; but the case had a grip on him. A glance at the office showed the depth of his fall. There were cases here that needed work. Other people. Real people who suffered just like the Merrimons did; but those cases paled, and he still did not know why. The girl had even found her way into his dreams. She wore the same clothes she had on the day she disappeared: faded yellow shorts, a white top. She was pale in the dream. Short hair. Eighty pounds. A hot spring day. There was no lead up when it happened; the dream started like a cannon shot, full-blown, color and sound. Something was pulling her into a dark place beneath the trees, dragging her through the warm, rotten leaves. Her hand was out, mouth open, teeth very white. He dove for the hand, missed, and she screamed as long fingers drew her down into some dark and seamless place.

When it happened, he woke sheeted in sweat, arms churning as if he were digging through leaves. The dream found him two or three nights a week, and it was the same every time. He'd climb from bed sometime close to three, shaky, wide-awake, then put cold water on his face and stare long into bloody eyes before going downstairs to pore through the file for whatever hours remained before his son woke up and the day put its own long fingers on his skin.

The dream had become his personal hell, the file a ritual, a religion; and it was eating him alive.

"Good morning."

Hunt jerked, looked up. In the door stood John Yoakum, his partner and friend. "Hey, John. Good morning."

Yoakum was sixty-three years old, with thinning brown hair and a goatee shot with gray. Thin but very fit, he was dangerously smart, cynical to a fault. They'd been partners for four years, worked a dozen major cases together, and Hunt liked the

33

guy. He was a private man and a smart-ass, but he also brought rare insight to a job that demanded nothing less. He worked long hours when they needed to be worked, watched his partner's back; and if he was a little dark, a little private, Hunt was okay with that.

Yoakum shook his head. "I'd like to live the night that made you look like this."

"No, you wouldn't."

Yoakum's grin fell off and his words were brisk. "I know that, Clyde. Just messing with you." He gestured over his shoulder. "I have a call you might want to take."

"Yeah. Why is that?"

"Because it's about Johnny Merrimon."

"Seriously?"

"Some lady wants to talk to a cop. I told her that I was the only real cop here today. I said, Emotional wrecks, yeah, got one of those. An obsessive compulsive that used to look like a cop. She could have that guy, too. Both, in fact. At the same time."

"What line, smart-ass?"

Yoakum showed his fine, porcelain teeth. "Line three," he said, and left with an easy swagger. Hunt lifted the phone and punched the flashing button for line three. "This is Detective Hunt."

At first there was silence, then a woman's voice. She sounded old. "Detective? I don't know that I need a detective. It's not that important, really. I just thought someone should know."

"It's okay, ma'am. May I have your name, please?"

"Louisa Sparrow, like the bird."

The voice fit. "What's the problem, Ms. Sparrow?"

"It's that poor boy. You know, the one that lost his sister."

"Johnny Merrimon."

"That's the one. The poor boy . . ." She trailed off for an instant, then her voice firmed. "He was just at my house . . . just this minute."

"With a picture of his sister," Hunt interrupted.

"Why, yes. How did you know?"

Hunt ignored the question. "May I have your address, please, ma'am?"

"He's not in trouble, is he? He's been through enough, I know. It's just that it's a school day, and it's all very upsetting, seeing her picture like that, and how he still looks just like her, like he hasn't grown at all; and those questions he asks, like I might have had something to do with it."

Detective Hunt thought about the small boy he'd found at the grocery store. The deep eyes. The wariness. "Mrs. Sparrow . . ."

"Yes."

"I really need that address."

Hunt found Johnny Merrimon a block away from Louisa Sparrow's house. The boy sat on the curb, his feet crossed in the gutter. Sweat soaked his shirt and plastered hair to his forehead. A beat-up bike lay where he'd dropped it, half on the grass of somebody's lawn. He was chewing on a pen and bent over a map that covered his lap like a blanket. His concentration was complete, broken only when Hunt slammed the car door. In that instant the boy looked like a startled animal, but then he paused. Hunt saw recognition snap in the boy's eyes, then determination and something deeper.

Acceptance.

Then cunning.

His eyes gauged distance, as if he might hop on his bike and try to run. He risked a glance at the nearby woods, but Hunt stepped closer, and the kid sagged. "Hello, Detective."

Hunt pulled off his sunglasses. His shadow fell on the boy's feet. "Hello, Johnny."

Johnny began folding the map. "I know what you're going to say, so you don't have to say it."

Hunt held out his hand. "May I see the map?" Johnny froze, and the hunted animal look rose again in his face. He looked down the long street, then at the map. Hunt continued: "I've heard about that map, you see. I didn't believe it at first, but people have told me." Hunt's eyes were hard on the boy. "How many times is it now, Johnny? How many times have I talked to you about this? Four? Five?"

"Seven." His voice barely rose from the gutter. His fingers showed white on the map.

"I'll give it back."

The boy looked up, black eyes shining, and the sense of cunning fell away. He was a kid. He was scared. "Promise?"

He looked so small. "I promise, Johnny."

Johnny raised his hand and Hunt's fingers closed on the map. It was worn soft and showed white in the folds. He sat on the curb, next to the boy, and spread the map between his hands. It was large, purple ink on white paper. He recognized it as a tax map, with names and matching addresses. It only covered a portion of the city, maybe a thousand properties. Close to half had been crossed off in red ink. "Where did you get this?" he asked.

"Tax assessor. They're not expensive."

"Do you have all of them? For the entire county?" Johnny nodded, and Hunt asked, "The red marks?"

"Houses I've visited. People I've spoken to."

Hunt was struck dumb. He could not imagine the hours involved, the ground covered on a busted-up bike. "What about the ones with asterisks?"

"Single men living alone. Ones that gave me the creeps."

Hunt folded the map, handed it back. "Are there marks on other maps, too?"

"Some of them."

"It has to stop."

"But—"

"No, Johnny. It has to stop. These are private citizens. We're getting complaints."

Johnny stood. "I'm not breaking any laws."

"You're a truant, son. You're ditching school right now. Besides, it's dangerous. You have no idea who lives in these houses." He flicked one finger at the map; it snapped against the paper and Johnny pulled it away. "I can't lose another kid."

"I can take care of myself."

"Yeah, you told me that this morning."

Johnny looked away, and Hunt studied the line of his narrow jaw, the muscles that pressed against the tight skin. He saw a small feather tied to a string around Johnny's neck. It shone whitish gray against the boy's washed-out shirt. Hunt pointed, trying to break the mood. "What's that?"

Johnny's hand moved to his neck. He tucked the feather back under his shirt. "It's a pinfeather," he said.

"A pinfeather?"

"For luck."

Hunt saw the kid's fingers go white, and he saw another feather tied to the bike. The feather was larger, mostly brown. "How about that one?" He pointed again. "Hawk? Owl?"

The boy's face showed nothing, and he kept his mouth shut. "Is that for luck, too?"

"No." Johnny paused, looked away. "That's different."

"Johnny—"

37

"Did you see in the news last week? When they found that girl that was abducted in Colorado? You know the one?"

"I know the one."

"She'd been gone for a year and they found her three blocks from her own house. She was less than a mile away the whole time. A mile from her family, locked up in a dirt hole dug into the wall of the cellar. Walled up with a bucket and mattress."

"Johnny—"

"They showed pictures on the news. A bucket. A candle. A filthy mattress. The ceiling was only four feet high. But they found her."

"That's just one case, Johnny."

"They're all like that." Johnny turned back, his deep eyes gone darker still. "It's a neighbor or a friend, someone the kid knows or a house she walked past every day. And when they find them, they're always close. Even if they're dead, they're close."

"That's not always true."

"But sometimes. Sometimes it is."

Hunt stood as well, and his voice came softly. "Sometimes."

"Just because you quit doesn't mean that I have to."

Looking at the boy and at his desperate conviction, Hunt felt a great sadness. He was the department's lead detective on major cases, and because of that, he'd taken point on Alyssa's disappearance. Hunt had worked harder than any other cop to bring that poor child home. He'd spent months, lost touch with his own family until his wife, in despair and quiet rage, had finally left him. And for what? Alyssa was gone, so gone they'd be lucky to find her remains. It didn't matter what happened in Colorado. Hunt knew the statistics: Most were dead by the end of the first day. But that made it no easier. He still wanted to bring her home. One way or another. "The file is still open, Johnny. No one has quit."

Johnny picked up his bike. He rolled up the map and shoved it into his back pocket. "I have to go."

Detective Hunt's hand settled on the handlebar. He felt specks of rust and heat from the sun. "I've cut you a lot of slack. I can't do it anymore. This needs to stop."

Johnny pulled on the bike but couldn't budge it. His voice was as loud as Hunt had ever heard it. "I can take care of myself."

"But that's just it, Johnny. It's not your job to take care of yourself. It's your mother's job, and frankly, I'm not sure she can tend to herself, let alone a thirteen-year-old boy."

"You may *think* that's true, but you don't *know* anything."

For a long second the detective held his eyes. He saw how they went from fierce to frightened, and understood how much the kid needed his hope. But the world was not a kind place to children, and Hunt had reached the limit with Johnny Merrimon. "If you lifted your shirt right now, how many bruises would I see?"

"I can take care of myself."

The words sounded automatic and weak, so Hunt lowered his voice. "I can't do anything if you won't talk to me."

Johnny straightened, then let go of his bike. "I'll walk," he said, and turned away.

"Johnny."

The kid kept walking.

"Johnny!"

When he stopped, Hunt walked the bike over to him. The spokes clicked as the wheels turned. Johnny took the handlebars when Hunt offered the bike back to him. "You still have my card?" Johnny nodded, and Hunt blew out a long breath. He could never fully explain his affinity for the boy, not even to himself. Maybe he saw something in the kid. Maybe he felt his pain more than he should. "Keep it with you, okay. Call me anytime."

"Okay."

"I don't want to hear about you doing this again."

Johnny said nothing.

"You'll go straight to school?"

Silence.

Hunt looked at the clean, blue sky, then at the boy. His hair was black and wet, his jaw clenched. "Be careful, Johnny."

CHAPTER FOUR

People were not right. The cop had that part straight. Johnny had peered over more fences and into more windows than he could count. He'd knocked on doors at all hours, and he'd seen things that weren't right. Things that people did when they thought they were alone and no one was watching. He'd seen kids sniff drugs and old people eat food that fell on the floor. He once saw a preacher in his underwear, hot-faced and screaming at his wife as she cried. That was messed up. But Johnny was no idiot. He knew that crazy people could look like anybody else. So he kept his head down. He kept his shoes laced tight and a knife in his pocket.

He was careful.

He was smart.

Johnny did not look back until he'd gone two full blocks. When he did turn his head, he saw that Detective Hunt still stood in the road, a distant speck of color next to a dark car and green grass. The cop was still for an instant, then one arm rose in a slow wave, and Johnny rode faster, careful to not look back again.

The cop scared him, and Johnny wondered how he knew the things he knew.

Five.

The number popped into his head.

Five bruises.

He pedaled harder, pumped his legs until the shirt on his

back clung like a second skin. He went north to the far edge of town, to the place where the river slid beneath the bridge and widened out until the current went flat. He rode his bike down the bank and dropped it. Blood pounded in his ears and he tasted salt. His eyes burned from it, so he wiped at them with a grubby sleeve. He used to fish here with his father. He knew where to find the bass and the giant cats that hugged the mud five feet down, but none of that mattered. He never fished anymore, but he still came here.

This was still his place.

He sat in the dust to untie his shoes. His fingers shook and he did not know why. The shoes came off, then he touched the feather to his cheek and wrapped it in his shirt. The sun put fierce heat on his skin, and he looked at the bruises, the largest of which was the size and shape of a large man's knee. It wrapped around the ribs on his left side and he remembered how Ken held him down with that knee, shifted his weight whenever Johnny tried to squirm out.

Johnny rolled his shoulders, tried to forget about it, the knee on his chest, the finger in his face.

You'll fucking do what I fucking say . . .

Open hand slaps to Johnny's face, first one side, then the other, his mother passed out in the back room.

You little shit . . .

Another slap, harder.

Where's your daddy now?

The bruise had yellowed out on the edges, gone green in the middle; and it hurt when he pushed it with a finger. The skin went white for a second—another perfect oval—then the color rushed in. Johnny scrubbed more salt from his eyes, and when he moved for the river, he stumbled once. He stepped in and river bottom pushed between his toes; then he dove, and warm water closed above him. It wrapped him up, shut out the world and bore him tirelessly down.

Johnny spent two hours at the river, too worried about Detective Hunt to risk more of his search, too ambivalent about school to make going worth his time. He swam across the river and back, made shallow dives from flat rocks baked hot by the sun. Driftwood lay in silver stacks and wind licked off the water. By late morning he was physically worn, stretched out on a flat rock forty feet downriver from the bridge, invisible behind a willow that dragged long strands in the black water. Cars made the bridge hum. A small stone clattered on the rock beside his head. He sat up and another pebble struck him on the shoulder. He looked around and saw no one. A third rock glanced off his leg. It was large enough to sting. "Throw another and you're dead."

Silence.

"I know it's you, Jack."

Johnny heard a laugh, and Jack stepped from the wood's edge. He wore cutoff jeans and filthy sneakers. His shirt was yellow white, with a picture of Elvis in black silhouette. He had a backpack on his back and more stones in his hand. One side of his mouth turned a sharp edge, and his hair was slicked back. Johnny had forgotten that it was Friday.

"That was for ditching without me." Jack walked over, a small boy with blond hair, brown eyes, and a seriously messed up arm. The right one was fine, but it was hard to miss the other. Shrunken and small, it looked like someone had nailed the arm of a six-year-old to a kid twice that age.

"Are you angry?" Johnny asked.

"Yes."

"I'll give you a free hit to make it even."

Jack held the hard smile. "*Three* hits," he said.

"Three with your girl arm."

"Two with the hammer." Jack cocked his good fist, and his smile thinned. "No flinching." He stepped closer and Johnny flexed his arm, pulled it tight to his side. Jack spread his legs, drew back the fist. "This is going to hurt."

"Do it, you pussy."

Jack punched Johnny in the arm, twice. He hit hard, and when he stepped back, he looked satisfied. "That's what you get."

Johnny rolled his arm, tossed one of the pebbles and Jack ducked it. "How'd you know I'd be here?"

"It's not rocket science."

"Then what took you so long?"

Jack sat on the rock next to Johnny. The pack came off and he stripped off the shirt, too. His skin was burned red, peeling on the shoulders. A silver cross hung on a thin steel chain. It spun as he opened the pack, winked silver in the sun. "I had to go home for supplies. Dad was still there."

"He didn't see you, did he?" Jack's father was a serious, hard-ass cop, and Johnny avoided him like the plague.

"Do I look like an idiot?" Jack's good hand disappeared inside the pack. "Still cold," he said, and pulled out a can of beer. He handed it to Johnny, then pulled out another.

"Stealing beer." Johnny shook his head. "You're going to burn in hell."

Jack flashed the same sharp smile. "The Lord forgives small sins."

"That's not what your mom says."

He barked a laugh. "My mom is one step away from foot washing and snake handling, Johnny man. You know that. She prays for my soul like I might burst into flame at any moment. She does it at home. She does it in public."

"Get out."

"That time I got caught cheating? Remember?"

Three months ago. Johnny remembered. "Yeah. History class."

"We had a meeting with the principal, right. Before it was done, she had him on his knees, praying for God to show me the path."

"Bullshit."

"No shit. He was so scared of her. You should have seen his face, all scrunched up, one eye squinting out to see if she was looking at him while he did it." Jack popped the top, shrugged. "Still, can't blame him. She's gone off the deep end and is trying just as hard to take me down with her. She had the preacher over last week to pray for me."

"Why?"

"In case I'm touching myself."

"I don't believe it."

"Life is a comedy," Jack said, but there was no smile left. His mother was scary religious, born again and taking no prisoners. She was on Jack all the time with threats of hellfire and damnation. He played it off, but the cracks showed.

Johnny opened his beer. "Does she know your dad still drinks?"

"She says that the Lord disapproves, so Dad put a beer refrigerator in the garage, his liquor, too. That seems to have settled it."

Jack chugged. Johnny took a sip. "That's some crap beer, Jack."

"Beggars and choosers, man. Don't make me hit you again." Jack chugged the rest of his beer, then stuffed the empty in the pack and pulled out another.

"Did you do your history paper?"

45

"What did I say about small sins?"

Johnny scanned the area behind Jack. "Where's your bike?"

"I don't know."

"What do you mean, you don't know?"

"I didn't feel like riding it."

"It's a six hundred dollar Trek."

Jack looked away, shrugged. "I miss the old one. That's all."

"Still no sign, huh?"

"Stolen, I guess. Gone for good."

The power of sentiment, Johnny thought. Jack's old bike was piss yellow with three gears and a banana seat. His dad bought it second-hand and it had to be fifteen years old. It had been gone for a long time. "Did you hop the train?"

Johnny's eyes slid to the stunted arm. Jack fell from the back of a pickup when he was four and shattered the arm, which turned out to have a hollow bone. He'd had an operation to fill the hollow core with cow's bone, but the surgeon must have been pretty bad, because it never really grew after that. The fingers didn't work that well. The limb had little strength. Johnny gave him hell about it because it made the arm a non-issue between the two of them. But that was just cover-up. When it came down to it, Jack was sensitive. He saw the glance.

"You don't think I can handle a train jump?" Angry.

"I was just thinking of that kid, you know."

They both knew the story, a fourteen-year-old from one of the county schools who tried to hop the same train and lost his grip. He'd fallen under the wheels and lost both legs: one at the thigh, one below the knee. He was a cautionary tale for kids like Jack.

"That kid was a wimp." Jack rooted through one of the outer pockets of the backpack and came out with a pack of menthols. He pulled out a cigarette with his bad arm and held

46

it between two baby fingers as he lit it with a lighter. He sucked in smoke and tried to blow a ring on the exhale.

"Your dad buys crap cigarettes, too."

Jack looked at the perfect blue sky and took another drag. The cigarette in his small hand looked unnaturally large. "You want one?" he asked.

"Why not?"

Jack handed Johnny a smoke and let him light it off the coal on the end of his own. Johnny took a drag and coughed. Jack laughed. "You are *so* not a smoker."

Johnny flicked the butt into the river. He spit into the dirt. "Crap cigarettes," he repeated. When he looked up, he caught Jack staring at the bruises on his chest and ribs.

"Those are new," Jack said.

"Not so new." Johnny watched the current carry a log past their rock. "Tell me again," he said.

"Tell you what?"

"About the van."

"Damn, Johnny. You know how to suck the joy out of a day. How many times do we need to go over it? Nothing's changed since the last time. Or the time before that."

"Just tell me."

Jack pulled in smoke and looked away from his friend. "It was just a van."

"What color?"

"You know what color."

"What color?"

Jack sighed. "White."

"What about dents? Scratches? Anything else you remember?"

"It's been a year, Johnny."

"What else?"

"For fuck's sake, man. It was a white van. White. Like I told you. Like I told the cops." Johnny waited and eventually Jack settled down. "It was a plain white van," he said. "Like a painter would use."

"You never said that before."

"I did."

"No. You described it: white, no windows in the back. You never said it looked like a painter's van. Why would you say that now? Was there paint spilled on the side?"

"No."

"Ladders on the roof? A rack for ladders?"

Jack finished the cigarette and flicked his own butt into the river. "It was just a van, Johnny. She was two hundred yards away when it happened. I wasn't even sure it was her until I found out she was missing. I was coming home from the library, same as her. A bunch of us had been there that day. I saw the van come over the hill and stop. A hand came out of the window and she walked up to the side. She didn't look scared or anything. She just walked right up." He paused. "Then the door opened up and somebody grabbed her. A white guy. Black shirt. Like I've said a hundred times. The door closed and they took off. The whole thing took like ten seconds. There's just nothing else for me to remember."

Johnny looked down, kicked at a stone.

"I'm sorry, man. I wish I'd done something, but I just didn't. It didn't even look real."

Johnny stood and stared at the river. After a minute, he nodded once. "Give me another beer."

They drank beer and swam in the river. Jack smoked. After an hour, Jack asked: "You want to check some houses?"

Johnny skimmed a rock and shook his head. Jack liked the game of it, the risk. He liked creeping around and seeing things that kids were not supposed to see. For Jack, it was an adrenaline thing. "Not today," Johnny said.

Jack walked to Johnny's bike, where the map was wedged into the spokes of the front tire. He pulled it out, held it up. "What about this?" Johnny looked at his friend, then told him about his run-in with Detective Hunt. "He's all over me."

Jack thought it was bullshit. "He's just a cop."

"Your dad's a cop."

"Yeah, and I steal beer from his fridge. What does that tell you?" Jack spit in the dirt, a universal sign of disgust between the two boys. "Come on. Let's do something. It makes you feel better. We both know it. And I can't sit out here all day."

"No."

"Whatever," Jack said, and shoved the map back between the spokes. He saw the feather tied to Johnny's bike. It dangled from a cord looped around the seat post. He took it in his hand. "Hey, what's this?"

Johnny stared at his friend. "Nothing," he said.

Jack ran the feather between his fingers. Light made it glisten at the edges. He tilted it against the light. "It's cool," he said.

"I said, leave it alone."

Jack saw the new angle in his friend's shoulders, and he let the feather drop. It swung once on its cord. "Jeez. It was just a question."

Johnny relaxed his fingers. Jack was Jack. He meant no harm. "I heard that your brother picked Clemson."

"You heard that?"

"It was all over the news."

Jack picked up a rock, rolled it from his good hand to his bad. "He's already being scouted by the pros. He broke the record last week."

"What record?"

49

"Career home runs."

"For the school?"

Jack shook his head. "The state."

"Guess your old man is proud," Johnny said.

"His son is gonna be famous." Jack's smile looked real, but Johnny saw how he tucked his bad arm more tightly against his ribs. "Of course he's proud."

They went back to drinking. The sun crawled higher, but the daylight seemed to dim. The air grew cool, as if the river itself had chilled. Johnny got halfway through his third beer, then put it down.

Jack got drunk.

They spoke no more of his brother.

It was noon when they heard the car downshift on the road. It stopped at the bridge, then turned onto the old logging track that led to the high bank above them. "Shit." Jack hid the beer cans. Johnny pulled on his shirt to cover the bruises, and Jack pretended that it was a normal thing to do. It was an old argument between them, whether or not to tell.

A high, metal grill pushed through the weeds that grew between the ruts of the track, and Johnny saw that it was a pickup, waxed. Chrome threw off glints of sun and the windshield was mirrored. When it stopped, the engine revved, then died. Three of the four doors opened. Jack stood up straighter.

Blue jeans. Boots. Thick arms. Johnny saw all of that as the older kids circled to the front of the truck. He'd seen them around. They were high school kids. Seventeen, eighteen years old. Grown men, or close to it. One had a pint of bourbon in his hand. All three were smoking cigarettes. They stood on a lip of earth where the bank fell away to the water. They looked down on Johnny, and one of them, a tall blond kid with a raspberry birthmark on his neck, nudged the driver. "Look at this," he said. "Couple of junior high faggots."

The driver's face showed no emotion. The guy with the bourbon took a pull on the bottle. Jack said, "Fuck off, Wayne."

Birthmark stopped laughing.

"That's right," Jack said. "I know who you are."

The driver thumped the back of his hand on Birthmark's chest. He was tall and well built, handsome in a postcard way. He regarded Wayne coolly, then pointed at Jack. "That's Gerald Cross's brother, so show him a little respect."

Wayne made a face. "That little dipshit? I don't believe it." He took a step, leaned over the bank and raised his voice. "Your brother should have signed with Carolina," he said. "You tell him Clemson is for pussies."

"Is that where you'll be going?" Johnny asked.

The driver laughed. So did the kid holding the bourbon. Wayne's face darkened, but the driver stepped forward, cut him off. "I know you, too," he said to Johnny, then paused and took a drag on his cigarette. "I'm sorry about your sister."

"Wait a minute," Wayne said, and pointed. "That's this guy?"

"Yes, it is."

The words came without visible emotion, and the blood fell out of Johnny's face. "I don't know you," Johnny said.

Jack touched Johnny's arm. "That's Hunt's son. The cop's son. His name is Allen. He's a senior."

Johnny looked up and saw the resemblance. Different hair, but the same build. The same soft eyes. "This is our place," Johnny said. "We were here first."

Hunt's son leaned out over the bank, but was clearly not disturbed by the confrontational tone. He spoke to Jack. "Haven't seen you around in a while."

"Why would you?" Jack said. "We've got nothing to say to each other. Gerald either, for that matter."

Johnny looked at Jack. "He knows your brother?"

"Once upon a time."

Allen straightened. "Once upon a time," he said, and there was no emotion in the words. "We'll find another place." He turned around, stopped, and spoke to Jack. "Tell your brother I said hi."

"Tell him yourself."

Allen paused, then offered an empty smile. He gestured to his friends, then got in the truck and started the engine. They backed up the dirt track, disappeared; then it was just the river, the wind.

"That's Hunt's son?" Johnny asked.

"Yeah." Jack spit in the dirt.

"What's the problem with him and your brother?"

"A girl," Jack said, then looked out over the river. "Water under the bridge."

The mood soured after that. They caught a garter snake and let it go, shaved driftwood with their knives, but it was no good. Johnny was talked out and Jack sensed it, so when a distant whistle announced the southbound freight, Jack pulled on his shoes and packed up. "I'm going to split," he said.

"You sure?"

"Unless you want to pedal me back to town on your handlebars." Johnny followed Jack up the bank. "You want to hook up later?" Jack asked. "Catch a movie? Play some videogames?"

The whistle called again, closer. "You'd better roll," Johnny said.

"Just call me later."

Johnny waited until he was gone, then unwrapped the pin-

52

feather from his shirt and slipped the string over his neck. Dipping his hands in the river, he dabbed water on his face, then smoothed the feather on his bike. The water made it gleam, and it slid between his fingertips, crisp and cool and perfect.

Johnny skimmed some more stones, then went back to the rock and lay down. The sun was warm, the air a blanket, and at some point, he dozed. When he woke, it was with a start. The day had slid to late afternoon: five o'clock, maybe five thirty. Dark clouds piled up on the far horizon. A breeze carried the smell of distant rain.

Johnny hopped off the rock and went to find his shoes. He had them in his hand when he heard the whine of a small engine. It approached from the north, fast. The whine climbed to a scream, a motorcycle, pushing hard. It was almost to the bridge when Johnny heard another engine. This one was big and running wide open. Johnny craned his neck, saw the concrete abutment that ran along the bridge and beyond that a slice of green leaves and sky gone the color of ash. The bridge began to shake, and Johnny knew that he'd never heard anything hit it so fast.

They were halfway across when metal hit metal. Johnny saw a shower of sparks, the top of a car, and a motorcycle that cartwheeled once before the body came over the rail. One of the legs bent impossibly, the arms churned, and Johnny knew that it was a mistake, a pinwheel that screamed with a man's voice.

It landed at Johnny's feet with a wet thump and the double snap of breaking bones. It was a man in a muddy shirt and brown pants. One arm twisted under his back, angle all wrong, and his chest looked caved in. His eyes were open, and they were the most amazing blue.

Brakes squealed on the road. Johnny stepped closer to the injured man, saw skin torn from one side of his face, right eye starting to go bloody. His good eye locked on Johnny as if the boy could save him.

Up on the road, the big engine gunned. Tires barked in reverse. Johnny felt the vibration when the car rolled back onto the bridge.

The injured man's jaw worked. "He's coming back."

"It's okay," Johnny said. "We'll help you." He knelt in the dirt. The man held out his hand and Johnny took it. "It's going to be okay."

But the man ignored Johnny's words. With a surprising strength, he pulled the boy closer. "I found her."

Johnny focused on the man's lips. "You found who?"

"The girl that was taken."

Johnny felt cold shock. The man's body seized, and blood shot from his mouth onto Johnny's shirt. Johnny barely noticed. "Who?" he said again, then louder. "Who?"

"I found her . . ."

Above them, the big engine idled. The injured man rolled his eyes up, his fear obvious. He pulled Johnny so close that he smelled blood and crushed organs. The man's eyes crinkled at the edges, and Johnny heard a single word. A whisper.

"Run . . ."

"What?"

The man's grip tightened. Johnny heard how the big engine rumbled and spat, then something like steel on concrete. The man's hand clenched so hard that nails cut Johnny's skin.

"For God's sake—"

The body seized again, spine locked tight, broken arm twisting.

"Run . . ."

Johnny looked down, saw a boot heel push dirt, and something clicked in his mind.

This was not an accident.

Johnny looked at the bridge and saw a hump of movement: a head and a shoulder, a man moving around the front of the car. It was a shadow man, a cutout. Johnny felt the blood on his hands, sticky wet and going cold.

Not an accident.

The man's body seized, head slamming dirt, boot heel drumming. Johnny tried to pull his hand free, had to jerk with all he had. Noise on the bridge. Movement. Fear was a knife that went in low and touched some deep place in him. Johnny had never been so scared in all of his life, not the day he woke up to find his father gone, not the times his mom winked out and Ken got that gleam in his eye.

Johnny was terrified.

Frozen.

Then he turned and ran, along the river, down the trail. He ran until his throat closed, until his heart tried to claw free from his chest. He ran fast and he ran afraid. He ran until the giant black monster stepped from the shadows and grabbed him up.

Then Johnny screamed.

CHAPTER FIVE

Levi Freemantle carried a precious thing on his shoulder. It was a heavy box, wrapped twice in black plastic and closed up with silver tape. Few men could carry it as far as Levi had, but Levi was not like other men. He ignored the hurt of it, the sense of it. He kept his feet on the path and moved his lips when words rose up in his mind. He listened to God's voice in his head and followed the river like his momma taught him when he was a boy. The river was the river, never-changing, and Levi had walked the river trail a hundred times, maybe. Not that he counted that good.

But a hundred was a lot.

He'd walked it a lot.

Levi saw the white boy before he heard him. He was coming straight at him, tearing down the trail like the devil was at his heels and hungry for white boys. His head rode low on skinny shoulders, face gone purple red, feet skipping over rocks and holes as branches snapped at his face and missed. The boy never looked back, not once, and it was like watching a hunted animal run.

Levi wanted to let the boy pass, but there was no way to hide. There was river and there was trees, but Levi stood six foot five and weighed three hundred pounds. People with guns were looking for him. Cops with bright metal on their belts, guards with clubs and nasty smiles. So Levi asked God what to do, and God told him to grab the boy up. Don't hurt him, God said. Just pick him up.

"Truly?" Levi whispered, but God did not answer; so Levi shrugged, then stepped from behind the tree and grabbed the boy up with one thick arm. The boy screamed, but Levi held him, gentle as he could. He was surprised, when God told him what to tell the boy.

"God says—" he began.

But Levi did not speak fast enough. The boy got one of Levi's fingers in his mouth and clamped down until the skin popped like a grape. His teeth went all the way to the bone, and blood pumped hard. It hurt, really hurt, and Levi flung the boy down into the dirt. He felt bad when he did it, like maybe he'd let God down.

But it hurt.

The boy rolled to his feet and took off like a rabbit, but Levi didn't think once about chasing him. He couldn't run with the heavy box on his shoulder, and he couldn't leave the box, not even for a minute. So he held his bloody finger and wished it would stop hurting like it did. The pain made him think of his wife, and that was a worse kind of hurt, so he kept one hand around the bloody finger and listened for the voice of God. When he finally spoke to Levi, he said it might be nice to know what the boy was running from.

Levi shrugged his giant shoulders.

"God talks and Levi walks."

That was a funny.

It took twenty minutes to get to the bridge. The blood on the rocks looked black and wrong, and Levi listened hard before laying his package on the ground and stepping out from under the willow tree. He wanted somebody to tell him what to do, but God had gone still. A finger of hot wind laid itself across his cheek and lightning flashed off in the west. The air was heavy with a dry, powdery smell that rose from the dust under the bridge and felt charged with static.

Levi thought he heard a voice in the river. He tilted his head, and listened for a full minute before deciding it was only water moving. Or a snake in the grass. Or a carp in the reeds at the river's edge.

But not God.

When God spoke, Levi felt cool air pile up above him; he felt peaceful, even when he remembered the bad he'd done.

So this wasn't God.

He stood over the body and his head wasn't working right. It wasn't that he was scared—although he did feel small, sharp nails on the back of his neck—Levi felt sad for the crooked man. Busted up and leaking red was wrong. So was the stillness, the open, flat-looking eyes.

Levi rocked from one foot to the other. He rubbed at the scars on his face, the right side where the skin looked melted. He didn't know what to do, so he sat down to wait for God to tell him.

God would know.

God was good like that.

CHAPTER SIX

Johnny came onto his own street just as the sun set and the light faded to purple. Night sounds rose in the woods. He limped, in pain, but his mind was flush with hope. It burned with it.

I found her.

You found who?

The girl that was taken.

Johnny replayed the words over and over, looking for some reason to doubt the emotion that pushed him through the pain that radiated up from his feet. Eight miles, most of it running, all of it without shoes. His feet were torn and cut, but his right foot was the worst, gashed by a broken bottle two miles after the hobgoblin with the black box grabbed him. Johnny could still taste the man's blood, the dirt on his skin. He tried not to think about it too much. Instead, he thought about his sister, his mother.

Johnny crested the second-to-last hill and a damp wind pressed against him. He saw lights strung out on the road-side. Windows. Houses. They looked small under the purple sky, crowded where the dark forest pushed them against the thin black road. Another mile, he told himself. One more hill.

His mother needed to hear what he'd heard.

He started down, and did not hear the car that rose on the crest behind him. He imagined what the news might do for his mother. Get her out of bed. Get her off the pills. It could be a whole new beginning. The two of them, and then Alyssa.

His father would come back.

They could get their old house.

The headlights found him and Johnny moved off the road. His shadow flowed left, then flickered out when the car pulled even and stopped. Johnny felt a spike of fear, then recognized Ken's car. It was a Cadillac, big and white, with sharp edges and gold letters that said, Escalade. Ken's window came down. His skin was almost tan enough to hide the bags under his eyes. "Where the hell have you been?" Johnny shook his head, winded. "Get in the car, Johnny. Right now."

Johnny bent at the waist. "I don't—" He shoved a fist into his side.

Ken jammed the transmission into park and threw open his door. "Don't talk back to me, kid. Just get in the car. Your mother's falling apart over this. The whole town is in an uproar." Ken climbed out. He was tall and heavy, shapeless in the way that Johnny thought only middle-aged men could be. He had a gold watch, thin hair, and laugh lines that made no sense to Johnny.

Johnny's words came with difficulty. "Falling apart over what?"

Ken gestured with a thick hand. "In. Now."

Johnny climbed in and slid across the smooth leather seat. Ken put the car in gear, and Johnny thought of the dead man.

I found her.

The house was lit up like Christmas: inside lights, outside lights, cop cars that angled in the drive and painted the yard with slashes of blue. Uniformed cops stood under the darkening sky, and Johnny saw guns and radios and slick, black clubs that hung from metal rings.

"What's going on?"

Ken opened his door and dropped a hand on Johnny's neck. Fingers dug into the thin straps of muscle and Johnny rolled his shoulders.

"That hurts."

"Not as much as it should." Ken dragged him across the seat and out of the car. His hand came away and he offered the cops a perfect smile. "Found him," he announced, and they stopped in the drive as Johnny's mother stepped onto the porch. She wore blue jeans and a brown shirt faded to the color of chocolate milk. Uncle Steve stepped out beside her. Johnny took another step, and his mother flew down the stairs, hair gone wild, eyes wet and crazy. She threw her arms around him, and her words blurred: "Oh my God. Where have you been?"

Johnny didn't understand. He'd come home after dark many times. Most days, she didn't know if he was in bed or not. Over his mother's shoulder, Johnny saw one of the cops lift his radio. "Dispatch. Twenty-seven. Please inform Detective Hunt that we've located Johnny Merrimon. He's at home."

A static-filled voice acknowledged what the cop had said. Then, some seconds later, the radio hissed again. "Twenty-seven, be advised. Detective Hunt is en route to your location."

"Ten-four, dispatch."

Johnny felt his mother's arms loosen. She pushed him back, and suddenly she was shaking him, screaming: "Don't you ever do that again! Not ever! Do you hear me? Do you? Say you do! Say it!" Then she grabbed him up again. "God, Johnny. I was so worried."

Johnny was shaken and squeezed, rattled so hard he could barely speak. The cops moved down the stairs, and Johnny saw his Uncle Steve, who begged with his eyes. Then Johnny understood. "The school called?"

His mother nodded against his neck. "They went into lock-down right after lunch. They called here and said they couldn't find you, so I called your Uncle Steve; but he said he dropped you off. He swore it. And then you didn't come home, and I thought . . ."

Johnny pulled out of her grasp. "Lockdown for what?"

His mother caressed one side of his face. "Oh, Johnny." Her fingers felt shaky and warm. "It's happened again."

"What has?"

His mother broke. "Another girl's been taken. Right off the school grounds, they think. A seventh-grader. Tiffany Shore."

Johnny blinked. His words came, automatic. "I know Tiffany."

"Me, too."

Her voice trailed off, but Johnny knew what she was think-ing. Tiffany Shore was in the seventh grade. Same as Alyssa had been when she vanished. Johnny shook his head. He thought of the dead man's words. When he'd said, *I found her,* he was talking about Johnny's sister, about Alyssa. Not Tiffany. Not some other girl. "That can't be right," Johnny said; but his mother nodded, crying, and Johnny felt the hope go cold. He felt it crumble to ash. "That can't be right," he said again.

She rocked back on her heels, looking for the right words; but one of the cops stepped forward before she could find them. "Son," he said, and Johnny looked up, "is that blood on your shirt?"

CHAPTER SEVEN

Levi waited with the broken body as the sun sank. The flies bothered him and his finger hurt so bad he wondered if God was testing him. He'd been to church and knew that God did that kind of thing; but Levi was nothing special. He swept floors to make money. The world confused him. But God's voice had been with Levi for seven days. It came like a whisper and was a comfort when the world seemed dark and tilted left. A week of whisper left a huge hole in a man's head when the whisper stopped, and Levi had to wonder why God was silent now. He was an escaped convict sitting in the dirt ten feet from a dead man. He'd been wandering loose for seven days.

I made the world in seven days.

The voice gushed into Levi like a flood, but it sounded different. It flickered in, faded out, and the thought felt unfinished. Levi held his breath, turned his head, but the voice didn't come again. Levi knew that he was not smart—his wife had told him that—but he wasn't stupid, either. Convicts and dead bodies looked bad together. The road was just above his head. So Levi decided that God would have to wait.

Just this once.

He knelt by the dead man and went through his pockets. He found a wallet and took the cash because he was hungry. He asked God to forgive him, then dropped the wallet in the dirt and straightened the man's body. He pulled the broken arm from behind his back and crossed his hands on his chest.

He dipped a finger in the tacky blood and made a cross on the pale, smooth forehead, then he closed the open eyes. He prayed to God to take the dead man's soul.

Take it.

Care for it.

He saw the flash of white when he stood.

It was in the dead man's hand, a scrap of fabric that poked between two fingers. It came out easily when Levi pulled. Pale and ragged, it looked like a piece of shirt that had been cut free or torn. It was as long as a baby's shoe, faded and dirty, with a name tag sewn into it. Levi couldn't read, so the letters meant nothing, but the fabric was kind of white and just the right size. He twisted it around his bleeding finger and used his teeth to tie it off, pull it tight.

In the shade of the willow, he stopped beside the heavy package wrapped in plastic. He ran one of his massive hands along the top of it, then hoisted it onto his shoulder. To any other man, it would have felt heavy, and the thought of it might have oppressed. But that's not how it was for Levi. He was strong, he had a purpose; and when the plastic rustled against his ear, he heard the voice of God. It told Levi he'd done good, and it told him to walk on.

He was fifty minutes gone when the cops showed up.

Detective Hunt's car rolled to a stop on the bridge. This far out, there were no street lamps, no houses. The sky above was black, with a deep purple line on the horizon to the west. Above them, storm clouds pressed low, and a hard, dry light thumped twice before the thunder came. A line of marked cars, lights flashing, pulled in behind Detective Hunt's car. Spotlights clicked on and lit the bridge. Hunt turned to Johnny, who sat in the backseat with his mother. Their faces were blacked out, and he saw strands of hair that stood out against the bright light from the cars behind them. "Are you okay?" he asked. No answer. Johnny's mother pulled him tight. "This the place, Johnny?"

Johnny swallowed. "This is it." He pointed. "That side of the bridge. Straight down."

"Tell me one more time what he said. Word for word."

Johnny's voice sounded dead. "I found her. The girl that was taken."

"Nothing else?"

"He told me to run. He was talking about the guy in the car."

Hunt nodded. They'd been through it six or seven times. Everything that had happened. "Nothing else to make you think he was talking about your sister? He didn't mention her name or description or anything like that?"

"He was talking about Alyssa."

"Johnny—"

"He was!"

Johnny's head tipped in the harsh glare, and Hunt wanted to touch the boy on the shoulder, tell him that it would be okay; but it was not his place to fix every broken thing, no matter how badly he might want to. He glanced at Katherine Merrimon. She sat, small and immobile, and he wanted to touch her, too; but those feelings were complicated. She was beautiful and gentle and damaged, but she was a victim, and there were rules about that. So Hunt stayed focused on the case, and his voice was hard when he spoke. "The odds are against it, Johnny. You should prepare for that. It's been a year. He was probably talking about Tiffany Shore."

Johnny shook his head, but remained silent. When his mother spoke, she sounded like a child herself. "I know Tiffany," she said.

She'd said that twice already, but no one mentioned it. Johnny blinked and saw an image of the missing girl. Tiffany was small and blond, with green eyes, a scar on her left hand, and a stupid joke she'd tell to anyone that would listen. Something about three monkeys, an elephant, and a cork. She was a nice girl. Always had been.

"The man on the bridge," Hunt began. "Do you remember anything else? Could you identify him?"

"He was just a shape. A sense of movement. I didn't see his face."

"What about the car?"

"No. Like I said."

Hunt peered through the windows as other cops began to exit cars and throw shadows against the stark concrete wall of the bridge. He was unhappy. "Stay here," he said. "Do not get out of this car."

He climbed out, shut the door behind him, and absorbed the scene. Heavy, damp air carried the scent of the river. Darkness welled up from beneath the bridge, and Hunt glanced north as if he could see the great swath of rough country that pushed down on Raven County: the stony woods and, at the foot of those hills, the twenty-mile stretch of swamp that vomited out the river. A drop of cold rain touched his cheek, and he gestured at the nearest cop. "Put a light over the side," he said. "Down there." He moved to the abutment as the cop pulled a light from the cruiser and shot a spear of light out into the night. It cut ragged patterns as the officer walked to the edge of the bridge, and when he put the light on the riverbank, it pinned the body on the dirt.

Johnny Merrimon's bicycle lay on the ground five feet away from it.

Jesus.

The kid was right.

Hunt felt his people move around him. He had four uniformed cops and Crime Scene on standby. He heard a staccato burst on the windshield, felt more drops spatter on the top of his head. The rain was coming, and it was coming hard. He gestured with an arm. "Get a tarp over that body. Move. I also want tarps over the railing, right here." He was thinking of paint scrapings, and of the glass shards that winked on the blacktop. "Somewhere around here, there should be a motorcycle. Find it. And somebody call for a tent." Thunder crashed and he looked up at the sky. "This is going to get ugly."

In the car, Johnny felt it when his mother began to shake. It started in her arms, moved to her shoulders.

"Mom?"

She ignored him and dug into her purse. It was dark in the low part of the car, so she held the bag up until headlights struck it. Johnny saw one eye when she tilted her head, then he heard the rattle and click of pills in a plastic bottle. She shook pills into her hand, tossed back her head and swallowed them dry. The bag fell back into darkness and her head hit the headrest hard enough to bounce once. Her voice, when she spoke, was devoid of emotion. "Don't ever do that again," she said.

"Ditch school?" Johnny asked.

"No."

A difficult pause. Ice in Johnny's chest.

"Don't make me hope." She turned her head. "Don't you ever do that to me again."

They got the tent up before the bottom fell out of the sky. Hunt squatted next to the body as the tent rattled and shook. The material snapped so loudly that he had to shout to be heard. Two uniformed officers held lights; a CSI tech and the medical examiner knelt on the other side of the body. Over

Hunt's shoulder, one of the uniforms said: "Water will be running under soon." Hunt agreed. Thunderstorms in late spring rolled in hard and left fast, but they could drop a lot of water. It was a bad break.

Hunt studied the blood-streaked face, then the splinter of bone where the arm bent at right angles. Grime caked the dead man's clothes; it was black, almost green, ground into the cloth and into the treads of his shoes. A smell lingered, something organic, something that went beyond river water and recent death. "What do we know?" Hunt asked the medical examiner.

"He's fit. Well muscled. Mid-thirties, I'd say. Wallet's with one of your men there."

Hunt looked at Detective Cross, who held a wallet in a clear plastic evidence bag. Cross was a big man whose face looked seamed and heavy behind the bright light. He was thirty-eight and had been a cop for over ten years. He'd made his reputation as a hard-nosed patrol sergeant who showed great courage under fire. He'd been a detective for less than six months. Cross spoke as he handed over the wallet. "Driver's license says his name is David Wilson. Organ donor. No corrective lenses. He lived on an expensive street, carried a library card and a stack of restaurant receipts: some from Raleigh, some from Wilmington. No sign of a wedding ring. No cash. Two credit cards, still in the wallet."

Hunt looked at the wallet. "You touched this?"

"Yes."

"I'm lead detective on this case, Cross. You understand that?" His voice was tight, forcibly controlled.

Cross drew back his shoulders. "Yes, sir."

"You're new at this. I understand. But being lead on this case means that I'm responsible. We catch the killer or not. We find the girl or we don't." His eyes remained fierce. A finger came up. "However this ends, I have to live with it. Night after night, it's on me. You understand?"

"Yes, sir."

"Don't ever touch evidence at my crime scene without permission. Do it again and I will fuck you up."

"I was just trying to help."

"Get out of my tent." Hunt shook with anger. If he lost another girl . . .

Cross left with a guilty step. Hunt forced a deep breath, then returned his attention to the body. The shirt was just a T-shirt, gray and stinking of sweat and blood and green black filth; the belt was plain brown and nondescript, with a brass buckle that showed heavy scarring. His pants were made of tough, worn cotton. One eye was partially open, and it looked flat and dull in the bright light.

"Hot as hell in this tent." The medical examiner's name was Trenton Moore. Small and sparely built, he had thick hair, large pores, and a lisp that grew more pronounced the louder he had to speak. He was young, smart, and dynamite on the stand, even with the lisp. "I think he's a rock climber."

"I beg your pardon."

Dr. Moore gestured with his chin. "Look at his hands."

Hunt studied David Wilson's hands. They showed calluses, scratches, and abrasions. The nails were clipped and even but dirty. They could belong to any construction worker he'd ever met. "What about them?"

The medical examiner straightened one of the fingers. "See that callus?" Hunt looked at the fingertip, a thick pad of tough skin. Dr. Moore flattened out the other fingers; they all had the same callus. "I had a roommate in college, a climber. He'd do fingertip chin-ups from the doorjamb. Sometimes he'd just hang there and chat. It was sick. Here, feel that."

Dr. Moore offered the hand and Hunt touched the callus. It felt like shoe leather. "My roommate had fingertips just like that." He pointed. "The upper body musculature is consistent. Overdeveloped forearms. Significant scarring on the hands. Of course, we're just shooting the shit here. I can't make any official comment until I get him on the table."

Hunt studied the placement of the hands, crossed over the dead man's chest. The legs straight and side by side. "Somebody moved him," he said.

"Maybe. We won't know anything for certain until the autopsy."

Creases appeared in Hunt's forehead. He gestured at the body. "You don't think he landed in that position, do you?"

The medical examiner grinned, suddenly looking all of twenty-five. "Just kidding, Detective. Trying to keep it light."

"Well, don't." Hunt gestured at the shattered arm, the crooked leg. "You think those were broken when the car hit him or when he came over the bridge?"

"Do you know for a fact that he was struck on the bridge?"

"His motorcycle was definitely moved postimpact. Somebody pushed it down an embankment. A couple of branches broken off a tree and tossed on top. Somebody would have found it eventually. We found paint scrapings on the bridge that match the color of the gas tank. I suspect that chemistry will match. And there's the kid. He saw it."

"Is he here?" Dr. Moore asked.

Hunt shook his head. "I sent him home with a uniform. Him and his mother. They don't need to be here for this."

"He's how old?"

"Thirteen."

"Reliable?"

Hunt thought about it. "I don't know. I think, maybe. He's a sharp kid. A little messed up, but sharp."

"What's his time line?"

"He says the body came over the rail two, maybe two and a half hours ago."

The examiner rolled his shoulders. "That's consistent. No lividity yet." He returned his attention to the body, bending low over the dead man's face. He pointed at the bloody cross on the forehead. "Don't see that very often."

"What do you make of it?"

"I deal in bodies, not motives. There's blood on the eyelids, too. You may get a print."

"How do you figure?"

"Just a hunch. Right size, right shape." Dr. Moore shrugged a final time. "Whoever killed this guy, I don't think he's very smart."

When Hunt emerged from the tent, the rain soaked his clothes, his hair. He looked at the bridge and tried to imagine the crunch of metal, the arc of the body, and how it must have been for the boy chosen by fate to bear witness. Hunt stooped for Johnny's bike, which had been cast aside when the tent went up. It made a sucking noise when he pulled it from the mud. Brown water ran off the pocked metal and Hunt walked it to the dry space beneath the bridge. A handful of cops sheltered there, some with cigarettes, only one of them looking very busy. Cross. He stood apart from the others, a light in one hand, Johnny Merrimon's map in the other.

Hunt walked over, still angry about the wallet, but Cross spoke first.

"I'm sorry," he said, and looked it.

Hunt thought of the year since he'd lost Alyssa: the nightmares, the futility. It was not fair to take it out on Cross. He was young at this, and he'd have his own black nights, given time. Hunt forced a smile. It wasn't much, but it was all he had. "Where'd you find that?" He pointed at the map.

Cross had a square jaw under brush-cut hair. He lowered the map and stabbed his flashlight downriver. "It was with the kid's bike." Cross flinched. "It's not evidence, is it?"

It was, but Hunt told himself to relax. "I'll need that back."

"No problem." Hunt turned to go, but Cross stopped him. "Detective . . ."

Hunt stopped and turned. Cross looked tall in the gloom, his skin olive green, his eyes intent.

"Listen," Cross said. "This has nothing to do with nothing, okay, but you probably should know about it. You know my son?"

"Gerald? The ball player? Yeah, I know him."

Cross's mouth drew down at the corners. "No, not Gerald. The other one. Jack. My youngest."

"No. I don't know Jack."

"Well, he was out here today with the Merrimon kid. He ditched school, too. But look, he was long gone before any of this happened. The school called me after the lockdown. I found the kid at home, watching cartoons."

Hunt thought about it. "Do I need to talk to him?"

"He's clueless, but you're welcome to talk to him."

"Doesn't seem relevant," Hunt said.

"Good. Because he tells me that your boy was out here, too."

Hunt shook his head. "I don't think so."

"Lunchtime or thereabouts. Your boy and a couple of his friends." Cross's face remained inscrutable. "Just thought you should know."

"And Jack is certain—"

"My son is lazy, not stupid."

72

"Okay, Cross. Thanks." Hunt began to turn, when Cross stopped him again.

"Listen, speaking of relevant. This guy who assaulted the Merrimon kid, the black guy with the scars on his face."

"What about him?"

"You're assuming that he had nothing to do with what happened here? With this victim? Is that right?"

"With this murder?"

"Right."

"No," Hunt said. "I don't see how he could. He was a mile or more downriver when it happened."

"Are you sure about that?"

"Your point?"

"We're assuming that three men came into contact with Johnny Merrimon. The dead man, Wilson, whoever drove the car that ran Wilson off the bridge, and the big black guy with the scarred face. Is that accurate?"

"That's our working theory, yes."

"But the kid didn't see the driver of the car. He saw a shape, a shadow, but he can't actually identify the driver, he can't say if it was the black guy or not." Cross raised the map. "This is a tax map for this side of town, and that's where the detail is. In town. Streets, neighborhoods. But here, top right, just on the edge. This is the river and this"—he pointed—"this is where we are. See the bridge?"

"I see it."

"Now follow the river."

Hunt saw it immediately. Just south of the bridge, the river bent into a tight loop; it wrapped around a narrow finger of land that was over a mile long but couldn't be more than a quarter mile across. Hunt felt a hard spike of anger, not at Cross, but at himself. "The trail follows the river," Hunt said.

"If the Merrimon kid stayed on the trail, he would need to cover a lot of ground to reach the place where he was grabbed, say ten or fifteen minutes at a dead run." Cross tapped a finger on the map. "If I left the trail and cut across here, I could walk to that same place in five minutes."

"Cut through the woods, and it's close."

"Really close."

Hunt looked out at the tent, a blur in the drumming rain. The man had been run off the road, crushed. "If David Wilson was killed because he learned something—"

"Knew something about the missing girl . . ."

Hunt bit down. "The man that killed him would want Johnny dead, too. And if he knew the way the river runs—"

"He could cross here and wait for the boy. Johnny runs for twelve, fifteen minutes. The killer walks for five, and there he is when Johnny comes around the corner."

"Damn." Hunt straightened. "Get on the radio. I want an all-points on a large black male, forty to sixty, with severe scarring on the right side of his face. His car will have visible damage, probably to the left front fender. Inform dispatch that he's wanted in connection with the homicide of David Wilson but may also be linked to the abduction of Tiffany Shore. Use caution in apprehending. We need to question him. Get that out now."

Cross pulled out his radio and called it in.

Hunt waited, and another wave of anger rolled over him. The past year had worn him thin, made him sloppy. He should have seen the river issue—the way it bent like that—not heard it from some rookie detective. But it was done. The girl was what mattered, so it had to be done. He let it go, drilled in on the matter at hand. Tiffany was missing for less than a day, eight hours, almost nine. This time, he would bring the kid home. He clenched his fists and he swore it.

This time it would be different.

He looked at Johnny's bike, heard the boy's voice in his head.

Promise?

Hunt reached for the large, brown feather that hung below the seat of Johnny's bike. It was tattered and sad looking, gritty between his fingers. He stroked it smooth.

Promise.

Behind him, Cross lowered the radio. "Done," he said.

Hunt nodded.

"What do you have there?"

Hunt let the feather droop back on the cord that secured it. It swung once, then stuck on the wet metal. "Nothing," he said. "A feather."

Cross stepped closer and lifted the feather.

"This is an eagle feather."

"How do you know that?"

Cross shrugged, looked embarrassed. "I was born in the mountains. My grandmother is half Cherokee. She was into all that totem stuff."

"Totem stuff?"

"You know. Rituals and sacred plants." He lifted a hand toward the river. "The river for purity. Snakes for wisdom. Stuff like that." He shrugged. "I always thought it was kind of bullshit."

"Totems?" Hunt repeated.

"Yeah." He gestured at the feather. "That's good magic."

"What kind of magic?"

"Strength. Power." Lightning thumped and he let the feather fall. "Only chiefs carry eagle feathers."

CHAPTER EIGHT

In the back of the patrol car, Johnny's mother slumped against his shoulder. Her head rolled when the curves came fast, bounced when the tires hit rough pavement. The river was behind them, the dead guy, too, and what was left of Johnny's faith in the wisdom of cops. Hunt refused to consider that this could still be about Alyssa, and that had made Johnny angry.

Maybe!

He'd said it loud, then repeated it when Hunt's eyes went soft.

Maybe it is!

But Hunt was busy and had his own ideas. He'd grown short with Johnny's insistence, then declined further discussion and ordered them home.

Leave it alone, he'd said. *This is not your problem.*

But the cop was wrong. Johnny felt it in his heart. It *was* his problem.

The patrol car stopped in the driveway. Rain hammered on the metal roof and Johnny studied the house, the light that faltered in the small, muddy yard. Shadows moved inside. Ken's car sat in the drive; Uncle Steve's did, too. The pills had taken his mother. Her eyes were closed, and small sounds tripped past her lips. Johnny hesitated, and the patrolman turned in his seat, his face distorted behind the glass divider covered with handprints and dried spit. "She okay?" he asked.

Johnny nodded.

"Well, this is it, kid." He hesitated, eyes still on Johnny's mother. "Is she going to need some help?"

Johnny defense mechanisms kicked in. "She's okay."

"Well, let's go."

Johnny shook his mother's shoulder. Her head lolled and he shook harder. When she opened her eyes, he squeezed her arm. "We have to go," he said. "We're home."

"Home." She repeated the word.

"Yes. Home. Let's go." Johnny opened his door and the rain sound changed from metallic clang to muted roar. Sheets of water fell on wet earth and drooping leaves. Warm air flooded the car. "Don't forget your bag," he said.

Johnny got her out of the car and turned for the shelter of the porch as the patrol car backed out of the mud and spun tires on the slick blacktop. He was on the porch when he realized that his mother was not with him. She stood in the rain, face turned to heaven, hands palm up. Her bag lay in the mud where she'd dropped it. Water fell black around her.

Johnny splashed to her side, the rain stinging hard from its long fall down. "Mom?" He took her arm again. "Come on. Let's go inside." She kept her eyes closed but spoke, her voice too low to hear. "What?" Johnny asked.

"I want to go away."

"Mom . . ."

"I want to wash into the earth and be gone from this place."

Johnny picked up her bag, squeezed her arm hard. "Inside. Now." He sounded like Ken, he realized; but she followed him.

Inside, the lights burned sulfur bright. Uncle Steve sat at the kitchen table, a row of beer cans in front of him. Ken paced, bourbon in a glass between his heavy fingers. They looked up as

Johnny led his mother in. "About time," Ken said. "The nerve of that arrogant cop, telling me that I couldn't come. Telling me that I could go home or wait here with him." He gestured at Uncle Steve, and the disdain was plain in his voice. Steve's head dipped between his shoulders. "I'm going to talk to somebody about that. He should know who I am."

"He knows who you are. He just doesn't care." The words popped out of Johnny before he'd thought them through. Ken stopped and stared, and Johnny knew it could go two ways. But then his mother came in behind him. She was blank-eyed and soaking wet; her clothing clung to her. Johnny took her arm as Ken stared. "Come on," he said. "I'll take you to your room."

"I'll take her." Ken stepped toward them, and Johnny felt something pop. "No," he said. "Just back off, Ken. She doesn't need you right now. She just needs to go to bed. She needs sleep and quiet and nobody messing with her."

Red suffused Ken's face. "Messing with her . . ."

Johnny thought briefly of the folding knife in his pocket. He put himself between Ken and his mother. The moment stretched until Ken decided to smile around his straight and brilliant teeth. "Katherine?" He looked to Johnny's mother. "Tell your son it's okay."

"It's okay, Johnny." The words traveled from some distant place. She swayed a bit, then said, "I'm fine." She turned from her son and shambled to the short and lightless hall. "Let's just go to bed." She put a hand on the wall, stopped for three long seconds, and Johnny watched water run down her face. When she turned, her voice had nothing left. "Go home, Steve."

Ken followed her to the end of the hall, looked back once, and shut the door. Johnny did not hear the lock drop, but he knew that it had. He wanted to punch the wall; instead, he looked at his Uncle Steve, who gathered his cans in silence.

He tossed them in the trash and collected his keys, a giant ring of them that opened every door at the mall. Paradise to any other kid. Just metal to Johnny. Uncle Steve stopped at the door. His eyes were troubled, and he looked at Johnny differently. He put an arm on the doorjamb. "Is this how it is?" he asked, opening one palm in a gesture that encompassed Johnny and the short hall to the locked door.

"Pretty much."

"Damn." Uncle Steve nodded, which Johnny thought was about all he could ever do. "About this morning . . ."

"What about it?" Johnny asked.

"She's just real pretty." Johnny turned away. "Thanks for not telling."

But Johnny, too, had nothing left. He went to his room and sat on the edge of his bed. He looked at the clock on the table and watched the tiny hand tick from one white slash to the next. He counted seconds until the headboard across the hall began its unholy thump; then he went in search of his mother's keys.

Ninety-four, he thought, and locked the front door behind him.

Ninety-four seconds.

He splashed through the mud and started his mother's car. At the bottom of the drive he opened the door, leaned out, and picked up a rock the size of a tennis ball.

When he left the house behind, Johnny steered with care. The windshield was fogged and only one headlight worked. He saw wet pavement, a hint of ditch. He wiped the glass with his hand and looked for the turn that would take him to the rich side of town.

He slowed as he turned onto Ken's street. The houses loomed, set back on huge lawns. Long walks curved across velvet grass and gates guarded the drives, the metal so black it looked cold. Johnny turned off the headlights as his tires crunched against the curb. He left the engine running. It would only take a second.

The rock felt perfect in his hand.

CHAPTER NINE

Detective Hunt drove fast down wet, narrow roads. The crime scene was three miles behind him, medical examiner packing up the body, Hunt's people still on scene. Things had changed after Cross showed him the map. Pieces had shifted in Hunt's mind, possibilities, variables. David Wilson was killed, Hunt believed, because he'd somehow found Tiffany Shore.

I found her, he'd told the boy, and now he was dead.

But where did he find her? How? Under what circumstances? And most important, who killed him? Hunt had drilled in on the car that ran him off the road, the man driving that car. That was logical, but the bend in the river impacted that logic. Hunt had assumed that there were three different men at or near the bridge when the deed was done: Wilson, now dead; the driver of the car that killed him; a random black male two miles downriver. Now Hunt had to question that. Maybe Johnny's giant was not just in the wrong place at the wrong time. Maybe he drove the car that killed David Wilson. Or maybe not.

Two men or three?

Damn!

Hunt needed to talk to Johnny, not later, but now, right this minute. He had new questions. He radioed dispatch and asked to be connected to the patrol unit he'd assigned to take Johnny and Katherine home. He looked at his watch and cursed as the connection was routed. Almost ten hours, that's how long Tiffany had been gone, and the stats were as cold and exact as only numbers could be. Few abductees made it past the first day; that's just how it ran.

Speed.

It all came down to speed.

I found her.

Hunt needed to ask Johnny about the man with the scarred face, about what he saw on the bridge. Hunt needed to know if the two men were one and the same. Not speculation or theory, fact.

"Connecting now," dispatch told him.

A second voice crackled on the radio. Hunt identified himself and asked the officer for Johnny's twenty.

"I just left his house. He was in the driveway last I saw him."

"How long ago, exactly?"

A pause. "Twenty minutes."

"Twenty minutes. Got it." Hunt clicked off. Another five would bring him to the house. *Come on, come on.* He accelerated until the car went light beneath him, steered at dangerous speeds over the slick black roads.

More than three hours since the motorcycle was struck. Whoever hit David Wilson could be anywhere by now, out of the county, out of the state, but Hunt didn't think so. It was risky to cover distance with an abducted child. Once an Amber Alert went out, the public became very aware. Most of these perverts wanted to grab the kid and go to ground. Johnny Merrimon was right about that. And while some abductions were carefully orchestrated, most were matters of opportunity. A child left in the car or untended in a busy store. A child walking alone.

Like Alyssa Merrimon.

She'd been walking home at dusk, alone on an empty stretch

of road. No one could have known she'd be there. No one could have planned for that. Same with Tiffany Shore. She'd lingered near the parking lot after the bell rang. It was a matter of opportunity. And desire.

Hunt braked for a red light, then turned left without stopping and felt the back end lose traction. He corrected the drift, straightened. He thought of evil and of the hard lump in the holster under his arm.

When word came in of Tiffany's abduction, Hunt had ordered a massive response. He'd sent patrol cars to verify the locations of all known sex offenders. Most were considered low probability: voyeurs, exhibitionists; but there were plenty of individuals convicted of rape or child abuse or some other heinous act. Hunt kept a short list of the worst: the deranged, sadistic individuals who were capable of just about anything. These men never got over the evil that drove them. There was no curing, no fixing. For these assholes, it was only a matter of time, so Hunt kept on top of them. He knew where they lived and what they drove; he knew their habits and their predilections. He'd seen photos, talked to victims, and seen the scars firsthand. None of those fuckers should be out of prison.

Not now.

Not ever.

Most were accounted for; they'd been located and interviewed. Almost all had given permission for a search of their homes, and all of the searches had come up negative. Those who had refused were under constant surveillance and Hunt got regular reports. He knew what they were eating and when; if they were alone or not, and if not, who they were with. He knew their locations, their activities. Awake or asleep. Static or on the move. Hunt fielded calls and kept his men sharp as they continued to work the list.

Hunt ran the names in his head. No one on the list stood six and a half feet tall. None had scars like the Merrimon kid had described. If Cross was right, that meant they had a new player, someone off the grid. And if Cross was wrong . . .

The possibilities were endless.

Hunt pulled a photograph of Tiffany Shore from his jacket pocket and glanced at it. He'd taken it from her distraught mother just a few hours ago. It was a school photo, and in it Tiffany was smiling and self-aware. He looked for similarities to Alyssa, but there were precious few. Alyssa had dark hair and fragile features; she looked young and small and innocent, with the same dark eyes as her brother. Tiffany had full lips, a perfect nose, and hair like yellow silk. The picture showed a graceful neck, nascent breasts, and a knowing smile that hinted at the woman she might one day become. The girls looked as if they had little in common, but they did.

They were innocent, both of them, and they were his responsibility.

His.

Nobody else's.

That thought still simmered in Hunt's mind when his cell phone rang. He glanced at caller ID. The Chief. His boss. He gave it four rings, then, against his better judgment, he answered.

"Where are you?" The Chief wasted no time. It was barely twelve months since Alyssa vanished, and now they had another missing girl. He'd be under his own pressures, Hunt knew: Tiffany's family, city government, the press.

"I'm en route to Katherine Merrimon's house. I'll be there in a few minutes."

"You're my lead detective. You should be at David Wilson's house or at the crime scene. Do I really need to spell that out for you?"

84

"No."

But the Chief spelled it out. "If we assume that Wilson found Tiffany Shore—and that *is* what we're assuming—then you should be backtracking his activities. Where he went. Who he talked to. Any choice he made today, any path that could have intersected with Tiffany Shore—"

"I know all that," Hunt interrupted sharply. "I sent Yoakum to his house. I'll meet him there shortly, but this comes first."

"Do I want to know why you're going to Katherine Merrimon's house?" Hunt heard the doubt, the sudden distrust.

"Her son may have information."

Hunt pictured the Chief: flunkies in his office, fat man's sweat staining his shirt. His voice was a politician's voice.

"I need to know that you're on this, Hunt. Are you on this?"

"That's a bullshit question." Hunt knew the source of the Chief's doubt, but could not hide the anger he felt. So he spent time on the Merrimon case. So what? Maybe he felt more than most cops would. It was an important case; but that's not how the Chief saw it. No. He heard about Hunt, awake every night at three in the morning; Hunt, showing up at sunrise on a Sunday to pore over evidence he'd already seen a hundred times; harassing judges to sign warrants that never panned out; working overtime, then off the clock; leveraging other cops, resources that should be spent on other cases. He watched Hunt work himself ragged. He saw the pale skin and the weight loss, the sleepless eyes and the stacks of files on the floor of Hunt's office. And there were other issues.

Rumors.

"It's not a question, Hunt. It's a demand, an imperative."

Hunt clamped his teeth, barely able to speak around the emotion he was choking down. He ran major crimes. Lead detective. That was his job, his life. "I said, I'm on it."

Hunt heard breath on the line, then a voice, muffled in the background. When the Chief spoke, his words came with precision. "I have no room for personal, Hunt. Not on this case."

Hunt stared straight ahead. "Got it. No personal."

"This is about Tiffany Shore. *Her* family. Not Alyssa Merrimon. Not her brother. And not her mother. Are we clear?"

"Crystal."

A long pause, then a voice that hinted at regret. "Personal gets you fired, Clyde. It gets you drummed right the hell out of my department. Don't make me do that."

"I don't need a lecture." He left the rest unsaid: *Not from some fat, politician cop.*

"You've already lost your wife. Don't lose your job, too."

Hunt looked in the mirror and saw the rage in his own eyes. He pulled air deep into his lungs. "Just stay out of my way," he said, and sounded like a reasonable man might sound. "Show a little faith."

"You've been burning the faith candle for a year, and it's burned pretty damn low. When the papers go to bed tomorrow night, I want to see a picture of Tiffany Shore sitting on her mother's lap. Front page. That's how we keep our jobs." A pause, Hunt unwilling to trust his voice and therefore silent. "Give me a happy ending, Clyde. Give me that, and I'll pretend you're the same cop you were a year ago."

The Chief hung up.

Hunt punched the roof of his car, then turned into Johnny's driveway. He noticed at once that the station wagon was gone. When he knocked on the front door, it rattled enough to make the house sound hollow. Hunt looked through the small window and saw Ken Holloway emerging from the dark hall. He wore shined shoes under slightly wrinkled pants, and worked to get his shirt tucked in. He cinched up an alligator belt, then paused at a mirror to smooth his hair and check his teeth. A revolver hung in his right hand.

"Police, Mr. Holloway. Put down the gun and open the door."

Holloway twitched, suddenly aware that he could be seen through the window. A deprecating smile rose on his face. "Police who?"

"Detective Clyde Hunt. I need to speak to Johnny."

The smile disappeared. "May I see a badge?"

Hunt pressed his shield to the glass, then stepped away from the door and lowered one hand to the butt of his service weapon. Holloway donated money to good causes. He served on boards and played golf with powerful people.

But Hunt knew the man.

It had taken a year of watching Katherine and Johnny: odd encounters, like the one at the grocery store; things said and not said; a limp or a bruise; the boy's naked eyes when he thought he was being tough. Hunt had pushed, but Katherine was gone most of the time, out of it, and Johnny was scared. Hunt had nothing solid.

But he knew.

Another step back cleared three feet between Hunt and the door. The dark bulk of Holloway's chest was visible through the slash of window. He looked meaty and tan, with a broad chest above a thick stomach. His face appeared behind the glass. "It's the middle of the night, Detective."

"It's barely nine, Mr. Holloway. A child has been abducted. Please open the door."

The lock disengaged and the door swung open a foot. Creases cut the flesh of Holloway's face, but Hunt saw damp spots at the hairline where he'd tried to make himself crisp. His hands were empty. "What does Tiffany Shore's disappearance have to do with Johnny?"

"Can you step away from the door, please?" Hunt kept his voice professional, which was hard. He'd as soon shoot Ken Holloway as look at him.

"Very well." Holloway pushed the door wide and turned, his hands slapping the sides of his legs.

Hunt stepped inside, eyes cutting left and right until he spotted the weapon, a .38 caliber revolver. Stainless. It sat on top of the television, barrel angled to the wall.

"It's registered," Holloway said.

"I'm sure it is. I need to speak with Johnny."

"This is about what happened today?"

Hunt smelled alcohol. "Do you really care?"

Holloway smiled without humor. "Just a minute." He raised his voice. "Johnny." No answer. He called again, then cursed under his breath. The hall swallowed him up and Hunt heard a door open, then slam closed. When he returned, he came alone. "He's not here."

"Where is he?"

"I have no idea."

Anger rose in Hunt's voice. "He's thirteen years old. It's dark out and raining. The car is gone and you have no idea where he is? As far as I'm concerned, that constitutes neglect."

"And as I understand the law, Detective, that's his mother's problem. I'm a guest in this house."

Their eyes locked, and Hunt stepped closer. Holloway was a two-faced user, slick and accommodating, but only when it served his needs. There might be buildings named after him at the college, but Hunt could not hide his dislike. "You need to be careful with me."

"Is that a threat?"

88

Hunt said nothing.

"You have no idea who I am," Holloway said.

"If harm comes to that boy . . ."

Holloway smiled coldly. "What's your name again? I have a meeting tomorrow with the mayor *and* the city manager. I'd like to get it right."

Hunt spelled it for him, then said, "About the boy."

"He's a delinquent. What do you want me to do about it? He's neither my son nor my responsibility. Now, do you want me to get his mother? I may be able to wake her. She won't know where he is, but I'll haul her out here if it will make you happy."

Hunt had admired Johnny's mother since they'd first met. Small but full of life, she'd shown courage and faith under unbearable circumstances. She'd stayed strong until the day she fell apart, at which point the collapse was total. Maybe it was grief, maybe it was guilt, but she was tragic and lost, adrift in the kind of horror that few parents could imagine. The thought of her with a user like Ken Holloway was bad enough. Seeing her dragged out of bed by him would be even worse, a degradation.

"I'll find him myself." Hunt moved for the door.

"We're not finished, Detective."

"No," Hunt said, "we're not."

His hand was on the door when Holloway's cell phone rang. He lingered as Holloway answered: "Yes." Holloway turned his back to Hunt. "Are you certain? Very well. Yes, call the police. I'll be there in ten minutes." He closed the phone and faced Hunt. "My alarm company," he said. "If you still want to find Johnny, you can start by looking at my house."

"Why do you say that?"

"Because the little shit just threw a rock through my front window."

"What makes you think it's Johnny?"

Holloway picked up his keys. "It's always Johnny."

"Always?"

"This is the fifth fucking time."

Johnny drove down dark streets, and rain put mercury streaks on the glass. Tiffany Shore's parents were rich, and lived just three blocks from Ken Holloway. Johnny had been to a party there once. He slowed as he approached Tiffany's house, then stopped on the street. He saw cop cars and shadows that moved behind draped windows. He watched the house for a long time, then looked at the neighbors on both sides. Warm light spilled out of those houses, and in the dark of the street, Johnny felt very alone, because nobody else knew. No one could understand what was happening behind the walls of Tiffany's house, what her family was suffering: the fear and anger, the slow drain of hope and the end of all things.

No one knew what Johnny knew.

Except her parents, he thought.

Her parents knew.

Hunt sat in his car and watched Holloway come out of the house. He gave a cold stare that Hunt was happy to return, then settled into his car. The big engine caught and the Escalade rocked onto the road. Hunt listened to the rain on his car and looked at the light spilling from Johnny's house. Katherine was asleep in there, and he pictured her buried under the covers, back curved against the night.

He powered up his laptop and keyed in Johnny Merrimon's name. Ken had filed complaints, but there was no record of any arrest. No warrants. Whatever Holloway believed about Johnny's involvement in the ongoing vandalism of his house, he had no proof of it.

Hunt thought about why Johnny would throw rocks through Holloway's windows. Only one thing made sense. Johnny wanted the man out of his house, away from his mother, and he'd figured out the one thing that would do it every time. No way would a man like Holloway leave his house unguarded. Not overnight.

Five times and never caught. Hunt shook his head and tried not to smile.

He really did like that kid.

For another two minutes, Hunt sat in the car and pored through the Tiffany Shore file. It was thin. He knew what she was wearing when last seen. He had a list of identifying marks. A dime-sized birthmark marred the back of her right shoulder blade; a fishhook scar still showed pink on her left calf. She was twelve years old, blond, with no major dental work, no surgical scars. Hunt had her height, weight, date of birth. She owned a cell phone but records showed no outgoing calls since yesterday. Not much to go on. What they did have was a couple of kids who heard her scream but couldn't agree on the color of the car she was pulled into. Hunt had also questioned her closest friends. As far as they knew, Tiffany had no secret boyfriend, no problems at home. She made good grades, liked horses, and had kissed a boy maybe once. A typical girl.

Hunt jotted a note in the file: *Were Tiffany and Alyssa friends?* Maybe they both knew the wrong guy.

Hunt thought of the things he did not have. He had no description of the perp, no calls of suspicious activity, and no ID on the car. Basically, nothing. What he did have was Johnny Merrimon and the things that David Wilson had told him before he died. He claimed to have found the girl that had been taken. Found her where? Found her how? Dead or alive? Whoever ran David Wilson off the road did so on purpose. But was it Johnny Merrimon's giant, as Cross suspected? Or was it someone else?

Hunt needed to find the kid.

He called the station, got one of his detectives. "It's Hunt. What have you got?"

"Nothing good. Myers and Holiday are still with Tiffany's parents."

"Are they holding up?" Hunt interrupted.

"Their doctor is there. The mother, you know. They're sedating her."

"Anything on Tiffany's cell?"

"Nothing. No hits on GPS, either."

"Is Yoakum still backtracking David Wilson?"

"He's at the house now."

"Do we know anything yet?"

"Just that Wilson was a professor at the college. Biology of some sort."

"What about prints?" Hunt asked.

"We got a thumb print from the victim's eyelid. We're running it now. Should know something soon."

"Volunteers?"

"Over a hundred so far. We're trying to get that organized for an early start. Should be working the countryside by six." A silence fell between the men, both thinking the same thing: *It's a damn big county.*

"We need more people," Hunt said. "Get the churches involved, the civic clubs. We had a hundred college kids when Alyssa Merrimon went missing. Call the dean." Hunt rattled off a number from memory. "He's sympathetic. See if he can make something happen. Also, I want Tiffany's school canvassed again tomorrow. Send the least intimidating officers you can find. Young ones. Females. You know the drill. I don't want to miss something just because some kid is too scared to talk to us."

"Got it. What else can I do?"

"Hang on." Hunt pulled up Katherine Merrimon's registration on his laptop. "Write this down, then put it on the wire." He gave the model, make, and license plate. "The kid is in his mom's car. It's a beater. Shouldn't be too hard to spot. Check Tate Street first, Ken Holloway's house. I doubt he'll be there, but it's worth a look. If anyone sees this car, I need to know immediately. Stop and detain. Call me when it happens."

"On it."

"Good. Give me David Wilson's address." Hunt reached for his pen, but saw movement on the porch of Johnny's house. A pale arm reached out.

What the hell?

He heard a scream, muted by the rain. His fingers found the lights, and bright beams slashed through the rain. "Holy shit."

"Detective—"

Hunt pressed the phone to his ear. "I have to go," he said.

"But—"

Hunt clicked the phone shut. His hand moved for the door, and he spoke again, even as rain hit his face.

"Holy shit."

But another scream drowned out the words.

CHAPTER TEN

Johnny stuck to the side streets and drove from one side of town to the other. Jack lived in a neighborhood with small houses and neat yards, a place full of cops and grocers and deliverymen. Swing sets and toys dotted the grass. On sunny days, kids played catch in the street. It was a good place, if you lived there, but strange cars stood out, so Johnny parked two blocks away and hoofed it through the rain. A light was on in Jack's room. Johnny peeked over the sill and saw his friend. He stretched across the bed, comic books strewn around him. He scratched himself as he read.

Johnny was about to tap the glass when Jack's door opened. Gerald walked in. Tall and muscular, he wore jeans and no shirt, a Clemson hat spun backward. He said something that pissed his brother off, because Jack threw one of his comic books, then pushed his brother out and locked the door.

Johnny tapped on the glass, watched Jack look up. He tapped again and his friend crossed the room. The window came up a few inches. Jack knelt at the crack. "Jesus, Johnny. Are you okay? I heard about what happened. Crap. I can't believe I missed it. A real live dead guy."

Johnny checked the door over Jack's shoulder. "Can you come outside?"

"I don't think so." Jack looked shamefaced. "You know about the lockdown, right? Tiffany Shore?"

"I know about it."

"The school called my dad when they couldn't find me."

"My mom, too."

"Yeah. Well. He caught me with his beer and I was still drunk. I'm in it deep. Mom's at church, praying for Tiffany's life and my eternal soul." He rolled his eyes, then hooked a thumb at the door. "Dickhead's in charge. He's supposed to keep an eye on me." Jack pressed closer to the crack. "But this dead guy. That must have been intense. What's happening now? I heard some of the stuff my dad said. Did he really have something to do with Tiffany?"

"Or my sister."

"I doubt that."

"It could be her."

"It's been a year, Johnny. You've got to be realistic. Odds are—"

"Don't tell me about the odds!"

Jack hesitated. "You're going out, aren't you?"

"I have to."

Jack shook his head, face gone serious. "Don't do it, man. This is not the night to be sneaking around. Every cop in town is out there. Whoever did this is going to be looking out. He's going to be alert."

Johnny shook his head. "Tiffany was taken today. It's early. That's when people make mistakes."

"Where are you going?"

"You know where I'm going."

"Don't do it, man. I'm serious. I've got a bad feeling."

Johnny did not back down. "I want you to come with me." Jack looked over his shoulder. The door was still closed. Johnny put his fingers on the sill. "I need help."

"I never agreed to go to those houses. That was always the line for me, and you know it."

95

"This is different."

"You're gonna get killed. Some freak show is going to catch you, and he's going to kill you." Jack's face bled out and he begged with his entire body. "Don't do it."

Johnny looked away, out into the dark neighborhood. "I choked, Jack."

"What do you mean?"

"The guy landed right at my feet. I heard his bones break. There was blood everywhere. One eye was about to pop out of his head."

"Get out. Really?"

"He knew where she was. You get that? Whoever ran him off the road did it on purpose so he couldn't tell." Johnny raised a fist. "I was right there."

"So?"

"I got scared. I ran."

"So you ran. So, what? I'd be in Virginia by now."

Johnny didn't hear him. His words came like he could still see it. "The guy was coming around the car." He shook his head. "I heard metal, like he was dragging a pipe. Big engine, just growling. And the guy, man, he was shitting himself he was so scared. He told me to run."

"There you go. He told you."

"Don't you get it, man? He knew where she was and I ran! She's my sister. My twin."

"Don't, Johnny."

"I have to make it right." Johnny's face filled the crack at the bottom of the window. "And it has to be tonight. This is my chance, Jack. I can fix it, but I don't know if I can do it alone. I need you to come with me."

Jack fidgeted, threw a desperate glance at the closed door. "Don't ask me, Johnny. I can't do it. Not tonight."

Johnny leaned back, disappointed and angry. "What's wrong with you, Jack? Earlier today, all you wanted to do was get out there and look. You couldn't wait to play outlaw."

Jack pleaded. "But this is not for play, is it? This just happened. This is fresh. For real. Say you find this guy . . . You're gonna get fucking killed."

"This is the time. Now. Right this second."

"Johnny—"

"In or out, Jack."

"Dude . . ." The answer was all over him.

Johnny saw it, plain as day. "No sweat," Johnny said, and then he was gone.

Katherine Merrimon stumbled down the last step and into the rain. She bent at the waist, lurched into the yard. "Johnny!" Her mouth shone pale and pink. She was barefoot and wild-eyed, her pupils dilated. She stumbled again, went down in the mud. An oversized T-shirt hung to her knees, and within seconds it was soaked. Mud shone on her legs.

She was frightened, probably medicated, so Hunt moved with caution. He'd seen mental breakdowns before, and that's what this looked like, like she was ripped at the seams. He held out his hands, fingers spread. "Mrs. Merrimon."

"Johnny!" Irrational. Face turned up as the rain beat down.

Hunt guessed that Tiffany Shore's abduction had scraped the soil off whatever poor grave she'd made for thoughts of her daughter's fate. She'd woken to an empty house, to another empty bed.

"Mrs. Merrimon," Hunt spoke softly.

She looked up, and even with the light full on her face, her eyes remained wide and dark. "Where's my son?"

Hunt knelt and placed his hands on her shoulders. "It's okay," he said. "Everything will be okay."

For that second, she calmed; then her face cracked, and when she spoke, her voice was so soft he barely heard it. "Where's Alyssa?" she asked, but Hunt had no answer. He watched the grief take her down. It broke her at the waist. She splayed her hands on the ground, dug her fingers into soft earth. "Make it stop," she whispered.

Hunt's duty was clear. She needed help. Johnny needed to be taken from her and placed in a stable environment. He should be on the phone to Social Services; he knew as much. But he knew something else as well. If he took her son, it would destroy the last good bit of her, and he couldn't do that. She rocked in the mud.

"Please make it stop."

"Katherine . . ."

"My babies . . ."

Hunt sat back on his heels, laid a hand on her shoulder. "Trust me," he said. When she looked up, eyes tortured and lost, he said her name again, then took her arm to help her stand.

Twenty minutes later, the rain had stopped. A marked car turned into the drive, and Hunt saw a flash of blond as the dome light winked on and Officer Laura Taylor made for the porch. She was in her late twenties, broad-bodied but with a narrow face. She'd had a thing for Hunt once upon a time, but that was ancient history. Now she was in love with a NASCAR driver out of Charlotte. The driver had no idea who she was, but that didn't bother her. Persistence, according to Officer Taylor, was a virtue.

She clumped up the steps and frowned as she spoke. "You're looking sharp, Hunt."

"What do you mean?"

She gestured at his clothes. "Wet clothes. Mud on your suit."

The gesture rose to include his head. "What are you, a surfer now?"

"A surfer?" Hunt touched his hair. Soaking wet, it hung below his collar.

"I can cut that for you."

"That's okay."

"Suit yourself." She pushed past him to glance through the open door. "You were pretty vague on the phone."

Taylor was a stickler for the rules, but Hunt chose her for a reason. Underneath it all, the cop, the regulations, and the ball-breaking attitude, Taylor was a soft touch. Hunt trusted her to do what was right. "I just need you to keep an eye on her," he said. "Make sure she doesn't do anything stupid."

"How bad is it?"

"She's in bed, calm for the moment; but she's on something, pills probably. She's lost it once. Could pop again. But she's a good person and tomorrow's another day. I think she deserves a chance."

When Taylor leaned back, she looked unimpressed. "Word around town is that she's pretty messed up."

"Messed up, how?"

"Don't get defensive."

"I'm not."

A smile under glittering eyes. "Bullshit. Look at you. White lips, those ropes in your neck. You look like I'm talking about your mother. Or your wife."

Hunt lowered his voice, forced himself to relax. "Messed up how?"

Taylor shrugged without sympathy and tilted her head toward the house. "She showed up at school once to pick up her daughter. That was four months after the girl got snatched. When they told her that Alyssa wasn't there, she refused to leave. Demanded to see her. Started screaming when they tried to explain. It got so out of control that the resource officer escorted her off the school grounds. She sat in her car for three hours, crying. And you know Officer Daniels?"

"The new guy?"

"He responded to a breaking and entering call about six weeks ago and found her asleep in her old house, just curled up on the sofa. Fetal, he said." Taylor looked around at the dilapidated house. "Messed up."

Hunt held his words for long seconds, and when he spoke, he tried hard to make her understand. "Do you have children, Laura?"

"You know I don't." She showed small teeth. "Children would interfere with the job."

"Then trust me on this. She deserves a break." Taylor held Hunt's gaze, and he knew she was doing the math. Taylor was a street cop, not a babysitter; and Hunt's request was not about channels or procedure. "Someone needs to be here in case her son returns. That's legit."

"And the rest of it?"

"Just make sure she doesn't wander off or take any more pills."

"You're hanging your ass out on this, Hunt, and you're asking me to bare my fine, sculpted backside, too."

"I know that."

"If she's this bad—booze, pills, whatever—then the kid should be in state custody. If something happens to him because you refused to take action . . ."

"That's my risk."

She looked out at the rain, and the worry showed. "People are talking. About you and her."

"The talk's unfounded."

Hard eyes. "Is it?"

"She's a victim," Hunt said coldly. "And she's married. I have no interest beyond a professional one."

"I think you're lying," Taylor said.

"Maybe," he replied. "But not to you."

Taylor drummed her fingers on the slick, vinyl belt that held her weapon, her cuffs, her Mace. "That's deep, Hunt. So profound it's downright female." The words were not unkind.

"Will you help me?"

"I'm your friend. Don't bring me into something sordid."

"She's a good woman and I lost her kid. That's it." The moment stretched. "Johnny Merrimon," Hunt said. "Would you know him if you saw him?"

"A kid shows up, I'll assume it's him."

Hunt nodded. "I owe you."

He turned but she stopped him. "She must be something special."

Hunt hesitated, but had no reason to lie. "They both are," he said. "Her and her son."

"Not to take anything away from these people, but why?"

Hunt pictured the kid, the way he understood his mother's vulnerability and did what he could to protect her when no one else would. Hunt saw him buying groceries at six in the morning, throwing a rock through Ken Holloway's window, not once, but five times, just to get him away from his mother. "I used to see them around town before all this happened. They were always together, all four of them. Church. The park. Concerts on the green. They were a beautiful family." He shrugged, and both knew that there were things left unsaid. "I don't like tragedies."

Officer Taylor laughed without humor.

"What?" Hunt asked.

"You're a cop," she said. "Everything is a tragedy."

"Maybe."

"Yeah, right." Her tone was disbelieving. "Maybe."

A hundred yards down the road, parked in a darkened drive, Johnny watched Hunt's car pull away from his house. He dipped down as it sped past, but another one still sat in the place where his mother normally parked. Johnny had seen the cars just in time, Hunt's sedan, the marked car with dark lights on the roof. He chewed on a fingernail, tasted dirt. All he wanted to do was check on his mom. Just once. But the cops . . .

Damn.

An old couple lived in the house where Johnny was parked. On warm days, the husband sat on the porch, smoked hand-rolled cigarettes and watched his wife garden in a faded housedress that gapped in the front and showed more white skin and blue veins than Johnny thought a body should have. But they always waved and smiled when he passed on his bike, the woman with stained hands, the man with stained teeth.

Johnny climbed out of the car and closed the door. He heard rustling sounds and water dripping, the churr of frogs on trees and the hiss of tires as another car angled down the hill and splashed its lights against the low-slung cottage. Ducking, he slipped around the side of the house and began working his way through the backyards that stretched between the car and his own house. He moved past sheds that smelled of lawn clippings and rot, a trampoline that had rusted springs and a dangerous tilt. He ducked clotheslines, went over fences, and caught glimpses of neighbors he barely knew.

He slowed as he drew near his mother's window. Her light burned yellow, and when he raised his head, he saw her sitting on the side of her bed. Tear-stained and splashed with mud, she sagged as if some vital string had been cut. She held a framed photograph, and her lips moved as she laid a finger on the glass and rolled her back to an unseen weight. But Johnny felt no sympathy. What leapt up in his chest was a sudden anger. She acted like Alyssa was gone for good, like there was no hope left.

She was so weak.

But when the photograph tilted, Johnny saw that it was not his sister's photo that had wrecked his mother.

It was his father's.

Johnny dropped below the sill. She'd burned them. Johnny remembered the day, a bright afternoon with fire in the backyard and the acrid smell of photographs charring down to nothing. He saw it like it was yesterday, how he'd stolen three of the photos from his mother's hand and run crazy circles as she'd stumbled and wept and screamed at him to give them back. He knew where all three of those photos were, too: one in his sock drawer, two in the suitcase he kept for Alyssa.

The one his mother held was different. In it his father was young, with parted lips and flashing eyes. He wore a suit and tie. He looked like a movie star.

For an instant, the image blurred in his mind, then Johnny knuckled moisture from his right eye and moved through the shaggy yard to the tree line. He pushed hard into the darkness, trying to forget the sight of his mother with that photograph. It made him sad, and sadness made him weak.

Johnny spit in the dirt.

This was no night for weak.

A small trail took him under trees that scratched the night sky with a canopy so vast and dense it gave a whole new meaning to dark. Beyond the old growth was a tobacco farm gone to scrub. The tall trees disappeared. Poison ivy crawled over bare earth and milkweed rose taller than his head. A hundred yards in, he hopped a creek that ran swollen and brown. Briars took skin from his arms. When he came to the old tobacco barn, he stopped and listened. He'd once found two older boys inside smoking pot. That was months ago, but Johnny never forgot the chase they gave him. He put a hand on the barn. The squared-off logs were ridged by age, and most of the chinking had crumbled to ruin, but it was solid enough. Johnny put an eye to a gap and peered inside. Darkness. Silence. He made for the door.

Inside, he stepped on an old bucket and reached above the lintel. It took all the length of his arm, but he felt it there, just where he'd left it. The bag came out with a dragging sound and a rainfall of mouse droppings. It was blue and moldy, still stained reddish-brown along the bottom seams. Johnny breathed in the smell of it, the stink of dirt and bird and dead plants. He dropped to the ground outside and felt his breath go shaky. Johnny peered into the scrub and listened hard.

Then he pulled dry wood from the barn and built a fire.

A big one.

CHAPTER ELEVEN

Hunt pulled into David Wilson's driveway as a high wind assaulted the last of the storm clouds. When he looked down he saw that small parts of the world had gone silver white: a puddle on the concrete drive, beads on the hood of his car. The street ended at the back of some faceless building that marked the edge of the college campus. Well-kept houses sheltered faculty families and a few students with parents wealthy enough to swing the rent. The lots were narrow, the trees tall and broad. Thin strips of green marked old joints in the concrete sidewalk. Weeds. Moss. The air smelled of growing things.

The rain that kept the neighbors in had also kept the police presence quiet, but Hunt saw signs that that would soon end. A man stood at the curb four houses down, a plastic bag hanging from his hand as he stared. Across the street, a cigarette sparked in the darkness. Hunt cursed under his breath and turned for the door. The house was a small Tudor with age-stained beams set into dark brick. A strip of grass separated it from its neighbor; a detached two-car garage filled the back corner. Hunt saw Yoakum through an undraped window and made for the door.

Inside, wood floors showed scars from long use and little care. Stairs rose to the right, the banister dark and slick. The kitchen was in the back, a glint of stainless steel and white linoleum that gleamed under hard lights. A uniformed cop nodded from the living room and Hunt nodded back. Another turned, and then a third. None of them looked Hunt in the eye, but he understood.

It all seemed very familiar.

David Wilson had been a professor, and the house felt like it: dark wood, exposed brick, a smell that was either fresh tobacco or old pot. Yoakum stepped in from the dining room and offered a smile that was perfunctory and meaningless. "I am not the bearer of glad tidings," he said.

Hunt studied the interior of the house. "Start at the beginning."

"The house belongs to the college. Wilson gets to live here as a perk. He's been here for three years."

"Nice perk." Hunt reconsidered the house, noticed more quick glances from other cops.

Yoakum saw it, too, and lowered his voice. "They're worried for you."

"Worried?"

"Alyssa was a year ago, yesterday. No one has forgotten."

Hunt looked around the room, eyes tight, mouth, too. Yoakum gave a shrug, trouble and worry in his eyes, too. "Just tell me about David Wilson," Hunt said.

"He's the head of the biology department. Well respected, as far as I can tell. Widely published. Kids admire him. Administration admires him, too."

"You made it plain to the college that Wilson's not a suspect? I don't want to ruin a good man's reputation for no reason."

"Material witness, I told them. Saw something that got him killed."

"Good. Tell me what else you know about David Wilson."

"You can start with this."

Yoakum crossed an oriental rug that was probably older than the house. He led Hunt to a wall that held a number of framed photographs, each of which showed basically the same thing: David Wilson with a different beautiful woman. "Bachelor?" Hunt asked.

"You tell me. Engine parts on the dining room table. Steak and beer in the fridge, and not much else. Seventeen condoms in the drawer of the bedside table."

"You counted?"

Yoakum shrugged. "It's my brand."

"Ah, humor."

"Who's joking?"

"Any indication of where or how he might have crossed paths with Tiffany Shore?"

"If there's a great big clue in this house somewhere, I haven't discovered it yet. If he really did find the kid, I'm guessing it was by accident."

"Alright," Hunt said. "Let's break it down. We know that he's lived here for three years. He's athletic, well paid, and smart."

"Athletic?"

"The ME thinks he may have been a rock climber."

"Smart man, that Trenton Moore."

"Yeah?"

"Come with me," Yoakum said, and threaded his way through the kitchen to a narrow door at the back of the house. He opened it and warm air gushed in. "Garage is through the backyard."

They stepped out onto wet grass. A privacy fence shielded much of the yard, and the garage loomed, square and blunt, at the far corner. Made from the same brick as the house, it was wide enough to hold at least two cars. Yoakum entered first and flicked on the lights. "Check it out."

Rafters spanned a gulf beneath the peaked roof. Oil stained

a dull cement floor. Two of the walls were made from peg boards, and on the pegs hung all kinds of climbing gear: coils of rope, carabineers, pitons, headlamps, and helmets.

"I'd say he was a climber."

"With some stupid-looking shoes," Yoakum said, and Hunt turned.

The shoes were ankle high, leather boots with smooth, black rubber soles that curved up the front and sides. Three pairs hung from different pegs. Hunt lifted a pair. "Friction shoes," he said. "They're good on stone."

Yoakum pointed at the rafters. "Guy's not scared of water, either."

"Kayaks." Hunt pointed to the longest of the kayaks. "That's oceangoing." He pointed to the short one. "That's river."

"There's no car registered in his name," Yoakum said.

"But oil stains on the floor." Hunt lifted a set of keys from a nail by the door: black plastic at the fat end. "Spare set, I'm guessing. Toyota." He looked at tire marks on the concrete. "Long wheel base. Maybe a truck or a Land Cruiser. Check with the college. Maybe it's registered to the biology department."

"We did find a trailer registered to David Wilson."

"For his dirt bike, probably. The one he was riding when he was killed wasn't street legal, so he probably took it out on a trailer. What he was doing out in the most forbidding corner of the county is the question. What he was doing and where he was doing it."

They left the garage and pulled the door shut, started back across the yard. "It's wild country up there. Lot of woods. Lot of trails."

"Good place to dirt bike."

"You think his car is still out there somewhere?" Yoakum asked.

They mounted steps to the back door, went inside and passed through the kitchen. "It has to be." Hunt pictured the county in his mind. They were a hundred miles from the state capital, sixty from the coast. There was money in town: industry, tourists, golf; but the north country was wild, riddled with swamps and narrow gorges, deep woods and spines of granite. If David Wilson was dirt biking up that way, then his car could be anywhere: back roads, unmapped trails, fields. Anywhere. "We need some designated units up there." Hunt ran some numbers in his head. "Make it four patrol cars. Get them up there now."

"It's pretty dark."

"Now," Hunt said. "And get the trailer's plate number to Highway Patrol."

Yoakum snapped his fingers and a uniformed officer materialized. "Make sure the state police have Wilson's plate. Tell them it's related to the Shore case. They already have the Amber Alert." The cop disappeared to make the call. Yoakum turned back to Hunt. "Now what?"

Hunt turned a slow circle, studied the shots of David Wilson with his collection of pretty females. "Bedroom. Basement. Attic. Show me everything."

CHAPTER TWELVE

Levi moved carefully on the mud and slick rocks. The river tossed bits of light that reminded him of something from when he was a boy. There was a rhythm, a pattern, like a kaleidoscope his daddy gave him the year before the cancer took him. The trail bent to high ground and Levi used his free hand to pull on roots and saplings to get him up the slick clay. He dug in the edges of his shoes for traction. When he reached the high, flat stretch, he stopped to catch his breath; and when he started again, the river lights winked out behind the willows and the ash, the sweet gums and the long-fingered pines. It went truly dark, and that's when he saw the faces. He saw his wife laughing at him and then suddenly not, her face gone reddish black and wet, almost by itself. He saw the man who was with her, and how his face went wrong, too, all red and crooked and flat on one side.

And the sounds.

Levi tried to stop thinking; he wanted to wash the images out of his head, pump water in one ear and flush it, dirty, out the other. He wanted to be empty, wanted to make room for when God spoke. He was happy then, even if it was just one word repeated over and over. Even when it was just a name that rang in his head like a church bell.

Sofia.

Levi heard it again.

Her name.

He walked on and felt warm water on his face. It took a mile for him to understand that he was crying. He didn't care. Nobody could see him out here, not his wife or his neighbors, none of the ones that made jokes when people said things he didn't understand, or laughed at how he went quiet when he found dead animals on the roadside. So he let the tears come. He listened for God, and let the tears run hot down his ruined face.

He tried to remember the last night he'd slept, but could not. The week behind him was a colored string of blurred images. Digging in the dirt. Walking.

That thing he done . . .

That thing.

Levi closed his eyes, so tired; and when his foot went out from under him, he fell on the slick clay. He landed on his back and slid down the bank, over stones that tore deep and cut. He struck his head on something hard, saw a burst of light, and felt pain explode in his side. It stabbed through him, horrible and jagged and raw. He felt something break, a violent tug, and realized that his box was gone. His arms flailed, touched plastic once and felt it glide away.

It was in the river.

God almighty, it was gone in the dark.

Levi stared out at black water and pinprick lights. His big hands clenched.

Levi couldn't swim.

He worried about that for a second, but was in the water even before God told him to jump. He landed, legs spread, arms out, and felt dirty water push into his mouth. He came up spitting, then went down again, his hands loud on the river, water fast and cold between his fingers. He struggled and choked and feared he would die, then found that he could stand in water that rose to his chest. So he stood and beat his way downriver, tore through bits of light until he found his package spinning idly behind a fallen tree.

He fought it to shore, crawled up the bank, and ignored the pain that tried to cripple him. He thought again of his wife.

She shouldn't have done the things she done.

He wrapped himself around the package. Pain all in him. Something not right in his body.

She shouldn't have done it.

Eventually, Levi slept, still curled around the package, moaning as his giant limbs twitched.

CHAPTER THIRTEEN

"Nothing." Hunt stood in the low basement at David Wilson's house. John Yoakum slouched beside him. Two bulbs hung from rust-stained sockets screwed into bare floor joists; a black furnace sat cold and still in the far corner. Hunt scuffed one foot on the floor and a puff of mold and dust rose and then settled. The room smelled of earth and damp concrete.

"What did you expect?" Yoakum asked.

Hunt looked into the crawl space that ran under the living room at the back of the house. "A lucky break. For once."

"No such thing as luck, good or bad."

"Tell that to Tiffany."

Fifteen hours had now passed since some unknown individual had jerked the girl into his car, and they were no closer to finding her. They'd been over every inch of the house and grounds with nothing to show for it. Hunt beat one palm on the bare wood of the basement stairs, and dust drifted down. "I have to check on my son," Hunt said. "I forgot to tell him I'd be late."

"Just call him."

Hunt shook his head. "He won't answer."

"That bad?"

"I don't want to talk about it."

"What do you want me to do?" Yoakum asked.

Hunt gestured up the stairs. "Clean it up. Close it down. I'll meet you at the station in half an hour."

"And when we're there?"

"We work the angles. We pray for some luck." Hunt put a finger in Yoakum's face. "And don't you say it."

Yoakum raised his hands. "What?"

"Not one damn word."

Outside, Hunt found a crowd of neighbors gathered on the sidewalk. Two uniformed officers kept them at bay, but he had to push through to get to his car. He was almost there when a thin, angry-looking man asked: "Is this about Tiffany Shore?" He raised his voice. "No one will tell us anything." Hunt moved past him, and the man pointed at Wilson's house, spoke even louder. "Is that man involved?"

Hunt almost stopped, then didn't.

Nothing he could say would make it better.

In the car, he turned the air on high and eased away from the crowd. He needed to go home, check on his son, throw some water on his face, but he found himself skirting the edge of town, then looking down the long, fast drop to Katherine Merrimon's house. Officer Taylor opened the door before he could knock. Her features were drawn, lips pressed tight. Hunt noticed that her hand rested on the holstered weapon. She relaxed when she saw who it was, then stepped onto the porch and closed the door behind her.

Hunt nodded. "Any sign?"

"Of the kid? No. Of that asshole, Ken Holloway, yes."

"Problem?"

"He showed up looking for Johnny. He was so pissed, he was red, kept going on about a ruined piano. A Steinman, Steinbeck."

"Steinway."

"Yeah, that's it. The rock that went through the window hit the piano, too." Taylor smiled. "I think maybe it's expensive."

Something tugged at Hunt's mouth. "Maybe. Did he give you any trouble?"

"Oh, yeah. Starts screaming for the kid's mother when I refuse to let him inside. I tell him to calm down, he starts telling me that he can get me fired." Hunt sensed her anger. "I'll tell you, if that boy had been here, I think he'd have been hurt."

"How long ago?" Hunt glanced at the street.

"An hour, maybe. He said he'd be back with his lawyer."

"Are you serious?"

She shrugged. "He wanted in the house and he wanted in bad."

"If he comes back," Hunt said, "and if he gives you any excuse, lock him up."

"Yeah?"

"I'm not going to have him scaring off my witness or messing up my investigation."

"And that's the only reason?"

Hunt bit down, looked at the house behind him. He smelled rot from the soffits and low clapboards, saw tears in the screens, cracks in the windowpanes. He remembered the house that Katherine lived in when Alyssa was torn from her, saw her dark eyes and heart-wrenching faith that God would return her child to her. She often prayed by a south-facing window, the light so pure on her perfect skin that she'd looked like an angel herself. And Ken Holloway had been there all along, offering a smile, money, support. That lasted a month. Once she was ground to dust, he'd dropped on her like a vulture. Now, she was strung out. Hunt was pretty sure he knew who was doing the stringing.

"I hate the guy," Hunt said, and his gaze went distant. "I hate him like I could kill him."

Taylor glanced away. "No way did I just hear that."

Hunt felt his shoulders rise, the blood in his face. "Forget it."

Taylor stared at him. "You sure?"

"Yes."

"You're solid?"

"Yeah. Solid."

"That's good." She nodded.

Hunt looked up the road and said, "You have to be kidding me."

Ken Holloway's white Escalade slowed on the street, then dropped a tire into the ditch as it turned into the drive. For a second, the car stalled; then the engine gunned and the tire clawed free. A raw gash gleamed black at the edge of the ditch. Clumps of mud and grass hung from the chassis on the right side. Through the window, Hunt could see Holloway's face: jaw set, flushed. Next to him sat a resigned-looking man that Hunt remembered seeing around the courthouse once or twice, a lawyer of some skill. His face shone pale and damp. He levered the door open, then looked with distaste at everything outside the vehicle: the house, the mud, the cops. His exit from the vehicle was the most dainty that Hunt had ever witnessed.

Hunt stepped down into the yard and Officer Taylor moved down with him. Holloway wore a pink shirt tucked into new jeans, boots that cost more than Hunt's service weapon. He was big, well over two hundred pounds. In his anger, he looked tall and threatening as he dragged his attorney through the mud. "Tell them." He aimed a finger, copper bracelet dancing on his wrist. "Tell them how it works."

The lawyer straightened his jacket. He had polished skin, perfect nails, and a voice to match. "I'm not even sure why I'm here," the lawyer said. "I've already explained to you—"

Holloway cut him off. "You're my attorney. You're on retainer. Now, tell them."

The lawyer looked from Holloway to the cops. He shot his cuffs as if he were in court. "Mr. Holloway is the owner of these premises. He wants access to his property."

"Demands access," Holloway interrupted. "It's my house."

Hunt kept his voice calm. "When I was here before, you said that you were a guest in the house."

"Semantics. I own the property."

"But Katherine Merrimon is the legal tenant."

"Mr. Holloway charges her a dollar a month," the lawyer said. "That hardly makes her a tenant."

"Rent is rent," Hunt said, and eyed the lawyer. "You know that."

"Nevertheless, he has the right to inspect the premises."

"At a reasonable time and with notice provided," Officer Taylor corrected. "Not in the middle of the night. If he wishes to call Mrs. Merrimon, he's welcome to do so."

"She is not answering the phone," the lawyer said.

Holloway stepped forward. "I want to see that child. He's damaged a valuable piece of private property and needs to be held accountable for that. I just want to speak with him."

"Is that right?" Hunt could hide neither the dislike nor the disgust.

"Of course. What else?"

"And if I told you that he's not here?" Hunt asked, stepping forward until a bare six inches separated the two men. He knew that Holloway had a temper. *Knew it.* Now he wanted to see it.

Begged to see it.

Holloway's eyes tightened, and Hunt recognized the first crack in the facade. The man didn't like being crowded, didn't like the challenge, so Hunt leaned even closer. He showed Holloway the contempt in his eyes, and saw him take the bait. At the last second, the lawyer realized, too, what was about to happen. He opened his mouth: "Mr. Holloway—"

"Do you have any idea who I am?" Holloway raised a finger and planted it square in Hunt's chest. And that was all it took. In one smooth, economical movement, Hunt gripped Holloway's wrist, spun the man in place and shoved his hand all the way to his shoulder blades. Holloway stepped forward to relieve the pressure, and Hunt kept the momentum going. He walked him to the Escalade and slammed him facedown across the hood.

"You just assaulted a police officer, Mr. Holloway. In front of witnesses."

"That's not assault."

"Ask your lawyer."

Holloway flattened one palm on the car and tried to push himself up. Hunt had to lean into him, and spoke again as he did. "And that's resisting an officer." The cuffs came out. He cinched the manacle around one thick wrist, clamping the steel as tight as he could, squeezing hard for that last click. Holloway cried out, and Hunt jerked the other hand behind his back. He put all of his weight on Holloway to keep him on the car, then ratcheted down the cuff. "Those are serious charges, Mr. Holloway. Your lawyer can explain them to you later."

Hunt hauled Holloway upright. The arrogance had vanished, but the anger was alive in his face. "You can't touch me," he said.

Hunt caught the chain of the cuffs and manhandled Holloway to Officer Taylor's car and opened the door. He put a hand on Holloway's head. "Nothing personal," he said, and stuffed him into the back. When he caught Taylor's eyes, there was no smile or irony in his voice. "Officer Taylor, would you please drive Mr. Holloway to the station and process him?"

Taylor kept her face straight, but could not hide her feelings. "Yes, sir."

Hunt watched them go: the squad car with Holloway's florid face pinned in the window, the big Cadillac with the girlish attorney behind the leather wheel. They rose on the hill and dropped from view, tomorrow's problem. The anger drained away, the hot spark of satisfaction. He stood alone in the yard, thinking of Katherine, and then he turned. Inside the house, he pressed an ear against her door. He spread his fingers on the sandpaper wood and for one second pictured himself walking into her room. She would be small and pale, very still on the bed, but she would smile, and her hand would rise.

Hunt felt that moment roll out like a mile of warm sand, but that's all that it was, a moment. An illusion. He was the cop who'd failed to bring her daughter home. He could no more change that fact than she could forget it. It would be unfair to even ask.

His hand fell away and he stepped to Johnny's door. It stood open and a small lamp pressed a yellow circle on the neatly made bed. The room was so different from the rooms of other boys. So empty. Hunt saw no toys or games, no posters on the wall. An open book lay facedown on the bed. More stood on the dresser, a long row pressed between two bricks. There was a photograph of Johnny's mother, three of Alyssa. Hunt lifted the nearest photo of the girl. Her smile was secretive and small. Dark hair dipped across her left eye, but the right one carried such a light; she looked as if she knew something special, as if she were waiting for someone to ask and might burst from the expectation of it. Her energy made Johnny seem stark and compressed, and Hunt wondered if he'd always been like that. Or had he merely changed?

Merely.

Hunt shook his head at the absurdity of the word. There was nothing *mere* about the boy Johnny had become. The evidence was everywhere: in his actions and his attitudes, in this bare-walled room and even in the books he kept. They were not a boy's books. Johnny had books on history and ancient religions, vision quests, and the hunting rituals of the Plains Indians. There was one on druid lore that weighed three pounds. Two more on Cherokee religion. They were library books, stamped with square white placards on the spines. Hunt picked up the one that lay open on the bed and saw that Johnny had checked it out fourteen consecutive times. Never overdue. Not once. Hunt pictured Johnny on his bike, pedaling eight miles each way to present his card and sign where they told him.

He examined the title—*An Illustrated History of Raven County*—then looked at the page to which it had been opened. On the right side was a black-and-white lithograph of an older man in a perfectly creased suit. A whitish beard covered the front of his collar and his eyes were specks of flint. The caption beneath read: "John Pendleton Merrimon, Surgeon and Abolitionist. 1858." Johnny's ancestor, Hunt realized. He looked a bit like Johnny's father, and nothing like the boy.

He flipped a few more pages, put the book back on the bed, and did not know that Johnny's mother was in the hall until he turned. Her legs descended from a shirt that barely covered her, and she was loose on her feet, one hand pressed flat to the wall as her shoulders cut small ellipses in the air. Her eyes were undressed wounds, her voice shockingly calm. "Do me a favor, Johnny." One palm turned to catch the yellow light. "Tell Alyssa I need to speak to her when she gets home."

"Katherine . . ." Hunt stopped, uncertain.

"Don't argue with me, Johnny. She should be home by now."

She turned, slid one hand along the wall and closed her door behind her. Bedsprings crunched and silence rippled through the house.

Before Hunt left, he turned on lights and checked the doors. In the yard, he tried to focus. There was still Tiffany Shore and the ruin of her parents; a wax-faced giant who might or might not be gone by now. There was Ken Holloway, Hunt's need to see his own son, and Johnny, out there somewhere doing God knows what. Hunt felt it all, a swirl, a massive weight, but he pushed it aside and stole one more moment. That's all it would ever be, and so he took it selfishly. He stood beneath a blanket of ink, and he thought of Katherine Merrimon, of her bruised eyes and her emptiness.

Nothing else seemed to matter.

CHAPTER FOURTEEN

Less than a mile away, Johnny's fire pushed against the night air; it curled orange and shot sparks into the sky. He squatted beside it, shoeless, shirtless. Yellow lines moved in the sweat on his chest, and soot marred his face where he'd dragged blackened fingers from cheek to jaw. His shadow was a stooped giant on the barn wall behind him. He reached for the blue bag that smelled of bird's blood, mildew, and dried vegetation. The buckles were corroded, stiff under his fingertips, and one of the straps had begun to rot. He opened the bag and took out a stack of crumpled papers. Writing covered both sides of the pages, but he didn't look at the words. That was for later, so he put the pages on the ground and weighed them down with a pebble the size of a quail's egg.

Next came a dark leather thong strung with rattlesnake rattles and the skull of a copperhead. The rattles he'd bought from a kid at school. The copperhead he'd killed himself. He'd spent four days in the woods looking for it, then found it sunning on a piece of old tin a hundred feet from his own back door. Meant to be, he'd decided. The snake wanted to be found. He'd killed it with a piece of cottonwood, then taken its head with the knife his father had given him for his tenth birthday.

A second leather thong held five more eagle feathers. They were twice the size of the one on his bike: three golden-brown wing feathers, two that were perfect and white, their hard, pointed ends as thick as his second finger. They still smelled of the bird, and three of them were edged with a rime of dried blood: eagle's blood, his blood.

He closed his eyes and slipped the thongs over his head. Feathers rustled. Rattles clicked against his skin.

Then he took out the Bible.

It was black and heavily fingered. Johnny's name was embossed on the cover, gold and shiny. It had been a childhood gift, presented in a satin box by a Baptist minister who'd told Johnny that the words inside were a gift from God.

A gift, young man.

Say it with me.

The same preacher came after Alyssa was taken. His voice did not waver when he promised Johnny that, yes, God still loved his children, that all Johnny had to do was pray. Pray hard enough, he'd said, and God will bring her home. So Johnny had. He'd prayed with all his might and all of his soul. He'd sworn his life to God if only he would bring her back.

Sworn it.

Everything.

Johnny remembered long nights of prayer, and his mother's fingertips, hot on his arm. He remembered her voice, and how it showed the last of her strength that he would ever see.

Pray with me, Johnny.

The desperate, hungry faith.

Pray for your sister.

Next time the preacher came, fingernails buffed and fat face shining, he'd told Johnny that he wasn't praying hard enough. "Do better," he'd said. "Believe more."

Johnny shifted his feet on the damp earth, crowded closer to the fire. He tore the cover off the Bible, and firelight flashed gold on the letters that spelled his name. He felt a burst of superstitious fear, then laid the cover on the fire and watched it burn. He watched until it was ash, then with one hand, he lifted the bag and emptied its contents onto the dirt. Dried leaves rained down, bits of branches and twigs bundled into piles. Cedar and pine, spruce and laurel.

The image of a child carved from birch bark.

A red ribbon that belonged to Alyssa.

He tied the ribbon around his wrist, then looked from the dried vegetation to the Bible, still in his hand. He hefted it, then laid it on the ground, and pages lifted in the heat as if knowing that they, too, were destined to burn.

The sight gave Johnny a grim satisfaction.

He needed older gods.

The need started months ago, and it started with a prayer. It was winter, furnace broken, no heat in the house, and cold burned his words to smoke as he prayed for his sister to come home. He woke at four, blades of air on his naked back, and prayed for his mom. He prayed for an end of pills, for his father to come back to her. He prayed for the slow, painful death of Ken Holloway. That's what sustained him, thoughts of salvation and the past, sweet, hot pleas for revenge.

An hour later, as the sun stretched some far horizon, Ken beat Johnny's mother bloody for reasons Johnny never understood. Johnny tried to stop him, so he came next. That's what started it: helplessness and blood, a failed prayer, and a gilded book that spoke of meekness and submission.

None of it gave Johnny strength.

None of it gave him power.

He laid cedar on the fire, then pine, spruce, and laurel. He stood close to the fire and let the smoke roll over him. His eyes watered and his lungs burned, but he sucked the smoke in and then pushed it out, first to the sky and to the earth, then to the four unseen horizons. He cupped smoke in his hands and wafted it across his face. He said words he'd learned in a book, then crushed juniper berries into his palms and smeared the juice on his chest. He shoved snakeroot into his pockets, lifted the child-image carved from birch bark and laid that, too, on the fire. It caught in a starburst of flame and pale, white smoke, and he did not look away until that, too, flew skyward. Then he tossed the remainder of his childhood Bible on the flames.

He recognized the split second when he could have taken it all back, snatched the book from hungry fingers, and made his way home, still his mother's child, still weak; but he let the moment pass. Pages curled, a black rose spread, and it was done.

He was ready.

The car still sat in the dark yard of the old couple who lived down the street. Johnny could see it as he cut through a neighbor's yard. The smoke smell hung on his damp skin and he was dark with berry juice and ash. He hopped a fence and found himself next to a patch of turned earth and fragile young plants. He started for the car but froze when a light flashed on in a rear window of the house. The old lady was there, the veined leaves of her hands very still on the yellow countertop of a bathroom sink. She dipped her head and tears followed one seam and then another. When her husband appeared behind her, he touched the side of her neck and spoke softly in her ear. For an instant something lighter moved on her face, something like a smile. She leaned her back into his brittle chest, and they froze like that, peaceful.

Johnny touched his own chest, felt sweat and ash and the deep thump of his heart. For an instant, he wondered what the old lady was crying about and what her husband had said to bring that flash of smile. He thought of his own father, and of how he'd always known what to do or say. Looking at the old couple, a bitter lump lodged in Johnny's gut, but he crushed it through sheer will. For one second, his teeth flashed white, then he crept past the window and was gone.

They never saw him.

Few ever did.

The car smelled old and stale. Pushing against the stiff leather of the seat, Johnny arched his back and shoved one hand into his pocket. The pages were crushed and rumpled, their scent reminiscent of pine resin and fire. He smoothed them on his leg and turned on a flashlight. The names were in his handwriting, the addresses, too. Notes and dates were scratched into the margins.

Six men. Six addresses. Registered sex offenders. Bad men. They scared him, but less than a day had passed since Tiffany Shore was taken, and Johnny figured it was probably the same man who took Alyssa. These were the worst that Johnny had been able to find, and he'd looked hard. He knew their routines and their jobs, what shows they liked and what time they went to bed. If one was acting differently, Johnny would know.

He drove out the fear and put his fingers on the key. His eyes, in the mirror, showed red lines and blackened lids. *He was untouchable*, he told himself, *a warrior*.

The engine turned, and he put the car in gear.

He was an Indian chief.

CHAPTER FIFTEEN

Hunt called Yoakum from the car. It was the dead of night, roads empty and scrubbed by the rain.

The phone rang twice. A third time.

After his brief moment of weakness, Hunt had forced down his thoughts of Katherine Merrimon. He'd spent less than a minute standing in her yard, but Hunt felt his guilt. Tiffany was still missing, so he focused all of his energy on the case: questions posed, actions taken. What were they missing? What more could be done?

The phone rang again.

Come on, Yoakum.

When Yoakum answered, he apologized. "It's crazy down here." He meant the police station.

"Tell me what's happening."

"We're doing the things you told us to do."

"Run it for me."

"The print we lifted from David Wilson's eyelid is in the system. No hits yet, but it's early. We have four cars combing the back roads for Wilson's Land Cruiser, which is, as you guessed, registered to the college. We're working up a list of Wilson's friends and relatives, anyone who might be able to tell us where he was today, what he was doing. We've already canvassed his colleagues at the college, but they're useless. There's a handful of known offenders that we've been unable to locate, but we have units on that. Two that we're looking for seem to be out of town. Houses locked up and dark. Newspapers stacked up out front. I've been told that one is in lockup in Wilmington, and should have confirmation on that soon. Two auxiliary officers are working up the search grid for the morning—"

"About the grid."

"Like you said. We're going to run the same search pattern we did for Alyssa Merrimon. Logical then, logical now. We just need the manpower." Yoakum paused. "Look, Clyde. You know all of this. You gave the orders. Why don't you go home and get some sleep. It's what? Like two in the morning? Have you checked on your kid, yet?"

Silence.

"Jesus, Hunt. Did you even call him?"

"I'm on my way to you," Hunt said.

"This is me talking as your friend, okay? You should go home. Get some sleep."

"Is that a joke?"

"No, actually. It's not. You were ragged this morning and I doubt you're any better now. What's going on down here, this is grunt work. We don't need you for this, so get some sleep. I need you sharp tomorrow. Tiffany needs you sharp."

Hunt listened to the tires on pavement. Trees flashed, black, at the edge of his headlights. "Maybe for an hour," he said.

"Maybe two," Yoakum replied. "Hell. Get crazy and go for three. I'll call if anything breaks."

"Okay. Fair enough." Hunt was about to disconnect when Yoakum said, "Look, Clyde. You're good at this. The job, I mean. But you need to keep it together."

"What are you saying?"

Yoakum exhaled, and the sound spoke volumes. "Just keep it tight, brother."

Yoakum hung up and Hunt turned the car for home. He knew that he would never sleep, but knew, too, that Yoakum was right. He should try. And his son . . .

Damn.

That was a whole different matter.

He parked in the drive and switched off the engine. The neighborhood was quiet, so he heard the music before he opened the door to his house. A muted throbbing. The wail of heavy strings. He let himself in and went upstairs, the wallpaper pale and slick against his shoulder. At his son's door, he knocked, doubting that it would be heard over the music. Eventually, he opened the door.

His first impression was that of pale skin and little motion, a flash of white blond hair and eyes that looked too much like his own. The boy would be eighteen in two weeks. He was big, athletic. He'd been a good student for most of his life. A good kid. But that had changed over the past year. He was disrespectful, intolerant. He sat on the edge of the bed, wearing gym socks, yellow shorts, and a shirt that read CANDY IS DANDY BUT SEX WON'T ROT YOUR TEETH. He held a car magazine and thumped his foot as the music screamed.

Hunt crossed the room and turned off the stereo. His son looked up, and in that instant Hunt saw what could easily pass for hatred.

"Can't you knock?"

"I did."

He turned a page, eyes back on the magazine. "What do you want?"

"You know what happened today?"

"Yeah. I heard. But not from you, thanks. I heard like everybody else did."

Hunt stepped farther into the room. "Were you out there? At

the river?" Silence from his son. Another page turned. "Did you ditch again? We've talked about this."

"Just leave me alone."

Hunt was looking at a stranger.

"I said, leave me alone."

Hunt hesitated, and his son stood. Muscles twitched and rolled under his skin. For an instant, Hunt felt his own hackles rise. There was such naked challenge in the boy's posture. But that impression lasted for little more than a few seconds. Hunt blinked and saw his son the way he'd been not very long ago. A gawky kid, full of curiosity and innocent enthusiasms. A kid who rose at six to make his own breakfast, built kites from balsa and packing paper. Hunt relaxed his posture. "I'll be downstairs. We need to talk, so take a few minutes and think about what you want to tell me."

His son ignored him. He crossed the room and started music that followed Hunt all the way down to the kitchen.

Hunt sat on a chair by the kitchen table and called Yoakum. "Any changes?"

"Didn't we just talk?"

"Yes. And I want to know if anything has changed since then."

"Nothing. How's the kid?"

Hunt reached for a bottle of scotch. "I think he wants to kill me."

"Does he need an alibi? Tell him to call me."

Hunt sloshed two fingers into a glass, sat back down. "What he needs is his mother. I can't relate to him anymore." Hunt took a sip. "He should have gone with her."

"The kid didn't have a choice, Clyde. She left and I don't recall her giving him an invitation to join."

"I could have forced the issue," Hunt said.

"He'll pull out of it."

"He's listening to grunge and ready to throw down with his own father."

"Grunge. Wow. Somebody call the evening news."

"Ha-ha." It was not a laugh.

"Stay home," Yoakum said. "Take care of the kid."

"The clock's ticking, John. I'll be there in ten."

"Don't do this again."

"Do what?" Hunt heard the anger in his voice. Yoakum heard it, too.

"Haven't you lost enough, Clyde? Truly."

"What do you mean by that?"

"For God's sake, man. Put your own kid first for a change."

Hunt wanted to respond. He wanted to say something fierce and scathing, but Yoakum slammed the phone down. Hunt laid the receiver back on its cradle, took another sip of scotch, then poured the rest of it in the sink. Yoakum was trying to do right. Hunt understood that, so he dipped his head and thought about the real problem. He was addicted to his job, but that was not the whole of it. In the still and dark of the kitchen, Hunt admitted, for once, that he did not much like his own son. He loved him, of course, but he did not like him. Not his attitudes, his beliefs, or his choices.

The boy had changed.

Hunt rinsed out his glass, and when he turned, Allen was standing in the door. They held stares, and the boy was the first to look away. "So I ditched. So what?"

"For starters, it's against the law."

"Can you ever just turn it off?" He slid a hand along the arm of a chair. "Why do you have to be a cop all the time? Why can't you just be a normal dad?"

"Normal dads don't care if their kids ditch school?"

Allen turned his head. "You know what I mean."

"A man was killed out at the bridge. You know that. Killed right where you'd been."

"Hours after I was there."

"What if something had happened to you? How am I supposed to tell your mom if anything bad ever happens to you?"

"Well, nothing did, so you're off the hook."

"You saw Johnny Merrimon out there? Jack Cross?"

"You know I did, or you wouldn't be asking. That's what cops do, right? That's how they interrogate their suspects."

"Other than today, do you ever see Johnny Merrimon?"

"He's in junior high. I'm a senior."

"I know," Hunt said. "But do you ever see him around? Do you ever talk to him?"

"No one talks to him. He's a freak."

Hunt straightened, a coal of anger in the hollow place behind his eyes. "He's a freak how?"

"He never talks, you know; and he's got those dead eyes." Allen rolled his shoulders. "He's messed up. I mean, twins, you know. How do you get over something like that?"

"What about Tiffany Shore?" Hunt asked. "You know her?"

The boy's head came around, and his eyes were unforgiving. "It never stops with you, does it?"

"What?"

"The damn job." His voice spiked. "The damn, fucking job!"

"Son—"

"I'm so sick of hearing about Alyssa and Johnny and what a terrible tragedy it all is. I'm sick of seeing you with that file, looking at her picture, going through it all night after night." He shoved a finger toward Hunt's study, where a copy of the Merrimon file had taken up permanent residence in the locked top drawer of his desk. "I'm sick of the way your eyes cloud up and you never hear *me* talking. I'm sick of hearing you up at three in the morning, pacing and muttering. Sick of your guilt and takeout food and doing my own laundry. Mom left because of your obsession."

"Now, just a minute."

"It's the right word, isn't it?"

"Your mother understood the demands of my job."

"I'm not talking about the job. I'm talking about what you bring home every night. I'm talking about your obsession with Johnny's mother."

Hunt felt his heart accelerate.

"That's why she left."

"You're wrong," Hunt said.

"She left because you're obsessed with that kid's mom!"

Hunt stepped forward and realized that his right hand was fisted. His son saw it, too, and raised his own hands. His shoulders squared up, and Hunt realized that the kid was big enough to take him.

"You going to hit me?" Allen wiped the back of one fist across the side of his mouth. "Go ahead. Do it. I dare you."

Hunt stepped back, uncurled his fingers. "Nobody's hitting anybody."

"That family is all you care about. Alyssa. Johnny. That woman. And now it's Tiffany Shore, and it's going to start all over again."

"These kids—"

"I know all about these kids! It's all I ever hear about! And it's never going to stop."

"It's my job," Hunt said.

"And I'm just your son."

His voice was subdued, the words explosive. They stared at

each other, father and son; then Hunt's phone trilled in the silence. Caller ID showed that it was Yoakum. Hunt held up a finger. "I have to take this." He opened the phone. "This had better be good."

Yoakum was curt. "We made the print on David Wilson's eyelid."

"Positive identification?"

"Yeah, and it gets better."

"How much better?"

"Like you would not believe."

Hunt looked at his watch, then turned back to his son. He held his eyes and detested the words even as he spoke them. "I'll be there in ten minutes." He closed the phone, lifted a hand. "Allen—"

But his son had already turned. He pounded up the stairs and slammed his door. Hunt stared at the ceiling, cursed in a whisper, then left the house as the volume ramped up and his son played the same messed-up song.

CHAPTER SIXTEEN

The police station was on a side street downtown. Two stories, red brick, functional. Hunt blew through the station doors and found Yoakum on the second floor, bent over a city map. "Tell me," Hunt said.

"The print is solid. Levi Freemantle. Forty-three years of age. Black male. Six foot five. Three hundred pounds."

"Damn. I thought the kid was exaggerating."

"No. He's big."

"Why does that name seem familiar?"

"Freemantle?" Yoakum leaned back in his chair. "Never heard it before tonight."

"Do we have a photo?"

"Not from DMV. He has no driver's license. Nor does he have a credit card or a bank account. Not that I can find."

"David Wilson was run off the bridge by a car."

"Maybe he has a license from another state. Maybe he just doesn't give a shit."

"What else do we know?" Hunt asked.

Yoakum rifled some papers. "He popped up on the radar a few years ago. Nothing before that. No arrests. No bank records or utilities or phone service. The guy was a ghost. He probably moved in from another jurisdiction. Since then, we have a number of arrests, a few convictions. He's done time, but nothing serious. A month here. Two months there. But get this, he walked off of a work detail a week ago."

"He's an escaped prisoner? Why haven't I heard about this?"

"It was in the paper last week, but buried on page nine. He's low priority, a nonviolent offender. He was not considered a threat. Besides, it's a county problem."

"What kind of work detail?"

"Minimum security. Road work on a two-lane out in the country. Litter collection. Weed trimming. He just walked off into the woods."

"Unbelievable."

Yoakum smiled, his teeth so smooth and white they looked painted. "Are you ready for the big news?"

"What?"

"He's done time, right. In and out. Well, get this. He was released from another stint just three days before Alyssa Merrimon was abducted."

Hunt felt a nail of excitement. "Do not kid me, Yoakum."

"We have an address. It's local."

"What about a warrant?"

"I sent Cross to get the judge out of bed."

"Has the judge signed off on this yet?"

"He will."

"You sure about that?"

"She's white. Her parents are rich." Yoakum shrugged. "Just a matter of time."

Hunt looked around the room, cataloging faces. "Come on, Yoakum. You can't say things like that. We've talked about this."

Yoakum rolled his shoulders, and his voice came surprisingly hard. "The world is what it is, unjust and tragic and full of crying shames. Don't hate me for it."

"One of these days your mouth is going to get you in trouble. So keep that shit zipped."

Yoakum popped gum and looked away. Hunt started reviewing what information they had. Levi Freemantle lived on Huron Street with Ronda Jeffries, a white female, age thirty-two. Hunt entered her name into the computer. Arrested twice for solicitation. No convictions. One bust for possession of a Class A narcotic. Convicted. Served seven months of an eighteen-month sentence. Good behavior. One conviction for public indecency. Simple assault. "Ronda Jeffries," Hunt said, "what's her relationship with Freemantle?"

"Shared address is all we know. Could be housemates. Could be more."

Hunt studied the arrest sheet for Levi Freemantle. It seemed incomplete. "These are bullshit arrests. Trespass. Loitering. Shoplifting, for God's sake. Nothing violent. No sex."

"It is what it is."

The sheet looked like a hundred others, so nondescript that Hunt felt like he knew the guy, like he knew a thousand of them; but six five and three hundred pounds was not something to forget. He double-checked the dates and confirmed that Levi Freemantle had been released from jail three days before Alyssa Merrimon was abducted. He'd walked off an inmate road crew one week before Tiffany Shore's disappearance. If it was a coincidence, it was a big one. Then there was David Wilson, murdered, who claimed to have found the missing girl. Freemantle's print was on the body. Johnny's description matched. The timing. The bend in the river.

Hunt put down the papers. "Call Cross. Find out where we are."

"He knows what to do."

"Call him, John."

Yoakum dialed Cross's cell and asked how long he would be with the warrant. When he hung up, his voice was flat. "He says he doesn't know. The judge won't be rushed."

137

"Damn it." Hunt stood. "Let's take a ride."

Yoakum grabbed his jacket and shrugged it on as he hurried after Hunt. "We're not going in without a warrant, are we?"

"Doing so would be stupid."

"That's not an answer."

Hunt ignored him, his feet loud on the hard, textured steps going down.

Yoakum spoke louder. "Damn it, Clyde, that's not an answer."

Huron Street turned sharp left off one of the main thoroughfares, then died on the wrong side of the tracks four miles from the city square. This part of town was near the front edge of the sand hills; you could tell from the temperature and from the vegetation. The sand held the heat, so the air was hotter. Trees grew smaller in the weak soil. The street ran narrow and short, with yards full of weed and dirt and dogs on strong chains. Hunt knew it well enough to take it seriously. Two years ago, he'd worked a murder scene on the third block in: a woman stabbed to death in her own bathtub. Turned out her son did it because she'd refused to loan him money. She died over fifty bucks.

Hard people.

A mean street.

Hunt took the left and slowed two houses in. He killed the lights, drifted over a shattered bottle, and stopped. The road stretched out, a river of dark and poverty that died at silver rails leading to better places. Small, blue light leaked through curtains in a house to the left. Crickets scraped in the weeds.

"This is a bad idea," Yoakum said.

Hunt moved his chin. "Last block down. On the right."

Yoakum's head swiveled. His lips drew tight as he peered down the dark stretch. "Jesus."

Hunt studied the street, too. He saw dull yards with dirt tracks that ran from the front stoop to the road, a mattress on the curb, sofas on porches. Cars sat on blocks. Even the sky seemed heavier than it should.

Two houses down, a pit bull paced side to side and eyed them from the end of its chain.

"I hate this shit," Yoakum said.

"Let's go in a bit farther."

"Why?"

"I want to see if there's a car at Freemantle's house. Or lights."

Hunt kept his headlights off and eased the car into gear. They rolled another twenty feet and the pit bull stopped pacing. Yoakum pushed back into his seat. "Bad idea," he said, and the dog lunged the full length of its chain, barking with such venom that it felt like it was in the car. Chains rattled up and down the street as other dogs joined in. Lights flicked on in two of the houses.

"Bad idea," Hunt agreed, and put the car in reverse. He whipped around the corner and shifted into drive.

After a minute of silence, Yoakum said: "That might be a problem."

"The dogs?"

"He'll hear us coming four blocks away."

Hunt looked at his watch. "Maybe not."

"How so?"

"Trust me."

Yoakum looked out the window. Hunt opened his cell and dialed Cross, who answered on the first ring. "I need that warrant," Hunt said. "I need it in twenty minutes."

"It's this judge." Cross's frustration showed. "He's going over the affidavit for the third time."

"What? The document is crystal clear. There's probable cause written all over it. Lean on him."

"I tried already."

"Which judge is it?" Hunt asked, and Cross told him. "Put him on the phone."

"He won't."

"Just do it."

Hunt waited. Yoakum looked sideways. "You're going to pressure the judge?"

"I'm going to threaten him."

The judge came on the phone. "This is highly inappropriate, Detective."

"Is there some problem with the warrant application?" Hunt asked.

"I have your affidavit and I will make my ruling once I've had the full opportunity—"

Hunt cut him off. "Twelve-year-old child dies while judge dallies over warrant. That's the headline if we're too late. I have connections at the paper, people who owe me. I'll make sure of it."

"You wouldn't dare."

"Fucking try me."

Thirty minutes later, the cops assembled in an empty lot behind one of the local banks. They had their warrant. It was ten minutes after three, dark and quiet. Overhead, a street light snapped and sizzled, then burned out with an audible crack. Five cops, six counting Hunt. He shrugged a vest over his head, slapped the Velcro in place and checked his weapon a second time. Yoakum met him at the back of the dark blue panel truck with the small gold shield on the back door. "You ready?"

Yoakum looked concerned. "We should wait."

"No."

"Going in dark is a needless risk. Strange house, hostile street. He'll hear the dogs when we're still four blocks out."

"We move now."

Yoakum shook his head. "You're going to get somebody hurt."

"Everybody here knows what they signed up for. This is not the Boy Scouts."

"And this is not some effete judge rubbing you the wrong way. This is the street. This is you putting good cops in harm's way when a few more hours might make a world of difference. The Chief is looking for an excuse to fry your ass, and getting somebody hurt is the best gift you could give him. Be smart, Clyde. For once. Put this in perspective."

Hunt seized his friend by the arm. He squeezed hard and felt bone. "What if it was *your* daughter? *Your* sister? That's the perspective, and you need to line up on it." Hunt dropped the arm and tried to turn away, but Yoakum wasn't finished.

"You're running on emotion."

Hunt studied his friend, eyes black in the night, face pale and clenched. "Don't go against me on this, John. I'm finding this kid and I'm finding her alive."

"It's on your head if somebody gets hurt."

"And on yours if she dies while we dick around in this parking lot. Now, are you done?"

Yoakum's features settled into determined planes. He cracked his knuckles and nodded. "I'm tired of talking anyway."

Hunt snapped his fingers and the other cops circled around: Yoakum, Cross, and three uniforms in full body armor. "This is who we want." He held up a poor copy of an arrest photo pulled from one of the old files. "He has severe scarring on the right side of his face. The kid that identified him said it looked melted, like wax. He's six and a half feet tall and weighs three hundred pounds. I don't think we'll find more than one guy with this description, so it should be easy."

A few nervous laughs. Hunt let them have it. "It's the last block before the tracks, last house on the right. It sits back from the road with an empty lot behind it, tracks on one side, an occupied residence on the other. I want those three sides covered before we go in. The streetlamps are mostly busted, so it'll be dark. The yards will be dead grass and flat dirt except for where the roots and trash make it not so flat. So watch your step. Once the van stops, Yoakum deploys first. He takes two of you with him." Hunt pointed at two of the uniformed cops. "You'll cover the back and sides in case he bolts. I'll take the rest and go in the front. Cross is on the hammer, but I'm first man in. Now, this guy is huge, so no messing around. Get him down and get him down fast. The girl may be stashed elsewhere, so control your fire. We need him alive and we need him talking."

"What about the dogs?" Yoakum interrupted.

Hunt looked at his watch. "Fuck the dogs." He opened the back of the van; one of the uniformed officers got behind the wheel. Inside, it smelled of gun oil and sweat. The men sat shoulder to shoulder. "I hate this shit," Yoakum said, and two of the uniforms smiled.

Yoakum always said that.

The engine caught and the truck turned a tight radius before sliding out onto the empty street. Through the back window, the tarmac was so shiny and black, it looked like volcanic glass. Hunt spoke to the driver. "Stop a block before the turn. There's a convenience store. It's closed."

Ninety seconds later, the truck eased into a deserted lot and jolted to a halt ten feet from a rusted Dumpster. Hunt looked at his watch. "Three minutes."

"Why wait?" Yoakum asked.

Hunt ignored the question. "Three minutes."

Fingers tightened and relaxed. Men stared at their shoes. Cross fingered the heavy sledgehammer. "Right on the lock," Hunt said. "Then get out of my way."

Cross nodded. Two minutes later, Yoakum nudged Hunt with an elbow. "Grunge, huh?"

"Not now, Yoakum." Another minute passed. The first hint of train came like a tide, so thin it was transparent.

"You feel that?" Yoakum asked.

Hunt looked around the dark space. "Here we go." He tapped the driver on the shoulder. "When I say."

The driver nodded, and the night air began to swell. A rumble approached from the south, grew deeper, louder. The vibration climbed into an avalanche of sound, and when the whistle cried, one of the men twitched.

"You're a freaking genius," Yoakum said.

Hunt put a hand on the driver's shoulder. "Now."

The truck ran out of the lot, went left and left again, hit Huron street dead center and tore down its length as dogs lunged and howled and choked on stiff collars. Then they were there. Hunt saw a car in the driveway, one window with a light burning. The van rocked to a halt. The doors split wide and spilled cop all over the street. Yoakum and his men ran for the sides, weapons ready, black boots so lost against the dark earth that they almost seemed to float.

Thirty feet away, the train tore through the night, a thunder-clap that shook the earth. Hunt gave the driver one second to catch up, then felt air tear his throat as he ran. Cross came up on his other side, and they took the yard in long strides, ate up the dirt and dead grass until the porch sagged under their weight. Hunt pointed at the space between the door handle and frame, then stepped back, flashlight in one hand, service weapon in the other. He nodded once and didn't even hear the sledgehammer strike. It burst the door with a spray of desiccated wood and a flash of bright, tortured metal. The caboose flashed past, brought the suck of vacuum and a fading clatter; then Hunt was through.

Inside, a lamp burned above a chair with torn cushions; something fluorescent at the back spread white light near the end of the hall. Hunt checked right, then tracked the gun left. Gaps in the wall showed black rooms and humps of furniture. Something hissed to the left, static from a speaker, the thump of a needle at the end of a long, vinyl groove. Hunt stepped aside and Cross pushed in after him, then the driver. The room was hot and close. Shadows danced on tobacco-colored walls but nothing else moved.

Hunt smelled it first, an oily burn that filled his sinuses. Cross caught his eye as the driver convulsed twice and buried his nose in the crook of his arm. "Steady," Hunt whispered, then pointed at the dark room to the left and sent the other cops that way. Hunt swung his light into the narrow hall, checked his stride at the door, then stepped into the rank gloom. The space was narrow and felt longer than it should be. Ahead, a sharp edge of white light cut a triangle on the carpet. Hunt called out: "Police. We have a warrant."

Silent. Still. Hunt moved down the hall and came to a kitchen on his right. A long tube of white flickered over a sink filled with dishes. He checked the room, found an empty liquor bottle, and an open window with a torn screen. He turned his back, moved deeper into the gloom, and saw the smear of blood on Sheetrock. He stepped past an open door, swung his light into the room, and flies exploded from the bodies.

The woman was white, possibly in her thirties, possibly Ronda Jeffries. It was hard to tell because most of her face was gone. She wore filmy lingerie, crusted with blood. One breast hung out, the skin more gray than white. Her face was crushed, jaw broken in two or more places, left eye distended from a shattered orbit. Her torso stretched toward the hall, her legs near the bed. One arm angled above her head, and on that hand two fingers were clearly broken.

The black male was not so horribly disfigured. In life he must have been large; but not now. Now he was reduced. Trapped gas distended his stomach, making his arms and legs look unusually small. His head was staved in on the right side, giving his face a slack, unfinished appearance. He was nude, slumped in an overstuffed chair as if he'd simply decided to sit.

Hunt reached for the wall switch and flicked on the overhead light. It made everything look worse, the violence more complete. Hunt felt the other cops arrive behind him. "Nobody in," Hunt said.

He knelt by the woman, careful of how he placed his feet. He studied the corpse from the bottom to the top. She had a pedicure, with acrylic beads set into the bright red polish. Calluses on the bottoms of her feet. Legs shaved to the knee. False nails, close to an inch long, made a spike of each finger. No visible scars or tattoos. Thirty-two seemed to be about the right age.

He did the same with the dead man, squatted by the chair and looked him over. Black. Forties. Strong. Maybe six foot two. He had old surgical scars on both knees. No jewelry. Gold fillings. He needed a shave.

Hunt stood. A glance showed work boots by the closet door, jeans, satin briefs the color of candied apples. He found the cinder block beside the bed. "Yoakum." Hunt gestured and Yoakum crossed the room. Hunt pointed at the cinder block. One side of it was greased with coagulated blood. "I'm thinking that's the murder weapon."

"Looks like it."

Hunt straightened. "Hang on." He stepped around the dead man's feet and over the female victim's arm. The other cops pressed against the open door but Hunt ignored them. He knelt by the door, ran his fingers across the carpet where parallel indentations stretched the length of a cinder block. When he stood, he found Cross at the door.

"What can I do?" Cross asked.

"Tape off the yard and the street. Get Crime Scene and the medical examiner out here." Hunt rubbed his face. "And find me a Diet Coke." He caught Cross by the sleeve as he turned. "Not from the refrigerator in this house. And clear this hall."

Hunt watched the hall empty, sensed Yoakum behind him and turned. Framed against the death and violence, his friend looked flushed and very alive. Hunt looked past him, and when he spoke, he kept his voice low. "It's early, I know, but I don't think this was premeditated."

"Because?"

Hunt flicked a finger toward the base of the door. "Dents in the carpet. It looks like they were using the cinder block for a doorstop." He shrugged. "Killers with a plan usually bring a weapon."

"Maybe. Maybe he knew the cinder block would be there."

"Too early," Hunt agreed. "You're right."

"So what's the plan?"

Hunt indicated the room with an open palm. "Seal this off until Crime Scene gets here. Canvass the street. Get a cadaver dog out here, just in case." Hunt stopped speaking, turned into the hall. "Damn!" It came from the gut, an explosion. He slammed a fist into the wall, then stomped into the living room. When Yoakum stepped into the room, Hunt had both palms pressed against the frame of the front door. His forehead made a dull, thumping sound as he tapped it against the wood. "Damn it." He hit his head harder.

"If you want to bleed," Yoakum said, "there are better ways."

Hunt turned, put his back against the splintered door. He knew that his face was naked. "This is not right."

"Murder never is."

"She was supposed to be here, John." Hunt felt a sudden need for fresh air. He tore open the door, tossed words over his shoulder with something like hate. "It was supposed to end today."

"Tiffany?"

"All of it. Everything."

Yoakum didn't get it, but then he did.

The hell that Hunt was living through.

His life as he knew it.

CHAPTER SEVENTEEN

The old station wagon coasted to a halt on a bent strip of narrow black. The road was empty, a dark, lonely stretch beyond the edge of town, bracketed by forest and quiet. Johnny eyed the house, where dim light pushed out from one of the windows. Two weeks had passed since the last time he was here, but the same vehicles rusted under the same trees, the same beer can balanced on the mailbox.

The house itself was a bare hint: a yellow gleam and a collection of hard edges that didn't seem to line up properly. A rotten-sweet poison seeped in from the dump a mile away. In daylight, the crows flocked and a distant gun barked as the junkman shot rats and cans. At night, the crickets called; but sometimes, for no reason, they fell silent. It was as if the world suddenly closed its mouth. Johnny always froze in that silence, and the air around him felt breathless and cold. Johnny dreamed of that sensation more than he cared to admit, but still he came.

Midnight. Dawn.

Six times.

A dozen.

Burton Jarvis was on the list because he was a recidivist. That was the biggest word Johnny knew: it meant, *sick motherfucker likely to do it again.* He was a registered sex offender who made his money stuffing gut-shot deer and hauling refuse on a flatbed trailer. His nickname was Jar, as in: "Look at the size of this freaking buck, Jar. Think you can stuff one that big?"

Jar didn't have what Johnny would consider friends, but a few men came by more than once. They passed computer discs between filthy palms and made small talk about how Thailand was still the best place to get laid. Johnny had found those men, too. Where they lived. Where they worked.

They were on his list.

One guy came more than the others. Sometimes he had a gun, and sometimes not. Tall and wiry and old, he had eager, shiny eyes and long fingers. He and Jar drank liquor from the same bottle and talked about stuff they'd done outside some village in Vietnam. They got all smoke-eyed when they talked about a girl they called Small Yellow. They'd spent three days with her in a strafed-out hut full of her dead family. *Small Yellow*, they'd say, bottle going up, one head shaking. *Fucking shame.*

Their laughter was not nice at all.

It took Johnny two trips to become suspicious about the shed behind Jar's house. It sat at the end of a narrow footpath through dense trees, hidden from the road and from the house. The walls were cinder block, the windows nailed shut and packed tight with pink insulation and black plastic. Johnny could not see in. Light never came out. The lock was half the size of Johnny's head.

That's where he went first.

The shed.

CHAPTER EIGHTEEN

By six o'clock the bodies were bagged. Hunt stood on the porch as the stretchers clattered through the door, the black vinyl looking awkward and slick. He eyed the street and the yard, both colorless under a dull, dark sky. The sun had yet to rise, but he felt it coming. Gray light gathered on treetops beyond the tracks and the eastern sky showed the barest hint of something new. Cop cars were all over the place, blocking off the street, angled at the curb. The medical examiner's van sat at the edge of the yard, back end yawning wide. A dusting of reporters stood behind yellow tape, but it was the neighbors that Hunt studied the hardest. The street left a narrow footprint. Small lots pushed the houses together. Somebody knew something. They had to. His eyes cut back and forth, lingered on an old white man in a yellowed shirt, a black kid with shifty eyes, gang colors, and homemade tats. He studied a wide-faced woman with pendulous breasts and a child in each arm. She lived next door but claimed to know nothing.

Didn't hear nothing.

Eyes full of hate.

Didn't see nothing.

One of the department's canine handlers appeared around the side of the house, his clothing smeared with filth, his face drawn. The dog, a black-coated mongrel, pressed against his thigh. Its tongue lolled out of its mouth as it gazed, unblinking, at the body bags. His handler shook his head. "Nothing in the crawl space or on the grounds. If there's another body, it's else-where."

"You're positive of that?" Hunt asked.

"Absolutely." He thumped the dog's head with an open palm.

Hunt felt something like relief, but was loath to put too much faith in the feeling. Just because Tiffany Shore was not here did not mean that she was still alive. He remained viscerally aware of the bodies behind him. "No chance that these threw the dog off?" He gestured at the bags.

"No chance at all."

Hunt nodded. "Okay, Mike. Thanks for checking."

The handler made a clicking sound with his mouth and the dog followed him out.

Nothing. They had nothing. Hunt thought about what Johnny Merrimon had said about the girl they'd found in Colorado: walled up in a hole dug into the side of the cellar, caged for a year with a mattress, a bucket, and a candle. Disgust was an organ in Hunt's gut. The more he thought about it, the more that organ churned. He tried to imagine if he'd been the cop to find that girl. What would he have done first: Would he have lifted her from that stained mattress or put six rounds in the bastard's face? He wondered if he could do it, forget seventeen years of cop and just pull the trigger.

Maybe.

More than maybe.

Hunt watched Trenton Moore secure the bodies in the back of his van. The medical examiner looked like Hunt felt: tired and gray, stretched as thin as the morning light. When he stepped back onto the porch, Hunt smelled coffee and formal-dehyde, a morgue smell. "Sorry to give you two more so quickly," Hunt told him.

Moore waved it off. "I was going to call you anyway," he said. "I have a preliminary workup on David Wilson."

"That was quick."

"What can I say? I love my job."

Hunt stepped to the far side of the porch, away from the door and the foot traffic. Moore followed him. "Talk to me."

"He was alive when he came over the rail. The boy told us that, and my findings are consistent. Most of the obvious injuries, you saw. Broken leg and arm; multiple fractures, actually. Full details will be in the final report. Extensive abrasions from contact with the concrete and the ground. Fractured orbit on the left side. He had seven crushed ribs, also on the left side, massive trauma to his internal organs, internal bleeding, a punctured lung; but none of these things killed him."

"Explain."

"I found a single large contusion on his throat." Moore indicated the front of his own throat, just above the collarbone. "The larynx was crushed, the esophagus. Massive weight was applied until the entire airway was damaged to the point of total obstruction." A pause. "He suffocated, Detective."

"But he was alive when Johnny left him. Breathing, able to speak."

"The contusion on his throat has a pattern. It's extremely vague, only visible under magnification and not enough to take an impression or get any kind of match, but it's definitely there."

"A pattern?"

Moore's expression was pained. "A tread pattern."

Hunt felt sweat cool on his neck.

"Somebody stepped on his throat, Detective. Somebody stood on his throat until he was dead."

Moore's report changed the tone of Hunt's morning. It

152

implied a viciousness that seemed colder, somehow, more cruel and personal.

Hunt walked into the house, unsettled and angry. The bodies were gone, but the black dawn felt darker still. At twenty-five minutes after six, Hunt's phone rang. It was his son. Hunt recognized the number and flinched. With all that was going on, he'd not thought of the boy. Not even once. "Hello, Allen."

"You didn't come home."

Hunt moved back onto the porch. He looked at the flat, gray sky, pictured his son's face. "I know," he said. "I'm sorry."

"You coming home for breakfast?"

Hunt's guilt intensified. The kid was trying to make things right between them. "I can't."

Silence then. "Of course not."

Hunt's fingers tightened on the phone. He felt his son slipping away, but had no idea what to do about it. "Son. About last night . . ."

"Yeah."

"I would not have hit you." Hunt heard breath on the line, then the kid disconnected. *Damn*. Hunt pocketed the phone and put his eyes back on the idlers. They watched the van with dark fascination; all of them except one. The old man in the stained shirt stood on the tracks, one hand clutching the waist of his ragged pants. His eyes drooped enough to show red skin at the bottom lids, and his other hand shook with a palsy as he sucked on a damp cigarette. He stared at Hunt, then gestured with a curl of his fingers.

"Yoakum," Hunt said, and Yoakum stuck his head through the door. "I'll be back." Hunt indicated the man on the tracks, and Yoakum studied the decrepit figure.

"You need backup?"

"Fuck off, Yoakum."

153

The bank crumbled under Hunt's feet as he climbed to the tracks. Smoke curled around the wine-dark root of the old man's nose, and, up close, Hunt saw that the palsy infected much of his body. He stood seven inches over five feet, bent at the shoulders and tilted right, as if that leg was too short. White hair rose in the breeze. He held out a hand, and his voice made Hunt think of soda crackers. "Can I have a dollar?"

Hunt studied the hand, saw the faded tattoo on the back of it. "How about five?" The old man tracked the bill out of the wallet, took it, and slipped it into one of his pockets. He licked chalky lips and flicked his eyes down the bank on the opposite side of the tracks. Following the gaze, Hunt spotted a tattered green tarp slung in the low brush beyond the kudzu. It faded into the trees, almost invisible. He saw a pile of empty cans, a ring of blackened earth. The man was homeless.

A raw and sudden fear flared in the man's eyes. Tension put new creases in the hollowed-out cheeks. "It's okay," Hunt told him. "No problems." He took out another bill and the old man's head bobbed as he cackled, a rasp of noise that ended in a hacking cough. Something brown hit one of the gleaming rails. Hunt had to look away, and when he did he saw the bottles scattered down the bank. Cheap wines, forty-ounce beers, a few pint bottles of inexpensive bourbon. "Did you see what happened here?" Hunt asked, pointing at the house.

The man looked vacant, then lost and afraid. He turned away and Hunt caught him by the reed of his arm. He kept his voice soft. "Sir. You motioned to me. Remember?"

The old man shifted in place, fingers curled and yellow at the tips. "Sh . . . sh . . . she liked to walk around naked." He gestured to the bathroom window. "She was laughing at me." One eye twitched. "F . . . fucking bitch."

Hunt spoke with care. "Are you referring to Ronda Jeffries?"

The man's chin made a violent twitch, but he didn't seem to understand the question.

"Are you alright?" Hunt asked.

Both arms rose. "Ain't I king of the world?" He made as if to walk off, and Hunt put two fingers on the hard bone of his shoulder.

"Sir, can you tell me what happened here?"

The man's left eye closed. "I just saw the shovel," he said, and stood on one foot to scratch his calf with the front edge of his shoe. "He got that shovel." He pointed. "Got it right out of that shed."

"Do you mean Levi Freemantle? Black male. Three hundred pounds." Hunt looked at the shed. When he looked back, the man's face had gone slack again. "Sir, you were saying?"

"What do you want?" He waved a hand as if chasing flies from his face. "I don't know you." He turned and shambled off down the tracks, looked back once, then swatted at more imaginary flies.

Hunt sighed. "Cross," he called, and waved him up the slope.

"Yes, sir?" Cross appeared on the tracks.

"Go get him," Hunt said. "He may have seen something. Maybe not. See what you can get, but go easy. When you finish, call Social Services and the veteran's hospital. Get them out here to help this guy."

"Veteran's hospital?"

Hunt gestured at the back of his right hand. "He has a tattoo. USN. The guy's a sailor. Show him some respect."

"Yes, sir."

When Hunt made it back to the front porch, Yoakum stuck his head out again. "I think you ought to see this," he said.

"What?"

"You remember the empty room on the southwest corner?"

"The bedroom?" Hunt asked, picturing it in his head. It was a small bedroom, stripped bare. A yellow shade in the window. Tape marks on the wall. It was remarkable only in its emptiness. "What about it?"

Yoakum's voice dropped. "You just need to see it."

Hunt followed Yoakum through the house. He pushed past technicians collecting prints, a photographer in a police jacket. Two uniformed cops made room for him as he approached the room. "It's in the closet." Yoakum opened the closet door and flicked the switch. Light spilled out, filling the closet, making its white walls seem brighter than they were. The picture, drawn with crayons on the back wall, was seven feet tall, childish and distorted. The man was outlined in black, had red lips, wide purple pants, and tremendous, stick-finger hands. The brown eyes were perfectly round, as if traced around the bottom of a mason jar. A series of lines rippled across the right side of his face, but looked sinuous and nonthreatening. He clutched a little girl to his chest and waved one hand, as if at a friend in the distance. The girl had oval eyes and a ribbon in her hair, a speck of pink almost lost against his wide chest. She had one hand up and wore a yellow skirt. Her smile was a violent gash of red.

"What the hell?"

"Exactly," Yoakum replied. "That is exactly what I said."

Hunt scanned the rest of the room. "No other drawings?"

"None."

"Somebody has to know something."

"We've canvassed the neighborhood, but they won't talk to cops. Not on this street."

"Is there any sign that a girl was held in this house?"

"The room's been cleaned," Yoakum offered. "That's odd in itself. The rest of the place is disgusting."

Hunt played his eyes over the bare walls, noted the spots where tape had been ripped off. The marks were angled, as if to hold sheets of paper by the corners. Hunt started in one corner and moved slowly along each wall. He studied the stained Sheetrock, the floor. He found crayon marks on the walls. There was not another picture, no kind of design. He found random squiggles and short, hard lines, like someone had drawn off the paper's edge. He looked behind the yellow shade, then stooped for something in the far corner. He picked it up by the edges, and Yoakum came over to examine it. "Is that a button?" he asked.

Hunt tilted it, squinted. "It came off a stuffed animal."

"What?"

Hunt looked closer. "I think it's an eye." He held out a hand. "Give me a bag." Yoakum passed over a plastic bag. Hunt placed the plastic eye in the bag and sealed it. "I want this room dusted." Hunt stood.

"Where are you going?" Yoakum asked.

"I'm tired of this shit."

Hunt stormed out of the house and onto the porch. People still stood in tight knots, captivated by the sight of cops who presented no actual threat. Looking at them, at their complacence and their disregard, Hunt felt his anger boil into rage. Pitching his voice to carry, Hunt said, "I want to talk to someone who knows what has been going on in this house." People froze. Blankness dropped into every single face. He'd seen it a million times. "People are dead. A girl is missing. Can anyone tell me what has been going on in this house?"

Hunt's eyes found those of the angry woman with a child on each hip. He focused on her because she was a mother, and because she lived right next door. "Anything might help." The woman stared, face cold and distant. Hunt panned the crowd, saw the anger and distrust. "A girl is missing!"

But he was a cop on the wrong street. He saw a paint can at the corner of the porch, label gone white, lid rusted shut. With a violence that surprised him, Hunt kicked the can. It arced into the yard, struck dirt, and exploded in a belch of gray. Hunt stared at the splatter, and when he looked up, he saw the Chief standing at the curb. He was fresh at the scene; his car still idled. He stood at the open door, arms crossed, frowning, his gaze intent on Hunt. Their eyes locked for a long second, then the Chief shook his head. Slowly. Resignedly.

Hunt counted two heartbeats, then turned for the open door.

The smell of death rolled over him.

CHAPTER NINETEEN

Burton Jarvis left the shed at twenty minutes past six. He'd been up all night, strung out on tequila and speed, and now a fuse burned behind his eyes, something hot and bright. Something like fear. He was angry and unsatisfied, full of sharp regret that had nothing to do with right and wrong. His mind spun on ideas of consequence and risk, the knowledge of things he probably shouldn't have done. Things that could get him caught.

But still . . .

He swayed in the damp gray space beneath the trees, felt the slash of grin spread on his face.

But still . . .

The smile wilted as he manipulated the big lock, died when the sweat sprang out on his skin. He staggered down the path from the shed to the house. His eyeballs itched, and it felt like somebody had poured wax into his sinuses.

Jar was not a nice man. He knew this about himself, but did not care. In fact, he took a perverse pride in watching young mothers drag their children into traffic just to avoid passing him on the sidewalk. After nine arrests and thirteen years behind bars, caring for his own needs had become his religion. He was sixty-eight, with bristled hair, two loose teeth, and eyes like raw oysters. Three packs a day kept him lean; the drugs and booze kept him out of prison. They dulled the edge, took the sting out of the places his mind liked to travel. With enough dope, he could get through the day.

Usually.

Jar kept a ramshackle house on twelve acres at the edge of town. The two-lane slithered past on its way to the landfill. In the front yard he had trees and dirt, a nineteen-year-old Pontiac, and a truck that spewed black smoke. In back, he had barrels of empty bottles and a ditch filled with trash.

And he had the shed. It sat on the back of the property, in a patch of woods so deep and dense he could have grown it just to serve this one purpose: to hide his shed. It was not on any tax map or plat. There was no permit. There was the shed, two miles of woods, and then there was the river.

Jar had seen the kid before, of course: a flash in the window, a blip of color in the deep brush. He had no idea what the little shit wanted, but had almost caught him once. He'd seen the boy at a rear window, then slipped out the front door and come up quiet and slick. He got a handful of hair but the kid tore free before he could snag a meaty part. Jar had chased him for a quarter mile before his lungs revolted. He remembered the moment, though: on his knees in the dirt, yelling with what breath he could find: *Come back here again and I'll kill you. I will fucking kill you.*

But the kid had come back, twice that Jar knew about. He never expected to see him like this. Not in broad daylight.

The car was what caught his eye first. It was parked along the side of the road, its leftmost tires all but in the ditch. Jar saw a slice of dull chrome through the trees and stepped out onto his porch. He was in underwear, stretched around the legs and old, but he didn't care. This was a barren street, the nearest neighbor more than a quarter mile away. Cars came by on the way to the dump, kids dragged loud cars, but that was about it. This was his patch of heaven, and he did whatever the hell he wanted to do. Besides, it was early. The sun hadn't even cleared the trees.

What the hell was a car doing parked in front of *his* house?

Most people knew better.

He reached inside and caught the bat where it leaned against the doorjamb. It had dents and scars from a time he beat the television to death over a fumble in a playoff game. Jar staggered when he hit the bottom step, his lower back full of dull pain and the odd sharp needle. Trees leaned into him as he walked. A branch took a swipe and peeled some skin off his cheek.

Fucking tree.

He hit it with the bat, almost fell down.

The car was an old wagon: yellow paint, wood-grain panels. It had bald tires and weather stripping sprung from two of the windows. It looked empty. Jar stopped at the end of his dirt drive and put bleary eyes up the road and down. Nobody coming. Nothing on the road but the wagon. The blacktop was warm and smooth, the bat busted up and full of splinters. It scraped against his leg and drove slivers of wood under the skin. He stopped and saw pinpricks of blood that looked as bright as candy on the white, hairless meat of his calf.

Fucking bat.

The car windows were down, the boy curled up on the front seat. He had on filthy jeans and ragged sneakers, feathers or something around his neck. That was weird. His chest and shoulders were bare and streaked with what looked like soot. His face was the same as Jar had seen at the window, smudged and thin and up to no good. He lay on his side, asleep, and Jar could already feel his fingers around the boy's bony neck.

This was the kid. The sneak that had Jar looking over his

shoulder every other night. Jar flicked his gaze up and down the road, looked back into the car. He saw binoculars on the floor, a half-empty bottle of water and a goddamn camera. What the hell was the camera for? The kid had a knife in his hand, a pocketknife, folded open.

Jar would have laughed, but he was too busy doing the math.

Nobody in sight. Thirty seconds to get the kid out of the car, another minute to get him behind the house.

It was doable.

But he was drunk and sloppy, worn-out; and people like Jar did not do well in prison. Plus, there was the car to worry about. He'd have to ditch it fast and untraceable. If the kid put up a fight, it would get ugly. Jar had a temper—he didn't deny that. There was the risk of somebody on the road: a random driver. The way the road bent, cars could pop up plenty quick. If somebody saw him dragging some boy out of a car, they'd call the cops for sure. And the cops were already riled up about the missing girl.

And luck only went so far.

A battle raged in Jar's mind. This was the kid, and he knew something. He had to. Otherwise, why'd he keep turning up? Just the sight of him made Jar's skin itch. There was something about this kid . . .

But Jar had a good thing going. He had liquor and space, long nights to remember other days. He had his shed and the occasional opportunity. Two good miles of empty woods.

But only if he was careful.

He rocked on the smooth tar, felt the fear begin to win. There was too much going on. He was drunk and unsteady.

But it was the same boy.

Jar realized that he'd been staring at the kid for over a

minute, standing and staring in his underwear on a public road. That's what made up his mind. His thoughts were ticking slowly, and that made for trouble. He'd learned that one the hard way. Nine arrests and thirteen years, all from stupid mistakes. Forget that. He'd get the plate number and find the kid later.

But the boy opened his eyes. He blinked once, started screaming.

Jar went through the window like a rat down a hole.

CHAPTER TWENTY

Johnny woke to a nightmare stained gray. He saw the sky through glass, then dishwater eyes dashed with blood, fingers tipped with yellow plaster. He knew it was a nightmare because he'd seen it before—same face, same broken nails. Johnny blinked, but nothing changed. The dirty man stood there, fingers going tight, and Johnny realized where he was. The scream tore out of his throat and Burton Jarvis came through the window so fast Johnny barely had time to move. He shoved himself away, but bone-hard fingers caught an ankle. Johnny screamed again and Jar grunted, the sound coming from the same deep, foul place of Johnny's dreams. Another hand closed around his ankle, and Johnny flew across the seat.

He lashed out with the knife, cut one arm and then the other. Red lines appeared, then opened, and Johnny tried to cut him again; Jar jerked him so hard his head slammed into the wheel. The door clanked, and then Johnny was on the street. His head struck pavement. A foot slammed down on his hand and the knife clattered away.

He tried to get under the car, but Jar caught him by the neck and flipped him onto his back. Gravel dug into his skull. The fingers squeezed and Johnny felt a long line of ice form on his chest. For an instant, it was that cold, but then the heat came, the pain, and Johnny knew that he'd been cut with his own knife. Jar screamed in his face, dirty words and insanity, ropes of spit. Another cold line opened and turned to fire. Johnny was dying, he knew it. The old bastard was killing him on the street.

The knife flashed. "You like that?"

He cut Johnny again.

And again.

"You like that, you little bastard?"

He was insane, raging; then the sky thundered and he was flying, a red flower on his chest. Sound compressed Johnny's eardrums, the cotton push of thunder and the wet thump Jar's body made when it hit pavement. Johnny closed his eyes and saw how the old man had come off the ground, the whiplash that left a strand of spit in the air. None of it made sense, but it hung there—fresh paint on Johnny's mind—then the pain hit. Johnny sat and agony sheeted his chest. His hand came up stinging red. He looked at his fingers, then away. He saw the bottom of Jar's feet. A twitch in the old man's leg.

What happened?

A stone rasped on the street behind Johnny. He saw the gun first, big and black and shaking in fingers squeezed white. They were small fingers, grimed at the nails. Her arms were skinny, the muscles taut and barely able to hold the gun. The muzzle cut wild circles in the air. A dirty blue shirt hung to her knees. Jar's name was on a patch over the pocket. There was an oil stain and a button missing near the bottom. Handcuffs clattered on her wrists. Her lips bled where she bit them.

She did not look at Johnny as she stepped past him. She looked at Burton Jarvis, whose leg still thumped, whose fingers curled.

Johnny understood. "Tiffany."

She ignored him. He saw the welts on her legs, the angry gashes under bright cuffs. "Tiffany, don't."

Her thumbs found the hammer. Metal clicked twice, and

Jar's leg went still. When Johnny stood, he could see Jar's face, the eyes wide and silver. The old man's hand rose. "Don't," he said.

Blood rolled from one nostril and trembled on the edge of Tiffany's lip.

She was going to do it.

"I need to talk to him." Johnny lifted his hands. "He knows where my sister is."

Tiffany hesitated. Blood ran from her lip to one perfect tooth. Her arms straightened.

"No," Johnny said.

But she pulled the trigger. The bullet tore through Jar's palm and blew through his teeth. The head rose and bounced. The leg went still.

Tiffany sat down on the road and stared into space. She placed the gun beside her as Jar's blood pooled against her leg. Johnny ran to the old man's side and dropped to his knees. He grabbed Jar's shattered head as if he could hold in all of the things that leaked out, but the eyes were dull and empty, the silver turned to lead. For a second, Johnny saw black, and then he screamed. "Where is she?" He screamed the question, kept screaming it, and then he was beating Jar's head against the road, slamming it until the sound went from hard to wet. Eventually Johnny stopped.

He was too late.

CHAPTER TWENTY-ONE

Levi woke disoriented, vision blurred, and it was the sound of a gunshot that woke him. He didn't think it was close, but sound did funny things on the river. The gunshot could have come from anywhere.

He blinked until his vision cleared. There was the memory of pain, and when he tried to sit, the pain woke up, too. Something sawed at his gut, and when he put his hand there, it came back red. He looked and saw the end of a broken branch sticking out of his stomach. It was as thick as a pool cue, a jagged stump of wood that jutted out on the right side, just below his bottom rib. He put a finger on the rough end of it and felt it move deep inside him. He blinked back tears and tried to pull it out.

The next time he woke up, he knew better, so he left it alone. It hurt when he moved, but not so bad he couldn't move at all. He had to not think about it—so he thought about not thinking. He struggled to his knees, placed his forehead on the box, and spread out his hands. He asked God for the strength to go another day, to do what needed doing. He felt sure that God would talk to him, but when he opened his eyes, he saw a crow on a limb. Black-eyed and unmoving, it stared at the box, and Levi felt a stab of fear. He didn't trust the birds. They were too still, too intent on the doings of people. And there were stories about crows, stories from his grandmother's grandmother, from way back—stories of crows and the souls of the newly dead.

Tales of souls that twisted and burned on the long fall down.

Levi spread his hands and leaned protectively above the box. For a long second, the crow considered him, then flapped to the top of another tree. Its trunk was charred from a lightning strike, and the fork on the river side had gone dead to white. The bird landed among a dozen of its kin, called once, and fell quiet. Not a single feather moved. They looked at Levi, and cold touched his heart. It was a murder of crows on a crown of dead wood. He heard it like a whisper.

A murder of crows.

The voice startled him. It was not God's voice. It was oily smooth and sweet. It filled his head and put the taste of sugar in his mouth. He tried to stand, and pain ripped through him again as his ankle crumpled. He bit down hard, then rolled onto his back. Hot air rose around him, and when he looked up, the birds took wing in a rustle and flap that made the dead wood groan. Levi gripped the ankle and felt the wrongness of it, the cantaloupe of swollen flesh. It was sprained, maybe broken, and he guessed it must have happened in his dash down the riverbed. He'd not even felt it. But he felt it now; he pushed on his foot and felt the blade in his nerves, so sharp and eager it made him cry.

He looked at a slash of gunmetal sky and heard the same strange whisper.

A murder of crows.

The voice scared him. "Where are you?" he pleaded, and he was talking to God. But no one answered. The sky was empty of crows, and the dead wood still moved, up and down, side to side, long after the birds had gone.

It took Levi an hour to find the courage to try and walk again. When the same blade went off in his ankle, he decided he had to crawl. So that's what he did, along the bank, upriver, weeping soft as he pulled the box behind him.

CHAPTER TWENTY-TWO

The hospital parking lot could not handle all of the news trucks. They'd packed in so dense that Charlie had to fight to keep a lane open in case an ambulance needed to deliver a patient. That was Charlie's job, guarding the parking lot, tending to the door and keeping people out. He stood under the portico, blinking under the bright lights.

This was his fifth interview.

He raised an arm, heedless of the crowd, eyes on the reporter from Channel Four. She was as pretty in real life as she was on television. She looked like a movie poster. "Right there," Charlie pointed. "The car came in that entrance, all erratic-like. Weaving. It hit that piece of concrete, bounced off, then ended up here." Charlie moved his arm again, pointing to the place where he stood. "Luckily, I'm quick on my feet."

The reporter nodded, and her face showed none of her doubt. Charlie carried enough belly for three men. "Go on," she said.

Charlie scratched at a thin spot on his head. "Well, that was about it," he offered.

The reporter smiled so brightly, Charlie felt the glow. "It was Johnny Merrimon behind the wheel?"

"That's right. I remembered his face from last year. Hard to forget it, really. They had pictures of his twin sister up pretty much everywhere. They look just alike. He was all cut up, though, and dirty. The car was just full of blood."

The reporter cut her eyes to the camera. "Johnny would be thirteen . . ."

"Had no business being behind the wheel . . ."

"But the girl with him was Tiffany Shore."

Charlie nodded. "The one that went missing. Yes. That was her. She was in the newspaper, too."

"Did Tiffany appear to be injured?" A light kindled in the reporter's eyes. Painted lips parted to show the glisten of her perfect teeth.

Charlie took his hand off of his head. "Don't know about injured. She was handcuffed and out of it. Bawling. Started screaming when we tried to get her out of the car. She wouldn't let go of Johnny's arm."

"And what about Johnny Merrimon. What was his state?"

"His state? Damn. He looked like a wild Indian."

"A wild Indian?"

The reporter shoved the microphone closer. Charlie swallowed, took his eyes from her mouth. "Yeah. He's got that jet black hair, you know, and those black eyes. He's lean as a ferret, and didn't have no shirt on. Had feathers and bones around his neck—I saw a skull, swear to God, a skull—and his face was done up all black and red, kind of striped." He made a motion with spread fingers. "You know, like face paint."

The reporter became excited. "War paint?"

"He just looked dirty to me. Dirty and white-eyed and wild, breathing like he'd just run ten miles."

"Was he injured?"

"Cut up, mostly. Sliced, I'd call it. Just sliced and all covered with blood and dirt. He had trouble letting go of the wheel. They had to pull him out of the car, too. It was a mess, I'll tell you." He nodded. "A mess."

She pushed the microphone closer. "Is it your understanding

that Johnny Merrimon saved Tiffany Shore from the man who'd abducted her?"

"I don't know about that." He paused to stare at the reporter's cleavage. "Neither one of them looked very saved to me."

Hunt stood in the bright hall, his reflection a twisted curve in the gleam of the well-scrubbed floor. A vein thumped in his temple, and a hot, acid flush rose from his chest. He was talking to his boss, the chief of police, and trying hard not to lay the man out.

"How in hell did you miss it?" The Chief was a slope-shouldered man with an expanding waistline, a reputation for intolerance, and a politician's instinct for survival. Normally, he had the sense to stay out of Hunt's way, but this was not a normal day. "For God's sake, Hunt, the man's a known pedophile."

Hunt counted silently to three. A doctor passed, then a thin nurse with an empty gurney. "We interviewed him twice. He gave us permission to search his home and we did. It was clean. He's not the only known offender. There were others deemed higher risk. Manpower is limited."

"That's not good enough."

Hunt ticked off points on a finger. "His last offense was nineteen years ago. He's been off probation for sixteen of those years. There are other registered offenders with worse records, and no way for us to know about the shed. No permits or utilities. Nothing on the tax maps. It's off the grid, totally dark. There could be ten thousand sheds just like it in this county and we'd never know. Then there's Levi Freemantle. I've never seen a lead that looked more solid. David Wilson said he found the girl. Freemantle's print was on Wilson's body—"

"I'm being crucified out there." The Chief stabbed a finger toward the front of the hospital. "On national television."

"Well, that's beyond my control."

The Chief's eyes narrowed. His voice fell dangerously. "You're enjoying this, aren't you?"

"Don't be absurd."

"They want to know how that kid found Tiffany Shore when we couldn't. He's thirteen, for God's sake, and they want to make him a hero."

"We don't know what happened out there."

"I look like an idiot! And speaking of the kid, thanks, too, for giving Ken Holloway an excuse to chew on my ass. I've had four calls from city hall. Four, including two from the mayor. Holloway is making serious allegations. He's threatening a lawsuit."

Hunt's anger kicked up a notch. "He assaulted one of your officers. You should care about that."

"Cry me a river, Hunt. He put a finger on your chest."

"He was interfering with my investigation."

"Interfering with something." The Chief's face made it plain that words were left unsaid.

Hunt's shoulders squared. "What does that mean?"

"Holloway maintains that you have a personal interest in Katherine Merrimon. An emotional interest."

"That's ridiculous."

"Is it? He says you've been harassing him. He says you antagonized him."

"He was becoming aggressive. I acted as I saw fit."

"Officer Taylor confirmed Holloway's side of it."

"She would never say that."

"She didn't have to say it, you idiot. In her small but entire life, Officer Taylor has never been able to hide an honest emotion. I just had to ask the question."

Hunt stepped away, and the Chief continued. "What I care

about is how your actions reflect on me, so I'm going to ask you straight out. Do you have a thing for Katherine Merrimon?"

"Just tell me what you want me to do."

"I want you to answer the damn question."

"The question is despicable."

Seconds stretched. The Chief was breathing hard. "Maybe you should take some time off."

"Forget it."

The Chief pushed out another hard breath, and for an instant he looked sympathetic. "Look, Clyde. We never found Alyssa. And the way this case has unfolded . . . people are asking questions."

"About what?"

The same look of sympathy. "About your competence. I've told you before, you take these matters too personally."

"No more so than any other cop would."

"This morning, you were yelling at a crowd of bystanders. You kicked a paint can all over your own crime scene." The Chief looked away, then shook his head. "It's been a long year. I think you need a break."

"Are you firing me?"

"I'm asking you to take a few weeks off. A month at most."

"No."

"Just like that?"

"Just like that."

The sympathy vanished. The anger surged back. "Then let me tell you what you *are* going to do. First of all, you're going to take any heat that comes from this entire, screwed-up business. If the press wants a whipping boy, I intend to give them you, and I expect you to take it. Same thing with city government. Same thing with Tiffany Shore's parents."

"Why would I agree to that?"

"Because I've been carrying you for a year."

"Bullshit."

"Second." He raised his voice, slapped two fingers into an open palm. "I want you to back off Ken Holloway. The man has more money than God, more friends in high places than either of us could dream up, and I don't need that kind of headache. Other than sleeping with a woman that apparently holds some interest for you, he's never done an evil thing in his life, far as I can tell. No arrests. No charges of any kind. So if he wants to put his finger on your chest, you take it like a man. And if he wants to slum it with Katherine Merrimon"—the Chief put one finger squarely on Hunt's chest, shoved hard—"you let him."

Hunt watched the Chief storm off. He was a little man, with a little man's priorities, and Hunt had larger concerns; so he buried the conversation, flushed it. Forgot it.

Ah, crap. Who was he kidding?

Threading his way through the winding corridors, he eventually reached the pediatric hall where they'd placed Johnny. Hunt was not allowed to see the boy, but he hoped to find the doctor and a change of heart. What he found instead was an austere woman who sat, knees clenched together, on a bench down the hall from Johnny's room. She had gray hair, pulled back, and a severely cut suit. Hunt recognized her.

Social Services.

Shit.

The woman caught his eye and began to rise, but he turned away before she could say anything. He made it to the lobby, but stopped when he heard Katherine's voice. "Detective Hunt?"

Standing beside the elevator bank, she looked like hell. Hunt crossed to her side, and they found themselves strangely alone in the crowded room. "Katherine," Hunt said. "How's Johnny?"

She rubbed one arm, then lifted hair from her eyes and Hunt saw that she was on the verge of a breakdown. "Not good. He was cut seven times, two of them pretty deep." She traced a finger beneath each eye before the tears spilled out. "It took two hundred and six stitches to close the wounds. He'll be scarred for life."

Hunt looked beyond her. "Is he awake?"

"Not now. He was, briefly."

"Did he say anything at all?"

"He asked about Alyssa. He wanted to know if we found her." Hunt looked away, but she put a hand on his arm. "Is it the same man?"

She was asking if Burton Jarvis was the man who took her daughter. "It's too early to say."

"Is it?" She squeezed, and Hunt saw the hope and dread that filled her up.

"I don't know," he said. "We're looking into it. We're checking. When I know something, you'll know it, too. I promise."

She bobbed her head. "I should get back . . . in case he wakes up."

She made to leave and Hunt stopped her. He thought hard before he spoke. "Katherine."

"Yes?"

"Social Services is going to want to speak with you."

"DSS? I don't understand."

"Johnny was gone all night. In your car. He was almost killed by a known pedophile." Hunt paused. "I don't think they'll let Johnny stay with you."

"I don't understand." Then, quickly, "I won't allow it."

"He came in wearing feathers. He had rattlesnake rattles

and a skull on a string around his neck. I don't know a judge that would let him stay with you. You've seen the press outside? That's national media. CNN. FOX. They're calling him the Little Chief, the Wild Indian. It's a story now, and that makes it political. DSS will take action because they have no choice."

The defiance melted. "What can I do?"

"I don't know."

"Please." Her fingers tightened on his arm. "Please."

Hunt looked up and down the room. In seventeen years, he'd never crossed the line, but here it was, as clear as any line he'd ever seen. In full control of himself, Hunt stepped over it. Why? Because some things mattered more.

"They'll do a full evaluation," he said. "That starts with a surprise inspection of your home."

"I don't—"

"You need to go home now. You need to clean up." Her hand moved up, touched a strand of limp hair. Hunt paused, but some things had to hurt. "You need to lose the drugs."

"I don't—"

Hunt stopped her. "Please don't lie to me, Katherine. Right now, I'm your friend, not a cop. I'm one friend trying to help another."

She held his gaze for as long as she could, then looked down.

"Katherine, look at me." She tilted her face, and it was naked in the harsh light. "Trust me."

She blinked away dewdrop tears, and her words came with effort. "I need a ride."

Hunt peered through the glass doors, took in the crowd. The reporters. The cameras. He found Katherine's hand with his own. "This way." Hunt led her down successive corridors, onto an elevator, then outside through a double door at the back marked FOR DELIVERIES ONLY. "Car's this way."

"What about my car?"

"Impounded. Evidence."

Twenty feet into the hot sun, she took back her hand. "I can manage." But when they got to the car, Hunt saw that she clearly could not. A flush burned her cheeks and her fingers twisted white. She pressed against the door and kept her head down.

At her house, Hunt pulled the car as close to her door as he could. "Do you have money for a cab? To get back to the hospital?" She nodded. "My number?"

She swept hair from her face, met his gaze, and some small pride glinted in her eyes. "I have several of your cards." She opened her door and heat spilled in. He watched her legs swing away, her hand on the top of the door. When she leaned in, her voice was clipped. "I love my son, Detective."

"I know."

"I'm a good mother."

She was trying to convince herself, but the wide pits at the center of her eyes made the statement a lie. Johnny was in the hospital, and she was still stoned. "I know you are," Hunt said; but that's not what he believed.

I know you were.

I hope you will be again.

Hunt put the car in reverse.

She stood in the dirt and watched him go.

Thirty minutes later, Hunt was at the shed, working the scene with Yoakum and several techs. His back was to the house. "Heads up," Yoakum told him.

"What?"

"Chief."

Hunt looked down the trail and saw the Chief push through the last bit of low vegetation. Two assistants followed him. A uniform held branches out of his way. "I just did this," Hunt said.

"Good things come in fat packages."

Hunt crossed his arms over his chest. If the Chief decided to check up, that was fine, but Hunt wasn't going to look happy about it. The Chief stopped fifteen feet away to survey the scene, hands on hips, chin at an angle.

"Did he see this in a movie?" Yoakum whispered.

"Button it, John."

"It's Patton. Shit. The man thinks he's George C. Scott."

The Chief lurched into motion and closed the last gap, his small entourage bunching up behind him. He nodded once to Yoakum and showed Hunt his serious eyes. "Walk with me."

Hunt turned his palms, taking in the dense woods, the thick undergrowth. "Where?"

The Chief studied the dense growth. "Give us a minute." His assistants melted away. "You, too, Yoakum."

"Me?" Hand on his chest. Eyes shocked.

"Get lost."

Yoakum got behind the Chief before he started goose-stepping, but Hunt was in no mood for humor. He stared at the Chief and the Chief stared back. Tension ramped up, but the Chief broke first. "About earlier. Maybe I was out of line."

"Maybe."

"And maybe I wasn't."

The Chief studied the tall trees, the wall of forest. The shed was a speck in a sea of green. "If you tell me that you're not too close to this, I'll accept it."

The gaze held. "It's just another case."

"Okay." A tight nod. "We'll play it like that, but consider this your absolute last final fucking chance. Now, before I change my mind and fire you for being such a poor liar, tell me what you've learned out here."

Hunt pointed toward the house, which was invisible beyond the trees. "We found where Jarvis tapped into his circuit box. The cable is buried two inches down. The shed is completely off the grid. And you saw the trail in. It's barely a footpath. None of this is visible from the road or the house. No permits. No utilities. It's a shell. A dead zone."

"Any luck with the kids?"

"They're sedated. The doctor won't let me see them."

The Chief stepped into the shed and Hunt followed. He felt his skin crawl. "As you can see, the walls are padded with mattresses, probably for sound baffling. The windows are packed with fiberglass insulation and sealed with industrial plastic. Again, to muffle sound, but also to keep the site black. Look at this." Hunt stepped to the far wall and pointed at a small, ragged hole. "This is where she tore out the hook that held her cuffs." The hook had been bagged and numbered. Hunt picked it up and felt cold metal through the slick plastic. He held it out for the Chief, who touched it once, then knelt and placed a finger on the hole in the wall. It was a shallow hole. The concrete was crumbly and dry. "Tough kid," Hunt said.

"So how'd she get out of the shed?"

Hunt led the Chief to the door and stepped outside. He gestured at the lock. It was a Yale, big and brass and solid. It was in the locked position, secured to the steel, U-shaped hasp. "He locked the lock, but failed to lock the door."

"Accident?" The Chief lifted the lock, let it drop and swing. "Or arrogance?"

"Does it matter?"

A shrug. "The gun?"

"Unknown. It could have been in the shed all along. She could have found it in his house. That was unlocked, too." Both men looked again in the direction of the house. Nothing was visible through the trees. Before dawn, though, with lights burning, Tiffany would have seen it. "I'm guessing he was intoxicated. We found liquor and drugs. The autopsy should tell us."

"Any sign that there may have been other children?" The Chief kept his tone professional.

"Are you asking about Alyssa Merrimon?"

"Not specifically."

The Chief was unflinching, his eyes implacable, as Hunt peered into the deep woods. "We'll need the dog," Hunt said. "If she's buried out there, I want to find her."

"Not much light."

Hunt's voice was bleak. "I've already made the call."

CHAPTER TWENTY-THREE

Behind the thin walls of a house that was not her own, Katherine Merrimon stared into the bathroom mirror. She'd recognized the lie in the cop's face, felt it like a slap. So she asked herself the hardest question.

Was she a good mother?

Her skin stretched across the bones of her face, washed out and too pale. Hair hung with more weight than it should, and her fingers shook when she raised them to her cheek. She saw how chipped her nails had become, the way dark flesh rose up around her eyes. She looked for something familiar, but the eyes were cardboard eyes.

An image of Johnny pressed into her mind. He was bandaged, bled white; and his first thought had been of his sister.

Alyssa.

The name channeled through her lips, almost took her down. She gripped the sink until one hand rose. She found the mirror, and with great loathing, she opened it. Pill bottles lined three shelves. Orange plastic. White labels. She picked a bottle at random: Vicodin. She got the top off, dumped three pills into her palm. They could take it all away, the kaleidoscope memories, the loss.

Sweat trickled down her back. Her mouth went painfully dry and she could feel how they would be on her tongue—the hard swallow and the short, bitter wait. But when she lifted her gaze to the mirror, she saw those cutout eyes, and they looked faded, like copies of copies. They were the same as Johnny's eyes, and they had not always looked like that. Not for either of them.

She tilted her hand and allowed the pills to fall. They made small sounds as they struck the porcelain. In a sudden frenzy, she scooped out all of the bottles, raked them into the sink. One by one, she tore them open, dumped the pills into the toilet. One bottle. Twenty. She emptied them all and flushed the pills down.

Fast.

It had to be fast.

She carried the empty bottles to the kitchen, threw them in the trash and hauled the bag outside. Time collapsed as she cleaned and scrubbed. Floors. The refrigerator. Windows. The hours became a hot blur of sweat and ammonia. She stuffed sheets into the washing machine, poured liquor into the weeds and threw bottles into the open can where they shattered and burst as she spun and went back for more. In the end, she confronted the same mirror. Blood hammered in the soft place beneath her jaw. She turned the water scalding hot and scrubbed her face until it hurt, but the eyes still looked wrong. She tore off her clothes and stepped into the shower; but it was not enough.

The dirt was on the inside.

Johnny woke alone in a strange room. He heard footsteps beyond the door, a muted voice. A doctor was paged over an intercom, and bits of memory came back. He touched the bandages on his chest, felt pain, then tried to sit as nausea pushed through him. Colors spiked at the edge of his vision: dull red through the window, flat white under the door. He looked for his mother and the walls twisted. When he sat, he saw remnants of soot under his nails, hints of berry juice and blood stains on his fingers. His feathers were gone, but that didn't matter anymore. He closed his eyes and felt Jar's impossible grip. He smelled car leather, felt the long, cold lines as Jar crushed his neck and slashed him with his own knife.

Johnny pulled his hands beneath the sheet, but still felt the warm, spongy hole in the back of Jar's head. He heard sounds that went from hard to wet and remembered that Jar was dead. Johnny rolled onto his side and closed out the light.

The door opened so quietly that Johnny didn't really hear it. He sensed the movement of air, the presence of someone by his bed. He opened his eyes and saw Detective Hunt, who looked haggard, his smile forced. "I'm not supposed to be here," he said, then gestured at the chair. "Do you mind?"

Johnny straightened against the pillows. He tried to speak, but the world was wrapped in cotton.

"How do you feel?" Hunt asked.

Johnny's eyes settled on the gun whose butt showed under the detective's jacket. "I'm okay." The words sounded thick and slow and false.

Hunt sat. "Can we talk?" Johnny did not respond, and Detective Hunt leaned forward. He made a steeple of his fingers and put his elbows on his knees. The jacket gapped open so that Johnny could see the worn holster, the black lacquer that seemed to coat the steel. "I need to know what happened."

Johnny didn't answer. He was transfixed.

"Can you look at me, son?"

Johnny nodded, but his eyes felt too heavy to lift.

"Johnny?"

Johnny stared at the gun. The checkered grip. The white bead of the safety.

His hand moved, all on its own, and the cop was dimming, even as Johnny stretched for the gun. He just wanted to hold it, to see if it was as heavy as it looked, but the gun receded into a ball of soft light. A weight came onto Johnny's chest. It pressed him into the mattress and he heard the cop's distant voice. "Johnny. Stay with me, Johnny."

Then he was falling, and somebody drove black spikes into his eyes.

Katherine ironed her clothes and dressed. She fought to keep her fingers steady, but the buttons felt very small. She dried her hair, combed out the tangles, and debated over makeup. In the end, she looked like a normal woman stretched over the bones of someone very ill. When she called for a cab, she had to think hard to remember the numbers on the house; then she sat on the sofa's edge to wait.

A clock ticked in the kitchen.

She kept her back straight.

When the sweat began to form, it started between the blades on her back. She imagined the taste of a drink and heard the lullaby of one more forgotten day.

It would be easy.

So very, very easy.

The decision to pray stole across her like a shadow. It was as if she'd blinked, then opened her eyes to an absence of light so distinct, it made her look up. The temptation rose from a deep place in her soul, a once-fierce heat now compressed to something black and cold. She fought the temptation, but lost, and when she knelt, she felt like a liar and a fake, like a traveler lost in a night of ceaseless rain.

Words, at first, refused to come, and it felt like God, himself, had closed her throat. But she dipped her chin and strove to remember how it felt. Nakedness. Faith. The humility to plead. And that's what she did. She begged for strength, and for her son to be well. She begged God for help, silently, ardently. She begged to keep what she had: her son, their life together. When she stood, she heard the sound of tires on gravel, and it sounded like rain. And then the sound stopped.

Ken Holloway met her at the door.

His suit was creased, the tie a rich purple, loose around his neck. Katherine froze when she saw the displeasure on his face, the sweat on his collar. She stared at the brush of hair that covered the back of his hand.

"What are you doing?" He cupped her chin with a thumb and two hard fingers. "Who are you so dressed up for?" She could not answer. He squeezed her chin. "I said, who are you so dressed up for?"

"I'm going to the hospital." Small voice.

Ken looked at his watch. "Visiting hours will be over in an hour. How about you pour us a drink and you can go tomorrow? First thing."

"They'll wonder why I'm not there."

"Who will wonder?"

She swallowed. "DSS."

"Bureaucrats. They can't hurt you."

She raised her head. "I have to go."

"Fix me a drink."

"There's nothing here."

"What?"

"It's gone. All of it." She tried to move past him. He stopped her with one massive arm.

"It's late." He ran a hand down the small of her back.

"I can't."

"I was in jail all night." He gripped her arm. "That was Johnny's fault, you know. Your son's fault. If he hadn't thrown that rock through my window . . ."

"You don't know that he did that."

"Did you just contradict me?"

185

Pain flared in her arm. She looked down at his fingers. "Take your hand off me."

He laughed, and she felt him move against her, the press of his chest as he filled the doorway. He began to drive her back. "Let go," she said. But he was pushing her into the house, his lips thin below unforgiving eyes. A sudden image of her son came to Katherine, his small chin in one still hand as he sat on the stoop and looked up the hill for some sign of his father's return. She'd chastised him for it, but she felt it now, the hope he must have felt. Her gaze slid up from Ken's arm and she looked up the same hill. She imagined the rise and fall of her husband's truck, but the hill was empty, the road a stretch of silent black. Ken made the same raw sound in his throat, and when she looked up, she saw a smile cut his face. "Tomorrow," he said. "Johnny. First thing."

She looked again to the hilltop, saw metal flash as a car rose at the crest. Her breath caught, then she recognized the car. "My cab," she said.

Ken stepped back as the cab began to slow. Katherine pulled her arm free, but felt him there, tall and thick and angry. "I have to go," she said, then pushed past him and met the cab in the drive.

"Katherine." His smile was broad, and to anyone else might have seemed genuine. "We'll talk tomorrow."

She threw herself into the cab, felt the seat on her back, smelled cigarettes, unwashed clothes and hair tonic. The driver had folded skin and a scar on his neck that was the color of damp pearl. "Where to?"

Katherine kept her eyes on Ken Holloway.

"Ma'am?"

Ken kept his smile.

"The hospital," she said.

The driver watched her in the mirror. She felt his eyes and met them. "Are you okay?" he asked.

She was sweaty and shaking. "I'll be fine," she said.

But she was wrong.

CHAPTER TWENTY-FOUR

Johnny stood with woods at his back, a narrow clearing before him. It was a scratch in a sea of trees, an imperfection; but from where Johnny stood, it was everything, a rolling thatch of green that bent to a silent breeze.

His sister stared at him from the center of the glade. She raised her hand, and Johnny found himself walking, grass at his ankles, then at his knees. Alyssa looked as she had the last time he'd seen her: pale yellow shorts, a white top. Her hair was as black as ink, her skin very tan. She kept one hand behind her back, and tilted her head so that strands of black fell across her eyes. She stood on a piece of rusted tin that pressed the grass flat. Johnny could smell the crushed-grass smell, the summer ripeness.

The snake curled at her feet. It was the copperhead he'd killed. Five feet long, brown and gold and silent. It tasted the air with its tongue, and when Johnny stopped, it raised its head.

Johnny remembered how it struck at him on the day he'd killed it. How close it had come.

Inches.

Maybe less.

Alyssa stooped for the snake, and her fingers closed around its midsection. The tail wrapped her wrist. The head rose higher as she straightened, and the snake met her gaze. Its tongue flicked out. "This is not strength," she said.

The snake struck her in the face, and when it withdrew, two holes appeared, followed by dots of blood that looked like small, perfect apples. She held the snake higher, took a step and the tin shifted beneath her feet. "This is weakness."

The snake struck, a blur that slowed only when the fangs snagged in her face. She faltered, and the snake hit her again. Twice. Once on the brow, once on her lower lip. More holes. More blood. She stopped walking, and suddenly her eyes shone, so brown they were black, so still they could pass for empty. They were Johnny's eyes, their mother's eyes. Her hand tightened on the snake, and Johnny saw that she was not afraid. Her face radiated violence and anger. Her lips paled and the snake began to struggle. She squeezed and her voice gained strength.

"Weakness," she repeated, fingers white, snake becoming frantic as she crushed it. It struck her hand, her face. It hit the neck and hung on, pumping its venom even as it writhed. Alyssa ignored it, moved her other hand from behind her back. In it, she held a gun, black and gleaming in the hard, hot light.

"Power," she said.

And ripped the snake from her neck.

Johnny woke with a start. The drugs had worn off, but the dream kept its grip: his vanished sister, and how she'd smiled as Johnny laid fingers on the warm, bright metal in her hand. He touched the bandages on his chest, then he saw his mother. She sat alone in a chair by the wall. Mascara stained the skin beneath her eyes. One knee twitched.

"Mom."

Her head came around and her voice caught. "Johnny." She found her feet in an instant, crossed the room and stood over him. Her hand smoothed his hair, then she bent and wrapped her arms around him. "My baby."

Detective Hunt came two hours after breakfast. He appeared

in the door, gave Johnny a tight smile, then crooked a finger at Katherine and moved back into the hall.

Johnny watched them through the glass. Whatever Hunt said, his mother didn't like it. They argued hotly. She shook her head, stared twice through the window, then dipped her chin. Hunt's hand touched her shoulder once, but she threw it off.

When the door finally opened, Hunt entered first, Johnny's mother right behind him. She offered an unconvincing smile, then perched on the edge of a slick, vinyl-covered chair in the corner. She looked as if she might throw up.

"Hey, Johnny." Hunt pulled a chair closer to the bed. "How are you feeling?"

Johnny looked from his mother to the glint of metal under Hunt's arm, the black and shining steel. "Is Tiffany okay?"

Hunt twitched his jacket closed. "I think she will be."

Johnny closed his eyes and saw her sitting in the dead man's blood; he felt the dry, hot skin of her arm as he'd tried to get her in the car. "She didn't know who I was. We've been in school together for seven years." He shook his head. "Halfway to the hospital, she finally recognized me. She wouldn't let go of me. Crying. Screaming."

"I'll find out how she is. First thing." Hunt paused and his voice went grown-up serious. "It was a brave thing you did."

Johnny blinked. "I didn't save anybody."

"Is that right?"

"That's what they're saying, isn't it?"

"Some people are saying that. Yes."

"He was going to kill me. Tiffany is the hero. They shouldn't be telling stories otherwise."

"TV people, Johnny. Don't take it seriously."

Johnny stared at the white wall and one hand touched the bandages on his chest. "He was going to kill me."

Katherine made a noise that sounded like a sob, and Hunt turned in his seat. "There is really no need for you to be here."

She rose from the edge of her seat. "You can't make me go."

"No one is suggesting—"

"I am not leaving." Her voice climbed, hands shaking.

Hunt turned back to Johnny, and his smile seemed real, though troubled. "Are you strong enough to answer some questions?" Johnny nodded. "We're going to start at the beginning. I want you to picture the man you saw on the bridge, the one driving the car that hit the motorcycle. Got it?"

"Yes."

"Now, picture the man that assaulted you after you ran."

"He didn't assault me. He just picked me up, kind of held me."

"Held you?"

"Like he was waiting for something."

"Is there any chance that it could have been the same man. The man on the bridge. The one that picked you up."

"They were different men."

"You barely saw the man on the bridge. You said he was a silhouette."

"Different shape, different size. They were a mile apart, maybe even two."

Hunt explained about the bend in the river. "It's possible that it was the same man."

"I know how the river runs. The middle of that bend is a swamp. If you tried to cut across it, you'd sink to your waist. The trail follows the river for a reason. They're different men, trust me. The one on the bridge didn't even look big enough to carry that box."

"What box?"

"Like a trunk," Johnny said. "Wrapped in plastic. He had it on a shoulder and it looked real heavy."

"Describe it."

"Black plastic. Silver tape. Long. Thick. Like a trunk. He held me with one arm, held the trunk with the other. Just stood there, like I said, and then he spoke to me."

"You didn't tell me that before. What did he say?"

"God says."

"What does that mean?"

"I don't know."

Hunt stood and walked to the window. For a long minute, he stared through the glass. "Does the name David Wilson mean anything to you?"

"No."

"What about Levi Freemantle?"

"David Wilson is the man that got knocked off the bridge. Levi Freemantle is the man that picked me up."

"You said that the names meant nothing to you."

Johnny rolled his shoulders. "They don't. But Freemantle is a Mustee name, so that has to be the big guy. That makes David Wilson the dead one."

"Mustee?"

"Yeah."

"What's mustee?"

"Indian blood mixed with African." Hunt looked vacant. "Lumbee, Sapona, Cherokee, Catawba. There were Indian slaves, too. Didn't you know that?"

Hunt studied the kid, not sure if he should believe him. "How do you know that Freemantle is a mustee name?"

"Raven County's first freed slave was a mustee named Isaac. When he was freed, he chose the name Freemantle as his last name. Mantle of freedom. That's what the name means."

"Before this case, I'd never heard of Freemantles in Raven County."

Johnny shrugged. "They've been around. Why do you think Levi Freemantle is the same man from the bridge?"

"Let's talk about Burton Jarvis."

"No," Johnny said.

"What?"

"Not unless you answer my question. That's only fair."

"This isn't the playground, Johnny. It's not about fair."

"He's very stubborn," Katherine said.

"Very well," Hunt said. "One question. One time."

Johnny dipped his chin, and his eyes never left Hunt's face. "Why do you think that Levi Freemantle is the same man from the bridge?"

"Freemantle left a print on David Wilson's body. It makes us wonder if Freemantle was the one that drove him off the bridge. If you could tell us they were the same men, Freemantle and the one you saw on the bridge, it would clean things up." Hunt did not mention the bodies found in Freemantle's house, the drawing of the giant stick figure holding a girl with a yellow dress and a blood-red mouth.

Johnny sat up straighter, and something pulled beneath the bandages. "Was David Wilson still alive when Freemantle got to him?"

"Unknown."

"But possible."

Hunt pictured the bloody prints on the dead man's eyelids. "Doubtful," he said.

"Maybe he told Freemantle where she was."

"I wouldn't go there, Johnny."

"What if he *was* talking about Alyssa. Maybe he told Freemantle where he found her."

193

"No."

"But, maybe—"

"It's doubtful that he was talking about Alyssa at all, and it's just as doubtful that he was still alive when Freemantle got to him." Hunt studied the kid, watched him do the math. "Don't even think about it," he said.

"Think about what?"

He was so wide-eyed and innocent, any other cop would buy it. "Your days playing at cop are over, Johnny. No more maps. No more adventures. Do I make myself clear?"

Johnny turned his head away. "You asked about Burton Jarvis. What do you want to know?"

"Start at the beginning. How did you find his house? Why were you there? What did you see? What happened? All of it. Everything."

Johnny pictured his first few times at the house: the dark and the shed, how the house looked through the trees and the noise of small animals in the deep woods. He thought of plaster nails and months of bad dreams, Jar's terrible friend and their talk of Small Yellow. The laughter that made Johnny's legs get weak. He could not suppress the anxiety, and his mother picked up on it. She stood and paced, worried, and the movement annoyed Detective Hunt. "Would you mind sitting down, Katherine?"

She ignored him.

"Katherine."

"How am I supposed to sit there like everything is okay?" She twitched, and her eyes glittered. "Social Services." She glared at Hunt. "I won't allow it!"

Hunt lowered his voice. "We agreed to leave Johnny out of this for now."

"I can't stand it!"

"I'm doing what I can, Katherine. You have to believe me."

"You told me that you'd bring Alyssa home. You told me to believe that, too."

Hunt paled. "This is not helpful."

"Is that what you were talking about?" Johnny gestured toward the hall. "DSS?"

"Social Services is concerned for your welfare, Johnny. Given all that's happened, they're required to make a full evaluation. That means interviews, home inspections. They'll talk to the school. But all of that can take awhile. In the meantime, they want to remove you from your mother's custody. Temporarily. For your own protection."

"Protection?"

"They think you're at risk."

"From me," Katherine said.

"Nobody is saying that!" Hunt lost his patience.

"This is wrong," Johnny said.

"Take it easy, son." Hunt looked at Johnny's mother, who was close to tears, then focused on the boy. "I'm talking to your Uncle Steve. I think I can arrange for you to stay with him while this runs its course."

"Steve is an asshole."

"Johnny!"

"Well, he is, Mom."

Hunt leaned closer. "It's Steve or a court-appointed guardian. With Steve, your mother can visit when she wants. You'll still be with family, at least until a final decision is made. If it goes to court, it's out of my hands. The judge makes the call and you take what you get. It's not always good."

Johnny looked at his mother, but her face was in her hands. "Mom?" She shook her head.

"I'm sorry," Hunt said. "But this has been a long time coming. In the end, it will be for the best."

"We need to find my father," Johnny said.

He didn't hear his mother's footsteps. Suddenly, she was just there, by the bed. Her eyes shone, large and dark and sad. "No one knows where to find him, Johnny."

"But you said he wrote. You said Chicago, maybe California."

"He never wrote."

"But—"

"I lied." She turned one palm, and it flashed white. "He never wrote."

Johnny's vision blurred. "I want to go home," he said, but Hunt was unforgiving.

"That's not going to happen."

Katherine stepped to her son's side. She lifted her chin, and Hunt saw the protectiveness, the thin measure of pride. "Please," she said, and took her son's hand.

"I want to go home," Johnny repeated.

And for an instant, Hunt was kind enough to look away; but this was the job. He admired a lot of things about the kid, but whatever fantasy world the boy lived in, it was time to knock it down, before somebody else got hurt or the boy got himself killed.

Hunt crossed the room and picked up the paper bag that held the boy's feathers, his rattles, and the lone, yellowed skull. He pulled out the necklaces and turned so that they hung at eye level. "You want to tell me about this?"

"What is that?" Katherine asked.

"Johnny was wearing these when he came in. He was painted with soot and berry juice, half dressed, his pockets stuffed with something they tell me is snakeroot, whatever that is. DSS is going to ask about that, about all of it. They're going to push, hard, and I think maybe Johnny should start by telling me."

Johnny stared at the feathers, saw that Jar had sliced one of them clean in half. Nothing, he realized, had changed. The cop was still a threat, his mother still weak. No one would understand.

"It's not normal," Hunt stressed.

"I don't want to talk about that."

"Tell me about Burton Jarvis."

"No."

"How did you find him? How many times did you go there?"

Johnny looked out the window.

Hunt dropped the necklaces, scooped up the pages that contained Johnny's notes. "Are these notes accurate? This indicates more than a dozen visits. And others, too. Not just at the Jarvis place."

Johnny glanced at the notes. "Those are just pretend."

"What?"

"Like a game."

"Johnny—" Disappointment hung on his features.

Johnny didn't even blink. "Last night was the first time."

"I understand why you feel the need to lie, son, but I need to know what you saw. You have five names on here, people that we're aware of, known offenders that we're watching. Then there's the sixth man. The one that came to Burton Jarvis's place on multiple occasions." Hunt studied the page. "There's a full page of notes on this man. You have a general description: height, weight, hair color. You have the make of his car and three different license plate numbers, all of which were reported stolen sometime in the past year. I need to know who this man is. I think you can help me."

"No."

"What is 'small yellow'? What does that mean?"

"You work for the same people as DSS."

"Damn it." Hunt's patience evaporated, and Katherine stepped between her son and the cop. She spread slender fingers, and her words came with rare conviction.

"That's enough," she said.

"Half of these notes are illegible. There may be information here that is important in ways that Johnny doesn't fully understand. He needs to talk to me."

Katherine looked at her son's writing. She scanned the notes, then read them more closely. It took some time, but Hunt waited. When she finished, she looked frightened. "If he answers your questions, will that help us with DSS? Or hurt us?"

"You have to trust me."

"Nothing is more important than keeping my son," she said.

"Not even getting Alyssa back?"

"Are you saying that might happen?"

"Your son, I believe, has discovered a previously unknown pedophile operating in the area. A smart one. A careful one. There could be a link."

"Is that likely?"

Hunt's doubt showed in his voice. "I don't know."

"Then I have to think about the child I still have."

"I'm worried for your son."

She held his gaze, and her voice was as sharp and brittle as a shard of glass. "You want us to trust you?"

"Yes."

"Trust the police?"

"Yes."

Katherine stepped forward, shoved the pages at Hunt. "You want to talk about this unknown pedophile. The smart one. The careful one. The one associated with the man that almost killed my son . . ."

Hunt tilted his head, and she pointed one finger at an ink scratch that only a mother could read. Her face paled into a porcelain mask of anger and fear. "That word," she said, "is not 'cup' or 'cap' or anything safe. It's 'cop.' It says the man with Burton Jarvis was a cop." She pushed the pages into Hunt's chest and stepped closer to her son. "This interview is over."

After Hunt left, Katherine stood by her son's bed. She stared at him for a long time but did not ask about the feathers or the notes or the things that Hunt had said. The color fell from her cheeks, and she looked calm. "Pray with me, Johnny."

He watched her kneel, felt the anger stir someplace low. For a moment, she'd been strong, and for an instant more, he'd been so proud of her. "Pray?" he asked.

"Yes."

"Since when?"

She scrubbed her palms on her jeans. "I think I forgot how good it felt."

Johnny heard the words as if a stranger had spoken them. It was so easy for her to quit, to throw up her hands and settle for feeling better.

"He doesn't listen," Johnny said.

"Maybe we need to give him another chance."

Johnny stared at her, so disgusted and disappointed that he could no longer hide it. He gripped the rail and felt as if he might bend metal with his fingers. "Do you know what I prayed for? Every single night until I realized that God doesn't care? That he never would. Do you know?"

His voice was brutal, and she shook her head, eyes both sad and startled.

"Three things only," Johnny said. "I prayed for the rest of our family to come home. I prayed for you to stop taking pills." She opened her mouth, but Johnny spoke over her. The words came fast and cold. "I prayed for Ken to die."

"Johnny!"

"Every night, I prayed for it. Family home. An end of pills. Ken Holloway to die a slow and painful death."

"Please, don't say that."

"What part? For Ken to die? Slow and painful?"

"Don't."

"I want him to die in fear like he's put on us. I want him to know how it feels to be helpless and afraid, and then I want him to go someplace where he can't touch us anymore." She laid a finger on his hair—sad eyes gone liquid—and he pushed her hand away. "But God's not about that, is he?" Johnny sat up higher, anger gone to rage, rage taking him fast to tears. "Prayer didn't bring Alyssa home. Or Dad. It never kept the house warm or kept Ken from hurting you. God turned his back on us. You told me that yourself. Remember?"

She did. A cold night on the floor of a depleted house, blood on her teeth and the sound of Ken pouring a drink in the other room. "I think that maybe I was wrong."

"How can you even say that after everything we've lost?"

"What God gives us can't be so absolute, Johnny. It can't be everything we want. He doesn't work like that. It would be too easy."

"Nothing has been easy!"

"Don't you see?" She begged with her eyes. "There is always more to lose." She reached for his hand but he jerked it away. In its place, she gripped the bed rail with both hands and light glinted in her hair. "Pray with me, Johnny."

"For what?"

"For us to stay together. For help in letting go." Her fingers, too, went white on the rail. "Pray for forgiveness." She held his gaze for a long second, but declined to wait for an answer. Her head tilted, and the words came quietly. Not once did she look to see if Johnny had his eyes closed, if he had, in fact, joined her in prayer; and that was just as well.

There was nothing like forgiveness in Johnny's face.

Nothing like letting go.

CHAPTER TWENTY-FIVE

Hunt felt so many things as he stepped out of the room: confusion and doubt about what Katherine had claimed to read in Johnny's notes; anger and frustration that the boy would not talk to him; relief that the kid was alive, and that Tiffany, too, had survived. Hunt pressed his shoulder blades against a cold wall and ignored the people who passed, the looks they gave. He was exhausted and worried, but hoped that the death of Burton Jarvis was the beginning of the end, that the old man's violent end was the first step in unraveling Alyssa's disappearance, too. He tried to convince himself that the sick bastard was alone in the terrible things he'd done; but something foul and slick worried through the back of his mind.

A cop?

Was it even possible?

Hunt tried one more time to decipher the tight scrawl of Johnny's notes. Some of it was in pencil, smudged. Parts were water stained, others marred by soot and pine sap and tears in the paper. Hunt could read just enough to know that there was more. He wanted to kick the door down and squeeze an answer from the boy.

Damn it!

The kid knew things. Hunt was certain of it. He pictured again, as he had so many times, the black eyes and wariness, the profound stillness of deep and careful thought. Johnny was messed up in so many fundamental ways, confused, twisted sideways; but the clarity with which he saw certain things . . .

Loyalty. Fierceness. Determination.

These attributes made the boy so much more than mere impediment. They made Hunt proud and protective. Johnny should know how rare these things had become, how precious in this world. Hunt wanted to put an arm around the kid, make him understand, and, at the same time, he wanted him to stop.

Hunt stepped into the parking lot, and the sun was too bright, the air too pure. Green grass and sunshine made no sense on a day like this. He looked up at the sixth floor. Johnny's room was at one end, Tiffany's at the other. The building gleamed white, and the windows threw back perfect blue.

Hunt moved for his car and was halfway there when he saw the man in the suit. Reedlike, hunched at the shoulders, he moved from a recess near the far corner of the building, ducked between two cars, and came up on Hunt's right side. Hunt catalogued him automatically. Hands in plain view, affable smile. He carried folded pages in one hand. A hospital administrator, Hunt guessed. A visiting relative.

"Detective Hunt?"

Thirties, wispy hair, skin slightly pocked. His teeth were white and straight. "Yes."

The man's smile broadened and one finger rose. He looked as if he were trying to place a familiar face. "Detective Clyde Lafayette Hunt?"

"Yes."

He handed Hunt the folded pages and his smile dropped away as Hunt took them. "You've been served."

Hunt watched him go, then studied the papers. He was being sued, by Ken Holloway.

Shit.

Levi Freemantle's probation officer worked in a warren of offices tucked away on the third floor of the county courthouse. Linoleum peeled from the hall floor and eighty years of nicotine stained the plaster walls. The office doors were dark oak under transom windows that leaned out on brass hinges. Sound carried from behind the doors: arguments, excuses, tears. It had all been heard before. A hundred times. A million. Lies came in a flood, which made a career probation officer one of the most astute judges of human nature that Hunt had ever seen.

He found Freemantle's PO in the ninth office down. The plaque on the door frame said Calvin Tremont, and the door stood open. Files were stacked on chairs and on the floor. A fan churned warm air from its place on a scratched metal cabinet. The man behind the desk was known to Hunt. Medium height, wide through the gut, he was close to sixty, with salted hair and lines that looked almost black where they creased his dark skin. Hunt knocked on the door.

When Tremont looked up, his face carried a ready frown, but it didn't last. He and Hunt had a solid relationship. "Hello, Detective," he said. "What brings you up here?"

"One of your people."

"I'd offer you a seat, but . . ." He spread his fingers in a gesture that included the files on both chairs.

"This won't take long." Hunt stepped into the office. "I left a message yesterday. This is about the same matter."

"First day back from vacation." He gestured again. "I'm not even through my e-mails yet."

"Good trip?"

"Family at the coast." He said it in such a manner that it could mean almost anything. Hunt nodded and did not push. Parole officers were like cops; they rarely did personal.

"I need to talk about Levi Freemantle."

Tremont's face offered up the first real smile Hunt had seen. "Levi? How's my boy?"

"Your boy?"

"He's a good kid."

"He's forty-three."

"Trust me, he's a child."

"We think your child killed two people. Maybe three."

Tremont's head moved like the neck joint was oiled. "I suspect that you've made a mistake."

"You sound certain."

"Levi Freemantle looks like the biggest badass on the street, like he'd kill you for a nickel bag, which is not always a bad thing when you have nothing. But I'll tell you straight, Detective. He wouldn't kill anybody. No way. You've made a mistake."

"You have his address?" Hunt asked.

Tremont nodded and rattled it off from memory. "He's been there about three years."

"We found two bodies at that address," Hunt said. "A white female, early to mid-thirties. Black male, approximately forty-five years of age. We found them yesterday. They've been dead for most of a week." Hunt gave it a moment to sink in. "Do you know a Clinton Rhodes?"

"Is he the dead guy?"

Hunt nodded.

"Not my case," Tremont said. "But he's been in and out of here for a long time. Bad dude. Violent. Now him I could see doing a murder. Not Levi."

"We're fairly confident."

Tremont shifted in his chair. "Levi Freemantle is pulling three months on a probation violation. He won't be out for another nine weeks."

"He escaped a work detail eight days ago."

"I don't believe it."

"He walked off and hasn't been seen since, except by a burned-out drunk who barely knows his own name, and by a young boy who puts him near the scene of another murder. That was two days ago. So you see, I've got three bodies, each with some connection to your kid."

Tremont pulled Freemantle's file and opened it. "Levi has never been convicted for a violent offense. Hell, he's never been accused of one. Trespass, shoplifting." He snapped the file closed. "Look," he said. "Levi is not the sharpest tool in the toolbox. Most of these crimes, hell—if somebody said, Levi, go in there and get me a bottle of wine, he'd just walk into the store and get it. He has no sense of consequence."

"Neither do most killers."

"It's not like that. Levi . . ." He shook his head. "He's child-like."

"I have a dead white female. Early to mid-thirties. Any thoughts on that?"

"He's been involved with a Ronda Jeffries. She's white, likes to party. Been known to turn a trick or two on the side. For fun, she likes big, bad men. Specifically, she likes big, bad black men. She got involved with Levi because that's what he looks like, the toughest mother on the street. She keeps him around because he's easy to handle and he does what she says. He makes a few dollars and gives them to her. He takes care of the house. Makes her look legit. When she needs a break, or another man, she generally finds some way to get Levi locked up for a spell. It's like I said, he'll do whatever she tells him to do. The first time he got arrested, it was for shoplifting. She took a bottle of perfume off a display counter and told him to carry it; then she walked him past the security guard and out the front door."

"Are they married?"

"No, but Levi thinks they are."

"Why?"

A smile. "Because they've slept together, and because . . ."
The words trailed off. "Oh, shit."

"What?"

"Who's taking care of their kid?"

Hunt felt a chill. "Their kid?"

"A little girl. Two years old."

Hunt reached for his phone.

"Got a smile that would melt your heart."

CHAPTER TWENTY-SIX

The hospital forced Katherine to leave Johnny's room at nine that night. In one sense, it was hard for her, but in another, it was a blessing. Ken Holloway had called the room four times, refusing to hang up until she agreed to meet with him. He'd been insistent and she'd been strong, refusing each time, explaining that now, finally, she had to put her son first. Eventually, she'd been forced to hang up on him. Twice. After that, she twitched in fear every time the door opened or a noise rose too quickly in the hall.

And then there was the dryness. She tried to be strong, but felt it in every part of her body.

The need.

She lingered by the bed for a final moment. Her son was asleep, his face, as always, like that of his sister. Same mouth. Same lines. She kissed him on the head, then met her cab at the rear entrance of the hospital.

The ride home was white-knuckled. They passed three stores advertising beer and wine, two different bars. She tightened her jaw and dug nails into her palms. When the downtown lights fell away, she allowed herself to breathe. There was dark road, the steady hum of tires on black pavement. She was okay. She repeated it.

I am okay.

The cab started down the final hill, and she saw the house from a half mile out. Light spilled from every window, stained the yard in bumblebee patterns of black and yellow.

She'd left the place dark.

Climbing from the cab, she started for the door, then hesitated. Her hand found the cell phone in her purse. She got as far as the porch, then changed her mind and stepped back. Everything was so still: the yard, the woods, the street.

That's when she saw the car. It was parked two hundred feet down the road, edged far onto the shoulder. It was too dark to make out the color. Black, maybe. A big sedan that she did not recognize. She stared hard, took a step toward it, and realized that she could hear its engine running.

She took two more steps and the car lights snapped on. Spitting dirt and gravel, the car made a tight, squealing turn and flew up the road, taillights growing small, then dropping away as the road fell.

Katherine tried to slow her breath. It was just a car. Just a neighbor. She turned back to the house and saw that the front door stood open a crack, a long slice of yellow that spread wide when she pushed.

Inside, music played.

"*Have yourself a merry little Christmas . . .*"

It was late May.

She turned off the music and moved down the hall. The house *felt* empty, but the music freaked her out. It was the one song, set to play again and again. She checked the bedrooms first, found nothing out of place. The bathroom was fine, too.

She found the pills in the kitchen.

The orange bottle sat in the exact center of the chipped Formica table. It was bright and shiny, its label a slash of perfect white. Katherine stared at it, felt her tongue thicken. The pills clicked when she picked the bottle up to read the label. It had her name on it, dated today.

Seventy-five pills.

Oxycontin.

In a rage, she tore open the door and flung the bottle into the yard. The lock twisted in her fingers as she drove it home. She checked every window, every door, then sat on the sofa by the front window. She kept her back straight, and felt the bottle out there, a presence in the dark. She ground her teeth and cursed Ken Holloway's name.

It wasn't going to be that easy.

Johnny left the hospital at noon the next day. They rolled him to the curb and he stood carefully. "You okay?" the nurse asked.

"I think so."

"Give yourself a minute."

Thirty feet away, cameras clicked and whirred. Reporters shouted questions, but the cops held them at a distance. Johnny took it in, one hand on the roof of Uncle Steve's van. He saw news trucks from the Charlotte stations, the ones in Raleigh. "I'm ready," he said, and the nurse helped him into the van.

"Nothing too stressful," she said. "Two of those cuts went plenty deep." She gave a final smile and closed the door. Behind the wheel, Steve studied the cameras. Next to him, Johnny's mother kept one hand up to shield her face.

Hunt stepped to the window once Johnny was secured in the back. When he spoke, it was of the deal he'd arranged with DSS. "This is only going to work if you all play by the rules." He moved from face to face, stopped on Steve's. "I need to know if you can handle this."

Steve glanced at Johnny in the rearview mirror. "I guess. Assuming he does what I tell him."

Hunt looked at Johnny. "This is a gift, Johnny. With all that's happened."

"How long does he have to stay away?" Katherine asked.

"It's up to DSS now."

"This is bullshit," Johnny mumbled.

"What did you say?"

Johnny kicked at the floor mat. "Nothing."

Hunt nodded. "That's what I thought." He stepped back, spoke to Steve. "On my taillights. All the way out."

The drive took twelve minutes, and nobody spoke. At the house, Hunt parked on the grass. Johnny and his mother climbed from the van. She stared at a distant streetlamp, touched her throat once, then went inside. Johnny followed her to his room. On the bed lay his clothes, neatly folded. Her voice was full of apology. "I laid them out last night. I didn't know what you'd want to take."

"I'll pack."

"Are you sure?" She gestured at his bandaged chest.

"I can do it."

"Johnny . . ."

He looked at her, saw how stretched she looked. She'd always been strong, and then, after the abduction, the exact opposite. This face now, it was different, as if the two sides of her were engaged in some fierce struggle. "I should not have lied to you," she said. "I should never have told you that he wrote."

"I understand."

"I didn't want you to know that we were so alone. I thought—"

"I said I get it."

She ran a hand over his hair. "So strong," she said. "So self-contained."

Johnny stiffened because those were the words she'd once

used to describe his father. Johnny had walked into a rare argument, the source of which was still unknown to him. But those had been her words: *You don't always have to be so self-contained!* He'd just smiled and kissed her, and that had been the end of the argument. Johnny's dad was good like that. When he chose to smile, no one could stay angry at him. To Johnny, even now, self-containment and strength were one and the same. Don't complain. Get the job done. He had that in full measure. What he lacked was the same easy smile. Whether he'd never truly had it, or whether he'd forgotten its feel, he could no longer say. Life, for Johnny, had become a matter of self-containment. He scooped up a pair of jeans, shoved them into a duffel. "Let's just do this."

She left the room and he heard the click of her door, the small crunch of bedsprings. He didn't know which side of her had finally won, the softness or the strength, but experience told him that she was under the covers, eyes shut tight. Her sudden presence in the door, moments later, took him by surprise. She held out a framed photograph, a color shot from her wedding day. She was twenty, all smiles, and the sun spilled perfect color across her face. Johnny's dad stood by her side, the same reckless smile bending his features. Johnny remembered the photograph. He thought she'd burned it with the rest. "Take this," she said.

"I'm coming back."

"Take it."

And Johnny did.

Then she hugged him with great tenderness; and when she returned to her room, the door stayed closed.

Johnny stopped behind the screen door, duffel pulling hard on one shoulder. Outside, the leaves twitched in a fitful wind. Hunt stood with his head down, hands shoved deep into his pockets. He peered out from deep-set eyes, staring at the house. He did not see Johnny; his gaze touched first one window, and then another, head unmoving, forehead creased in the center. He shifted when Johnny nudged the door with one foot. "You're not supposed to be carrying that." He lifted the bag from Johnny's shoulder. "You're going to pull those stitches."

"They felt okay." Johnny stepped into the yard and Hunt stopped beside him.

"Before we go."

"Yeah?"

"When you saw Levi Freemantle . . ." Hunt hesitated. "Did he have anybody with him?"

Johnny considered the question, looking for danger. He'd refused all of Hunt's questions, but could not see how this could cause trouble with DSS. He saw the hope on the detective's face, watched it fade as he shook his head. "Just the trunk."

Hunt's eyes were tortured, his voice tight. "Nobody at all?" Hunt could not ask the rest of it: *No child? No small girl that could melt a heart?*

Johnny shook his head.

Hunt paused, then cleared his throat. "Here." He held out one of his cards, and Johnny took it. "You can always call me. You don't even need a reason." Johnny tilted the card, then tucked it into his back pocket. Hunt looked one last time at the house, then forced a smile. His hand touched Johnny's shoulder. "Be good," he said, and tossed Johnny's bag into the back of the van.

Johnny watched Hunt's car ease into the road, then turn. The van door squealed when he opened it. He climbed in, Steve's lips twisted in forced cheer. "Guess it's just us."

"This is bullshit," Johnny said.

Steve's smile fell away. He started the car, and pulled out of the drive. He licked his lips, cut his eyes right. "Can you tell me what happened?"

He was talking about Tiffany Shore.

"I didn't save anybody." It was automatic now, metallic. Johnny kept his eyes away from the house. He feared his reaction if he looked at the shell he'd left his mother in, the vacuum wrapped in flaked paint and rotted wood.

Steve accelerated. "Still, your dad would be proud."

"Maybe."

Johnny risked a final glance as the house grew small behind them. The swaybacked roof seemed to straighten, its blemishes faded, and for an instant the house shone like a dime. "Are we going to be okay with this?" Johnny asked. "Me staying with you? It's not my idea, you know."

"Just stay out of my stuff." The van crested the hill, and Steve twisted his jaw like it had popped out of joint. The road dropped into shadow. "You want to buy some candy or comics or something?"

"Candy?"

"That's what kids like, isn't it."

Johnny said nothing.

"Feels like I owe you."

"Well, you don't."

Steve inclined his head toward the glove compartment, more relaxed. "Reach in there and grab my smokes."

Papers and other junk stuffed the glove compartment. Cigarette packs. Receipts. Lottery tickets. Johnny pulled out a wrinkled half pack of Lucky Strikes and handed them to his uncle. Then he found the gun. It was wedged into the back corner, tucked away beneath the owner's manual and a coffee-stained map of Myrtle Beach. The grip was brown wood, nicked, the metal blued with a silver shine on the hammer. Cracks discolored the dry leather holster. Next to the gun rested a faded cardboard box of shells that said: .32 HOLLOW POINT.

"Don't touch that," Steve said easily.

Johnny closed the glove compartment. He watched whiskered trees march beside them, the dark spaces between that hinted of giant men the color of smoke. "Will you teach me how to shoot?"

"It ain't that hard."

"Will you?"

Steve glanced sideways, appraising, then flicked a skin of ash out the window. Johnny kept his features still, and he was proud of that, because *still* was not what he felt. He was thinking of his sister and of a giant man with a melted face and a mustee name.

"What for?" Steve asked, and Johnny showed his most innocent eyes.

"Just 'cause."

CHAPTER TWENTY-SEVEN

S teve worked the van through town. He passed storefronts
and columned mansions, the parklike town square with
its canopy of twisted oaks and the statue erected more than
a century ago to honor a proud county's Confederate dead.
Johnny saw a brush of mistletoe in a tree, and thought of a girl
he'd once dared to kiss, whose face now he could barely recall.

A different life.

Once past the square and the sun-dashed campus of the local
college, Steve turned onto the four-lane that led to the mall. It
was Ken's mall. He owned it. "Where are we going?" Johnny
asked.

"I have to stop by work. It won't take long."

Johnny sank into his seat. Steve sensed it. "Mr. Holloway
won't be there," Steve said. "He never is."

"I'm not scared of Ken."

"I can take you to my place first."

"I said I'm not scared."

A half laugh. "Whatever."

Johnny forced himself to sit up. "Why does he care so much
about my mother?"

"Mr. Holloway?"

"He treats her like crap."

"She's the prettiest woman in this part of the state, or hadn't
you noticed?"

"It's more than that."

Steve shrugged. "Mr. Holloway doesn't like to lose."

"Lose what?"

"Anything." Johnny's confusion showed, and Steve saw it. He narrowed his eyes and pushed smoke through his lips. "You don't know, do you?" He shook his head. "Christ, almighty."

"What?"

"Your mom used to go out with Ken Holloway."

"I don't believe it."

"Well, you'd better." Steve took another drag, drawing the moment out. "She was eighteen, maybe nineteen. Just a girl, really." He shook his head, pursed his lips. "Hotter than a three-dollar pistol, your momma. Could have gone to Hollywood, maybe. New York, for sure. Never did, of course, but could have."

"I still don't believe it."

"He was older, but even then he was the richest man around. Not like he is now, mind you, but rich enough. It'd be hard for a pretty girl to resist the kind of attention he could apply if he set his mind to it, and your mother was no different from most other girls. Flowers. Gifts. Fancy dinners. Anything he could think of to make her feel important."

"She's not like that." Johnny was angry.

"Not now. But young people like to feel bigger than the place they come from. It lasted for a few months, I guess. But then your dad came back to town."

"Back from where?"

"The service. Four years. He's what, six years older than she is? Seven? Anyway, she was just a kid when he left, but that changed." Steve laughed and blew out a low whistle. "Boy, did that change." Johnny stared out the window, and Steve continued. "Your old man fell for her like a ton of steel."

"Her, too? For him I mean?"

"Your mom was like a butterfly, Johnny. Pretty and light and delicate. Your old man loved that about her, cherished it. He was as gentle and patient as you'd need to be for a butterfly to land in your hand."

"And Holloway?"

Steve stubbed out the cigarette, spit out the window. "Holloway just wanted to put her in a jar."

"And she figured that out about him?"

"You should have seen him when she said she was leaving him for your father."

"Angry?"

"Angry. Jealous. He pursued her hard, tried to change her mind, but three months later your folks were married. You came a year later. It was as sharp a rejection as I ever saw, and I don't know that Holloway ever got over it."

"But Dad did work for Holloway. All those houses he built. Holloway was over all the time."

"Your daddy sees good in all people. It's part of what makes him so fine. But Holloway was just waiting to bury him."

"Dad didn't know?"

"I told him as much, but your daddy always thought he could handle him. He's prideful like that."

"Confident," Johnny said.

"Arrogant."

Blacktop slid under the truck. The fan belt made a sudden, screaming noise. "You work for Holloway."

"Not all of us have a choice, Johnny. That's a life lesson for you. Free of charge."

Steve stopped the van at a light. In the distance, Holloway's mall rose like a battleship. Johnny watched Steve's face, and when he spoke, it was of his mother. "Did you want to date her?"

Steve's eyes were as flat as a snake's. "Hell, son." The light turned green. "Everybody did."

The parking lot was slammed, which reminded Johnny that it was Saturday. Steve parked near the employee entrance at the back. When he opened the door, his mirror splashed sun into Johnny's eyes. "Come on," he said.

"Can I wait in the van?"

"Too dangerous back here. Homeless. Drug abusers. God knows what else." Johnny watched as Steve touched the objects on his belt: Mace, radio, cuffs. "Come on. I'll show you something cool."

Inside, a key card granted access to a narrow door, metal stairs, and a third-story hallway that led to an office marked SECURITY. Steve swiped his card and leaned a shoulder against the office door. "Kids never get to see this."

The security office was large and complex, with a bank of video monitors that covered an entire wall. Two guards sat in black swivel chairs, hands on keyboards and joysticks, changing images on the screens, zooming in and out, observing. They turned as Johnny stepped in, then did a double take.

One of them was twenty-something and fat, with hair mowed short and a razor-burned face. His smile was at once awe filled and dismissive. "This the kid?"

Steve put a hand on Johnny's back, propelled him farther into the room "My nephew. Sort of."

The fat guard offered a meaty hand, and Johnny studied it warily before shaking it. "Good job, kid. Wish I could have been there."

Johnny looked at his uncle, who offered two words. "Tiffany Shore."

The guard made a shooting motion. "Pow."

"I don't want to talk about it," Johnny said.

But the guard was eager. "You see this?" He whipped a news-paper from the counter. "Front page. Check it out."

The picture was of Johnny, taken through the window as he sat in the front seat of his mother's car. His hands still gripped the wheel. His mouth hung open, face shocked and empty. Blood sheeted everything, dark where it had dried, bright where it wept red on Johnny's chest. Feathers and rattles shone black on his skin, the skull as yellow-wet as a stone soaked in honey. Tiffany angled across the seat beside him, sun so fierce on her face that it shattered in her eyes. Men with clean clothes and long arms reached through the door to pull her out, but she was fighting, mouth tight, fingers desperate on Johnny's arm.

The caption ran below the photograph: "Stolen Child Found, Pedophile Killed."

Johnny's voice came in a choked whisper. "Where did they get this picture?"

"The security guard at the hospital took it with his cell phone. They're using the same picture on CNN." The fat guard shook his head. "Probably paid him a fortune."

Steve stepped in front of Johnny and pushed the paper away. "He doesn't need to see that."

The guard shifted as he took in Johnny's face, saw how shadows multiplied in the hollow places. "I didn't mean nothing."

"Is the boss in?" Steve interrupted.

The guard hooked a thumb at an office door but kept his eyes on Johnny. Johnny followed Steve's gaze and saw a window and white blinds sheathed in dust. An eye peered out and the blinds snapped shut. "Shit," Steve muttered. "Has he been looking for me?"

"Should he be?"

Steve shrugged, but looked nervous. "Anything exciting?"

"One shoplifter. Two D-and-Ds."

Steve explained. "Drunk and disorderly." He tapped Johnny on the shoulder and crossed the room. "Come here," he said, and Johnny followed him past the bank of monitors to a wall of glass that was nine feet high and twice as long. The view was onto the Food Court. Steve tapped the glass. "Mirrored," he said.

Johnny peered through the windows and could see everything spread out below: storefronts and food stands, escalators, people. The fat guard ambled up, cupped both hands and breathed deeply. "This must be what God feels like." Johnny wanted to laugh at the absurdity of the comment, the sheer smallness of it.

Then he saw Jack.

Red-faced, humiliated, awkward-looking Jack.

He stood at the edge of the crowd, a small, tan boy with a shriveled arm and no meanness in his entire body. He stood, taking it, because fighting back would get him nowhere, and because walking away would imply that he actually cared about the shame that was being heaped upon him. His tormentors were seniors, lean, muscled kids with self-aware smiles.

Johnny cringed when he saw spit go down the back of Jack's shirt; but his anger spiked when he saw Jack's brother, who stood ten feet away and did nothing to stop it. He was surrounded by fawning girls, four at least.

Johnny pointed. "Do you see that?"

Steve leaned forward. "Gerald Cross? Yeah, I see it. The girls have been like that ever since he signed with Clemson. He'll go pro in a year. His contract will be ten million, minimum."

"Not him."

"Then what?"

"Can I go down there?"

Steve shrugged. "Go. Stay. I'm not your daddy."

Johnny pounded down the stairs, through the security door and into the crowd. He smelled pizza and scorched beef, the crush of overheated bodies and, somewhere, an unchanged diaper. He angled for Jack and heard his name whispered. Fingers pointed.

That's the guy.

It took Johnny a minute to understand, but then he did.

The story was everywhere.

By the time he crossed the Food Court, a dozen people were watching him, but he didn't care. One of the seniors was snapping rabbit punches at Jack's bad arm, hitting beneath the meat of the shoulder, right where the hollow bone had the least protection. Jack was trying to hide it, but Johnny saw that his friend was about to cry.

Johnny bulled his way into the group and punched the senior as hard as he could. He connected with the kid's mouth, felt whiskers, teeth, and the ripe softness of a burst lip. The guy stumbled left, caught himself, and his hands came up, fisted. He drew back to throw a punch, then recognized Johnny. "Holy shit," he said.

Johnny stared at the startled brown eyes, the stained teeth, and the long hair spiked with gel. The kid spit blood and stepped away. "Damn freak."

Johnny shook with rage, with a long year's silence and with all of the things he'd repressed since waking in a hospital room stained red. The senior mistook the trembling for fear and started to smile, then looked over Johnny's head at the suddenly watchful crowd. He lowered his hands, tried to laugh it all off. "Easy, Pocahontas."

No one else laughed. Johnny was a celebrity of the darkest kind, a strange, wild kid with eyes that were savage and black.

He'd seen things no boy was supposed to see. He'd lost a twin, found Tiffany Shore, and maybe killed a man.

He was war paint and fire.

Insane.

Johnny held up a single finger, then looked into his friend's bright, brimming eyes. "Let's get out of here."

He started to leave, then saw Gerald, who stood three rows back, tall and broad, with sandy hair and skin the color of fired clay. Johnny pulled Jack into his wake, and the crowd parted. He stopped in front of Gerald and saw how the pretty girls stepped back, how naked Gerald looked without them.

Johnny dragged Jack from his shadow and draped an arm around his neck. He did not see how his friend lowered his eyes and rolled a curve into his spine, did not see the shame and the fear and the quick, nervous twitch. Gerald towered over Johnny, ten inches taller, a hundred pounds heavier. He was summer sweat and green grass, a hero in the making, but no one watching could doubt who was in charge.

Johnny held up the same finger, stabbed Gerald in the meat of his chest. "He's your brother, you dick. What's wrong with you?"

The boys stalked through the press of silent people. Johnny looked straight ahead and tried to avoid eye contact, but he did see one person he recognized, another senior, tall with white-blond hair and wide-set eyes. It was Detective Hunt's son, Allen. From the river. Alone, in steel-toed boots and a jean jacket, he leaned against a column near the back of the crowd. A toothpick rolled between his teeth, and he guarded his eyes. When Johnny looked at him, he neither blinked nor moved. Just the toothpick. Side to side.

The security door accepted the key card that Steve had given him. The door clicked open and Johnny pushed through, into a cool, open space that smelled of damp and cement. Stairs rose to the right and beneath them was a low, gray space. Jack threw himself onto the floor, back against the wall, feet drawn up. Johnny sat next to him. Chewing gum made dark marks on the floor. One of Jack's shoes was untied, and his jeans, at the knees, were stained with grass.

"Well," Johnny said. "That sucked."

Jack put his face on his knees and Johnny looked up. His fingers explored a rivet, then a weld line. When Jack's face came up, Johnny saw wet spots that turned the grass stains black.

"How did you get us in here?"

"Uncle Steve."

Jack sucked in two quick breaths, smeared mucus along the back of his bad arm.

"Those guys are dicks," Johnny said.

Jack sniffed. "Shit munchers."

"Yeah. Asswipes."

Jack laughed, a nervous expulsion, and Johnny relaxed. "What was that all about?"

"He wanted me to say something," Jack explained. "I wouldn't do it." Johnny looked the question and Jack shrugged. "Jocks rule. Gimps drool."

"Fucking Gerald. How's your arm?"

Jack rotated his arm at the shoulder, then pressed it across his chest. He pointed at Johnny's chest. Bandages were visible above the buttons. "You're bleeding, man."

"I tore some stitches."

Jack stared at the bandages. "Is that from the other night?"

The bandages darkened. Johnny pulled the shirt closed.

"I should have gone with you, Johnny. When you asked me for help, I should have gone."

"It wouldn't have made a difference," Johnny said.

Jack beat a fist on his leg. "I'm a bad friend." The fist sounded like a hammer on meat. "I am"—he paused, hitting again—"a bad friend."

"Stop that."

"I didn't do anything for Alyssa."

"You couldn't have."

"I saw it happen."

"There was nothing you could do, Jack."

But Jack ignored him. "I didn't do anything for you." He hit again, hard.

"Stop it, Jack."

Jack stopped. "Is it true?" He looked at Johnny. "The stuff that they're saying about you? You know?" He made a motion over his face, fingers wiggling.

Johnny knew what he meant. "Some of it, I guess."

"What the hell, Johnny?"

Johnny looked at his friend, and knew, without a doubt, that Jack could never understand Johnny's desperate need to believe in something more powerful than his own two hands. Jack had never felt the loss or the fear. He had never lived the nightmare that had become Johnny's life, but he wasn't stupid, either.

Johnny had to tell him something.

"You remember that book we read in English? *The Lord of the Flies?* About those boys on the deserted island and how they go feral with no adults around to tell them different. They make spears and blood paint. They run wild through the jungle, hunt pigs, beat drums. You remember?"

"Yeah. So?"

"One day they were normal, then one day the rules didn't matter anymore. They made up their own rules, their own beliefs." He paused. "Sometimes I feel like those boys."

"Those kids tried to kill each other. They went insane."

"Insane?"

"Yeah."

Johnny shrugged. "I really like that book."

"You're an idiot."

"Maybe."

Jack picked at a thread on his jeans, looked around at the concrete and stairs. "I thought you hated your Uncle Steve."

Johnny explained about DSS, Detective Hunt. "That's why."

"I wouldn't do anything special for that cop," Jack said.

"What do you mean?"

He waved a hand. "Stuff I hear from my dad. Cop stuff."

"Like what?"

"Like he's sweet on your mom. That they've been . . . you know."

"Bullshit."

"That's what my dad says."

"Well, your dad's a liar."

"He probably is."

A silence fell. They were awkward together for the first time. "You want to spend the night?" Johnny asked. "It's just Steve's place, but, you know—"

"My dad won't let me hang out with you."

"Why not?"

"*Lord of the Flies,* man. He thinks you're dangerous." Jack tipped his head against the wall. Johnny did the same. "Dangerous," Jack said. "Dangerous is cool."

"Not if we can't hang out."

They fell into another long silence. "I really loved your dad," Jack said. "He made me feel like the arm didn't matter."

"It doesn't."

"I hate my family."

"No, you don't."

226

Jack wrapped his arms around his knees and his fingers went white where he squeezed them. "You remember last year? When I broke my arm?"

The arm was weak; it broke easily. Johnny remembered at least three times that Jack had been in a cast. Last year, though, had been a bad one, with breaks in four places. Fixing it took more surgeries: screws and pins and other bits of metal. "I remember."

"Gerald's the one that did it." The small hand danced at the end of its narrow wrist. Jack's voice fell down a well. "That's why my dad gave me the new bike."

"Jack—"

"That's why I never ride it."

"Shit, man."

"I hate my family."

CHAPTER TWENTY-EIGHT

Hunt stood in the Chief's office. Flags graced the corners of the room, and on one wall hung pictures of his boss with various state functionaries: the lieutenant governor, a former senator, a two-bit actor who looked vaguely familiar. Photos of his children were spaced along the credenza. The local paper sat on the desk. So did the papers from Wilmington, Charlotte, and Raleigh. Johnny's picture was on the front page of each of them. Face paint and feathers, blood and bone.

A wild Indian.

The Chief filled his chair, tilted back, hands crossed on his stomach. Anger carved deep lines at the corners of his eyes. He was tired, with unwashed hair that glistened on his forehead. The county sheriff, a lean man in his sixties, with cracked skin on his knuckles and leathery bags beneath his eyes, stood against the wall. He'd been sheriff for almost thirty years and was as feared for his temper as he was respected for his abilities. He studied Hunt with dark, impenetrable eyes and looked no happier than the Chief.

Hunt refused to flinch.

"Do you have any idea," the Chief began, "how many people work for this department? How many officers, how many trainees?"

"I am well aware."

The Chief gestured at the sheriff. "And in the Sheriff's Department? Any idea?"

"A lot, I'm sure."

"And how do you think those people would feel if we let you root around in their personnel files? Their confidential personnel files?"

"I have reason to believe—"

"We've seen your reason." The sheriff's voice cut through the room. He shifted but kept his shoulder on the wall, his thumbs in his heavy, black belt. "And neither one of us can tell *what* that word says. Maybe it's 'cop', but maybe it's something else. Maybe this kid is mistaken."

The Chief leaned forward. "Or full of it."

"Or crazy as a shithouse rat."

Hunt stared at the sheriff. "I respectfully disagree."

"Are you some kind of expert now?" The Chief thumped a finger on the newspapers. "Just look at him."

The photograph damned the boy to ready judgment: feathers, wild hair, Tiffany frozen in terror, and his eyes shocked to utter blankness.

"I understand how that looks, but this is a smart kid. If he thinks he saw a cop, there's a reason for it."

The sheriff interrupted. "The boy claims he made it up. You said so yourself. Now, that's all I really need to hear."

"He's worried that DSS will take him away from the only family he has left. He thinks a cop was involved with Burton Jarvis." Hunt could not contain his frustration. "He's terrified. He's protecting himself."

"Do you have any other reason, beyond this kid, to think that one of ours, a cop for God's sake, might be involved in this unholy mess?"

"Tiffany Shore's handcuffs were police issue."

"Found at any decent surplus store," the sheriff said.

"It's strong circumstantial evidence, especially in connection with Johnny's observations."

"We're done discussing that boy's *observations*," the Chief said.

"Is there anything that links Tiffany Shore's cuffs to either department?" The sheriff's features barely moved. "Serial numbers? Anything?"

"No."

"Anything at the scene? In Jarvis's past? On his property?"

"No. But at the very least, the kid has identified a dangerous predator who has so far avoided detection. The files are a logical place to start. If he's right, then we take a bad guy off the street. If he's wrong, no harm done."

"No harm done? For God's sake, Hunt." The Chief splayed his meaty hands on the desk. "Giving you access to those files would piss off every employee I have and probably violate more employment laws than I care to count. Not to mention the image problem we'd have if word gets out."

"And it would," the sheriff said.

"The kid has already made me look like an ass on national television, and you—my lead detective, my right arm, or so I've been told—you have managed to drag this department into a lawsuit with one of the city's most respected businessmen."

"That lawsuit is crap and you know it."

The Chief ticked off points on his fingers. "Police brutality. Harassment. Intentional infliction of emotional distress. False arrest. Is there anything else? I'm running out of fingers."

"There may be a pedophile with a badge running loose in this county. That's the issue, and it should concern both of you. Ignoring that possibility puts children at further risk. *You*"— Hunt stressed the word, repeated it—"*you* would be putting children at further risk."

The Chief came out of his seat. "If you repeat anything like that outside of this office, I will have your ass and I will burn it."

"Ignoring this won't make it go away."

"That's enough."

"If another child goes missing because of self-serving public relations concerns—"

"Why are we listening to this son of a bitch?" the sheriff demanded. "If we lose another kid, it'll be because of his incompetence. That's the bottom line here and everybody knows it. Just look at him, for Christ's sake."

Hunt bristled and the Chief tried to settle everyone down. "Jarvis is dead. Tiffany is safe. That's what matters."

The sheriff barked a laugh. "Thanks to a twelve-year-old girl and a thirteen-year-old punk."

"I'll handle my own people," the Chief said, and stared the sheriff down. "Is that clear?"

The sheriff returned to his post on the wall and nailed Hunt with a finger. "Well, you tell supercop to keep his eye on the ball. 'Cause I think he's losing it. I think he's trying to make himself look better by dragging other cops through the mud. My people. Your people. Us, for all I can tell."

The Chief held up a hand and spoke to Hunt, a red flush climbing his neck as he did. "Are we clear on this issue of cop pedophiles? I don't want to hear one damn word about this."

"I think your stance is painfully clear."

"Good. Because you should be looking into the circumstances of David Wilson's death, Levi Freemantle, Burton Jarvis's *known* associates. Not figments. Not maybes. *Known*, as in factual. If someone else is involved with Jarvis, that's the way to find him. I want every loose end nailed down. We will reconsider your request to examine personnel files if and when Johnny Merrimon decides to talk about what he saw."

"If he saw it," the sheriff said.

"If he saw it," the Chief agreed. "What he saw. How it happened. All of the usual things we, as cops, like to hear before going off half-cocked. Is that clear, Detective?"

"Yes."

"Then get the hell out."

Hunt did not move. "There's more, I think."

"You think?" The sheriff's scorn was pronounced.

"The Freemantle case."

"Have you found him?" the Chief asked.

"Not yet."

"Then what?"

"We have ID on the bodies: Freemantle's girlfriend and a guy she was probably sleeping with. We're pretty sure Freemantle did it. No forced entry. Looks extemporaneous. Crime of passion, maybe. We think he walked in on them."

"Extemporaneous," the sheriff said. "That's a big word."

"Freemantle walked off a work detail that morning. Probably went straight home and caught them in the act. His probation officer says the girlfriend was pretty much a whore."

"Fine. A good, clean case. I like it."

Hunt pushed out a breath. "They have a daughter."

"And?" The Chief's entire body swelled.

"She's missing."

"No." The Chief stood. "No, she's not."

"What?"

The Chief kept his voice calm and level, but a fierceness underlay it. "No one has filed a missing persons report. No one has called us for help."

"That doesn't mean it's not true."

"She could be with relatives, a grandmother, an aunt. Levi Freemantle probably has the kid. He's the father, isn't he? He hasn't lost custody rights yet."

Hunt stood, angry. "You're just going to ignore this?"

"Ignore what?" The Chief turned his palms flat. "There is nothing to ignore. There's no case here."

"I get it," Hunt said.

"You do?" The fierceness moved to implicit threat.

"No one wants another missing kid, so you bury it. You stick your head in the sand and pretend there's no problem."

"If you utter one word about another missing child . . ."

"I've had enough of your threats."

The Chief straightened. "Don't you have enough on your plate?"

"I want you to think hard about this," Hunt said.

"And if I don't?"

Hunt looked at the sheriff, the Chief. "I think that would be bad for all of us."

CHAPTER TWENTY-NINE

Johnny went home to Uncle Steve's two-bedroom apartment. It was a dump, even from the outside. Steve opened the door and looked embarrassed. "This okay?" he asked.

Johnny smelled beer and dirty clothes. "Sure."

Steve showed Johnny his room and closed the door when Johnny asked him to. The room held a single bed with a table and lamp. A closet. A dresser. Nothing else. Johnny dropped his bag and opened it. He put the photograph of his parents on the table, then opened his shirt and checked the bandages. Red spots had soaked through in a diagonal line eight inches long. It was the worst of the cuts, but the blood was dry and Johnny guessed it would be okay. He buttoned up.

At sunset, Steve called out for pizza and they ate in front of a game show that he described as educational in nature. Afterward, Steve put his hands on his knees, looked awkward. "I have a lady friend . . ." His fingers shifted on the weave of his fine polyblend pants.

"I'll stay in my room. Or you can go out if you want. It won't bother me."

"Go out?"

"Sure."

"What about DSS?"

"If they come, I won't answer the door. We can say we were out for dinner."

Steve looked at the phone, the door. Johnny made it easy for him. "I've been alone plenty of times. You don't have to worry."

Relief softened Steve's hard-edged mouth. "I'd just be gone for a few hours."

"I'm thirteen."

Steve rose and pointed. The nail on his finger was brown and broken. "Stay out of my stuff," he said.

"Of course."

"And don't let anybody inside."

Johnny nodded solemnly and saw that Steve still needed help. "I'll probably just read. Homework, you know."

"Homework. Good idea."

Steve left and Johnny watched him all the way to the curb. Then he went through Steve's stuff. Methodically. Carefully. He felt no guilt, no remorse. If Steve was going to get stoned or drunk, Johnny wanted to know. Same thing with guns and knives and baseball bats.

Johnny wanted to know where they were.

If the gun was loaded.

He found vodka in the freezer, a bag of pot in a casserole dish. The computer was password protected, the filing cabinet locked. He discovered a hunting knife on the floor of the bedroom closet and a sex manual on the shelf. An interior door led from the kitchen to the garage, where he found a pickup truck with worn tires and gouges in the dirty white paint. Johnny stood under the bright light and ran his hands along the hood, the mud-caked fenders. The truck was old, a beater, but it had air in the tires and the needle lifted off the peg when Johnny turned the key to check the gas. He stood in the garage smell and thought hard about things he should probably not do; but two minutes later he sat at the kitchen table, truck key in front of him, phone book open.

There was one listing for Levi Freemantle.

Johnny knew the street.

He picked up the key but jumped when the phone rang. It was his mother, and she was distraught. "Are you being a good boy?"

Johnny tilted the key in the light. "Yes."

"This is only temporary, honey. You need to believe that."

Johnny heard a noise through the phone, a crash. "I believe it."

"I love you, baby."

"I love you, too." Another sound.

"I have to go," she said.

"Are you okay?"

"Be a good boy." She hung up.

Johnny stared at the phone, then put it down. The key was warm in his hand.

No one had to know.

CHAPTER THIRTY

Katherine put the phone on the floor, next to her leg. Against her back, the front door was hard and cold. She pushed against it, even as a fist slammed into it from the outside. "Go away, Ken!"

Above her, the deadbolt held fast. Another blow, this one low. A kick. "You are my girlfriend. This is my house."

"I changed the locks!"

"Open this damn door!"

"I'll call the cops. I swear I will."

The door shuddered from successive blows; the knob twisted but held. "I just want to talk!"

"I'm dialing." A lie.

Silence, sudden and complete. She held her breath and listened. She imagined his own ear to the door, his fingertips pressed white on the dirty paint. The silence built. Ten seconds. A minute. She screamed when he kicked the door a final time. Then she felt vibration as he descended the steps. His car started and headlights stabbed through the tattered lace curtains as he turned in the yard and sped up the road.

She collapsed against the door, shaking so violently her jaw hurt. He had to be drunk or coked up. But she'd made a decision. Johnny first. No drinking, no pills. And that meant no Ken Holloway.

Katherine bit down on the heel of her hand. At least Johnny was not here. At least he was safe.

She waited until her heart slowed and her breathing settled. Five minutes. Maybe ten. She was about to stand when she heard stealthy movement in the yard: gravel under foot, a rasp of bare earth. Fear paralyzed her so badly that she literally could not breathe. Outside, an old plank bent with the sound of wind through a dead tree. Weight on the porch. A thump against the door, very quiet. Katherine heard the bottom step groan and then silence.

Total, terrifying silence.

She had the phone in her hand but decided that 911 was not good enough. She wanted Hunt, trusted him. Keeping low, she moved to the kitchen. His card was in the top drawer. He answered on the first ring. She spoke in a whisper.

"Do not open the door," he said. "Whatever you do. I'll have a car there before you know it."

She kept the phone in her hand even after they'd disconnected. She crept to the window and risked a glance. She saw shadows and trees, the friction of light and dark as low clouds raced across a rising moon. Nothing on the road. Nothing in the yard. She leaned right, pushed her cheek into the glass. She saw part of the porch but not enough. At the door again, she listened and heard a scratching sound, like a fork on wax paper. She heard it twice, faintly, then the unmistakable sound of a muffled cry. Faint. Somehow familiar.

She heard it again. It was outside the door. On the porch.

Katherine looked at the phone, then heard the cry again. For one wild second, she thought it was a baby. Someone had left a baby on her porch; but that was insane, she knew it; but the sound came again, and she found her fingers on the deadbolt, one hand on the knob.

She froze, thinking of Ken.

In the distance, an engine turned over. The sound rose then

238

drifted south. The cry came again and she felt air on her cheek as the door opened to the length of the security chain. She did not remember making the decision to open it.

On the porch was a cardboard box sealed with silver tape. An envelope sat on top of it. The box shifted and the sound from within came more clearly. Johnny's name was written on the envelope. "Oh my God." She studied the yard, found it empty, and stepped out. The envelope was unsealed, a single piece of paper inside. The message was typed and unsigned.

You saw nobody. Heard nothing. You keep your damn mouth shut.

Katherine stared in dread at the box. She knelt and peeled back the line of bright tape. It came off with a tearing sound. Inside was a cat. Alive.

Its back was broken.

Katherine fell backward into the house, frozen, and one thought filled her head.

Johnny.

She punched in the number for Steve's apartment but misdialed. She tried again, fingers clumsy. "Please, God," she said.

The phone rang six times, ten; but no one answered. In mortal fear, she hung up the phone. Then she called Hunt again.

CHAPTER THIRTY-ONE

Johnny opened the garage door and started the truck. It ran rough and spilled blue smoke, but it was drivable. He stuck to side streets until he hit the four-lane, then he stepped on the gas and the truck jolted beneath him. He slowed as he approached Main Street, then cut right down a one-way to avoid traffic.

He drove slowly. Neighborhoods decayed the closer he got to the tracks. Johnny heard music and raised voices, the crump of a misaligned door slamming shut. He found Huron Street and turned left. Parked cars cluttered the narrow street and glass winked in the gutter. Weeds grew tall from cracks in the curb and a dog exploded at him from the darkness. It was a patch of brown on black, a jagged outline that jerked to a halt at the end of its chain. Johnny drove on, but there were other dogs in other yards. He imagined fingers on thin curtains, people stained television blue as they bent to peer through filthy windows. And it was not just imagination. To the left, a man stepped through his front door and onto the porch. He had pale feet, wore jeans with no shirt, and sucked on the cigarette that hung between his lips. Johnny ignored him and drove on.

Freemantle's house solidified ahead and to the right. It was a lightless hulk pinned on a dark lot. Behind it, pale gravel spilled down the bank that led to the tracks. Johnny smelled creosote, rock dust, and oil. He pulled to the curb and killed the engine. Behind him, in a house the color of mustard, a baby cried.

Johnny stepped onto the street and the baby fell quiet. The dogs settled down. Stepping into Freemantle's yard, Johnny saw yellow tape strung between the posts that held up the porch roof. Ducking beneath the tape, he cupped his hands around his face and tried to see inside. Nothing. More dark. Johnny pulled down more yellow tape. The door swung open at his touch. Johnny stepped inside, but there was no one. The house was empty. He flipped on lights and saw blood on the wall.

That scared him.

That was real.

The blood was streaked and black. Gray powder stained light switches and doorknobs. In the back room, the blood was worse. So was the smell. Oily and thick, it stuck in his throat. Dried blood was a desert on the floor. Tape marked where the bodies had fallen.

Two bodies.

A desert of blood.

Johnny turned and ran for the front door. The hall constricted and his shadow twisted as he ran. The door stood open, a hard, black empty space with yellow tape that slapped at his arms. He leapt off the porch, landed badly, and tore skin from his palms. He stumbled once more, then cranked up the truck and got the hell out. The dogs rose to send him on his way.

Hunt bulled his way through town. He crested the last hill doing eighty and felt the car rise on its shocks; then he was in the trough, foot pressing down as the needle swung to ninety. He braked hard at Katherine's drive, hung a right, and slid to a halt.

Lights burned in the house. Darkness gathered in the trees.

No squad car.

Hunt spilled out, lights thumping blue behind the grille of his car. He scanned the tree line and the yard, one hand on his holstered weapon. It was quiet and still; the porch felt hollow beneath his feet. He hammered on the door, sensed movement inside and stepped back, checking the yard behind him once again. The lock disengaged and the door opened a crack, then swung wide. Katherine Merrimon stood in the light, tear-stained and small, an eight-inch butcher's knife gripped between fingers squeezed to bone.

"Katherine—"

"Any word on Johnny?"

Hunt stepped through the door. "I've already sent a car to Steve's apartment. It's probably there already." Hunt held out a hand. "May I have the knife?"

"Sorry." She handed it over and Hunt placed it on the counter.

"You're okay," he said. "I'm sure that Johnny is, too."

"He's not okay."

"We don't know anything yet."

"I want to go to Steve's."

"And we will. I promise. Just sit down for a minute." He got her onto the sofa and then straightened. The box was on the table. "Is that it?" Hunt asked.

She nodded. "I think it's dead, now."

Hunt approached the box, saw the silver tape, torn free, and beside the box an envelope and a sheet of paper. "I couldn't leave it outside," Katherine said. Hunt used a pen to lift the flaps. A film glazed the cat's eyes. Its tongue protruded.

"It's dead." Hunt closed the flaps, then read the note: *You saw nobody. Heard nothing. You keep your damn mouth shut.*

Katherine crossed the room and stood beside him, looking down. She was shaking. "Do you think Ken did it? It came ten minutes after he left."

"I doubt it."

"You sound certain."

"I'm not, but it feels wrong. Why drive off and come back? Why announce himself like that? And why do it in the first place?"

"What does it mean?" Katherine asked.

Hunt read the lines again. "I think it has to do with Burton Jarvis."

"What?"

"The news coverage has been extensive." He held her eyes. "You saw Johnny's notes?"

"Of course."

"He was there, Katherine, at Jarvis's house. No matter what he wants me to believe, Johnny was there a lot."

"Somebody thinks that Johnny saw him?"

"Johnny identified five of the six men who visited on a regular basis. Just five."

"And number six?"

"Number six was careful. He changed license plates three times that we know of. He's worried that Johnny can identify him."

"Are you talking about the cop?"

"We don't know that it was a cop."

"Johnny thinks it was."

"He's wrong. He has to be."

"But what if he's not?"

Hunt lacked an answer. In its place, he offered a hand. "Let's go find your son."

It was late when Johnny turned into Steve's development. He weaved between the buildings, made the final left, and stopped a hundred yards short. Steve's van was back. Cop cars were parked in the street in front of his apartment. Hunt's car was there, too. That meant Social Services.

Johnny cursed himself. He should have come back more quickly. He should not have gone at all. They'd take him away for good, now. Sure as apple pie. Sure as anything.

He killed the engine and opened the door. A stand of pines rose to the right of the road, halfway to the building. Johnny kept his shoulder on warm metal, maneuvered between parked cars until the trees were close, then he sprinted for cover. He dove into a bed of needles, pulled himself up, and scrambled for the darkest pocket he could find.

Jack was already there.

"Damn it, Johnny! You scared me."

Johnny smelled the bourbon on his friend, saw the bottle clutched to his chest. "What are you doing here, Jack?"

Jack shifted, sat up against the trunk of a pine tree. "Where else would I be?"

"Do you know what's going on?"

Jack pointed at the police cars. "When I got here, that's what I found."

"How'd you get here?"

"I walked."

"It's four miles."

Jack shrugged.

"Are you drunk?" Johnny asked.

"Are you preaching?"

"No."

"You sound a little preachy."

Johnny ignored the dig. "Is my mother in there?"

"I think I saw her once. Truth is, I don't really know. I've just been waiting for you." Johnny maneuvered closer to the edge of the trees. Jack hissed at him. "Don't do that, Johnny. For all I know, my old man's in there, too. I can't handle that."

"Your father?"

244

"He's trying to make an impression. Working overtime and all. He wants to make detective first grade by the time Gerald goes pro." He took a pull on the bottle. "Like it matters."

Johnny slid back into the gloom. Jack was slurring his words, slipping off the tree trunk. He could barely sit up straight. "What's wrong with you?" Johnny asked.

"Nothing." Sullen. Johnny turned his attention back to the apartment. "If you must know . . ." Jack spoke too loudly.

"Shut up, J-man! Jesus."

Jack lowered his voice. "If you must know, I had a fight with my dad. Somebody called him about what happened at the mall."

"Let me guess. He took Gerald's side."

Jack shook his head. "I expected that anyway. This was about you. He said we couldn't be friends anymore, said it was my official warning. The last warning." Jack waved a hand and staggered to his feet. "But don't worry. I told him to fuck off."

"You did not."

The bottle went up. "As good as."

Johnny studied the window. "If I go in there, they'll take me away for real."

"Who?"

"DSS. They'll take me from Steve's and lock me up with some stiff-necked do-gooder who makes me take a bath three times a day and won't let me out of the house."

"That or somebody looking for a check from the state. They'll feed you bread and water. Make you sleep on the floor. Make you their slave."

"Shut up, Jack."

"I'm serious."

"No, you're not."

Jack stumbled closer and squinted at the windows. When he

spoke this time, he really was serious. "They're probably worried. Your mom and all."

"I can't think about that right now."

"Why not?"

Johnny took Jack by the shirt and pulled him up. "Come on," he said.

"Where?"

"Just come on."

He marched Jack to the truck. "Wait here."

"Dude . . ."

But Johnny wasn't listening. Ignoring the cop cars, he tried the door on Steve's van. Locked. In the yard, he pried a loose brick from the edge of the sidewalk. A straight walk back to the van, brick up in his right hand. He smashed the van's window, reached in and opened the glove compartment.

At the truck, he snatched the bottle out of Jack's hands and tossed it into the dark. He handed Jack the box of shells. "Hold these."

"What is that?"

"And this." He shoved the pistol into Jack's hands.

"Oh, shit."

Johnny opened the door and looked hard at his friend. "You coming this time?"

"Oh, fuck," Jack said, and Johnny fired up the truck.

Johnny kept it at the speed limit, then coasted to a stop at the top of the hill. Below them, the road stretched all the way to Johnny's house.

"What are we doing?"

"I need to get something."

"Anybody there, you think?"

"One way to find out."

Johnny took them down the hill and the house came up on

the right. A few lights burned. Nothing in the driveway. He eased the truck in and switched off the engine. The night air was still. Nothing moved in the house. "Looks empty." Johnny climbed out and tried his key in the front door. "It doesn't work," he said.

"Is it the right key?"

Johnny tried again. "She must have changed the locks."

"Why?"

"Holloway, I guess."

"That's good, right?"

"If that's what it means."

"Well . . ." Jack looked around, and Johnny threw a rock through the window. "Jesus, Johnny! Freaking warn me next time."

"Sorry."

"Who throws a rock through his own window?"

Johnny turned, his voice intense. "Don't you get it?" He pointed up the road, back the way they'd come. "The cops know I ran off from Steve's, so they'll call Social Services for sure. They'll put me some place I don't even want to think about. They'll lock me down and that'll be it. Game over."

"Huh?" Jack was drunk.

Johnny gripped his shoulder and squeezed. "This is my last chance to find her. You think I give a crap about Ken's window? Steve's van? None of that matters."

Johnny released his friend with such force that Jack staggered. Johnny picked up a broken branch and used it to knock shards from the window frame. When he tossed the branch down, he made sure Jack knew who was in charge. "Wait here," he said. "Keep an eye out."

He climbed through the broken window, flicked on the overhead light. The place looked the same but felt different. A pang

247

of loss stabbed him in the heart, but he ignored it. Going first to his mother's room, he pulled open the bedside table drawer and scooped out the cash he found there. Two hundred bucks, give or take. He took two twenties and put the rest back. In his room, he opened his backpack and stuffed in clothing and a blanket. From his closet, he took two jackets, one made of denim, the other of cotton twill. Turning to the bed, he scooped up his copy of *An Illustrated History of Raven County*. It fell open to the page dedicated to John Pendleton Merrimon, Surgeon and Abolitionist. For a second, he touched the picture of his namesake, then he turned the page. The bold heading read: "The Mantle of Freedom: Raven County's First Freed Slave." There was the story of Isaac Freemantle, and there was a map.

On the map was the river and a trail.

The trail led to a place.

Johnny snapped the book closed and stuffed it in the pack.

The gun went in on top of it.

In the kitchen, he found canned food and peanut butter, a large flashlight and a box of matches. He pulled bread off the shelf, two cans of grape soda from the refrigerator. For an instant he considered writing his mother a note, but the moment passed. If she knew what he planned, she would only worry more. He walked outside and tossed the cotton jacket to Jack. "Here." Johnny pulled on the jean jacket. Jack was starting to sober up. Johnny saw it in his damp, miserable face, in the wary manner in which he looked down the stretch of lonely road. "You don't have to come," Johnny said. "I can do this by myself."

"Johnny, man. I don't even know what you're doing."

Johnny looked into the deep woods behind the house. He thought of the gun that weighed down the pack. "I'll tell you when you're sober. If you still want to come, then you can come."

"Where are we going now?"

"Camping."

Jack looked blank, and Johnny put a hand on his shoulder. His mouth was a sharp line, his eyes very bright. "Think of it as an adventure."

CHAPTER THIRTY-TWO

Hunt stood by the fireplace and kept a wary eye on Katherine Merrimon. She sat on the sofa in Steve's living room, shaking and flushed. Every few minutes she would stand and stare through the window. Yoakum was in the kitchen. So was Cross. Steve paced and threw frightened looks at Hunt. He tried to speak to Katherine, but she slapped him. "It's your fault," she said.

"That damn kid."

She slapped him again.

"I'm going outside," Steve said. "I need a smoke."

"Don't come back." She didn't even look at him.

"Katherine . . ."

She stared into the dark and Hunt stepped forward. "Go have your smoke, Steve. Give us a few minutes."

He opened the door. "Fine. Whatever."

Hunt waited for the door to close, then took Katherine's arm and led her to the sofa. "We'll find him."

"You don't know that."

"I will do everything that I can do to bring your son home. That's a promise." Both of them recognized the empty nature of the promise. Katherine folded her hands in her lap. "Nothing matters more to me, right now. Do you believe me?"

"I don't know."

"I promise, Katherine. I swear."

She nodded, shoulders turned in, hands still folded into

a small, perfect package. "Do you think somebody took him?"

Hunt could barely hear her. "No," he said. "Absolutely not."

"Maybe somebody decided that a threat wasn't good enough."

Hunt turned on the sofa. "There was no forced entry, no sign of a struggle. Steve's truck was taken. Johnny knows how to drive. He had access to the key."

"I need him back. Do you understand?"

"Yes."

"I need my son home."

Hunt watched her stare through the glass. Yoakum appeared in the kitchen door. "Clyde," he said, and motioned with a finger.

Hunt walked to the kitchen. "What is it?"

Yoakum led Hunt into the kitchen and stopped at the small table. "You see anything here that bothers you?" Hunt looked at the table. It was mostly bare. There were a few magazines, some mail, yesterday's newspaper and an open phone book. He was about to shake his head when Yoakum said: "Phone book."

It took a second, then Hunt saw it. Levi Freemantle, 713 Huron Street.

"Oh, shit."

"Why would he care about Levi Freemantle?"

"He thinks Freemantle knows where Alyssa is."

"Why would he think that?"

"He thinks that David Wilson might have told him before he died." Hunt closed the book. "This is my fault."

"No one could have guessed he'd do something like this."

"I could have." Hunt scrubbed his hands over his face. "The

kid's capable of just about anything. It was stupid of me to think he'd just let this go."

"I can be there in eight minutes."

"No. The kid trusts me, more or less. Better if I go."

"Well, you'd better hump it."

They went back into the living room, but Steve burst in before they made it across the rug. He pointed a finger at Katherine, then closed his hand into a fist. His lips were drawn, his face red. He pumped his hand, as if trying to control his temper.

"What is it?" Hunt asked.

Steve cut his eyes to Hunt. His words were clipped, and he stabbed a finger toward the street. "That little shit stole my gun, too."

Ten minutes later, Hunt had been through every room in Freemantle's house. He called Yoakum from the living room. "I missed him."

"Any sign he was there?"

Hunt stepped onto Freemantle's porch and fingered the torn, yellow tape. Up the street, dogs howled. "Tape's down. Door's open."

"Should we put an all-points on the truck?"

Hunt considered. "What if Johnny was right? What if the sixth man was a cop?"

"I don't see how that's possible."

"But what if? What if we put out an all-points and the wrong cop finds him?"

"You think we should keep this quiet?"

"I don't know. Thinking this way feels twenty kinds of wrong."

"I'm with you. Hang on a sec. What?" The phone was muffled. Hunt heard muted voices, then Yoakum was back. "Aw, shit."

"What?"

"Cross says he already called it in."

"Nobody authorized that."

"He says a runaway kid in a stolen truck carrying a stolen gun is a no-brainer. Frankly, I can't disagree with him, especially since . . ."

Yoakum paused and Hunt imagined him stepping away from Katherine. "Since what?"

A door closed. Yoakum spoke in a whisper. "Since he's out looking for a stone-cold killer."

Johnny had to go two roads over to find the entrance to the abandoned tobacco farm. The gate was unlocked, the track overgrown with weeds and low brambles. Jack closed the gate behind them. He'd never been to the old barn. "Where are we going?"

"You'll see." Headlights cut into the darkness. Feathers of pine reached in and turned from black to green. Sap glistened on knotted trunks, then winked out as they passed.

They bounced through ruts and deep gouges made by spring rains. When they came out of the woods and into the abandoned fields, the sky opened above them: high, lonely stars and a trace of moon behind tissue clouds. "This was a plantation once," Johnny said. "Then just a bunch of farms." The track cut right, straightened, then split. Johnny went left. "You can still see where the big house burned." He jerked his head. "Over there. Chimney stones in a pile. The old well shaft."

"Yeah?"

"It's overgrown now. I found it six months ago."

The barn loomed ahead, a wall of grayed-out logs on a foundation of chiseled granite. Milkweed rose, pink and green, and fingers of ivy clawed up the length of the back corner. Black showed where chinking had crumbled to dust. Johnny pulled around to the other side and stopped. The doorway gaped. Charred wood and ash marked the fire pit. Johnny put the truck in park. "Give me the pack." Jack shrugged it off. "Don't turn off the engine until I say." Johnny dropped the pack on the ground and pulled out the flashlight. He disappeared inside the barn, found the moldy blue backpack and three stubs of candle. "Alright," he said.

Jack switched off the engine and the headlights winked out. The night collapsed to a twitching beam of light that flashed on white skin, wide eyes, and filthy clothes. "Ken's house is that way." Johnny pointed with the flashlight. "Through the trees. Not far."

"How'd you find all this?"

Johnny squatted and dug the matches out of the pack. "Getting out of the house when things got bad. Looking for snakes."

"About the snakes—"

"Hold this." Johnny handed the light to Jack, then put the candles on a slab of granite and lit them. Jack watched and said nothing, but Johnny felt him there. "I've slept out here more than a few times. It's not bad. Inside is full of spiders. Mosquitoes are worse out here."

"I'll take the mosquitoes."

"Me, too."

Jack put the light on the blue pack. "What's that?"

"Let's make a fire." Johnny stood and began foraging for wood. Eventually, Jack helped him. They gathered twigs and fallen branches. The fire was still small when Jack found the scrap of Bible. It was pebbled leather, black; part of the spine, two inches long and charred. Some of the gold letters could still be seen. Jack held it for a long minute, and Johnny could tell that he knew what it was. He watched Jack's tiny fingers trace the letters, then he stood, took it from him and threw it on the fire. Rocking back on his heels, Johnny watched his friend. Jack was not what most would call a good boy, but Johnny knew for a fact that he believed in the devil.

"I'm not going to burn in hell, if that's what you're thinking."

Jack's small arm moved. He pointed at the fire. "What are you doing, Johnny?" His head shifted and red light filled up his eyes. "I've been good and I've been quiet. About all of this." He moved his fingers over his face again. "What they said in the paper. The things you've been keeping secret from me. Snakes and charms and voodoo shit." He shook his head. "But this ain't right. Whatever this is, you can't go burning Bibles. Even I know that."

"It's just a book."

"You take that back."

Johnny raised his voice. "It's just a book and it doesn't work. It doesn't make a difference." Jack's mouth opened, but Johnny rode his words down. "The preacher said it would, but he was full of shit, too."

"I think I might be sick."

"Well, go over there if you're going to do it." Johnny stabbed a finger at the darkness. "I'm going to eat some dinner and I don't need to be smelling your puke."

Jack closed his eyes, and when he opened them, he looked better, less green. When he spoke, Johnny knew that he'd decided to let it go. "What's that?" Jack asked, pointing at the pack.

An eddy of smoke wafted against Johnny's face and he narrowed his eyes. "You really want to know?"

"I asked, didn't I?"

Johnny unhooked the straps and dumped the contents of the

bag on the ground. He separated the bundles of vegetation. There were four of them, each tied with string. He put them in a row, caught Jack's eye and touched each in turn. "Cedar," he said. "Pine. Spruce. Laurel."

"Yeah. So?"

"They're supposed to be sacred." He touched them again, each in turn. "Wisdom. Strength. Courage. Perseverance. You're supposed to burn them."

"Is that an Indian thing?"

"Indian. Some other things." Johnny scooped up the bundles and threw them into the darkness beyond the fire. They landed with a crunch, and Johnny spat on the dirt. "You hungry?" he asked. "I'm hungry."

They ate peanut butter sandwiches and drank grape soda. Jack kept his eyes on his friend and looked away when Johnny caught him staring. Johnny ignored him. He didn't want to talk about the things he'd done and he sure as hell wasn't going to let Jack judge him. He wiped peanut butter fingers on his jeans and picked up the gun. It was heavy and smooth. He opened it up and saw that it was loaded.

"There's no safety on that," Jack said. "Careful where you point it."

Johnny snapped the cylinder closed. "You know guns?"

Jack rolled his shoulders. "Dad's a cop."

"Can you shoot?"

"Straight enough, I guess."

Johnny slipped the gun back into its holster. They fell into silence and night sounds rose up around them. Moths danced about the candle flames and their shadows licked the ground. Jack tossed his can into the fire to see if it would burn; paint blistered and burst. "Johnny?"

"Yeah."

Jack kept his eyes on the fire. "Do you think cowardice is a sin?"

"Are you scared?"

"Do you think it's a sin?" Insistent. Thin jaw clenched.

Johnny tossed his own can into the fire. Long seconds passed and he didn't blink until he felt his eyes go bone dry. "That man at the river, David Wilson. He knew where my sister was. He knew, and I ran away before he could tell me." Johnny looked at his friend. "So, yeah. I think cowardice is a sin."

"God or no God." Jack's eyes were wide and still.

"That's right."

Jack stared into the dark and wrapped his arms around his knees. "What are we doing out here, Johnny?"

Johnny poked at the fire with a stick. "If I tell you, there's no wimping out. No take-backs. So you need to tell me now if you're in or out."

"Hard to do if I don't know what we're talking about."

Johnny lifted his shoulders. "I'll take you home right now, but not if you know what I'm doing."

"Jesus, Johnny. I wouldn't tell anybody."

"In or out?"

Across the fire, beyond the curtain of smoke and scorched air, Jack scrubbed a forearm across his nose. Orange glazed his eyes until he turned his head, then the color fell away and he was just a dirty boy with a washed-out tan and hair that stood out in all directions. "You're pretty much all I have that's good, Johnny. I don't guess there'll be any take-backs." He turned back and his eyes were so simple and brown they made Johnny think of a dog's eyes. "May as well tell me."

"Come here." Johnny dug into the pack from home. He pulled out the book on Raven County but did not open it. Jack came around the fire, sat in the dirt, and Johnny explained it from the beginning: David Wilson going off the bridge and what he'd said; Levi Freemantle, how he'd grabbed Johnny up by the river; the blood Johnny had found in Freemantle's house.

Jack bobbed his head. "Dang, Johnny. That was in the papers, too. Same day as you. Not his name, I don't think, but they found bodies in that house. Two people with their heads bashed in."

"I kind of figured somebody was dead when I saw all the blood."

Jack's face scrunched up. "Was there a lot of it?"

"It was everywhere, and I mean like paint."

The boys were silent for a minute.

Like paint.

Then Jack shook his head. "I don't understand what this has to do with us."

Johnny clicked on the flashlight and opened the book to the page about Isaac Freemantle. He pointed at the map. "Here's town." He moved his finger north, made a circling motion. "This is mostly swamp." He moved his finger slightly. "This is where the granite rises up and you have that huge stretch of woods where those old mines are. You remember?"

"Yeah. Fourth-grade field trip. They made us hold hands so nobody wandered off and fell into a hole." He was embarrassed, Johnny knew, by the memory. Nobody had wanted to hold Jack's bad hand. There had been pushing and shoving. Some girl had said it was gross.

Johnny traced his finger south, to the trail that ran beside the river. "This is where I ran into him, right about there. Over here is the bridge."

"Got it."

Johnny continued tracing the path along the river. His finger stopped near the edge of the swamp. There were two words

258

there: Hush Arbor. "This is where he was going. This is where we'll find him."

"You're talking over me, man."

Johnny closed the book. "This goes back, okay. Back to slave times."

"What?"

"Slave times. Concentrate. See, slaves came over with their own religions. African stuff. Tribal stuff. Animal gods and spirits in the water, fetishes, charms. Root work, they called it. Hoodoo. But that was good for the white folks, just fine, in fact, because nobody here wanted them learning about Jesus and God and stuff. They didn't want a bunch of slaves thinking they were equal in the eyes of God. Do you see? If you're equal, then nobody should own you. That was dangerous thinking if you owned slaves."

"So, they didn't want the slaves to learn."

"But they did. African slaves, Indian slaves. They learned to read and they took to the Bible; but they had to do it in private, 'cause they understood the danger of it, too. They were smarter than the slave owners thought they were. They knew they'd be punished for their faith. Sold off, Killed, maybe. So they'd worship in the woods and in the swamps. Secret places. Hidden places. You see?"

"No."

"Think of them as hiding places for church. They called these places 'hush arbors', and they'd go there to worship in secret, to hide their faith from the whites that didn't want to share their religion."

"Hush arbors? Like the place on the map."

Johnny nodded. "They were too smart to build a church because they knew somebody would find it. But woods are just woods, a swamp is just mud and water and snakes and shit. So that's where they'd go. They'd sing their songs to God, dance on the dirt, and testify to their new faith."

"That's in the book?"

Johnny looked away, hesitated. "Some of it. Not all of it."

"Not all of what?"

"There was a slave named Isaac, who was a preacher of sorts. He taught those who couldn't read. He spread the word, even though he knew the danger of it." Johnny swatted a mosquito, rolled it off his neck and squeezed blood between thumb and fingertip. "They were discovered eventually, and three slaves were lynched right there in the hush arbor, strung up from the trees that made their church. They were going to hang Isaac, too, but his owner intervened. He stood the mob down with a gun in one hand and a Bible in the other. They say he called God down from the heavens and threatened to shoot the first man who took a step. Nobody had the courage to chance it. He saved that slave's life."

Jack was enthralled. "What happened next?"

"He took Isaac home and hid him for three weeks, waited for the mob to cool down, waited for some guilt to set in, I guess. Then he gave that slave his freedom, and he gave him the land where his people had worshipped."

"And been lynched."

"That, too."

"And you want to find this guy there?"

"Isaac Freemantle lived there the rest of his life. Maybe Freemantles still do. The trail goes right to it. Probably how they got to town and back."

Jack frowned. "How do you know all this? You say it's not in the book."

"My great-great-grandfather's name was John Pendleton Merrimon. Same name as me."

"Yeah. So?"

"He was the one with the gun and the Bible." Johnny tossed a stick on the fire. "He's the one that set Isaac free."

"Get out."

"Truth."

"And you want to go out into the swamp, to find this guy's great-grandson or whatever, a killer, so you can ask him about Alyssa?" Johnny nodded in absolute certainty, and Jack shook his head. "You think he owes you?"

"I don't think he knows who I am."

"You're an idiot. I mean, you are off the fucking reservation."

"Off the reservation." Johnny's voice was bitter. "That's funny."

"It's not a joke. This is stupid, Johnny. It's mental."

"No take-backs. That's what you said."

Jack scrambled to his feet and sparks popped in the fire. "Jesus, Johnny. This guy just killed two people. He'll kill us, too. Sure as shit."

Johnny rose as well. "That's why I took this." He pulled Steve's gun from the holster, and fire devils danced in the metal.

"You're insane."

"And you're coming with me."

Jack looked around, as if for help; but there was nothing there. Light pushed dark and the sky pressed down. Jack opened his hands and begged with his eyes. "It's been a year, Johnny."

"Don't you say it!"

Jack swallowed, took a desperate look at the scrub beyond the fire; then he said it. "She's fucking dead, man."

Johnny swung with all he had. The blow struck the side of

Jack's face and he went down in the dirt. Johnny stood over him, his breath like glass in his throat, the gun a dead weight in his hand. For that instant, his oldest friend was not his friend, but his enemy; Johnny wondered why he'd ever thought that Jack could be more than that. Then he recognized the terror in his friend's face.

The heat drained out of Johnny, and he became aware of the sky, suddenly dark and huge. He saw himself through Jack's eyes, and knew, *freaking knew,* that he was the crazy one. But that changed nothing.

"I have to go."

Johnny's fist fell open. Jack pushed back in the dirt.

"Please, don't make me go alone."

CHAPTER THIRTY-THREE

Hunt drove Katherine Merrimon back to the small house at the edge of town. He tried once to make conversation, but she was unresponsive. Stopping in the drive, he peered through the glass and frowned. "When you saw the strange car on the street the other night, where was it parked?"

Katherine pointed and Hunt looked up the street, past the distant light. "It was just sitting there. Its engine was running. I'd never seen it before."

"What kind of car?"

"I thought it was a police car."

"Why a police car? What makes you say that?"

"It had that look. A big sedan. The shape of it. It looked like a cop car."

"Lights on the roof?"

"No. Just the shape of it." She gestured at the car in which they sat. "Like this."

"A Crown Victoria?"

"It just looked like this. American. Big. I don't know. It was dark. I don't care about cars. I don't know about them."

"And it took off when?"

"When I started walking toward it."

"Which direction did it go?"

She pointed, and Hunt frowned again. "I don't think you should stay here, not with all that's happened."

"Where else would I stay?" She waited for an answer. "Your place?"

"I'm not like that, Katherine."

"All men are like that." She could not hide the bitterness.

She held his gaze and Hunt was struck by the intensity of it. So jaded, so weary. *Damn Ken Holloway,* Hunt thought. *Damn him for making her like that.*

"I was thinking of a hotel. Something anonymous."

She must have heard the hurt in his voice. "I'm sorry," she said. "That was unfair. You've been nothing but aboveboard."

"So you'll do it?"

"Johnny might come home. I need to be here for that."

"Katherine—"

"No."

"Then I want a squad car on the street."

"No to that, too."

"It's not safe here," Hunt said. "Things are happening that we don't understand."

"A police car would scare Johnny. If he did run away, I want him to know that he can come home. How will he know that if the cops are parked in front of the house?" Katherine opened her door. "Thank you for the ride, Detective. I'll be fine from here."

Hunt stepped out of the car and put his hands on the roof. "I'd like to check the house."

"I need to be alone."

Hunt studied the street because her pain was killing him. He'd seen her courage before, and he'd seen that courage fail. It had been like watching a redwood fall or a river die. He looked at the dark house, then at her. "Please," he said.

"If you insist."

Hunt found the broken window three seconds later. "Back in

264

the car," he said, and drew his service weapon. "Get in the car and lock the doors."

She bolted for the door.

"Katherine!"

"I changed the locks. Don't you see? It's Johnny."

Hunt caught her on the steps and pulled her back. "Wait," he said. "Just wait." Then he called out. "Johnny." He tried the door. It opened easily. "Johnny. It's Detective Hunt and your mother." Nothing. Hunt held up a hand. "Stay here."

Inside, Hunt flicked on the lights. Glass shards glittered on the carpet. He checked the back rooms, turned on every light. When he came down the hall, he found Katherine in the living room. He holstered his weapon. "Nobody. It's empty."

She sat on the sofa and held herself still.

"Is anything missing?" She said nothing, and Hunt stepped closer. "Has anything been stolen?"

She looked up, eyes wet and vacant.

"I'm going to check the yard," Hunt said. "I need you to look around and tell me what you see."

"It won't do any good. I haven't *seen* anything for most of a year. I wouldn't know if something was missing."

Hunt understood the comment, but let it go. "Check Johnny's room. Start there."

"Alright."

She moved to the hallway. Johnny's light burned. She heard Hunt leave the house, then she stood in the entrance to Johnny's room. She realized, looking in, that it was unfamiliar to her. How many times had she been in this room, she wondered. Three times? Five? And how many times sober? None, she thought. The year behind her was a blur of days. She ate. She slept. Ken Holloway came and went.

Her son's room was strange to her.

Her son, she realized, was strange to her.

She checked the closet, but did not know what should be there. Same thing with the drawers and the shelves. There was no recollection of buying clothes, or of washing them. Johnny had been doing that, she realized. He cooked. He cleaned. She covered her mouth, overwhelmed.

Where was her son?

She found the suitcase under the bed. It was old and battered, vaguely familiar. She dragged it out and heaved it up onto the bed. She opened it and froze.

Alyssa's face.

Johnny's and her husband's.

Photos covered the inside of the lid. It was a collage of sunshine and her children; life, like a promise. Her eyes burned, her throat closed, and she touched one of the photographs.

Alyssa.

She had one arm around her brother's neck. They were grinning like imps.

Johnny.

In the suitcase, she found an eight-by-ten photograph of her husband. He wore a blue T-shirt and a belt of tools. He stood sideways to the camera, an angular, strong man with a wide smile and hair so black it gleamed. Dark glasses hid his eyes, but she knew what they would look like, blue and sharp and unflinching. For a moment, she was overwhelmed with regret for the blame she'd dumped on him, for the horrible thing she'd said. Then the anger spiked: It *was* his fault! She should never have been walking home alone.

But the anger was wasted. "Where are you, Spencer?"

There was no answer to that. He was gone.

Her fingers touched the other items in the suitcase, Alyssa's things. Her stuffed animals, her diary.

How?

She'd burned this, all of it. Burned everything during three bad weeks of drug-fueled insanity. She lifted a stuffed lamb from the bottom of the case and pressed her face into it, trying to find some small scent that lingered.

"Katherine."

Hunt's voice was a distant thing. The toy came away wet. "Go away," she said.

"Property's clear." He was in the hall. His steps put a vibration in the wood and the vibration found her knees.

"Don't come in here."

He stopped in the door.

"Don't come in." She felt a break, somewhere deep, a flow of memory so keen and strong that it took down every wall she'd built. Without the drugs, she was naked in the river.

"Katherine—"

"Leave me alone." The lamb was soft in her hands. "I'm begging you."

Hunt backed away, and she heard the front door close. She looked at the lamb: the shiny, black eyes, the fleece so white it could be a cloud on a perfect day. She buried her face and drew in a breath, but there was no girl smell left. There was the scent of an old suitcase and of the unclean space beneath an empty bed.

She waited for Hunt's car to leave, then rose on numbed legs and opened the door. The night air was a fog that tasted of growing things. She crossed the drive to the edge of the yard, to the high weeds where she'd last seen the wink of white and orange. It took several minutes to find the bottle of oxycontin and carry it back inside. She locked the door. Her fingers shook and the pills tumbled out. She selected four of them, spilled them on her tongue and swallowed them dry. Then she went back to Johnny's bed, cupped the lamb beneath an arm and laid herself on the covers. She stared at the photographs, and for ten long minutes she endured the pain; then a soft and heavy hand pressed her into the mattress; it took her to a place where she could bear to touch the pictures that her son had hidden for so well and so long. She could say their names without hurt, and in her mind's eye, she could see them move.

Hunt made a slow drive through the area. He checked side streets and driveways, but saw nothing that looked out of place. Houses were quiet and still, their driveways cluttered with pickup trucks, utility vans, and tired cars. No big sedan with its engine running. No silhouette behind glass.

When he circled back to Katherine's street, he chose his place with care: far enough from her house to be unobtrusive, close enough to see if anyone came calling. She didn't want a patrol car on the street. Fine. But he refused to leave her alone, here on the dark edge of things. He pulled off the road, rolled down his window and turned off the engine. He checked the time. Late.

Pushing down a twinge of guilt, he dialed his son and told him to lock the house, set the alarm.

"You're not coming home, tonight?"

"I'm sorry, Allen. Not tonight. Did you get some dinner?"

"I'm not hungry."

Hunt looked at his watch again. He cursed his wife for leaving, then remembered the things his son had said. Maybe it *was* his fault. Here he was again, another night away from his family because of the job. He stopped himself.

Not because of the job.

Not entirely.

He looked down the road to where Katherine's drive spilled gravel onto warm blacktop. He saw lights through the trees, and wondered if he would be here, watching, if it was just another victim. If it was anyone but her.

"Listen, Allen—"

But the signal was dead. No one was there.

Hunt hung up the phone and settled lower in his seat. He watched for strange cars, and for Ken Holloway. He thought of her alone in that swaybacked house, and when, hours later, he dozed, he dreamed of taking her away from it. They were in his car, windows down, and he saw her the way she'd been. Wind whipped her hair. She put a hand on his face, said his name, and light made clear, sweet water of her eyes. It was a good dream, but he woke cramped and unhappy. The sun was low, in his face, and the dream was as false as a trick of light. His phone was ringing.

"Yeah." Hunt scrubbed sleep from his eyes and sat higher.

"It's Yoakum."

The sun sliced in mercilessly. Hunt dropped his visor. "What is it, John?" Hunt glanced at the time: 7:21.

"I'm out at the Burton Jarvis site." Yoakum paused and Hunt heard a voice in the background. A dog chuffed twice. "You need to get out here."

Hunt's fingers found the key in the ignition. "Talk to me."

"We've got a body."

"Is it Alyssa Merrimon?"

Yoakum cleared his throat. "I think we've got a lot of bodies."

The Jarvis house was dark and silent when Hunt rolled into the drive. No patrol cars. No other detectives. There was Yoakum, pale and unshaven, popping mints from a metal tin. His shoes were slicked with mud, his pants wet from the knees down. Next to him stood Mike Caulfield, one of the department's few officers dedicated to the canine unit. A veteran of thirty years, he was tall and stooped, with large, callused hands and a lick of hair so black that it had to be dyed. He wore thorn-proof overalls, equally wet and muddy. On a leash, at his side, sat the same mongrel dog that he'd used to search Levi Freemantle's property. They met Hunt when he stepped out of the car.

"Yoak." Hunt nodded, looked at the dog handler. "Mike." They looked oppressed, both of them. The dog neither moved nor blinked. He watched his handler. "You haven't called in support yet?"

Yoakum snapped the lid on his tin of mints. "I wanted you to see this first." They started walking toward the woods behind the house. "Tell him, Mike."

Mike's head bobbed. "I woke up early this morning. Normally, when I do that, I like to go hunting; but I decided to give this place one last run." He gestured ahead. "I've been working a grid, see, in a pattern out from the shed. But I decided, screw that, just for once, just to stretch my legs. I got out here at five and took a straight line for the river. That's about two miles."

They walked past the shed, still draped with yellow tape. Mike moved without hesitation, ducking branches, talking as he moved. "I got a bit more than a mile in when Tom started perking up. Another hundred yards, and he went ape shit." Mike ducked his head again, embarrassed. "Relatively speaking."

"I was at the station early," Yoakum said. "I took the call."

They pushed through a thicket, crossed a narrow stream that ran quick and light across a bed of exposed granite. The sun angled between gray-skinned trunks. The temperature rose. Yoakum slipped once and went down on a knee.

"What's that smell?" Hunt asked. It was sickly sweet and furtive. A hint one moment, then a good, strong stench the next.

"The dump is that way." Mike pointed. "A mile or two. You can smell it when the wind gets up."

They walked farther, and Hunt saw the dog's ears come up. His head rose, nose up and sniffing; then he dipped his nose to the ground and started pulling. The handler caught Hunt's eye. "See what I mean?"

They passed through a final thicket and entered a wide, shallow depression. Hardwoods towered like monuments. Dead leaves, damp and rotting, made a carpet of the forest floor. Three orange flags protruded from the earth. They were small, mounted on thin, stiff wire. Otherwise, the earth was undisturbed. "You're sure these are bodies?" Hunt asked.

Mike gave the dog a hand signal and he sat, eyes intent, nostrils flaring, but otherwise perfectly still. "Thirty years, Detective Hunt, and this is the best dog I've ever handled. You'll find human remains under those flags."

Hunt nodded and stared out at the flags, so bright and small in the vast, subdued depression. They were widely spaced, maybe fifty feet apart. "Three more. Damn."

Mike and Yoakum exchanged a glance. Hunt caught it. "What?"

"I only had three flags," Mike said.

"Meaning?"

Mike patted the dog. "Meaning, I'll need more."

Hunt stared at the wiry, leather-faced dog handler. His ears were drooping knots of cartilage, his nose long and hooked and ruddy. His lips hung with unnatural stillness, and Hunt knew that he was waiting for the question. "Are you saying that there are more bodies out there?"

Mike blew his nose into a bandanna. He nodded once, and the skin of his neck folded. "I think so."

Hunt looked at Yoakum. "How long did Jarvis own this property?"

Yoakum's face was bleak. "Twenty-four years."

"Jesus Christ."

"What do you want me to do?" Yoakum asked.

Hunt looked up, saw leaves that moved and jagged cracks of blue. "Call it in. Get everybody out here."

Yoakum stepped away and opened his phone. Mike honked his nose one last time, then shoved the bandanna back into a pocket. "What about me?" he asked.

"Work the dog," Hunt said. "We'll improvise some flags."

"Yes, sir." Mike made a motion with his hand and the dog moved without hesitation. Nose down, tail up, it set off in a straight, determined line.

Hunt felt a breeze on his neck.

The dump smell rose.

CHAPTER THIRTY-FOUR

The sun was less than a hint behind the trees when Johnny nudged Jack with a foot. The fire was dead and gray, the blanket heavy with dew. "It's time," Johnny said.

Jack blinked up at Johnny, who was dressed and ready. He scratched at his neck. "I'm eaten alive."

"Me, too." Johnny held out a hand and pulled Jack to his feet. "Want some breakfast?"

"What do we have?"

"Canned sausage or peanut butter. We're out of bread."

"Any grape soda?"

"No."

Jack shook his head. "I'm good."

Johnny knocked dirt off the blanket, then took a leak on the side of the tobacco barn. His hands were smudged with soot from the fire. He thought of sacred things that weren't sacred after all, and of the gun tucked under his jacket. He'd sat up late, spinning the cylinder, tilting its barrel against the light. He'd rubbed a wet thumb on the site, aimed at the fire and tried to keep his arms steady under the weight of it. He thought of Levi Freemantle and told himself that he knew what he was doing, then decided that it didn't really matter. In the end, only Jack had a choice.

"You don't have to come."

Jack shrugged on the jacket. "You're my best friend."

"I'm serious," Johnny said.

"So am I."

Johnny stuffed the blanket in the pack, then cinched up the straps. "Thanks, J-man."

"Don't go pussy on me."

"I'm not. I'm just saying—"

"I know what you're saying.

Johnny opened the truck door. "Ready?"

"Rock and roll."

Johnny drove through the stubbled field and under the surrounding trees. Out of the woods, they passed through the same gate, then followed the two-lane north toward the county line. Johnny stuck to the roads that he knew, then cut east, through a trailer park, to an unfamiliar road that turned, in a slow bend, away from town and the clutter that surrounded it. They rode past small vineyards and stone walls, went deeper into open country still dotted with antebellum mansions perched above rolling fields. Once, he stopped. He compared the map in the book with a road map of Raven County. "Do you know where we are?" Jack asked.

But Johnny didn't answer. He stared down the road, then doubled back to a stretch of old, cracked pavement that grew increasingly narrow. He checked road signs twice, then made a left onto a single-lane stretch of black that descended for a few miles until it turned hard right and ended at a gravel road. Johnny stopped. Except for crows on a wire, nothing around them moved. "You smell that?" Johnny asked.

"No."

"The river. It bends east just outside of town, then cuts back. I think we're about twelve miles north of town. Maybe a little east." He pointed down the gravel road. "I think this is it."

Jack looked around at the trees, the fields, the windswept silence. "You think this is what?"

"Let's see." Johnny turned right and the tires spit gravel. A half mile farther, he passed a shot-up yellow sign that read: END OF STATE MAINTENANCE. Immediately, the forest pushed in. The river smell intensified. The road turned north again. Johnny pointed right. "The river's that way. We're going parallel." He drove for another mile and passed the first gate. It stood open, but the sign was unmistakable. PRIVATE PROPERTY. NO TRESPASSING.

Johnny ignored it.

The second gate was closed, but unlocked. It was age-stained aluminum, bowed in the middle as if backed into by a truck. It hung from a cedar post, and part of its lower edge pressed upon the road where it had buckled. "Get the gate."

Jack got out of the truck and dragged it open. Grass bent beneath it at the road's edge, and Johnny moved the truck through. Jack closed it after he'd passed.

They dropped into the flood plain, saw the river, black and oily slow, and Johnny pointed at a broad swath of flattened grass where the river had spilled over its banks in the last big storm. "It's going to get swampy."

The road bent away from the river, and swamp began to push in from both sides. The road rose a few feet, until it was a high strip above soft earth and dark water that flashed beyond gashes in the trees. Johnny rounded a bend and almost struck a snapping turtle that basked in the middle of the road. Its shell was two feet across, black with dried algae. He steered around it and it opened its hooked mouth as they passed.

The road dipped a final time, then rose onto a causeway that crossed a wide stretch of still water. They drove into the hollow place, then up onto the hump of earth. On either side, shallow water stretched away, its surface marred by fallen trees, half submerged, and tussocks of grass that broke the surface where the bottom rose. Across the causeway, dry land clawed from the swamp. It was an island of sorts, a mile of hardwoods and vine. Johnny stopped the truck. Ahead of them, gravel grew sparse, then nonexistent as the road turned into a tendon of rutted, black earth that crossed the bog and disappeared into forest. Giant limbs swept the ground and roots stretched the length of a man before plunging into the earth.

Johnny crossed the causeway, stopped in the last patch of sun and killed the engine. The air hung silent, then swamp sounds began to return. They started small and rose like notes from a flute. At the water's edge, a heron stabbed its beak into the mud and came up empty. It stalked a few feet, then froze, one eye tilted at the water. The boys climbed out of the truck. Johnny saw the sign from ten feet out. Half-covered by honeysuckle and some other creeping vine, it seemed as old as everything else, weathered boards nailed to a tree. Johnny pulled off the vines. The words were carved into the wood beneath, deep cuts, black at the bottoms as if burned.

HUSH ARBOR, 1853.

"This is it." Johnny stepped back.

"The place where they hanged those people."

"That was a long time ago."

"This is a death place, Johnny. We shouldn't be here."

"Don't let your imagination get away from you."

"It's up and gone."

Johnny ignored the comment for a long moment. Honeysuckle put a sugar scent in the air, and he put two fingers on the rough-cut letters. "Just a place," Johnny lied. The heron speared a frog, tore it from the mud. "Just a place."

Jack skimmed a rock and spread ripples in the tar-colored water. The heron took wing, frog still twitching in his beak. "Do you really think somebody lives out here?"

Johnny looked up, twisted his head. "No power lines. No phone lines. Maybe not."

"That's the best news I've heard all day."

Johnny peered under the trees. He moved under the branches and felt the temperature drop. The canopy rose into a cathedral quiet.

"What about the truck?"

Johnny looked back. His friend clung to the sunlight, one hand on hot metal. "Too loud. We leave it."

"Really?"

"Yeah."

Jack stepped into shadow. "Quiet, now," Johnny said. And the forest swallowed them up.

Cops descended on the Jarvis scene: city cops, the sheriff's office. Someone mentioned the state police, but Hunt shot that down. In seventeen years, he'd seen nothing but conflict and disruption when too many fingers found their way into the pie. Keep it local. Keep it tight. But they had seven flags, now, too many for the local medical examiner. Dr. Moore approached Hunt with mournful eyes, all of his normal exuberance crushed. He wore latex gloves stained with dark matter. For most of two hours he'd worked his way through layers of earth on a single, flagged site. He'd found bone and teeth, some small bits of rotted cloth. Hunt kept everyone but Yoakum at a distance. They milled about on the edge, speaking in hushed tones as the sun climbed.

"Doc." Hunt looked the question.

Moore shook his head, then mopped his face with a mud-stained handkerchief. "It's a child," he said. "Female. Nine to twelve years of age, I'd estimate."

Hunt caught Yoakum's eye. "How long?"

"How long ago did she die? Years. I can't say for certain. Not yet."

"Cause of death?"

The man compressed as he stood. His shoulders fell. His lips turned down. "There's a hole in the skull." He gestured at the curve of bone behind his right ear. "Too early to say more than that."

"Gunshot?" Yoakum asked. "Blunt trauma?"

"Both. Neither. It's too early."

"And the other sites?"

Moore cast sad eyes at the flags. "I'll need help. I've already called the chief medical examiner in Chapel Hill. He's sending people."

"What else can we do for you?" Hunt asked.

Moore tipped his head, indicating the police officers massed on the edge of the scene. "Get rid of them."

"Are they in your way?"

"It's not helpful."

Hunt nodded. Moore was right. "I'll make it happen."

"Thanks." Moore raised a hand, then trudged back to the shallow grave.

"Want me to do it?" Yoakum asked, staring at the Chief.

Hunt allowed a tight smile. "Don't think I can handle him?"

"I think he's looking for an excuse to fire you and bring in the state cops. That would keep it clean, take the pressure off him, the department." Yoakum gestured at the field of flags. "No one could blame him. This is big, maybe too big to stay local. You're his lead detective. Firing you could give him a legitimate excuse to wash his hands and bring in the SBI. Politics, Clyde. Ugly business. You should let me talk to him."

"No." Hunt pointed at the ME. "Stay here. Make sure he gets anything he needs."

"Your funeral, brother."

Hunt left Yoakum with the remains of their unknown victim

and walked to the Chief. The man was rumpled and flushed. Here in the woods, on site and out of place, he looked even more like a politician than a cop. As Hunt approached, uniformed officers stepped aside so that an aisle opened. The Chief spoke before Hunt could.

"What did the ME say?"

Hunt looked from the Chief to the sheriff. Both men looked pinched, and Hunt guessed that his face bore the same expression. Memories of their last meeting still poisoned the air. "He said he wants these people out of here."

"I'm talking about the body. What did he say about that?"

"Female. Nine to twelve years old. Time and manner of death as yet undetermined."

"Is it Alyssa Merrimon?"

Hunt looked at the sheriff and shook his head. "This one has been in the ground for years."

The Chief peered across the swale. Skin folded at the bottoms of his eyes pulled back to show bright pink crescents. "Six more out there. Maybe we'll get lucky."

"I wouldn't call that lucky," Hunt said.

The sheriff's lips turned at the corners. "You still think you'll find her alive?"

Hunt returned the hard stare. "Maybe."

The sheriff said, "You're such a Boy Scout, Hunt. I swear to God."

"I've had enough of your cr—"

"That's enough," the Chief said. "From both of you."

Hunt forced the tension from his frame. "You'll let me clear these people out of here?"

The Chief nodded. "Keep whoever you need, send the rest home."

"I don't need anybody from the sheriff's office."

Hunt waited for a reaction from the sheriff. Jarvis's house was inside the city limit, but out here, in the deep woods, they were pretty much standing on the city line. If he wanted to push a jurisdiction claim, he could. The sheriff broke first. "Perkins." He snapped his fingers and an unfamiliar deputy crossed to his side. "Round our people up. Get them out of here." He smiled at Hunt, rocked the hat back on his head, and spoke in a low voice. "When you fuck this up and are long gone, I'll still be running this county."

"Don't count your chickens."

Another cold smile. "Have a nice day, Detective."

Hunt watched him go. The Chief was waiting when he turned, but his face showed none of the animosity Hunt expected. Instead, he looked deflated, troubled. He lifted the hat from his head and scrubbed the sleeve of his shirt across his forehead. He dipped his head toward the flags and spoke softly. "If those are all children . . ." He trailed off. "God help us."

"Maybe he already did. Jarvis is dead."

"Do you think Jarvis did this?" He nodded again at the flags. "All of this?"

Hunt watched Trenton Moore begin excavation on the second site. "Maybe." A pause. "Maybe he had help."

"You still believe there's a cop involved?"

"You know about the dead cat? The threat warning Johnny Merrimon not to talk?"

"I do."

"His mother says that before that happened, she came home from the hospital and saw a car parked near the house. Late at night. Engine running. He was just sitting there."

"Hardly against the law."

"There's nothing out there. Some houses, a stretch of empty road. There is no legitimate reason for someone to be there.

When she approached the car, it sped off. This was right after Johnny was identified in the Burton Jarvis story. His name was in every paper, on every channel. His picture, as you know. He would not have been hard to find."

The Chief turned his palms, impatience crossing his features. "So?"

"She says it looked like a cop car." Color pushed into the Chief's face, but Hunt ignored it. "Whoever Johnny saw out here with Jarvis—"

"If he saw anybody."

Hunt raised his voice. "Whoever Johnny saw out here had the presence of mind to put stolen plates on his car. If a cop had something to hide, that's what he'd do."

"That's what anyone would do."

"I want access to employee files."

"I can't do that."

"I want you to reconsider."

The Chief hesitated. "I'll think about it."

"When will I know?"

"Give me a day. Alright? Give me a day and some peace of mind."

"I need something else. If there *are* bodies under those flags, and they are all children . . ."

"Go on."

"No way did they all come from Raven County. Not even over a two-decade stretch of time." He shook his head. "We'd have known."

"Agreed."

"I need some people to contact surrounding counties, nearby metropolitan areas." The Chief was already nodding. "We need to look for other missing children."

They fell into silence, each man alone with his thoughts.

Hunt pictured grieving parents in museum bedrooms, surrounded by pink animals, dress-up clothes, and framed photographs, carefully dusted. He hoped to bring them closure, some small measure of peace. He wanted to deliver the remains of their children home to them, tell them that the monster responsible was dead, sent out of this world not by time, disease, or the police, but by one of his victims, by a small girl with the strength to pull the trigger. Hunt found poetry in that. Maybe they would, too.

The Chief's thoughts were more basic. "The media will eat this up. I expect you to manage that, Hunt. No leaks. No unnamed sources. Keep your people quiet. Keep this shit locked."

"Leave Yoakum and two uniforms here. Put a few units on the road to discourage media or anybody else that gets curious."

The Chief frowned and palmed sweat from his forehead. "It'll be a circus."

"Another reason to send everybody else out of here."

Hunt heard footsteps approaching and turned in time to see Cross moving quickly downslope. He glanced at the sealed area, then made a line for Hunt and the Chief. His face was flushed, his collar dark with sweat. "Hunt," he said. "Chief." He was eager, excited.

"What are you doing here?" Hunt asked.

"Looking for you."

"Well, you've found me. What is it?"

"We have a location on David Wilson's truck," he said.

"Where?"

"North. Dumped in a ravine."

"Show me."

Hunt left the Chief alone in a shaft of yellow light, head

bent, fingers working the brim of his hat. Hunt looked back twice, the Chief small and unchanging until the endless ranks of trees marched between them. They climbed out of the woods and walked past the shed, the empty house. Hunt looked at neither. "How did we find it?"

"Somebody called it in."

"Who?"

"Wouldn't give a name. He found it early this morning, an hour before sunrise, maybe. He sounded drunk. When I asked, he admitted that he'd been out shining deer. He said the spotlight lit it up pretty good."

"Do we have people on scene?"

"I came straight for you. I knew you'd want it."

"Are we sure it's his car?" Hunt asked.

"The caller had the license number. Registered to the college. Has to be it."

"Did we get a phone number on the caller?"

"Pay phone at a convenience store."

"That's unfortunate. Any idea if he touched the vehicle? A drunk out shining deer at five in the morning . . . I doubt he'd hesitate to scrounge around."

"Unknown. He gave the location, then pretty much hung up on me."

They came out of the woods and into the bright, morning sun. Hunt stopped at the road's edge. "You could have called me."

"I was hoping you'd take me with you."

Hunt studied the younger man. His face was intent, determined. "You're up for promotion. Is that right?"

"A good word from you would go a long way."

Hunt considered it. "I haven't slept much," he said. "You drive."

CHAPTER THIRTY-FIVE

The boys moved slowly. The road was soft underfoot, the trees alive with birds and twists of shadow. Vines drooped to the ground, gray and smooth and thick as a large man's wrist. Not far away, a woodpecker hammered for its breakfast.

"This place gives me the creeps," Jack said.

"Just keep your eyes open."

The forest darkened, and noise fell off with the sun.

"The screaming willies."

"Shut up, Jack. Jeez."

They walked for twenty minutes. None of the wheel ruts on the road looked recent, but that meant nothing. Freemantle was on foot when Johnny last saw him. Once through the trees, the road widened out, flattened, and the forest began to open up. They passed an overgrown orchard, apple trees heavy with bloom. Muscadine vines crawled over a collapsed trellis.

"We're getting close," Johnny said.

"To what?"

"Whatever's out here."

The road came to a crumbled gate, then turned right and disappeared around an elbow of brambles and heavy growth. The gun came out of the holster and Johnny tilted it awkwardly. "Does this have a safety?"

"No. I told you. Jesus, watch where you point it."

"Sorry." Johnny aimed the barrel at the ground. Wind lifted leaves to show their dull, silver bottoms. At the bend in the road, there were granite posts where the gate had fallen. The gate itself was on the ground, grass between the pales, its soft wood slowly rotting. White paint still showed in the grain.

Johnny edged his head past the granite, then pulled it back.

"What?" Jack asked.

"Nothing." He stopped. "Come on."

They passed between the granite posts and the forest curved away. They saw shells of buildings, a house that had burned to the ground. There were blackened timbers, a bone of chimney. A granite step sat where the front door had been. A claw-foot tub lay on its side, spilling char and a few green shoots of some wild plant. An iron bed frame protruded from the rubble. So did other items too hard to burn: shattered crockery, a cooking pot, the steel handle of a well pump rusted solid. Johnny picked up a door hinge and saw hammer marks in the metal.

"What a mess." Jack spoke for both of them.

The barn still stood, as did a smokehouse with an open door and steel hooks that hung on chains rusted red. Johnny saw a padlock on the door of a shed. Another building stood next to it. It had a single door, narrow windows, and two small chimneys. Like the main house, a single block of stone made a step to the door. It was worn smooth in the center. Peering through the glass, they saw a fireplace and a brick oven. A plain table and iron cookware. "This was the kitchen," Johnny said. "They used to build them separate from the house to reduce the risk of a fire."

"That's ironic."

Johnny stepped back and looked at the burned house. "No electricity out here, so it could have been a candle."

"Or lightning."

"Maybe."

"Check that out." Jack pointed.

Johnny turned. He saw a post, eight feet high, and a brass bell turned green. "That's strange."

"What?"

Johnny pushed through weeds as high as his waist. "It's a slave bell. I saw one just like it in the civil rights museum in Wilmington. They rang these to call the slaves in from the fields."

"Why would a freed slave keep a slave bell?"

Johnny peered under the bell. "I don't know. A reminder?"

"Screaming willies, man." It came as a whisper.

Johnny checked inside the barn. Except for the farm implements he expected to see—all of them dusty and unused—it was empty. He rattled the lock on the shed and peered through the cracks in the door. "Junk."

"Can we go?"

Johnny surveyed the area. Everything stood out in the stark sunlight. The trees made a wall around the clearing. "Not yet." He pointed to the far end of the clearing, where a gash split the trees. "Through there," Johnny said.

They moved cautiously. The trees rose up, and then they were under them. A footpath ran fifty yards to another clearing. At the end of it, the sunlight lit up a waist-high stone wall and, beyond that, a hint of green grass. In the stone was another wooden gate. This one stood in fine repair. Its paint shone, white and perfect.

"I've never been so unhappy to see fresh paint," Jack whispered.

They crept closer, heard a bird drop low, then veer off, felt the compression of leaves underfoot.

"What is that?"

A wet sound, a chuffing.

Johnny shook his head. "I don't know."

They ducked low, sprinted the last few yards, and crouched below the wall. The stone was warm, the sound close. It rose from beyond the wall. Johnny peered through the pales of the gate. He saw trimmed grass, and rows of carved stone.

Ducking back, he said, "It's a cemetery."

"What?"

Johnny held the gun against his chest and felt his heart thud against the steel. Breath snagged in his throat. "It's a freaking cemetery."

"Is he in there?"

A wide-eyed nod, the smallest of whispers. "Yes."

Jack licked lips gone chalky white. "We have to get out of here."

"He's just sitting there."

"Doing what?"

Johnny eased up the stone. The cemetery was small. Forty headstones, maybe. A tremendous oak tree stood in the center, magnolias in each of the back corners. The headstones stretched in rows, some silver gray, some black, all feathered with lichen and moss.

Levi Freemantle sat in the center, legs splayed in front of him. His clothes were filthy and torn. Blood smears showed at the knees and in the creases of his hands, a stain of it on the right side of his shirt and pants. One shoe was off, spilled over in the bright, clean grass. His foot and ankle were swollen to the point that they seemed to be a single, fused appendage. His finger was ripe with infection from Johnny's bite. It was wrapped in cloth stained yellow. The skin strained so hard that it shone. He had a shovel in his lap. Beside him was a coffin.

"What's he doing?"

Johnny didn't answer right away. The light was so perfect that he could see every detail: streamers of silver tape dulled to

287

lead; dried mud caked on the coffin, gouges in the wood, water stains. Freemantle's knees were scraped nearly to the bone. Moisture glinted on his ruined face. Something jutted from his side. Johnny slid down the wall and pressed his back into the stone. "He's burying a body."

"Oh, shit."

"And crying like a fifth-grade girl."

Jack closed his eyes. Johnny raised the pistol so that the cylinder pressed against his forehead. He smelled gun oil and his lips moved without sound: *The gun is power. I have the gun. The gun is power.*

I have the gun.

He started to stand, but Jack pulled him down. "Don't do it." Jack squeezed harder, begged. "Don't do it, man."

"The fuck's wrong with you, Jack?" Johnny pulled his arm free. "You think this is a game? You think this whole year has been a game? This is why we came."

Jack's terror was as plain on his face as the dirt. His whole body shook, but he nodded and lowered his hand. "Okay, Johnny."

"I don't have a choice."

"I said, okay."

For a second, Johnny was held by the quiet, utter panic on his friend's face, then he shoved himself to his feet and brought the gun up the way they did it in the movies: two hands on the grip, barrel as straight and steady as he could make it. Levi Freemantle stood, shovel in his hand, but he didn't even notice Johnny. Head bent toward the ground, he stared at a shallow scrape he'd made in the earth.

Freemantle held his bad foot off the ground so that the shovel supported much of his weight. His tears were unabashed, and Johnny watched as he tried to dig a hole for the coffin. He stood on his good foot and used the bad one to drive the shovel, but pain twisted his face. He shifted his weight to the other foot, but the ankle crumpled.

He fell.

Climbed back to his feet.

Tried again.

Johnny opened the gate and stepped into the cemetery. Fifteen feet away, twelve, Freemantle oblivious. Johnny risked a glance at the coffin. It was small, a child's coffin. He stepped closer and Freemantle looked up. His damp eyes jumped from Johnny's face to the bare place in the ground. He hobbled a step, shovel blade rising, then crunching back into the earth. Johnny saw sadness and pain and dirt and blood, what looked like a piece of wood sticking out of his side. "Stop," Johnny said.

Freemantle did as he was told, then raised a hand, palm up and flat. He gestured to the place where he'd scraped in the dirt, then finally looked at the gun. He looked at it for a long time, like he wasn't sure what it was or why it was pointed at his chest. When he spoke, his words were thick. "Did you come to help me?"

"What?"

"I been asking for help, but he won't talk to me."

"Who?"

"Is he talking to you?"

"I don't know what you mean."

The scars twisted on his face. One eye had a milky lens at its center. "I can't make the hole."

Johnny risked a glance at the wall. Jack shook his head. Johnny looked at the coffin. "Do you remember me?"

A nod. "You was running and I picked you up."

"Why?'

"God said."

"God said to pick me up?" Another nod. "Why?"

"He didn't say."

"Johnny."

It was Jack, but Johnny ignored him. "What else did God tell you?"

"She's my baby." Freemantle pointed at the coffin. On his ruined face the tears gathered and fell. "I can't make the hole."

Johnny looked once at Jack.

Then he lowered the gun.

CHAPTER THIRTY-SIX

Cross drove with a deft hand through the outskirts of town, then north. Hunt watched neighborhoods slide by, then light industrial. His thoughts were neither of the discovered car nor of David Wilson, but of the seven small flags, and of Alyssa Merrimon. He could not shake the thought of her under that damp earth. Her young life ended, her family destroyed. Thoughts descended, too, of Hunt's own hell: a year of sleepless nights and anguish, twelve months of failure, his own family gone to ruin. All that time, and he'd never been able to let go. What was job? What was personal?

When his phone rang, he looked at caller ID and it felt prophetic. "Hello, Katherine."

"Any word on Johnny?" She sounded bad.

"No. Nothing."

"He should have called by now. Johnny would have called."

"We have units out looking for him. He's a smart kid. We'll find him." He paused, aware of Cross in the car. "I'm sorry I haven't come by to discuss this in person. I would have, but . . ."

"He should have called."

"Katherine?" Concern was in his voice. She picked up on it.

"It was a bad night," she said.

"Are you okay?"

"I'm better now, but I need my son home."

"We'll find him," Hunt said.

She hesitated, and when she spoke, her voice came powder soft. "If you promise me, I'll believe you."

Hunt understood the desperation those words implied. He closed his eyes and pictured her in that house. She sat on Johnny's bed, one lip caught between porcelain teeth. She was holding her breath, fingers clenched, lashes long and black on the skin beneath her eyes. "I promise," Hunt said.

"Swear it."

"We'll find him."

"Thank you, Detective." Her breath traveled down the line. "Thank you, Clyde." She hung up, and Hunt closed the phone. He rubbed his eyes and felt grit beneath the lids.

Cross passed a car, then eased right. "Johnny's mom?" he asked.

"Yes."

They drove on, left the business district behind, and rolled into open country. Cross kept his hand steady on the wheel. He cleared his throat. "You should know that rumors are flying." Hunt stared at him. "At the station," Cross continued. "People are talking."

"What rumors?"

"That you think a cop's involved with Burton Jarvis. Involved with these dead kids. Maybe with Alyssa Merrimon."

"Rumors can be dangerous things."

"I'm just saying—"

"I understand what you're saying."

A hundred yards flowed under the tires. When Cross spoke, it was with care. "The Chief told the office staff not to let you anywhere near the personnel files. You, specifically. That's where the rumor started. I just thought you should know."

Hunt watched the grass, the sky. He thought of the many

ways he'd like to punish the Chief. "Do we have somebody at David Wilson's car?"

"It's in the county, so we had to bring in the sheriff. One of his deputies is on site. He knows better than to touch it."

"I hope you're right."

"Not much farther."

The vehicle was a late-model Toyota Land Cruiser, black. It was angled, nose-down, in a rocky, brush-choked ravine that had to be thirty feet deep. The trailer was still attached, though it had twisted sideways and jackknifed onto the roof. "Has anybody been down there?"

The deputy shook his head. "Sheriff said to cooperate, so that's what I'm doing. Nobody's been down there."

Hunt surveyed the route down. It was loose rock and thin soil. Trees grew along the lip, weeds and brush. "You have rope in the trunk, Cross?"

"Yes."

"Get it."

Hunt tied off the rope and dropped it down the incline. He and Cross descended, shale sliding underfoot. Hunt was first down. A ribbon of water snaked down the gulley and ran under the car. The roof had collapsed under the weight of the trailer. The front end was damaged, paint scraped from the sides. A spiderweb of cracks stretched across the windshield. "Don't touch anything."

Cross peered through the window. "Keys are in the ignition." He shifted. "It's still in drive."

Hunt used a handkerchief to open the passenger door. Heat flooded out. Stale car smell. The seat leather was worn shiny on the driver's side. Backseats were down, the cargo area crammed with climbing gear. Hunt saw a motocross jacket and muddy boots. A gasoline can was wedged behind the driver's seat. No

293

sign of blood from an accident. "Looks like somebody ditched it."

"A good place for it," Cross said.

Hunt used the same handkerchief to open the glove compartment. He prodded papers with a pen, then closed it. He studied the floorboards, then peered under the seats. "Hello," he said.

"What?"

Hunt reached under the seat with the pen and came out with a brass casing. He straightened and Cross pushed closer. "Forty-five." Hunt pulled an evidence bag from a pocket and slipped the casing into it. He held it to the light that filtered down. "Let's get some people out here."

Hunt and Cross waited for the technicians to arrive. They stood on the gravel shoulder, staring at the battered vehicle. It took twenty minutes: two crime scene vans, four technicians. "I want it worked up where it is. Prints, fibers. Everything that you can do here and now, I want you to do it. Time is an issue. When you're done, you can haul it out of there and take it to impound."

The lead technician studied the vehicle, the slope. "Are you serious?"

"There's rope. You'll manage." Hunt looked at the sky. Black clouds were rising in the south. "Just get it out of there before the rains come. I don't want another day like the last one." Hunt watched the technicians get to work, then called Yoakum and filled him in.

"It's a good break," Yoakum said.

"What about there?"

"Dr. Moore confirmed a second body."

"And?"

"Another child. Not Alyssa Merrimon."

Hunt forced his fingers to relax. "Rain's coming."

"I know. They're saying three hours, maybe four."

"Any media?"

"Not yet."

Hunt looked at the wrecked Toyota, debating where he would be most useful. The crime scene techs were working up the car. The medical examiner had the bodies. "I feel like we're missing something."

"No shit."

"Something obvious."

"What do you want to do?" Yoakum asked.

"Sit tight. I'm coming to you." Hunt disconnected.

A voice rose from the gulley. "Detective."

The technician stood at the bottom of the ravine, next to the open driver's side door. Hunt called down. "Yeah."

"It looks like the car's been wiped." He gestured inside. "The steering wheel is clean, the door handle, the gearshift." He raised his shoulders. "I think it's wiped."

"What about the casing?"

The tech stabbed a finger toward the van. "Michaels has the casing." Hunt faced that way. The back doors of the first van stood open. Gear was mounted inside, a small table bolted to the wall. One of the techs had the casing on a sheet of clean, white paper.

"Michaels?"

"Just a sec." He continued working. When he straightened, he said, "We have a print."

Hunt left Cross on the street, and returned to the Jarvis site just as the medical examiner was scraping soil from a third body. Yoakum stood to the side, hands on his hips, lips pursed. He was a big man, bent at the neck, but in the damp, shadow-filled swale he looked small and depressed. "Number three," he said.

Hunt looked at the two body bags already laid out and ready for transport. They looked flat and close to empty. "Let's get out of here." He turned, but Yoakum did not follow. He stared at the bags, the suspected graves with bodies yet to be exhumed.

"Somebody should die for this," Yoakum said.

Hunt stepped back. In all of the years he'd worked with Yoakum, he'd never seen a crack in the armor. Yoakum was brutally efficient. Yoakum told jokes. He did not show feelings. "Somebody did," Hunt said.

The man's face was all angles in the forest light. "You think Jarvis was alone in this?"

"I don't know."

"They're just babies."

"Come on, John. Let's do the job."

Yoakum shook his head, and Hunt knew what he was thinking.

Somebody should die.

They slogged upslope and out of the woods. On the road, engines idling, were two news vans. They angled in next to the marked cars and the medical examiner's van. Yoakum saw them first. "Movie people," he said.

"Shit."

The Chief had left two uniformed patrol officers on the street. They stood, arms spread, trying to ignore the cameras and microphones shoved in their faces. When the newscasters saw Hunt, they began directing questions his way. "Is it true you've located more bodies?"

"No comment."

"Why is the medical examiner on site?"

Hunt and Yoakum pushed past the uniformed officers. Hunt raised his voice. "Nobody gets past," he said.

"Detective Hunt—" It was the reporter from Channel Four. "Detective—"

Hunt refused to break stride. He made for his car and the reporter dogged his steps, camera crew trailing in her wake. "Is it true that you're looking for Johnny Merrimon?" Hunt turned, unsure and suddenly furious. She pushed the microphone forward, her face in profile to the camera, eyes bright and eager. "Is it true that he's missing?"

Hunt looked beyond her. Another news van was coming down the road. "No comment." He put his hand on the door, opened it.

"What about allegations of police involvement with Burton Jarvis?"

"What did you say?" She repeated the question, and Hunt felt color bleed out of his face. "Get more units out here," he said to Yoakum. "You"—he pointed at the reporter—"come with me." Her smile grew and she gestured at her crew. "Just you," Hunt said. He didn't wait for a reply. He walked twenty feet down the road, knowing that she would follow. When he turned, she was three steps behind him, coiffed and flawless in a tight, red sweater. Behind her, the third news crew arrived and began prepping to film. "Why would you ask that question?"

She did not back down. "Is it true?"

"I can't comment on an ongoing investigation. Why did you ask that question?"

"My sources are protected." She lifted her perfect chin, put her hands on her hips.

Hunt loomed over her. "I'd rather you not spread that kind of rumor." He stared hard into her hungry blue eyes. "It's counterproductive."

"Do you deny it, then?"

Hunt thought of Johnny Merrimon's notes, the Chief's edict

about personnel files, the police-issue cuffs used to secure Tiffany Shore. He thought of the dark sedan parked on the street at Katherine's house, the cat with its crushed vertebrae. The threat designed to keep Johnny quiet. "Your source is mistaken."

"Can I quote you on that?"

"You can tattoo that on your forehead." Hunt walked away and she followed. Another van rolled to a stop as Hunt rejoined Yoakum. It was from the Office of the Chief Medical Examiner in Chapel Hill.

The reporters swarmed, shouting questions.

The camera crews ate it up.

Hunt threw himself behind the wheel of his car and Yoakum spilled in next to him. The big engine caught and Hunt waited until the reporters cleared his path before he gunned it. Yoakum picked up on his mood. "What?"

"They know about Johnny."

"How?"

"They know a cop may be involved."

"What the hell?"

Hunt kept his eyes on the road. "Somebody's talking."

CHAPTER THIRTY-SEVEN

Yoakum followed Hunt into the police station. People stopped working when they entered the bullpen. Silence fell and Hunt pushed through the stares, the mounting tension, and Yoakum trailed behind him. They entered Hunt's office and Yoakum closed the door. "That was awkward."

"Can't blame them. Court TV is parked on Main Street."

Yoakum stared through a smudged window, and his goatee looked yellow white in the dirty light. "That's not what that was about."

"No? We went from abduction to multiple homicide in a matter of hours. We've got dead kids and national media. People are talking and people are scared. We're in the thick of it, you and me. Why wouldn't they stare?"

"That was about two things only."

"Is that right?" Hunt was angry, frustrated, but Yoakum refused to back down.

"That was about you looking for a cop—one of them—and that was about you going down."

"Going down for what?"

"Johnny Merrimon."

This time Hunt looked out the window. "Nobody has said anything—"

"They will if the kid doesn't turn up soon. The media is involved, now. They know he's missing. Eventually they'll figure out that you kept Social Services out of it, and everybody knows about you and that boy's mom."

"There's no story there."

"You may believe that, but I don't. It doesn't matter anyway. Keeping Johnny away from Social Services was your call. The reasons won't matter if something happens to him. You'll be crucified."

"I think you're wrong."

"Because you know the kid. Others don't. They know his life is shit. They know he lost a twin and his old man. They know his mom is a freak job, and they know what they saw in the papers. You've seen the pictures. Johnny comes off like he's lost his mind, like any sane person would lock the kid down for his own protection."

"As opposed to what?"

"As opposed to giving him to a dumb-shit, security-guard relative that can't run his own life. Damn it, Clyde, don't you see? There is nothing that will make your decisions appear reasonable if something bad happens to that kid. Ken Holloway will make sure of that. So will the Chief, the press, the attorney general." Yoakum raised a rough, callused finger. "You'd better pray that boy turns up unharmed."

Hunt studied his friend. He looked old, creased. "Worry doesn't suit you, John."

"I expect the worst and the worst rarely disappoints. You know that. That's why thirty years of this crap has never touched me."

"And this case?" Hunt sensed the difference in his friend, the coiled anger.

A pause. "This case is different."

"Because they're kids?"

"Because all of them together don't add up to one of me. And because it has been going on for years in our own

300

backyard. I'll tell you, Clyde. I've never felt this way."

"What way is that?"

"Somebody should die. For this—" Yoakum's features drew down and he stabbed a finger against the surface of the desk, raised his voice. "Somebody should die."

"Keep your voice down."

"It's true."

"As far as I know, they still have the death penalty in North Carolina."

"Defense lawyers." Yoakum made it sound dirty.

A silence fell between them, and when Hunt spoke, he kept his voice low. "What if Johnny is right? What if a cop was involved with Burton Jarvis? What if a cop has been protecting him? Helping him?"

"No way."

"Seven kids . . ."

"I just can't see it."

"Somebody's talking to the media, John. If I was a dirty cop and wanted to derail an investigation, that'd be a good way to start: Spread rumors and kick up dust, distract the people that were looking for me."

Yoakum thought about it. "Let's say there's a second perp, somebody involved with Jarvis, with these kids. Could Johnny make an identification?"

"Maybe. He won't talk to me."

"What about Tiffany Shore?"

"No reason to think a second person was involved with her abduction, but one could have been. Right now, she's sedated, more or less catatonic. Doctor's hopeful, though. Maybe tomorrow."

"Is she under guard?"

"No."

"Maybe she should be. If it's a cop."

"Maybe she should."

Hunt looked down at his desk. Alyssa's file still sat on the corner of it, right next to the Tiffany Shore file. He flipped open the first file and saw Alyssa's photograph, the dark eyes and hair, the face that looked so much like her twin brother's. "Is it possible? One of our own?"

"Darkness is a cancer of the human heart, Clyde. You know I believe that."

Hunt lifted the second cover and studied Tiffany Shore's fine-boned features. He touched one photograph, then the other. "I can't just sit around."

"What?"

"You don't have to be involved."

"With what?" Yoakum asked, but Hunt ignored him. He left the office and turned for the narrow hall that led to the back of the building. People stared, looked away, and then he had the hall to himself. Pushing through a fire door, Hunt took the stairs down two at a time. The basement level had a poured concrete floor and metal doors off the main hallway. Storage. The evidence room. A small room at the back held the department's personnel files. Cops. Support staff. Maintenance. The records were kept in locked cabinets behind an unlocked door.

Moving fast, Hunt stopped once to pull a fire extinguisher from its bracket on the wall. The records room was nine feet by eleven, concrete scrubbed and white under fluorescent light. The cabinet he wanted was dead center at the back wall. Hunt eyed the lock on the top drawer. It was cheap. It would give.

Hunt hefted the extinguisher, but stopped when Yoakum stepped into the room behind him. "I told you not to get involved."

"No." Yoakum eased the door closed. "That's not what you said."

Hunt looked back at the locked drawer, hesitated.

"Do it," Yoakum said.

Hunt turned his head a fraction, put a single eye on his partner. A hot flush colored Yoakum's face and the fluorescent lights put pinpricks in his eyes.

"Do it," Yoakum said again. "Screw the Chief. Screw the chain of command." Hunt lowered the extinguisher, and Yoakum crowded behind him. "Do it for Alyssa."

"Are you pushing me?" Hunt asked.

"Do it for Johnny. Do it for his mother."

"What are you doing, John?"

Yoakum stepped even closer. "Reminding you that there's a difference between doing the job and doing personal."

"Sometimes the job is personal." Hunt stared at his partner until Yoakum took a step back. "Don't try to manipulate me."

Before Yoakum could respond, the door to the hallway opened and a desk officer, young and female, entered, then stopped when she saw them. Her eyes registered the extinguisher in Hunt's hands, the tension between the two men. "I'll come back later," she said, then left.

In the sudden silence, Yoakum held up a finger and thumb, less than an inch between them. "Sometimes it's that fucking close."

"What?"

"Getting fired over something stupid."

The stare held for long seconds, then Hunt, still angry, turned for the hall. He snapped the fire extinguisher back into its holder, and when he turned, Yoakum was waiting.

"Don't hate me 'cause I'm beautiful," Yoakum said, and Hunt felt weight come off his shoulders.

"Why would Johnny think it was a cop?" Hunt asked.

"Because it was?"

"Why would a kid think someone is a cop? What would make a thirteen-year-old boy believe that? A badge? Something the guy said? Something he did?" Hunt fingered the cuffs on his belt. "Handcuffs? A gun?"

"A uniform?"

They stood in the damp concrete smell, thinking about it. Johnny was a strange kid, but he had good instincts, and he was smart. That's what no one else seemed to get. If Johnny thought a cop was involved, there had to be a reason. Hunt tried to picture it: dark of night, two men in a dump house, Johnny at the window . . .

"Did you read the reports on the stolen plates?" Hunt asked.

"What?"

"License plates."

"I read it. So?"

"Whoever Johnny saw at Jarvis's house used stolen plates on his car. Three of them that we know about. Of the three that were stolen, one owner had no idea when or where he'd lost it. The other two were fairly confident."

Something shifted at the back of Hunt's mind and Yoakum saw it.

"What?"

"Two of the plates were stolen from cars parked at the mall."

"It's a good place to steal plates."

"So is the airport, the hospital, or a dozen different strip malls."

Their eyes met, and both had the same thought at the same time. Cuffs. Guns. Uniform.

Security guard.

CHAPTER THIRTY-EIGHT

Johnny dug in the dirt. He felt his stitches pull, but he ignored the pain. He was doing this for a reason. He told himself that. Repeated it. Levi Freemantle sat slack-lipped, with one hand spread on the raw pine coffin, his eyes intent on Johnny, and on every scoop of dirt that came out of the ground. He nodded as the boy struck a rock, then pried it out and heaved it up.

"Thank you."

Johnny barely heard it, but that didn't matter. He'd heard it twenty times already, small offerings that came as he worked. He nodded and dug. The sun beat down as thunderclouds stacked up in the south. Johnny looked at Jack and offered the shovel. "You want to take a turn?"

"No, thanks. I'm good."

For ten minutes Jack had stood with the gun raised. When he finally lowered it, only Johnny noticed. Now Jack sat on the stone wall, gun in his lap. He swatted mosquitoes and looked bored.

In a way, Johnny was glad that Jack refused to dig. Johnny knew nothing about Levi Freemantle, not why he was there or how his daughter had died, but he understood the man's loss in a way that Jack never could.

So he dug and he hurt. He thought about the things that David Wilson said at the bridge: *I found her. The girl that was taken.* Johnny had run in panic and blind fear before Wilson could tell him what he meant. But Freemantle had come after. Johnny eyed the big man, shovel falling, then coming up heavy.

He'd come after.

If Freemantle found David Wilson alive, then maybe Wilson told *him* where he'd found the girl. Maybe Freemantle knew.

Johnny tossed out dirt, and Freemantle dipped his head.

Maybe.

Johnny heard the word as he dug.

Maybe.

After more than an hour, two crows landed on a low branch of the oak tree that stood at the center of the cemetery. Johnny only noticed because Freemantle went still, then leaned across the coffin. He stared at the black birds, fear and hate on his face. One bird dropped to a headstone, a black knot that threw out its wings at the last moment. It cocked its head at the coffin, then lifted oiled feathers as it preened. Suddenly, Freemantle was on his feet. He charged the bird, stumbling, screaming. Jack twitched and the gun came up.

There were words in the scream, Johnny was certain, but there was no understanding them. The bird flapped to another tree, and Freemantle returned to where he'd been sitting. He stared long at the bird, then closed his eyes and made the sign of the cross.

Johnny looked at Jack, who shook his head, white-faced, and held on to the gun like grim death.

Two more crows landed in the trees, then another three. Johnny returned to work and the minutes stretched as a wind kicked up. The soil was loose and easy to dig, but Johnny dug deep. He ignored the pain in his hands, the greasy, peeled skin that oozed clear, sweet-smelling liquid. He ignored his back, the pull on his stitches, the sweat that stung his eyes. He had all day to get what he wanted, so he planned it out, the best approach, the questions he would ask once the big man's child was in the ground.

Johnny glanced at Freemantle.

The blade bit.

He shoveled hot, sandy earth as storm clouds massed over crow-flecked trees.

When Johnny climbed from the hole, the sun was dim behind the storm's leading edge. Treetops thrashed. An ozone smell hung in the air. "It's coming," Jack said.

The hole was not as deep as it might be, but it was the right size, the right shape. "That's all I've got," Johnny said. "All I can do."

"I have rope." Freemantle gestured at the coffin.

"All right."

They moved the coffin to the edge of the grave. Once there, they slipped rope through the small metal handles and worked the coffin down. It looked pitiful in the raw, rough hole. The ropes came out with a rasping sound, and Freemantle folded them together, big hands deft but slow. "I'd like to do this last part by myself." He ducked his head. "Barn's dry if you want to lay up." Freemantle looked at the compressed, purple sky, the leaves gone silver. "She never did like storms." He turned back, lifted the shovel and a yellow light pulsed in the belly of the clouds.

"Lightning," Johnny said.

But the big man did not hurry. He dropped a handful of earth into the grave. Leaves clattered in the wind. "Lightning falls." He dropped more earth on his daughter's coffin. The wind grew. Jack was already through the gate, but Johnny had no desire to follow. Freemantle stared down at the coffin, unmoving. "God sounds like my daddy."

"Is that right?"

Freemantle nodded. "Not like the other voice."

"Other voice?"

"Like chocolate gone soft in the sun. Sticky sweet. Hard to swallow away." He looked up at the storm. "I hear him when the crows come close."

Freemantle hefted a stone and threw it at a group of crows in the low branches of the oak tree. He came close, then paused for a long time, and Johnny didn't push him. The man was crazy insane. Johnny looked for Jack, but Jack was gone. "I'm scared of lightning," Freemantle said. He raised his face to the storm but did not appear frightened, in spite of what he'd said. "God won't talk to me anymore."

The grief was tangible. The loss.

"Here. Wait." Johnny took the shovel from Freemantle and stepped to the oak tree. The crows called raucously, then flew off, and Johnny used the shovel blade to gouge a circle in the bark. "That's supposed to protect you from lightning. Only on oak trees, though. It won't make a difference on any other kind of tree."

The big man stood, solemn and tense, good eye moving from the scarred bark to the boy. "Black magic."

"No."

"Says who?"

"The Celts. They're dead now. A long time dead."

"How you know it works if all them Celts is dead?"

"I read it somewhere. It's not important."

Freemantle shook his head, doubt all over his tortured face. "Lightning falls," he said again. "All you can do is pray God it don't fall on you." He faced the mound of fresh-dug earth. "She should have words as the dirt goes in." He turned, face full of hope and inexplicable trust. "Do you have a Bible?"

"I don't." Suddenly, Johnny was embarrassed. "But I know

some words." Johnny saw no reason to share his own beliefs on the matter, not here with this strange man and his fear of crows and lightning and voices like sugar. "I'll say them for you."

A burst of rain hissed in the treetops. Freemantle's face twisted in relief as Johnny stepped closer and felt the man's great height beside him. The scars were puckered and gray, the bad eye iridescent when the yellow light burst. Johnny thought back to long nights reading the Bible, to hours of his mother's fevered prayer and his own search for meaning. For a long moment, his mind was blank, then he said the only words he could remember. "Our Father who art in heaven . . ."

Cold rain fell hard.

". . . hallowed be thy name."

Levi Freemantle wept as he buried his daughter.

Johnny stood in the rain and waited for lightning to fall.

CHAPTER THIRTY-NINE

Hunt and Yoakum waited in the first-floor lobby of the big building downtown. Ken Holloway's office was on the fifth floor, but the receptionist, an iron-faced woman north of fifty, was being difficult. Outside, the day was growing darker by the minute. Blown litter scraped across the concrete walk, then lifted and spun in the wind. "We don't need an appointment." Hunt's shield filled his cupped palm.

The woman stood behind a massive teak counter, a phone system to one side, buttons flashing red and green. Holloway's company filled the entire building. A glance at the directory showed the scope of it. Real Estate Sales, Development, Commercial Construction, Consulting, Property Management. Holloway owned the mall, several of the largest buildings downtown, all three theaters, two golf courses; and that was just in this town. Holloway's interests stretched across the state.

"This is a criminal matter," Hunt said. "I can be back in twenty minutes with a subpoena and a warrant."

The woman's phone buzzed and she answered. When she hung up the phone, her voice was cold and clipped, her face unbending. "Mr. Holloway is one of the kindest people in this town, and everyone here is aware of your harassment. There will be no shortage of people to testify against you if there is anymore of that here today." The mask fell away and she smiled. "Mr. Holloway will see you now." She extended an arm. "The elevator is to your right."

They crossed the marbled floor and stepped into the elevator. Yoakum pushed the button and the doors slid together. "Delightful," he said.

"The receptionist?"

"A peach of a woman."

Holloway's office covered most of the entire floor. Hunt saw a conference room, a few secondary offices, but the rest was wide-open space. Holloway stood behind his desk. To the right stood his attorney; to the left, a uniformed security guard, armed. Three walls of plate glass offered a view that included most of downtown, including the police station, which looked dingy and small. From this height the storm was a fast-approaching wall of purple and black.

"Detectives," Holloway said.

Hunt stepped onto an oriental rug and moved past a conference table that cost more than his car. He stopped in front of the desk. Holloway's smile was forced, his fingertips white on the desk where they took his weight. "You remember my attorney. This is Bruce." He indicated the guard.

Hunt stared Bruce down. He was in his forties, tall and black in a crisp blue uniform with a gold shield on his chest and matching patch on one shoulder. The man's face showed no expression. The weapon was a semiautomatic. "You got a carry permit, Bruce?"

"He does," Holloway said.

"Can't he answer for himself?"

"No."

"He's a grown man."

"Not so long as he works for me."

Hunt raised an eyebrow at Bruce, tilted his head, and shrugged. "We're investigating a possible link between a criminal matter and one of your employees. We need the names and employment records of all of your security guards, particularly those at the mall."

"What kind of criminal matter?"

"We'd like the names."

The lawyer leaned over the desk. "I have advised my client to answer no questions absent a court order to do so."

Holloway raised his hands to show that he had no choice, and Hunt met the attorney's gaze. "Is that final?"

"Yes," the attorney said.

"You'll advise your client against any interference in our investigation?"

"Of course."

"He is to alert no one of this visit. The investigation is ongoing."

Holloway put on his professional smile. "We have nothing to discuss outside of court, Detective Hunt. Not my employees, your investigation, or your uncommonly poor choices. Not Katherine Merrimon or her troubled little bastard of a son."

Hunt held the gaze, then turned on his heel.

"Oh, but first," Holloway said. "I guess you should know that Katherine Merrimon has refused to see me further. Changed the locks. Hysterics. The usual."

Hunt stopped, walked back to the desk. "Is that right?"

"We filed eviction papers this morning. She'll be on the street in thirty days."

"She'll manage," Hunt said.

"Will she?"

Hunt's vision constricted until all he saw was Holloway's oiled smile. He felt a pull on his jacket and realized it was Yoakum. "Come on, Clyde."

Yoakum turned but Hunt did not budge. He eyed Bruce, then Holloway. "Do all of your guards carry weapons?" he asked.

"I'm not going to answer your questions," Holloway said. "I thought I made that clear." Hunt eyed the security guard. "He won't tell you anything, either."

Bruce kept his mouth shut, his back straight; but when Holloway stopped looking at him, he laid one finger on the butt of his weapon.

The attorney inclined his head. "Have a good day, Detectives. The receptionist will be happy to validate your parking."

They crossed the room, shoes soft on the rugs, loud when they hit wood. The elevator doors opened, then closed. "A nice office," Yoakum said. Hunt remained silent, nails biting into his palms. "Nice view."

They passed the receptionist, who glared but was ignored. On the sidewalk, the building rose tall and dark above them. Electricity charged the air, and Hunt's voice seemed to carry much of the same raw energy. "You saw it?"

"I did."

"His guards carry."

"Not all of them."

"But one."

"Yep."

"One carries."

They walked to the car and wind made their pants legs flap and stutter. A uniform, a badge, and a gun. A thirteen-year-old-kid could mistake that person for a cop.

Easy as anything.

Easy as pie.

At the car, Yoakum put his hands on the roof. Hunt was on the other side, the street empty behind him. "I need to say something," Yoakum said. "And I don't want you getting bent out of shape about it."

"What?"

"We don't need to see the employee files."

"They might help."

"But we don't *need* them."

Hunt shrugged. "I wanted to see him. I wanted him to know that I'm looking."

"That's not enough reason."

"You're probably right."

"Then why come here at all? Why involve Holloway if there's no need? You knew he wouldn't answer your questions. He hates you."

Hunt stared back, eyes shuttered.

"Oh, shit."

"Get in," Hunt said.

They slipped into the car; the wind noise fell away. "He'll call his people," Yoakum said. "That's how he is." Hunt started the car. "He's probably on the phone right now."

"Maybe." Hunt put the car in gear, checked traffic, and pulled away from the curb.

"You set him up," Yoakum continued. "He'll call his people and you'll charge him with obstruction."

Hunt kept his mouth shut.

He drove for the mall.

The mall was a monolith of concrete and stucco. Slab-sided and bleak, it rose against the dark sky. Glass doors flashed from gray to purple as people filed out, eager to beat the storm home. Hunt threaded through traffic and steered for the back. He rounded the corner and a few hard drops cracked against the windshield. They passed Dumpsters and loading docks and old cars.

They were halfway down the back wall when Hunt slammed on the brakes. His door clanked open and he was out before Yoakum called. "What are you doing?"

But Hunt was already moving. "Ma'am?" Hunt called out to a woman who stood, bent, on the outer edge of the nearest loading dock. "Ma'am?" The woman was in her sixties, attractive. Silver-white hair bobbed at the collar of her expensive dress. Hunt gave her his best smile. "Hi. Detective Hunt." He flashed the shield. "Sorry to bother you."

"May I help you?" She was thin-boned and elegant. The diamond at her throat looked to be two carats and real.

A few more drops struck the macadam. "I couldn't help but notice . . ." Hunt gestured at what she held in her hand.

"Tuna fish." She tilted the can, embarrassed. The top was off, tuna gone bad. She gestured at the edge of the dock, where she had just placed a fresh can. "There's a dear of a cat. I can't abide seeing it rooting around in the Dumpster."

"Is the cat tired of tuna?" He tipped his head at the spoiled can.

"I haven't seen her in a few days."

"What does the cat look like?" Her puzzlement showed, her hesitance, so Hunt offered his best smile. "If you don't mind. I'm a cat lover, too."

She beamed, stepping closer. "Brown tabby with gold eyes and two white paws." She raised both shoulders, smiled brilliantly. "Just full of life."

Hunt stepped up onto the loading dock. "May we come through your store?"

"I don't know—"

"I have to insist."

The store sold clothing. Hunt and Yoakum pushed through storage, then past the dressing rooms. Women looked up, startled, but Hunt ignored them, making for the escalators. "Clyde. Slow down."

The crowd was still large, storm notwithstanding. Families, kids—a surge of color and noise.

"Clyde!"

Hunt drove through the crowd, Yoakum trailing in his wake. "This is the guy."

"Who's the guy? What are you talking about?"

"It's the same cat from Johnny's house. Brown tabby with two white paws. This is our guy."

"Who is?"

"Whichever guard carries a gun."

"Johnny's cop."

Hunt took the escalator at a run. He emerged into the food court, shouldered past a group of shoppers and made for the door marked SECURITY. It was locked. Hunt pushed the buzzer.

"Security."

Hunt recognized the voice. "Steve. This is Detective Hunt. Buzz the door."

"Is there a problem?"

Hunt slammed a palm on cold metal. "Buzz the fucking door."

The door buzzed and Hunt took the stairs two at a time. Yoakum pounded concrete behind him. They rounded the landing, weapons out. Steve met them at the top of the stairs, door cracked open behind him. "Step aside, Steve."

"Whoa. Hey." Steve's hands went up when he saw the guns.

Into the security office. Fat security guard at the monitors, another standing in front of the broad glass window overlooking the food court. Both were startled, scared. Neither carried a weapon. "Office," Hunt said, then saw the closed door, the windows with slatted blinds. "You." He jabbed a finger at the standing guard. "Sit." The guard scurried to the nearest chair. Hunt motioned to the office door and Yoakum flanked it. Steve looked dazed.

"Anybody in there?" Hunt asked.

"Mr. Meechum? He left."

"Who is Meechum?"

"The boss man."

Hunt gestured Steve away from the door, then looked at Yoakum and counted down from three. The door opened easily, and they were through, into the empty office.

"I was saying—" Steve filled the open door. "Mr. Meechum just left."

"When?"

"Five minutes, maybe."

"Describe him," Hunt said.

"I don't know. Sixty-five. Skinny but strong. Thin hair, busted-up nose. Kind of a dick."

"Does he carry a sidearm?" Hunt asked. "Is he in uniform?"

"Jeans, usually. A kind of safari shirt. But he wears a pistol on his belt. He's the only one here that's allowed to."

"What kind?"

"Huh?"

"The gun. What caliber?"

"Forty-five, I think."

Hunt met Yoakum's eyes, and both understood. *Same as the shell casing found in David Wilson's car.*

"Does he carry cuffs?" Yoakum asked.

"We all do."

"John." Hunt gestured to the desk in the office. It was old and scuffed, nothing special. A bank of monitors sat on its surface, tied into the mall's surveillance system. Three of the monitors were fed by cameras overlooking the food court. Each one showed the same thing: a table of young girls, maybe fourteen, maybe less. The shots were zoomed in. Hunt could see braces, dimples, the ready laughter, the toss of hair. "This is our guy."

Yoakum leaned in. "Motherfucker."

"Why did Meechum leave?" Hunt asked, and there was a terrible certainty in him.

Steve did not hesitate. "He got a call from Mr. Holloway. I don't know what they talked about, but I put the call through myself."

"When?"

"Just now. Right before you got here."

"Steve," Hunt said. "We're going to need Meechum's address."

"I don't know his address, but you can walk to his house in two minutes."

"How's that?" Hunt asked.

"He lives behind the mall. A few weeds, a ditch or two, and you're at his back door."

"Show me," Hunt said.

"Now?"

"Right this minute."

Steve licked his lips, threw a nervous glance around the room. "Really?"

"Yeah." Hunt's hand fell hard on his shoulder. "Really."

Cold rain drummed against Hunt's face when he opened the door onto the back lot; it slashed in at an angle, beat itself to mist on the blacktop. Visibility was muted, as if light itself had been sucked from the air. A car rolled past, windshield fogged over, blades throwing water off the glass in wide, crystal arcs. "Where?" Hunt raised his voice.

Steve pointed. The heavy door clanged shut behind him. "There. Between those trees." Hunt saw the trees, two scrubby cedars sprouting from the edge of a ditch across the lot. "There's a trail. It's not long."

"I need you to show me."

"Aw, man." Steve looked up at the rain. "You're going to get me wet *and* fired." Nobody laughed.

"Now," Hunt said.

They dashed across the flooded pavement, slipped between a parked Suburban and a battered Ford with plastic taped over one window. Behind the cars, the ditch was already flooded. Dark water carried fast-food wrappers, plastic bags, and cigarette boxes downcurrent. The trail began at the trees, ran narrow and straight through the tall weeds of a vacant lot. Yoakum's hand fell on Hunt's shoulder. "Backup?" He held up his radio.

"We're not waiting."

"Good." Yoakum put the radio in his pocket and racked the slide on his weapon. "I hate waits."

"Which house?"

Steve leaned left to see between the two scrub cedars. A line of small houses backed up to the field of weeds. Hunt saw narrow patios and busted grills, a few bikes. Steve pointed again. "See the gray house with the red bike on the back patio?"

"Yeah."

"Third one to the left of that."

Hunt counted left, saw a low ranch with flaking paint and a dead holly at the corner. No lights. No movement. He pointed it out to Yoakum.

"Does he live alone?" Hunt asked.

"I think so."

"You stay here." Hunt checked Yoakum. "You ready?"

"Right as rain."

They hopped the ditch and slipped into the field, bent at the waist, weapons out and angled low. Weeds grew tall and put long, wet fingers on them as they moved. Thunder crashed. The trail was wet and slick.

They stopped in the last bit of cover before the bare yard that wrapped Meechum's house. A smell hung in the air, a chemical reek that came from nowhere.

They dashed the last twenty feet, put their backs to the wall beneath the largest window. Water sheeted from blocked gutters. The chemical smell was stronger, something burning. Hunt eased up to the window. The curtains were drawn but gapped open in the middle. It was the living room, a dingy space with old furnishings and low ceilings. The carpet was yellow orange, the walls cheap pine panels. Meechum was as Steve had described him. Wiry and crooked, he bent above his computer, shirt dark with sweat. In the fireplace, computer discs were mounded and aflame. "He's burning evidence," Hunt said, dropping down, making for the back door. "You're on the front door. We go in sixty seconds."

Yoakum moved to the front and left Hunt alone in the rain. He risked one more look through the rear window. Hair rose wild from Meechum's head. He stabbed the keys, then slapped the side of the computer, slapped it again. Hunt did not see the ax until Meechum reached for it. It leaned against the desk, a hickory shaft and a blade that was rusted black except where it gleamed silver along the bit. It came up and Meechum's face locked, lips back, eyes tight; then the ax came down with a grunt, a crash of plastic, and shattered glass.

The computer.

Damn it.

Hunt dropped from the window, bolted for the door. He tried the knob. Locked. He put his shoulder to the wood, found it flimsy and cheap. The doorjamb splintered under his weight, and he was in the kitchen, linoleum slippery under his muddy feet. A hint of motion through the door to the living room and Hunt's weapon came up as he entered. "Police! Police, God damn it!"

The computer was staved in at the top, Meechum above it, ax up and frozen as he stared at the drawn pistol. Hunt saw panic in his eyes. "Don't." Hunt stepped farther into the room, squared up his line of fire. The room stank of burning plastic.

Meechum shook his head, lizard of a tongue darting out.

"Just put down the ax." Hunt looked for Yoakum, then heard glass break at the front door.

"Just put it down," Hunt said.

The man's face twisted. His chest pumped as black smoke snaked up the chimney. Hunt saw the decision firm up in Meechum's face, even as motion winked in the door behind him. Hunt saw a flash of metal, Yoakum, gun up, rounding into the room.

The ax head lifted as Meechum's spine bent.

"No," Hunt yelled, but it was too late.

Meechum swung the ax, and Yoakum shot him through the heart.

The body dropped facedown, a small twitch in two bent fingers. Hunt crossed to the fireplace and kicked discs away from the flames. Seizing the poker, he dug deeper, spread the flaming plastic out and tried to save what he could. Eventually, Yoakum helped him. Five discs were unscathed, another dozen charred. Ten were ruined beyond hope of recovery.

Hunt stepped back. His shoes were blacked, his throat stinging. He stared at Yoakum, whose face was placid. "Did you have to kill him?" Hunt asked.

Yoakum looked at the body. "He went for you with an ax."

"He went for the computer."

Yoakum's face showed neither apology nor regret. "Bad angle. My view of you was obstructed. I couldn't see if you had a gun up or not. The ax was coming down as I entered the room. I thought he was going for you."

"I wish you hadn't killed him."

"It was a clean shoot."

Hunt paused, very still. "I never said it wasn't."

"It was clean." Blood scent rose in the room. Yoakum holstered his weapon, eyes dark and glassy smooth. "Squeaky," he said, and turned away.

Five minutes later, backup arrived, and with it came the Chief, and the questions, none of which were easy. Cops flooded the house. The storm continued. By sundown, the body was gone, the discs bagged and delivered to the department's best computer technician. The Chief called Hunt and Yoakum into the kitchen. "One last time. Tell me this is the guy."

"We think he was associated with Burton Jarvis."

"Why?"

"Stolen plates. The dead cat from the mall. Johnny Merrimon's notes—"

"Don't talk to me about that kid's notes."

"His descriptions line up," Hunt insisted. "Age, height, hair color. We've been through this three times."

"Do it again."

So he did. Hunt explained everything. The Chief did not interrupt. He barely blinked.

"We saved some of the discs," Hunt concluded. "The hard drive looks intact. It should tell us more."

The Chief stared from one man to the next. "I want both of you at the station," he said. "I want your statements. Beyond that, I don't want either of you to say a word to anyone about this, not to each other, not to your girlfriends or any other cops—not until I have your statements locked. Are we clear?"

"Yes."

The Chief pointed at the door. "Statements. Now."

"I'm ready for a beer," Yoakum replied. "How about we do statements tomorrow?"

The Chief was not amused. "Statements," he said. "From both of you. Separately. Then I want you to go home and get some sleep. Tomorrow I need to figure out what to make of this cluster fuck."

"Cluster fuck," Yoakum repeated, an edge in his voice.

"What would you call it?" The Chief refused to back down.

"The shoot was clean."

The Chief put his hands on his hips, thrust out his soft, round jaw. "A man was gunned down in his own living room. It had damn well better be."

Hunt drove his own car but Yoakum was ordered to ride with a patrolman. "I don't like the feel of this," Yoakum had said, but both men understood. The Chief did not want them discussing their statements while they drove. He wanted them unrehearsed and unprepared. Hunt did not see Yoakum when he arrived. He was met at the door by an internal affairs officer named Matthews. He was new to the jurisdiction, so Hunt knew him by sight and reputation only. He was supposedly smart, supposedly a decent guy. He had washed-out eyes and a disapproving mouth; he limped slightly as he led Hunt to an unused conference room. At first, the questions were standard, of the sort asked after any shooting, and if they were longer than usual, more involved, it was because the shooting was fatal. Hunt took it in stride. He'd been through it before.

The questions took an unexpected turn thirty minutes in.

"You and Detective Yoakum are friends, is that right?"

"We're partners."

"That answer is nonresponsive, Detective."

"John Yoakum is my friend."

"Have you ever seen Detective Yoakum fire his weapon in anger?"

"No. Of course not."

"Has he ever used excessive force?"

"How much force to apply is a judgment call. Detective Yoakum has always exercised impeccable judgment."

"In your opinion?"

"Yes."

"As his friend."

"As lead detective of major crimes." Hunt felt heat under his shirt. "As an officer with seventeen years' experience. Are we finished yet?"

"A few more questions."

"Get on with it then."

Matthews drummed the head of a pencil on the table and slouched back in his seat. "Detective Yoakum was in your office earlier today?"

"Yes."

"What were you discussing?"

Hunt's patience evaporated. "We've had more than a few things to discuss lately."

Matthews's lips turned, but the smile did not touch his eyes. "Of course." The pencil tapped. "Tiffany Shore. The murdered children." He could have been talking about a pot dealer or a speed trap.

"I'm going to give you exactly one more minute," Hunt said. "Then I am walking out of here."

Matthews leaned forward. "While in your office today, did

Detective Yoakum say that someone should die for what was done to those children?"

Hunt said nothing.

"Did he say that?"

"I think we're finished." Hunt stood.

"You haven't answered my question."

Hunt kept his voice tight. "What was or was not said in my office has no bearing on what happened today. Meechum had an ax. Yoakum did what he thought he had to do."

"Are you sure about that, Detective?" Matthews tipped his chair back against the wall, and Hunt saw that there was no joy on the man's face. "Think about it."

Hunt spoke to no one as he left the station. His watch said seven when he stepped out of the station and into pounding rain. He walked, unfeeling, to his car. Inside, in the moist, close air, his hands found the wheel, the ignition. He looked for news crews but saw none. Maybe it was the weather.

Someone heard.

Through his closed office door, someone heard what Yoakum said.

Hunt squeezed the wheel and replayed Yoakum's heart shot. The ax was up, Yoakum rounding into the room as the blade started down. It looked the same, but felt different.

Or did it?

After a minute, Hunt called his son at home. Seven rings, then music in the background. Hunt tried to hide his fatigue, his unsettled nature. "Hey, Allen."

"What?"

"Have you had dinner yet?"

"I'm smoking crack and watching porn. What do you care?"

Hunt bit down on his own emotion. "I'll be home soon. Want me to bring something?"

Outside, Yoakum emerged from the front door of the station. He looked once at Hunt, then raised a hand and made a gun of his fingers. Hunt flicked the lights. Yoakum pulled the trigger, then walked to his own car, as oblivious of the rain as Hunt had been.

"Chinese," Allen stated, "but bring it in an hour."

Yoakum opened his door, closed it. They were on opposite sides of the lot, the two of them. Facing each other.

"Why an hour?"

"Because I'm doing stuff."

Hunt was so tired of the wall between them, the sturdiness of it, the way it grew taller every day.

Yoakum slid into his car and Hunt felt it when the engine fired. "How about a movie after we eat? Like we used to."

"I don't think so."

"Just like that?"

"Yeah. Pretty much."

Yoakum pulled out of the lot as the kid hung up. Hunt closed his phone and watched him go. They should talk, but Hunt wasn't ready to do that. Not yet. Not even close. He had an hour. Katherine was only ten minutes away. He thought about it, then started the car. He drove five miles under the speed limit, car sure-footed on the glassy roads, but as the edge of town approached, he found himself driving faster. He wanted to see her, he realized. In that minute, rain beating the road to a river of black mist, he wanted it more than anything else.

His car rose on the hill then dropped, lights slashing down, small houses strung out below. They were well spaced, hints of spilled light and drab color tucked back into the trees; but that's not how it was at Katherine's house. Hunt slowed and ducked his head to see through a windshield slightly fogged. Her driveway was empty, her car still impounded, but news trucks lined the street. Nine of them. A dozen.

Hunt's head turned as he slid past. CNN. FOX. WRAL. A bunch more. He turned into the drive, passing close to the nearest trucks, and doors slid open as news crews spilled out into the storm. They were too savvy to come onto Katherine's yard, but shouted questions from the street as soon as Hunt stepped into the rain.

Have you found Johnny yet?

Is it true that he's led you to a serial child murderer?

The cameras were prepped for bad weather. The talent wore slickers but grew quickly damp and smudged. The questions continued. No order. No pretense at decorum. They'd been waiting in the rain, and Hunt was already making for the house.

Detective, is it true that the body count stands at seven?

That was Channel Nine. Hunt knew the guy.

Is Alyssa Merrimon among the dead?

Louder.

Detective? Detective?

The questions came faster, shouted through the downpour. Hunt turned his back. Katherine answered on the second knock, small and pale and beautiful.

Mrs. Merrimon—

A flurry. Hunt put himself between her and the cameras. Her smile was not as forced as Hunt feared it might be. "May I come in?" he asked.

She let him in, closed the door. "Johnny?"

"Not yet."

She stepped aside and Hunt shrugged off his wet coat. Only one light burned in the house. She cracked a curtain and peered out. A cup of coffee sat cold on the small table by the sofa. "Is it true?" She showed one dark eye, then looked back outside. "What they're saying?"

"What are they saying?"

"That you found a mass grave. That you would never have found it without Johnny."

"It's true."

"I can't bear to ask."

"We have no reason to believe that Alyssa's body is there. But . . ."

"But what?" She turned from the window, eyes fragile, chin tilted.

"We've not exhumed all of the bodies yet. The rain forced us to stop."

"So, tomorrow?"

"Tomorrow, we'll see."

She wrapped her arms around herself. "Can I offer you some coffee? Or tea? I don't have anything hard."

"Coffee would be great." She sounded terrible, Hunt thought, but was keeping it together better than he'd hoped she might. "I only have a few minutes."

"Coffee." She turned.

"Thank you, Katherine."

She poured coffee into a mug and handed it to him. "So there's nothing? No word at all?"

She was asking about Johnny. "No," he said. "I'm sorry." She looked at the window and at the storm beyond. Then she sat on the sofa and Hunt sat next to her. "He's a tough kid," Hunt said. "We're looking."

"Can't you do more? Anything? An Amber Alert?"

"Those are never used unless there's clear evidence of an abduction, and we don't believe he's been abducted. All evidence is that he's out on his own. Somewhere. Given his past behavior . . ."

She closed her eyes, beat fists on her thighs. "Johnny . . ." She shook her head. "Damn it, Johnny. Where are you?"

"He's smart, Katherine. He'll be okay. We'll find him."

When she opened her eyes, her face was glass, and Hunt could tell that she was moving the conversation forward. "Ken has come three times today."

Hunt hid his sudden worry. "I thought he'd moved on. He said as much."

"That's not what Ken Holloway does. If he told you that, he was lying."

"Threats?" Hunt asked.

"He rattled the door, whispered a few ugly things."

"Did he make any threats?" Hunt pushed. He could charge Holloway for communicating threats. It would go well with the obstruction charge. They were small charges for a man like Holloway, but they would get him locked up, if only for a little while. They would keep him away from Katherine.

"Can we just sit?" she asked. "Can we just sit in the quiet?"

Hunt let it go, the anger and the concern. "Sure," he said, and they sat as his coffee cooled, and as the news crews gave up and climbed back into the vans. After a moment, Hunt noticed that she was clutching something in her hands, pressing her palms together and squeezing her hands between her legs.

"I was in Johnny's room earlier today. You know . . ."

She trailed off and Hunt could see her there, touching the boy's things, working hard to suppress the fear and doubt.

"I found these." She unfolded her hands and Hunt saw a stack of his business cards. They were wrinkled, palmed and damp. She looked up, met his eyes. "Nineteen of them."

A shocking clarity shone in her face and Hunt felt a strange and sudden embarrassment. "I wanted Johnny to know there was someone to call," Hunt said. "If things got bad."

She nodded, unsurprised. "After I discovered these, I looked around the house and found all of the ones you've given to me. I threw a lot away, I know that, but I still found another dozen."

"It's my job," Hunt said.

The clarity never wavered. "Is it?" Hunt looked away. "You've always been there for us."

"Any good cop would do the same."

"I don't think so." Her shoulder brushed, once, against Hunt's, and he felt a charge, a blue spark that snapped and stung. "Thank you," she said, and they sat in the quiet, the two of them, side by side. She drew her legs up, tucked her hands back into her lap and laid her head on his shoulder. Hunt felt the narrowness of her arm pressed against his, the warmth of her skin as cold rain battered the window. "Thank you," she said again.

And Hunt held himself very still.

CHAPTER FORTY

The storm was so fierce that Johnny saw nothing of the sun as it dropped behind the curve of the earth. The rain fell, stinging cold, and the temperature came down with it. The air went from gray to blue to near black, but Johnny didn't move, not even when lightning fell in a hot-white flash that split the air with a sound like breaking stone. He hunched into himself. He sat against the wall and watched Levi Freemantle scrape the last sodden dirt onto the grave, then smooth it with the shovel and sit. Water came off the big man in sheets, and he settled into wet earth as if the mud rose around him. Nothing felt real. Johnny barely twitched when Jack leaned over the wall and said, "Johnny."

Seconds passed. "You left me," Johnny said.

Jack leaned farther over the wall, his head close. "You're going to get killed out here."

"Lightning falls."

"What is that supposed to mean?"

"Nothing. I don't know." The sky lit up. Johnny pointed at the old oak tree. "That's the tree they hung them from."

Jack looked at the gnarled tree, its giant limbs spread and restless, black when the lightning fell. "How do you know?"

A roll in Johnny's shoulders. "Can't you feel it?"

"No."

"The cemetery's built around it. Three headstones at the

base of it." He raised a finger. "See how small they are. How rough they were cut."

"I can't see shit."

"They're there."

"You're losing it, Johnny."

Johnny said nothing.

"There's a stove in the barn. I got a fire going."

Johnny stared at Freemantle. "I can't leave."

"You've been out here for hours. He's not going anywhere. Look at him."

"I can't take the chance."

"Have you thought about this? Really thought it through? He's burying his kid, man, and from the way her coffin looked, I'd say he was burying her for the second time. That means he dug her up from some other grave. Do you even know how the girl died? Or why he carried her all this way to put her in the ground with no one around to see it?"

"We saw it."

"We don't even know if it's really his kid."

Light spilled from a distant cloud. "Look at him." Both boys looked at Freemantle, slumped into himself, shattered by a grief so true it was unmistakable.

Jack lowered his voice. "Have you asked yourself why he's covered with blood or how he got so injured? The real reason he grabbed you up the other day?"

"God told him to."

"Don't go smart-ass on me, man. When this guy comes in from the rain, we're going to have to figure out what to do with him. I don't want to be the only one thinking about that."

"I just have one question, and as soon as he's done with this"—Johnny gestured at the rain, the grave, the mud—"I'm going to ask him."

"And if he won't answer?"

"I helped bury his daughter."

Jack's voice rose. "If he won't answer?"

"Give me the gun," Johnny said.

"You threaten him, he'll kill us."

Johnny held out a hand. Jack looked at the giant in the mud, then dropped the gun in Johnny's lap. It was cold and wet and heavy.

"I'm this close," Johnny said.

But Jack was already gone.

Johnny watched the man and the rain and the silent, rising mud. After a minute, he dug into a pocket. When his hand came out, it held a feather, small and white and crushed. He held it for a long time, watched it go limp in the pounding rain. He thought hard about throwing it away, but in the end he closed his fingers and waited, gun in one hand, last feather in the other.

Hours later, lightning dwindled in the north. The forest dripped. Freemantle looked up at the racing clouds, the hint of moon behind them. It was the first time he'd moved since smoothing the earth above his daughter. There'd been no more sign of Jack, no more entreaties to come in out of the rain. There'd been the slow march of hours, the flash and noise, the storm that drove the cold water down. There'd been hard stone at Johnny's back, and there'd been the two of them, twenty feet apart and unmoving. That had never changed.

Johnny tucked the feather back into his pocket, slipped the gun under his shirt.

Freemantle pushed himself up and stared after the storm. "I thought I'd get hit." In the dark, his eyes were spilled ink, his mouth a gash of surprise and disappointment. It was after midnight, time a hard road behind them. Freemantle picked up the shovel, his discarded shoe. Using the shovel as a crutch, he walked past Johnny. "It doesn't matter. It's done."

"I need to talk to you."

"I'm done."

The white gate swung on silent hinges. Freemantle moved slowly and Johnny fell in behind him. "Please."

"I'm tired."

Tired, Johnny thought. And sick. He could smell infection in the air that came off the big man. He stumbled once as the barn drew near. Johnny put out a hand, but it was like trying to catch the weight of a tree. His skin was hard and hot. He almost went down. "Tired," Freemantle said, and then they were at the barn.

Inside, Johnny saw dust and straw and metal tools, two big lanterns that hung from chains. Heat rolled over them as they stepped through the door. In the far corner, an iron stove stood on slabs of slate. Its sides were rounded, and coals glowed behind the grate. Jack was laid out on a mound of straw, his jacket folded for a pillow. He jumped when Freemantle closed the door.

"It's okay," Johnny said, stepping closer. Jack's eyes caught the glow from the stove. "You crying?" Johnny asked.

"No."

It was a lie, but Johnny let it go. In the closed confines of the barn, the shadows stretched long. Freemantle looked immense and dangerous. Johnny kept the pistol out of sight. "My name's Johnny. This is Jack."

Freemantle stared. His eyes were tinted yellow, lips cracked deep enough to show hints of meat. "Levi." He pulled off his shirt and hung it on a nail close to the stove. His chest and arms were padded with muscle. There were long, thin scars that looked like knife wounds, a hard tight pucker that could have come from a bullet. The branch in his side was jagged and black.

"That looks bad," Johnny said.

"It only hurts if I try to pull it out."

A smell rose, wet and earthy. Where Levi stood, water dripped onto stone, faded to a dark hint, and was gone in the heat. His eyelids drooped. "Almost there," he said.

"What?"

He opened his eyes. "Forgot where I was."

Johnny opened his mouth, but Jack spoke first. "Why did you carry the coffin out here?"

Freemantle pinned him with yellow, fevered eyes. "Why did I carry it?"

"I'm just asking."

"I can't drive. Momma said driving was for other folks." His eyes drifted shut and his body leaned left; he staggered once to stop from falling. "Momma said . . ."

"You okay, mister?"

His eyes snapped open. "Who wants to know?"

"My name is Johnny, remember?"

"I don't know nobody named Johnny."

"You need a hospital. You need a doctor."

Freemantle ignored him and limped to a shelf on the far wall. Johnny saw machine oil, rat poison, hooked metal tools, and rags gone stiff with age. Freemantle picked up a rusted box cutter and a plastic bottle smeared with cobwebs. He sat by the fire and cut the legs off of his pants, throwing the rags on the ground by the stove. The top came off the bottle and he poured brown liquid into the wounds on his knees.

Jack appeared next to Johnny. "That's for animals," he whispered.

"Bullshit."

335

"It says for veterinary use only." He pointed and the boys watched. Whatever it was, it hurt when he poured it.

"Are you okay?" Johnny finally asked. Freemantle nodded, then tipped the bottle over the wound in his side. "You need antibiotics."

Freemantle ignored him. He tried to pull the rag from his finger, but the flesh was so swollen that the cloth bit like wire. He cut it free, and Johnny saw the shredded wound his teeth had made. He turned his face away as Freemantle poured more of the liquid on the finger. Twice. Three times. His muscles locked up, relaxed, and then he lay down on the stone. "You boys shouldn't be out here."

"I just want to talk."

"I'm done," Freemantle said.

"How did your daughter die?"

"Jesus, Jack. Shut up." Johnny's whisper was fierce. He was here, now, and Jack was going to fuck it all up.

"They say you killed those people." Jack's voice was tight. "If you had a good reason, then I won't worry so much about you killing us." Jack was ready to bolt. Already he was angled for the door.

Levi Freemantle sat up slowly. His eyes looked even more yellow, his skin like ash. "Killed what people?"

He knew what people. Johnny saw that as plain as day. A wariness moved into the man's eyes. A new tension took his shoulders. Johnny's fingers settled on the pistol under his shirt. Freemantle saw the movement, and their eyes met. He remembered the gun. Johnny saw that, too.

Suddenly it all fell away. Freemantle slumped. "They can have me now. Shoot me. I don't care."

Johnny's hand came away from the gun. "Because you've buried her."

336

"Because she's gone."

"How did she die?"

Freemantle pulled a wet envelope from the front pocket of his pants. It was crushed, so damp that the paper was almost pulped. Much of the ink had smeared, but Johnny recognized Freemantle's name. The address was the Department of Corrections. Freemantle tossed the envelope and Johnny picked it up. Inside was a newspaper clipping. Bits of paper came off on Johnny's fingers. "Somebody had to read it to me," Freemantle said.

"What is it?" Jack asked.

But Johnny was trying to read. The headline was clear enough. "Toddler Dies in Hot Car."

"The little ones are a gift." Freemantle tilted his head and the bad eye caught fire. "The last true thing."

"They left his daughter in the car." Johnny squinted. "They went drinking in some bar at the beach, and they left her in the car."

"My wife," Freemantle said. "Her boyfriend."

"There was an investigation. The cops ruled it accidental."

"They buried her without a preacher, just put her in the ground with people that don't have names or family. My wife never even told me. I wasn't there to say goodbye." He paused again, then his voice broke. "Sofia went in the ground without her daddy there to say goodbye."

"Who sent this to you?" Johnny held up the clipping. It was from one of the newspapers at the coast.

But Freemantle had gone distant again, eyes unfocused, hands turned up on his knees. "I left my baby a picture so she wouldn't miss me. I drew it in her closet so she could see it every day and not be sad that her daddy was gone. She liked to play in her closet. She had a doll baby with tiny white shoes." He

337

held up two fingers, an inch apart. "She had some crayons for coloring, some paper I brung home from the store one day. That's why I drew us in the closet, 'cause she felt so good in there, 'cause it was her play place." He tilted his big head. "But a picture can't take care of nobody. Picture can't keep a baby girl safe."

"I'm sorry." Johnny meant it.

"Who sent the clipping?" Jack asked.

Freemantle smeared fingers across his face. "A neighbor lady with two babies of her own. She never liked my wife. She found out about what happened and sent that to me in jail. That's why I walked off, so I could stand over my baby's grave and make sure it was done right and proper, but it was just bare dirt that rose up in the middle. No flowers, no stone. I sat down and put my hand on the dirt. That's when God told me."

"Told you what?"

"That's when he told me to kill them."

The boys looked at each other and both had the same thought.

Insane.

Crazy fucking insane.

"God told me to bring my baby here." Freemantle looked up, and new life stirred in the desert of his face. "The little ones are gifts." He cupped his giant battered hands. "The last true things. That's why God told me to pick you up."

"What?"

"Life is a circle. That's what he said to tell you."

"Johnny . . ." It was Jack, a bare whisper. Johnny held up a hand.

"God told you to tell me that?"

"I remember now."

"What does that mean?"

338

"Johnny . . ." Jack's voice hinted at panic. Johnny tore his eyes from Levi Freemantle. His friend was pale and rigid. Johnny followed his gaze to the pile of filthy fabric by the stove. Shreds of pants. The twist of bandage from the infected finger. Jack pointed and Johnny saw it. A name tag sewn into the cloth Freemantle had used for a bandage. A name tag. A name.

Alyssa Merrimon.

Bloody and stained.

Johnny looked at Freemantle, who drew a shape in the air with one finger.

"Circle," he said.

And Johnny pulled the gun.

CHAPTER FORTY-ONE

Hunt was late getting home. The dinner was cold in the bag, but Allen made no comment. They ate in the kitchen, together but silent, and tension came off them in waves. At the door to his son's room, Hunt apologized. "It's just the case," he said.

"Sure."

Hunt watched his son kick off grungy shoes. "It'll be over soon."

"College starts in three months." He pulled off his shirt and tossed it after the shoes. Fine hairs textured his chest, rose from the hollow place at the base of his neck. His son was all but grown, Hunt realized, as close to a man as a boy could get and still have boy in him. Hunt paused, knowing that there was nothing he could say that would make this better.

"Son . . ."

"She never calls."

"Who?"

"Mom," he said, and there was nothing but boy in his face.

"I don't know what to say."

"Don't say anything."

Hurt, angry boy.

"Allen, I—"

"Just close the door."

Hunt could not move.

"Please," Allen said, and the look on his face was a blow to the gut, a hammer stroke. A stone settled on Hunt's heart and it carried the weight of a million failed expectations, the certainty that it should not be like this for his son.

"Please," Allen said again, and Hunt had no choice.

"Good night, son."

Hunt closed the door, then went downstairs. He stuffed cartons and paper bags into the trash, then poured a slug of scotch that he knew he would never finish. The day was all over him: death and despicable men, the lives of children cut short, and a host of still-unanswered questions. He wanted a shower and ten hours of sleep. Under his fingers, his face felt like an old man's face. He walked into his study, unlocked the desk drawer and pulled out the Alyssa Merrimon case file. He stared for a long time at her picture, glanced over the notes, the jotted questions, but his mind was on Yoakum. He replayed the moment that Meechum had died, the smell of gun smoke and Yoakum's steady hand, his eyes, so glassy smooth and still.

The call came at twelve thirty. "You awake?" Yoakum asked.

"Yes."

"Drunk?"

Hunt closed Alyssa's file. "No."

"I am."

"What is it, John? What's on your mind?" Hunt knew the answer.

"How long we been doing this?" Yoakum asked.

"A long time."

"Partners?"

"And friends."

A silence drew out, Yoakum's breath on the line. "What did you tell them?" he finally asked.

"I told them what happened."

"That's not what I'm asking and you know it."

Hunt pictured his friend, saw him in his own small house, a glass in his hand, in his living room, staring at the ashes of a long-dead fire. Yoakum was sixty-three. He'd been a cop for over thirty years; it was all he had. Hunt didn't answer the question.

"You're my friend, Clyde. He was going for you with an ax. What was I supposed to do?"

"Is that the reason you took the heart shot?"

"Of course."

"It wasn't anger? Not payback?"

"For what?" A different anger was waking.

"You know for what."

"Tell me, Clyde. You tell me for what."

"For those kids. For seven graves in a patch of muddy woods. For years of bad shit in our own backyard."

"No."

"All this time, Yoak. All this time and I've never seen you do personal. Today looked personal."

"A killer came after my partner with an ax. He came after my friend. You could call that personal, but you could call that the job, too. Now, what did you tell them?"

Hunt hesitated.

"Did you tell them it was a clean shoot?"

"We stuck to the facts. They asked for my opinion, but I didn't give it."

"But you will."

"Tomorrow," Hunt said. "Tomorrow, I will."

"And what will you tell them?"

Hunt reached for the scotch. In the low, cut-crystal glass, a small light kindled in the liquid. He replayed the moment in his mind, the ax starting down, Yoakum stepping into the room. What *had* his angle looked like? Did he have to take the kill shot? The computer was off to the side, but by how much? Hunt put himself in Yoakum's shoes. He thought he could see it, the way it could have looked.

But Yoakum spoke before Hunt could. "Have you filed that obstruction charge against Ken Holloway?"

In the aftermath of Meechum's shooting, Hunt had almost forgotten about Holloway's phone call. "No," he said.

"But you will?"

"I will."

A silence invaded the line, and it was an ugly one. Hunt knocked back the scotch. He knew where this could go, and prayed that it would not.

"None of this would have gone down if we'd left Holloway out of it," Yoakum finally said. "We'd have taken Meechum clean at the mall. No shooting. No burned discs. That was you, Clyde, your call. *That* was personal."

The phone seemed to hum in Hunt's hand. "Good night, Yoakum."

A heavy pause. "Good night, Clyde."

The line went dead.

Hunt poured another scotch.

CHAPTER FORTY-TWO

Freemantle stared at the gun. It shook in Johnny's hands. Johnny's voice shook, too. "Where is she?"

Jack pushed closer, alarmed. "Johnny, what are you doing?"

"Where's my sister?"

"I don't know your sister." An ember popped in the stove. "I don't know you."

Johnny stooped for the scrap of cloth with Alyssa's name on it. He held it out. "This is my sister. Her name is Alyssa Merrimon. This is her name." Freemantle kept his eyes on Johnny's face. "Look at it," Johnny said.

Freemantle shrugged and looked. "I can't read."

"She was taken a year ago. That's her name."

"I don't think he knows," Jack said.

"He has to."

"I would tell you if I knew."

"He doesn't know," Jack said.

"Where did you get this?" Johnny shoved the bloodstained cloth at Freemantle. "Where? When?"

Giant shoulders rolled, muscles tight under the skin. "I got that from broken man. Right after you bit me."

"Who?"

"Broken man." He said it like it was a name. "Broken man was by the bridge. I got that from broken man's hand. He was holding it."

The gun dipped. "After you picked me up?"

344

"God told me to see what you was running from, so I did."

"David Wilson," Johnny said. "Was he alive when you found him?"

Freemantle's head tilted, and he closed his eyes, thinking. "Put the gun down," Jack whispered. Johnny hesitated. "You really think this man has Alyssa? You're going to get somebody killed."

Johnny let the muzzle settle until it pointed at the dusty floor. "Was broken man alive?"

Freemantle's eyes stayed shut. "There was voices in the river. Whispers. Dandelion words." He made a floating motion with his fingers. "I was so tired . . ."

"Voices?" Johnny keyed on the word. "Did the broken man say something? Anything?"

"I don't remember."

"You have to."

The big hands turned palm up. "The crows was coming. I was scared." They were a foot apart, the boy, the man. "I'd tell you if I could." Freemantle lay down on the warm stone. "Maybe I'll know in the morning. That happens sometimes." He closed his eyes. "I'm sorry about your sister. I'm done now."

Johnny stared at Freemantle. He stared until his legs went numb. He felt despair, like hunger, and when he finally turned, Freemantle was snoring.

Johnny put the gun on a shelf. He looked at beams and posts and bits of sharp-edged metal. He turned his face to the roof as a dark pit opened in his chest. He was torn, and then he was empty. The pit was a vacuum.

It was Jack who broke the silence. "Why is he scared of crows?"

"I think he hears the devil when the crows get close."

345

"The devil?"

"He hears one voice. Why not the other?"

"What if it's true?" Jack put his arms around his knees. He rocked on a trunk and couldn't meet Johnny's eyes. "What if he really hears God's voice? What if he really hears . . . You know."

"He doesn't."

"But what if?"

"Nobody does."

Jack pulled his knees tighter. Dirt rimed his face. "I don't like crows, either. Been scared of them since I was little. What if that's why?"

"Come on, Jack."

"You know what they call a group of crows?" His voice was small and strained.

Johnny knew the answer. "A murder," he said. "A murder of crows."

"Maybe there's a reason for that." Jack looked at Freemantle. "What if God sent him here for a reason, too?"

"Look, Jack. This guy killed two people because they let his daughter die in a hot car. If thinking God told him to do it makes living with that fact any easier, then I guess that's what he had to do. The crows, the other voice . . . that's just guilty conscience catching up."

"Yeah?"

"Yeah." They both stared. "But he knows something."

"I'm scared, Johnny."

Johnny's eyes glittered. He watched Freemantle by the fire, nodded as the night grew thin.

"He knows something."

Jack fell into a fitful sleep as wind sighed through the cracks, a small voice that, twice, gusted into something terrible. The fire burned low. Johnny moved from anger to grief to unwanted sleep that took him down hard. He dreamed of stinking wood and sharp, yellow eyes, of a hard fall through shattered limbs and of his sister's hopeful smile. She squatted in the dirt of a low cellar: filthy skin, tatters for clothes. A single candle burned, and she looked up, startled. *Is that you?* she said, and Johnny bolted up with a scream trapped behind his teeth.

For that instant, he did not know where he was or what had happened, but he knew that something was wrong. He felt it in the close, hot air.

Something was wrong.

Levi Freemantle sat in the dirt, cross-legged, not three feet away. He was sheeted with the same sweat, shadows gray on his black skin. His hands were cupped in his lap, the pistol in his hands. He was staring at it, tilting it toward the stove. His finger found the trigger.

"It's loaded," Johnny said.

When Freemantle looked up, Johnny had the sense that his sickness had spread, that little awareness remained behind the vacant eyes. He turned the gun and gazed into the muzzle. The moment drew out. Johnny held out his hand. "May I have that?"

Freemantle ignored him. His hand swallowed the grip. "I got shot once." Johnny could barely hear him. Freemantle touched the bullet scar on his stomach. "Little boys shouldn't have guns."

"Who shot you?"

"My wife."

"Why?"

He looked at the gun. "Just 'cause."

"May I have that?" Johnny leaned closer and Freemantle handed him the gun. It could have been an apple. Or a cup of water. Johnny took it, pointed it at Freemantle's face. He was scared. The dream still had him. "Where's my sister?"

The muzzle was eighteen inches from Freemantle's eyes.

"Where is she?" Louder. Twelve inches. Ten. The gun, this time, was deathly still, but Freemantle was as unconcerned as an ox facing a bolt gun.

"When she shot me." His voice was low. "She said it's 'cause I was stupid."

Six inches. One hand cupping the other, finger tight on the trigger.

"You shouldn't call people stupid," Freemantle said. "Calling people names is mean."

Johnny hesitated, and Freemantle lay down. The gun still pointed at the empty place where his eyes had been, his yellow-stained, bloodshot, slaughterhouse eyes.

CHAPTER FORTY-THREE

Hunt woke at five, restless, still tired. He showered and shaved, moved through the small house, paused at the door to his son's room and listened to the sounds of his deep and steady breathing. It was a bad day coming. He felt it in every fiber, every bone. For this day to end well, he thought, it would take a miracle.

Downstairs, the kitchen was overly warm and smelling of scotch. Hunt rarely drank. He was hungover and disappointed in himself.

Screw Yoakum.

Screw that phone call.

But that was not fair. As much as he'd hated to hear it, the man was right. Hunt put events in motion the second he stepped out of the elevator and into Holloway's office. Meechum's death was his fault. He might as well have pulled the trigger.

Hunt flicked the curtain and looked out. No stars shone, but there was no call for rain, either. The medical examiners would be back in the woods in a matter of hours. They'd get the last bodies out today. Maybe one was Alyssa. Maybe not. Maybe Johnny would turn up. Then again . . .

Where are you, Johnny?

Hunt opened the window to let cool air spill across his hands, his feet. A damp breath licked his face, and for a moment the hangover faded. He looked once more at the soaking grass, the water that stood in shallow, mirrored pools. Then he made

349

coffee and waited for the sun to find itself in the troubled skies of Raven County.

His son still slept when he left.

Pale mist gathered in the black trees.

The Chief had set the meeting for nine o'clock—late in cop terms—but Hunt could not wait that long. The sun still hung below the courthouse as he drove down Main Street, then turned left and rolled past the police station. Already the curb was lined with news trucks. Cameramen stamped their feet. Reporters checked makeup. They knew the cops would move soon. They would make the long, slow roll to the black woods at the edge of town, where the last bodies would be culled from the damp, grasping soil.

The story would grow.

The day was ripe with opportunity.

Hunt drove around the block to the small parking lot at the rear. It was not yet seven, but Yoakum was there, waiting. He sat on the edge of a concrete barrier at the south end of the lot. His back pressed against a chain-link fence and bowed it out. Behind him, weathered-looking men in hard hats drank coffee and ate fast-food biscuits while dozers and cranes idled, damp and dull in a gray light so weak it made the turned earth look frozen. A bank would rise, Hunt thought. Maybe an office building. Holloway's probably. And the wheels of commerce would turn.

Yoakum was rough, unshaven; a cigarette hung at the edge of his mouth. He took a drag and flicked it through the fence as Hunt stepped into the warming air and walked the last twenty feet.

"Morning, John." Hunt was neutral, guarded. Their friendship was an understood thing, and this doubt between them was untouched ground.

"Clyde." Yoakum fished out another smoke, ran it between his fingers. He did not light it, and had trouble looking Hunt square in the face. He put his eyes on the roofline of the police station, then on the shoes that still showed traces of mud from the field behind Meechum's house.

Hunt waited.

"About last night," Yoakum began. "I was drunk. I was wrong."

Hunt kept his face immobile. "Just like that?"

Yoakum sparked the cigarette. "I was not myself."

Steel eyes. Doubt. Hunt said nothing, and Yoakum changed the subject. "You see this?" He lifted a stack of folded newspapers from the barrier on which he sat.

"Bad?"

Yoakum shrugged, handed over the papers. Hunt flicked through them. The headlines were sensational. There were photos of the medical examiner's vehicles framed by the deep and secret woods, photos of thin body bags being loaded through wide double doors. Reporters speculated on body count, hinted at police incompetence. They spoke of a security guard, shot dead by an unnamed cop. They recapped the story of how Tiffany Shore had been found, and they all asked the same question: *Where is Johnny Merrimon?*

"They know that we have an all-points out on Johnny." Hunt shook his head.

"Kid's a damn hero."

There was something in Yoakum's voice, and Hunt could not decide if it was bitterness or just another hangover. "The kid's missing."

"I didn't mean anything bad by that." Yoakum gestured at the papers. "Just that we come off like idiots."

"Occupational hazard these days."

"No shit."

"They're already stacked up out front. A dozen trucks. You see them?"

"They don't have my name yet." He was talking about Meechum, about the shooting. "You couldn't pay me to go in through the front door."

Hunt didn't blame him. The story would grow. Yoakum would be chewed up in the process. "They'll have it soon enough," he said.

Yoakum nodded, looked at the back of the station, a concrete wall stained with moisture. "Let's get this over with." ·

They crossed the lot together, but a tension remained between them, an awareness of the late night phone call, of things said and unsaid. At the door, Yoakum stopped. "Last night, Clyde." He looked embarrassed. "I was in a dark place. You understand?" Hunt started to speak, but Yoakum cut him off, opened the door, and edged a shoulder inside. "You do what you have to do," he said, then turned away.

Inside, an energy charged the air; Hunt saw it in the brisk movements, the eyes that danced their way. Yoakum was treated like a hero. Handshakes. Back slaps. Cops hated pedophiles, and Meechum's house had yielded a trove of damning evidence, the most frightening of which was a thick sheaf of photographs taken by the mall's surveillance cameras. The girls ranged in age from ten to fifteen, fresh-faced and awkward. Pictures showed them sitting in the food court, riding the escalators. Meechum had made bold notations in black marker: *Rachel, Jane, Christine*. He was uncertain of some of the names. Those had question marks: *Carly? Simone? April?*

Some photos had addresses noted on the low corners. They lived on quiet streets, family streets. Other photographs had ages scratched in dark marker, beneath the names, the faces:

Rachel, 12. Christine, 11. They'd come from the locked bottom drawer of Meechum's desk, and had made Hunt sick, when he saw them, sick and furious. More than that—the sight had made him murderous. Right or wrong, killing the bastard had been a good thing. There was, in fact, a certain beauty in how the case had unfolded. Burton Jarvis died in the street, half naked and begging for his life, put down by one of his victims. Meechum was gunned down in his own home, shot through the heart by one of the department's most senior detectives.

Beauty.

Justice.

Most of the cops were smiling, but not the Chief. The Chief was bleached out, with bright spots of scarlet in the center of his meaty cheeks. He stood in the door to his office, looking out. Seven fifteen in the morning, and he was already stained with sweat. Behind him, shadows moved. Hunt saw men in the Chief's office. Strange men in dark suits. Men who looked like cops.

"Five minutes," the Chief said, then closed the door.

"We're going early," Hunt said.

Yoakum rolled his shoulders. "I'm catching a smoke."

Detective Cross watched Yoakum thread through the crowded room, then rose from his desk and approached Hunt. "Can I talk to you in private?"

Hunt led Cross to his office and closed the door. Cross was ragged, his shirt coffee-stained and wrinkled. He'd failed to shave, and Hunt noticed that most of his whiskers were coming in white. "What's on your mind?"

"Any word on the Merrimon kid?"

"We're hopeful."

"But not yet?"

"Is there a problem?" Hunt asked.

"My son, Jack. I can't find him."

"What does that mean, you can't find him?"

Cross ran thick fingers across the brush of his hair. "We had a fight. He snuck out of the house."

"When?"

"Last night." A pause. "Maybe two nights ago."

"Maybe?"

"I'm not sure about the first night. Maybe he left then, maybe it was the next morning. I was out of the house early and didn't see him. With everything in the papers, you know, my wife's worried. More than she might otherwise be. She doesn't handle worry very well."

"She's worried, but you're not."

Cross fidgeted, and it was clear to Hunt that he was more than worried. He was genuinely frightened. "Do you know my wife, Detective?"

"I met her some years ago."

Cross's head moved. "She's a changed woman. The last few years . . ." He paused, struggling. "She's become very religious. She's been at the church for most of the past thirty hours, not really eating or sleeping, just praying, mostly for Jack. She's worried that he may be out with the Merrimon kid. If I could tell her that he's not—"

"Why is *that* her worry? Why Johnny?"

Cross cast a concerned gaze across the room. He lowered his voice. "She claims to see a darkness on Johnny's soul. A stain." He cringed as he said it, apologetic. "I know, I know; but there it is. She thinks that Johnny is bad for Jack. She's more worried about that than anything else. She's not right, you understand." He squinted, tilted his head. "She's struggling."

"I'm sorry to hear it." Hunt paused. "Are *you* worried about Jack?"

"Ah, he's done this kind of stuff before. Normal teenage junk. But two nights, if it is two nights . . . That's unusual."

"What was the fight about?"

"Jack worships that Merrimon kid. I mean, truly. Like a brother. Like a saint, even. I can't break him of it."

"And that's why you fought?"

"Jack's a weak kid, more like his mother than his brother. He's frightened and easily led. My wife's irrationality aside, Johnny *is* a bad influence. A rule breaker. Damaged, you know. I told Jack to stay away from him."

"Johnny's a good boy, but he's been pulled apart by all of this."

"Exactly. He's fucked up."

"He's traumatized."

"That's what I said."

Hunt buried his frustration. Not everyone saw Johnny the way he did. "What can I do for you, Cross? You want Jack's name added to the all-points?"

"No. God, no. Just let me know if you hear anything. His mother is upset, not thinking straight. She blames me. The sooner I can tell her that he's okay . . ."

"I understand."

"Thanks, Hunt. I owe you."

Cross left. Hunt stood in the door and saw Yoakum come back inside. His face had lost none of the anger. He was barely into the room when the Chief's door swung wide. "Hunt. Yoakum."

The Chief preceded them through the door. He circled his desk but remained standing. Hunt stepped in first. To the right, he saw the two unknown men. Both were north of fifty, tall and square with lined, uncompromising faces. One had silver hair, the other brown. No fat between them. Big hands. Calluses.

Badges hung on their belts. Guns. Hunt came farther into the room, got a closer look at the badges. State Bureau of Investigation. From the look of them, they were senior in the Bureau, professional, hard men.

Yoakum came in behind Hunt. He moved right, put himself between Hunt and the state cops. It was warm in the office, close. All five men were big men. All five knew that something was wrong. Problem was, some knew more than others.

The Chief made introductions. "Detectives Hunt, Yoakum. These are agents Barfield and Oliver—"

"Special agents," Oliver corrected.

No one shook hands. On the desk lay copies of Hunt's statement about yesterday's shooting. Yoakum's was there, too. "Special Agents Barfield and Oliver are from the Raleigh office. They were nice enough to come down early this morning."

"This morning," Barfield said, unsmiling. "That's funny."

"Why is that funny?" Hunt asked coldly.

"It was closer to last night than this morning," Barfield said.

Hunt looked at the Chief. If they were here from Raleigh, they must have been on the road since before dawn. "Why are we talking to the SBI?"

"Just take it easy," the Chief said. "All of you. We're going to do this right." He looked at his detectives. Hunt was leery. Yoakum looked bored. "I need your weapons."

The words were quiet, but fell into the room like a grenade. They had power, those four words, the power to ruin lives, rain collateral damage. Nobody moved. The moment drew out until Yoakum broke the silence. "I beg your pardon?"

"I need your weapons." The Chief put one finger on the desk. "And I need them now."

"This is bullshit." Yoakum could no longer feign indifference.

"Just do it." Hunt kept his eyes locked on the Chief, but drew his service weapon and placed it on the desk. Grudgingly, Yoakum followed suit. He watched the state cops, who remained flat-eyed and stoic. "Now what?"

The Chief took the weapons and put them on a credenza against the back wall. It was a telling moment. The guns were out of reach. Turning back, the Chief was clearly unhappy. "We've been over your statements," he said. "All very proper. All very bloodless. But I need to know if it was a clean shoot." He stared straight into Hunt's eyes. "And I need you to tell me."

Hunt felt Yoakum's sudden attention. The room was silent. "This is all highly unusual." Hunt looked from the state cops to the Chief. "This is not how it's done."

"Please." The Chief's voice was surprisingly soft.

Hunt tried to think clearly, to recall every detail of the shooting: how it happened, why it happened. But what came to him were feelings about John Yoakum. More than thirty years on the job. Four years of working side by side. They were partners, friends and colleagues.

And Meechum deserved to die.

The Chief waited, dull-faced and miserable, while Yoakum stared at a fixed point on the wall. "The shoot was clean," Hunt said.

Stiffness bled out of Yoakum. A trace of a smile touched his lips.

"You're certain?" the Chief asked. "You have no question?"

"From where Yoakum stood, it looked as if Meechum was coming at me with an ax. He made a split-second decision. It was the right one."

Special Agent Barfield spoke: "We still have to do this."

"What's he talking about?" Hunt asked.

The Chief shook his head, eyes briefly closed. Whatever the

357

agent meant, Hunt could tell that the Chief agreed. "Detective Yoakum, I need to ask you to go with these officers."

"What?" Yoakum's anger popped.

"To Raleigh. They have some questions. Better that they're not asked here."

Yoakum took one step back. "I'm not going to Raleigh."

Barfield held up his hands, fingers spread. "No reason we can't do this quietly. Discreetly."

"Why don't you discreet my ass?" Yoakum said. "I'm not going anywhere until somebody tells me what's going on."

The Chief said, "These questions need to be asked by someone not affiliated with this department. I've invited the SBI to assist."

"Spin control," Hunt said in disgust.

The Chief shook his head. Barfield laid a hand on Yoakum's shoulder. It was not a threatening move, not aggressive. Yoakum shrugged it off. "Don't touch me."

"Nobody's arresting you."

"Arresting me! What the—"

"Settle down, John."

"Fuck you, Clyde. What questions?"

Barfield reached out with the same hand, stopped short of touching anything. He tilted his body, indicating the door. Yoakum knocked his hand away. "Not until I know what these questions are about."

Barfield dropped his arm. "Your off-duty weapon is a Colt .45." It was not a question.

"What of it?"

"Where is that weapon now?"

"That's none of your business."

"Detective Hunt recovered a .45 shell casing from the wreckage of David Wilson's car."

"So?"

Hunt risked a glance at the Chief. At the sight of his face, a hollow place opened in his stomach.

Barfield's face showed no emotion. "It has your print on it. We'd like to talk to you about that." Again Barfield raised an arm, indicating that Yoakum should precede him through the door. "We can keep this quiet." But Yoakum swatted the hand away, a loud stinging blow; and suddenly, all was motion. "That's it," Barfield said. He and Oliver moved in unison. They seized Yoakum and forced him across the desk, facedown, right arm jack-hammered behind his back. Hunt stepped forward, hands up and reaching for the fabric of Oliver's jacket. It was instinct, pure and simple.

"Stay out of it, Hunt." Loud. Commanding.

Hunt looked at the Chief and froze, felt the rage in his face. Barfield was twisting the arm, cuffs out. Oliver had his full weight on Yoakum's shoulder blades. Barfield slapped a cuff onto Yoakum's wrist, and Yoakum fought it, a smear of blood on his top lip.

"Chief."

"Shut up, Hunt." Then to the SBI agents, "Is this really necessary?"

"He assaulted a state policeman."

Cuffs on, they hauled Yoakum to his feet. Hunt stepped between them and the door. "Whatever's going on, there's an explanation. Don't take him out like this. Those are his colleagues out there. Press all over the street."

"Stand aside, Detective." Barfield was red-faced. Oliver was the picture of dispassion. "We're just doing our jobs. Your own Chief asked us here."

Yoakum stood between the SBI agents. His shirt had pulled from beneath his belt. One button was sprung and his fury was a tangible thing. "Get your fucking hands off me," he said.

Hunt looked for the Chief. "You're going to let them haul him out in cuffs?"

"You arrested Ken Holloway for less."

"That's different."

"Is it?" The Chief was not going to help.

"We have room for two," Oliver said, and the threat was implicit.

Yoakum said, "This is bullshit, Clyde."

"Stand aside, Detective. I won't ask you again."

"Chief. Damn it."

"They have a job to do, same as us."

Hunt stood firm. "I will not allow this."

"Stand aside, Hunt," the Chief said. "Or I swear to God, I'll have them arrest you, too."

"You wouldn't."

"Get out of the fucking way."

Hunt looked at his friend, who tossed his hair and spit pink saliva on the Chief's floor. "Don't sweat it, Clyde." Hunt refused to move. "Go on and step aside."

"John—"

"Pretty day for a drive," Yoakum said, and Hunt felt himself step left. The door opened and they hauled his partner out in cuffs.

Through the bullpen.

Out the front door.

CHAPTER FORTY-FOUR

Johnny watched the sun rise from the loft door. His legs dangled over a dark drop that smelled of mud and bruised grass. He was thirsty and his body hurt all over. Nobody else was awake, the fire long dead. The sun appeared first as a line of pink, then as an edge of yellow that lifted above the trees. Johnny leaned far out and stared down.

"Don't jump." It was Jack, behind him.

Johnny turned. "Ha-ha."

Jack crossed the loft, sat down next to his friend. Hay hung in his hair. His heels drummed wood, then he leaned out, too. "I saved your life. You owe me."

"Owe you that." Johnny punched him on the shoulder.

"Dick." Jack looked across the field of weeds beaten flat. The forest was still black beneath the leaves. Swamp sounds rose on a sudden breeze. "I'm hungry."

"Starving."

"We should go home."

Johnny glanced at the ladder, the trapdoor that led down. "Still think he's talking to God?"

"I think he's dying."

"Really?"

"Yeah. Really."

Johnny rose, dusted his hands on his jeans. "I should talk to him."

Jack stood, too. "It stinks down there."

He was right. Freemantle was lying on his side, knees drawn up. He smelled like death. His bad arm was stretched out in the dirt, and when Johnny touched his skin, it felt like hot, dry paper. Johnny looked from the wound in his side to the swollen hand. The skin on the finger had split from the pressure. "All I did was bite him."

"The human mouth is a gross place."

"You kissed what's-her-face."

"That's different. Besides, you bit him to the bone, and it's been days. He's been carrying a body, in the woods. And he put animal medicine on it. That was just stupid."

"I don't think he's stupid."

"No?"

"It's not the right word."

Jack pushed out a breath. "We need to get out of here, like now, before this guy wakes up and kills us."

And it was as if Freemantle heard him.

His eyes snapped open, wide, dark, and wild. One hand stabbed out and caught Jack by the neck. His voice was a croak and he pulled Jack close. "God knows." Johnny felt the force of the words and grabbed his arm, but Freemantle's skin burned fever hot, his fingers driving into the soft parts of Jack's neck. "God knows," he said again as his fingers fell open and Jack scrambled back.

"Keep him away," Jack yelled. "Jesus Christ. Keep that crazy motherfucker off me."

Johnny was frozen. He stared until the madness left Freemantle's face. "What happened?" Freemantle looked confused, eyes now shocked and scared, chest pumping. He raised his ruined hand and stared at it as if he'd never seen it before. He lowered it into his lap, and rolled back onto his side. He ignored the boys, pulled his knees to his chest. "Where am I?"

When Johnny turned, he found Jack all the way across the barn, back jammed against the wall, small hand at his throat, good one making the sign of the cross. His lips were bled of color, eyes bright.

"We've got to go. We've got to go now."

"Are you okay, Jack?"

But Jack was washed out and blinking, the words dead in his throat. He opened his mouth, closed it and both boys stared at Freemantle, whose eyes were squeezed to tears as he shook on the cold stone. His lips moved without sense, and a spare, dry sound passed between them.

Jack crossed himself again.

Red finger marks showed on his throat.

CHAPTER FORTY-FIVE

When Hunt came back into the Chief's office, he was shaking with a rage so raw he was not sure he could contain it. He still saw the reporters' frenzy and how Yoakum had refused to blink or bow his head as they swarmed him. Hunt shoved the door, heard it drop into the frame, but the Chief had little patience for his anger. He slumped into his seat, reached back for Hunt's service weapon and put it on the desk. He pushed it forward. "That could have gone better."

Hunt stared at the gun. "I should pick that up and shoot you."

"Don't be melodramatic, Hunt. If this was your office, you'd have done the same thing."

Hunt picked up his service weapon and slipped it back into its holster. "That was an ambush, pure and simple."

The Chief flapped a hand. "You're the one who suggested that a cop might be involved."

"Involved with what?"

"Jarvis. Meechum."

Hunt pointed at the door. "That's what they think? That's what they want to talk to him about?"

"We have to protect ourselves. We have to protect the investigation and the reputation of this department. To do that, we had to bring in somebody from the outside, somebody impartial, removed. I don't like it, either, but there it is. This is how it's done."

"Who are you trying to convince? Me or you?"

"Don't give me that, you sanctimonious prick. None of it would have been necessary if you'd kept the media shut down. Kept your people quiet."

"None of my people talked."

"You're lead detective, Hunt. Anybody involved with this case is your responsibility."

"This is bullshit."

"Aren't you the one that has argued, all along, that a cop is involved with Burton Jarvis? That's what the boy saw, right? That was in his notes. A cop at Burton Jarvis's house."

"A security guard. Not a cop. We established that yesterday, the second we took Meechum down."

"Did you?"

"Did I what?"

"Did you establish that it was a security guard at Jarvis's house?"

"Obviously."

The Chief leaned back in his chair. "Whose idea was it to go to the mall?"

"Yoakum's."

"Who came up with the idea that a security guard might be mistaken for a police officer?"

"Yoakum. Both of us."

The Chief drummed his heavy fingers on the scratched surface of the desk. "Katherine Merrimon saw a car parked up the street from her house. She thought someone was watching the house. She thought it could be a cop car."

"That had to be Meechum. He drives a sedan."

"But not a cop car. Yoakum drives a cop car."

"She had an impression. That's all."

The Chief rose up in his seat, eyes tight, skin wrinkled at the

365

corners. "You'd have never found Meechum without Yoakum's deductive reasoning. Isn't that right? Yoakum led you to the mall."

"He should get a medal."

"Except, what if it's not reasoning. What if he knew?"

"Knew what?"

"What if he was involved with Jarvis and Meechum all along? Not two men working together, but three."

"That's absurd," Hunt said.

"You keep saying that."

"We need to find Johnny Merrimon. He could clear this up in a second."

"If he'll talk to you."

"He will," Hunt said. "This time, he will."

"So find the kid, and call me when you do. Call me the second he turns up. As soon as he says it wasn't Yoakum at Jarvis's house, I'll call the SBI. In the meantime, Yoakum's in the hot seat."

Hunt shook his head. "This is still wrong."

"Stop for a second and think. Burton Jarvis is dead. Meechum knew we were close because Holloway called him and told him. He was running scared. Had we taken Meechum alive, he'd have talked. Giving up a dirty cop would have bought a lot of slack from the DA. Yoakum would know that, so he'd have reason to want Meechum dead." The Chief finally rose. "Now, I'm going to ask you again. Was the shoot clean?"

"I know Yoakum."

"What have I told you about doing personal?"

"I know John Yoakum."

"Do you? Do you, really?" The Chief waited. "What does he do on the weekends? Where does he take his vacations?"

Hunt had to admit it. "I don't know. He never talks about it."

"He's never been married. Why is that?"

"How is this relevant?"

"You know," the Chief declared. "Hell, we all do. He's said it often enough."

Hunt knew the words. Yoakum said them whenever the crime was particularly vicious, the betrayal most gruesome.

Darkness is a cancer of the human heart.

"So, he's a cynic. Most cops are."

The Chief shrugged. "Maybe he was talking about himself."

The bullpen reverberated with low talk that died fast when Hunt stormed out of the Chief's office. The door crashed into the wall, knocking a picture off center. He felt the stares, the speculation; it was a weight of metal, but nobody spoke, nobody asked, so Hunt took it on himself. He stopped in the middle of the room, raised both arms. "What just happened is bullshit. If anybody asks—media, family, whoever—that's what you tell them." He spun a circle and said it loud. "Bullshit."

The word hung in the air. No one but Cross could meet his eyes, and even he was shaking his head. Hunt bit down on the angry words. Yoakum had never looked for friends in the department, never made the effort. He was a loner, a professional. What of it? What was wrong with that? He did the job. He lived his life.

Hunt left through the back door.

Already, the moisture was burning off the tarmac, off the broad, drooping leaves of a lonely tree by the edge of the road. Beyond the fence, heavy equipment shuddered and spat smoke. The lot smelled of diesel and mud and hot metal. Hunt slid into his car, started the engine, and set the air on high. He wrapped his hands around the wheel, let the cold air blast sweat on his

367

face, and pictured Yoakum as he was dragged out in cuffs. Then he pictured Johnny. Johnny's mom. He thought of how Yoakum had looked standing in that low, dank place by the river as the bodies came out. How angry he'd been. How disgusted.

No way did Yoakum have anything to do with that.

No way in hell.

He put the big car in reverse, whipped out of the slot, then racked the transmission into drive. There had to be an explanation, some reason that a shell casing found in David Wilson's wrecked Land Cruiser had Yoakum's print on it. If that explanation was anywhere, it would be at Yoakum's house. Hunt tried not to think of the other side of the same coin: If Yoakum *did* have anything to do with the missing children, that evidence would most likely be found there, too. Hunt didn't have a warrant or a key, but he didn't care. A rock through the window would do just fine. A pry bar in the door. This was not about being a cop. This was about friendship. It was about faith and trust and the sharp, hot burn that kindled at the thought of the Chief's betrayal. He'd sold Yoakum out to make the department look good, to make it look clean even as the case descended farther into the stink. "Bullshit." Hunt muttered it under his breath.

But the print . . .

He shook his head.

The print was tough.

Hunt sliced through traffic, hung a left on the four-lane that led across town. Yoakum's neighborhood was an old one, thick with bungalows that sat on elevated yards above concrete sidewalks buckled by tree roots the size of a man's leg. The neighborhood was transitional but well-kept, shaded and quiet.

Hunt decided on the pry bar.

He made a quick right and, three blocks later, a left.

Yoakum's house was one-story with a peaked roof and cedar shingles aged to dull silver. Bright color shone in the flower beds. The shrubbery was cut back, trees tended.

A blue panel truck sat in the driveway. White letters stood out against the paint.

SBI.

Hunt eased the car to the curb, still a half block away. Neighbors were in their yards: faded women in bright robes, old men, a few long-haired kids who should be doing better things. Their faces all showed the same thing: surprise, concern. At Yoakum's house, men in windbreakers with stenciled letters moved in and out of the front door. Hunt saw neither Oliver nor Barfield, but that didn't matter.

The SBI was in Yoakum's house.

They had a warrant.

CHAPTER FORTY-SIX

"He tried to kill me," Jack said. "You saw it. Jesus. That big motherfucker tried to kill me dead."

"If he wanted you dead, you'd be dead." Johnny knelt beside Freemantle. "Don't be such a girl."

"Don't touch him, Johnny. What are you doing?"

"I'm not touching him. Chill." Johnny leaned closer to Freemantle. "He's just sick." Freemantle's lips were moving, and there were words there, Johnny thought. He leaned closer.

". . . house is on fire . . . Momma's on fire . . ."

Johnny heard it.

". . . house is on fire . . . Momma's on fire . . ."

The words slipped away. Johnny looked up. "Did you hear that?"

"No."

"Come help me."

"Screw that."

"He needs medicine or a hospital."

"Fine," Jack said. "We'll go home and call the ambulance. Let them worry about it."

"If we call an ambulance, they'll call the cops and I won't find out what he knows."

"Let the cops ask him. That's their job."

"The cops want him for murder. They think Alyssa is dead. They won't ask him anything. Not fast enough anyway." Johnny pushed on Freemantle's shoulder but the man didn't stir.

"So what do you want to do?"

"I don't know, man. Alright? I'm making this up as I go. I just need one more chance. Some time, that's all. God damn it, Jack, just help me."

"Fine. What do you want me to do?"

"Watch him. I'm going to get the truck."

"That's twenty minutes."

But Johnny was already gone. Jack looked down at Freemantle's cracked lips, eyes that rolled behind paper lids. "This sucks," he said, then picked up the pistol. He pointed it at Levi Freemantle, then sat on the dirt.

Levi burned in a black fire. He knew it was fire because he'd been on fire before. He'd been on fire in a burning house, his momma in his arms, her hair gone up like a torch. He didn't know why the house was burning or why he was in it now. Seemed like that had happened a long time ago.

But he was burning.

Pain so bad it was under his skin.

He heard voices, far away; and he tried to tell them.

. . . house is on fire . . . Momma's on fire . . .

But they couldn't hear him. And nobody came to help.

Nobody came.

Skin so hot.

Burning . . .

Johnny ran all the way, and was sucking wind when he made it to the truck. He climbed in, closed the door. The key was slick between his fingers, but the engine turned over. Blue smoke rolled in the still air. Gospel on the radio. Johnny drove for the barn and left the motor running. Jack stood in the door and looked miserable.

"How are you going to get him up?"

Johnny didn't answer. He hopped out of the truck, went into

the barn, and knelt by Freemantle. He called his name, then touched his arm and looked up. "This guy's on fire."

"Duh."

"No. It's gotten worse. He's burning up."

". . . Momma's on fire . . . house is on fire . . ."

"What the hell?" Jack leaned closer. "Did you hear that?"

Johnny pointed toward the burned house. "I think his mother died in that fire." Johnny pushed on the man's shoulder one last time, shook him hard. He rocked back on his knees. "We can't get him in the truck by ourselves."

"He came around once."

"We should throw water on his face."

"That only works in the movies."

"Shit," Johnny said.

"I say we leave him here and get the hell out."

Johnny shook his head. "We wait."

"Enough's enough, Johnny."

"I stole the truck. I make the call."

So they waited, blue smoke in the air, gospel on the radio.

CHAPTER FORTY-SEVEN

Hunt drove twice through Yoakum's neighborhood, but each time he passed Yoakum's street, the SBI van still sat in the drive, so he let it go. He called Cross to check on the situation at the Jarvis site. He got him after four rings. "Yeah. The medical examiner is here. First body should be up within the hour. He thinks we'll get them all out today. Midafternoon, maybe. By sundown, for sure."

"How about media?"

"About what you'd expect. You coming out?"

"Anything to see?"

Cross paused. Voices were muffled in the background. "Not yet."

"Call me when there is."

Hunt clicked off. He was at an intersection on the poorest side of town. The houses were old, with cracks in the clapboards. Gray undershirts hung on clotheslines. He saw rusted oil tanks, granite block foundations that raised the floor joists off the damp earth. Years of debris settled beneath the nearest house, and Hunt saw a smooth spot in the dirt where dogs slid in and out. A hundred years of failed sharecroppers had settled on this side of town, and it showed. Hunt was a mile from the freed slave cemetery, surrounded by poverty and hopelessness, the lingering shadow of past injustice.

The light turned green.

Hunt did not move.

Something shifted in the back of his mind. A car honked behind him, so he drove through the intersection and pulled to the curb as the driver behind him gunned his engine and blew past. Hunt saw neon under the chassis, spinners on the hubs, and gang colors hanging from the rearview. Trustless eyes stared out of a guarded face, bass-heavy music thumped from the speakers, but Hunt forced the image out. His mind had been in the past.

Sharecroppers. Wet clothes.

The pink tongue of a mongrel in the shade . . .

He replayed the last minute.

And then he thought he had it.

He reached for the phone to call Yoakum, and then he remembered that Yoakum was in the backseat of a state cruiser halfway to Raleigh. He dialed Katherine Merrimon instead. She answered, hopeful but sounding tired. "I needed to see if you were home," Hunt said.

Sudden life. "Johnny?"

"Not yet. I'm coming over."

It took twenty-three minutes with traffic. She wore faded jeans, cut short, sandals, and a wrinkled shirt that hung from the bones of her shoulders. "You look tired," Hunt told her. And she did. Her eyes had retreated into their sockets. She had less color than usual.

"Ken showed up at three in the morning. I couldn't get back to sleep."

"Here? He came here?"

"I didn't let him in or anything. He beat on the door, made some more ugly comments. He was drunk. He just needed to bark."

An angry stillness settled behind Hunt's eyes. He knew the

look of an abused woman lying to herself. "Don't you dare make excuses for him."

"I can handle Ken."

Hunt forced himself to calm down. She was getting defensive, and there were better ways to handle the problem. "I need to go in Johnny's room."

"Okay." Inside, she led him down the dim corridor to Johnny's room. Hunt flipped on the light and looked at Johnny's bed. When he did not see what he wanted, he moved to the row of books on Johnny's dresser. He scanned the spines. "It's not here."

"What's not?"

"Johnny had a history book about Raven County. Like this." He made a shape with his hands, indicating its size. "It was on his bed a few days ago. You know anything about it?"

"No. Nothing. Is it important?"

"I don't know. Maybe." He started walking.

"You're leaving?"

"I'll stay in touch."

At the door, she laid a hand on his arm. "Listen. About Ken. I appreciate that you're being protective. If he becomes aggressive or makes threats or anything like that, I'll call you. Okay?" She squeezed his arm lightly. "I'll call."

"You do that," he said, but gears were already grinding in his mind. She stayed in the open door as he walked away, and did not go inside until his car was in the street. Her house still hung in the rearview mirror when Hunt got Officer Taylor on the phone. "I'm at Katherine Merrimon's house," he said.

"Why am I not surprised?"

"I need a favor."

"You're running out of markers."

"It's Ken Holloway. Check his office. Check his house. I want you to find him, and I want you to arrest him."

A silence followed. Hunt knew that she was replaying the last time, thinking about the lawsuit and how she'd like to keep her name off the next piece of paper filed in the Clerk's Office. "And the reason?"

"Obstruction. He tipped Meechum that we were coming to question him. I'll do the paperwork this afternoon, but I want him locked up now, as in right now. Any heat, I'll take it; but I want the bastard locked up."

"Is this arrest legitimate?"

"A week ago, you'd have never asked me that."

"A week ago, I would not have felt the need to."

"Just do it."

Hunt clicked off, then called information and asked for the number of the Raven County Public Library. The operator gave him the number, and then connected him. "Circulation desk." The voice belonged to a man. Hunt told him what he wanted and heard keys rattling on a keyboard. "That book is checked out."

"I know it is. Do you have more than one copy?"

"Checking. Yes, we do have another copy."

"Hold it for me," Hunt said. "And give me your name."

Hunt hung up the phone and steered for the library. Yoakum was out of his hands. The Jarvis site was under control. That left Johnny. A messed-up kid. A runaway with a stolen gun.

Freed slaves.

Freemantle.

Hunt knew the name because he'd seen it in Johnny's book. It had been just a glance, but he remembered the sense of it now: "John Pendleton Merrimon, Surgeon and Abolitionist." There had been another photograph on the next page. He'd barely noticed it at the time, but he had it now.

Isaac Freemantle.

And there had been a map.

Hunt accelerated, his back pressing into hot seat leather. Johnny knew where to find Freemantle, and Freemantle was an escaped convict, a killer.

Hunt reached for the lights. He blew down Main Street doing seventy-five, pulled into the lot, and left the engine running. Two minutes later, he was back with the book. He thumbed pages until he found the right one. He studied the photograph of John Pendleton Merrimon: the broad forehead, the heavy, masculine features. He wore a severe black suit and looked nothing like Johnny, except for the eyes, maybe. He had dark eyes.

Hunt read of Isaac, who chose the name Freemantle to signify his new freedom. And there was a picture of him, too, a large man in rough clothes and a slouch hat. He had massive hands and a patchy beard shot with white. Johnny had told Hunt that Freemantle was a mustee name, and Hunt thought that he could see the trace of Indian in Isaac Freemantle's features. Something in the eyes, perhaps. Or in the planes of his cheeks.

The map filled the opposite page. There was the river, the swamp, a long jut of land with water on three sides.

Hush Arbor.

Hunt compared the map in the book with the road map in his glove compartment. Hush Arbor, whatever it was, lay in the most deserted part of the county. Nothing there but woods and swamp and river. There was no record of Freemantles having a phone or utilities in Raven County, so the information could be meaningless, dated by a century and a half, but Hunt needed the kid. For a dozen reasons, he needed the kid.

Hunt put the car in gear.

Hush Arbor was north and west.

CHAPTER FORTY-EIGHT

Officer Taylor went to Ken Holloway's office first. She drove downtown and pulled into the big parking lot that framed Holloway's building on two sides. She moved slowly, looking for a white Escalade with gold letters. Didn't find it. Leaving her cruiser in front of the building, Taylor checked her belt, then walked to the big glass doors. She liked the way the belt rode on her hips. Serious metal. Heavy-duty gear. Taylor loved being a cop. The authority that came with the badge. The blue uniform that never wrinkled. She liked to drive fast. She liked to arrest bad people.

Her shoes made small, rubbery sounds on the waxed marble floor.

A woman sat behind a large reception counter, and Taylor felt her eyes all the way across the vaulted space. The woman was crisp and richly dressed, her gaze judgmental, her voice superior. "Yes?" she said, and Taylor disliked her at once.

"I'm here to speak with Ken Holloway." She used her cop voice, the one that said, *Don't make me repeat myself.*

The receptionist arched an eyebrow. Her lips barely moved. "To what is this pertaining?"

"It's pertaining to my wanting to see him."

"I see." She pursed thin lips. "Mr. Holloway is not in today."

Taylor pulled out a pad and pen. "And your name?" People hated the pad and pen. They disliked being on record with a cop. The receptionist reluctantly gave her name and Taylor wrote it down. "And you say Mr. Holloway is not in?"

"Yes. I mean, no. He is not in."

The receptionist had paled into submission, but Taylor never smiled when she used her authority. She used minimal language and kept her face neutral. "When was the last time you saw or spoke with Mr. Holloway?"

"He's not been in since sometime yesterday."

"And others in this building would be willing to confirm that?"

"I believe so."

Taylor made a slow perusal of the room: the art on the walls, the directory, the elevators. She placed a card on the counter. "Please have Mr. Holloway call that number when he comes in."

"Yes, ma'am."

Taylor held eye contact, then left the way she entered, slow and steady, one hand on the wide, vinyl belt. Back in the car, she keyed up the laptop and checked DMV records for all vehicles owned by Ken Holloway. In addition to the Escalade, he owned a Porsche 911, a Land Rover, and a Harley-Davidson. Taylor made one more sweep of the parking lot, but saw none of those vehicles. A note went in the pad, next to the receptionist's name: *probably telling the truth*.

Holloway's house was on one of the big golf courses on the rich side of town. The course was private, built around a palatial clubhouse of stone and ivy. No house on his street cost less than two million dollars, and Holloway's was the biggest, a white monolith on four acres of manicured lawn. Halfway up the drive, Taylor passed a statue of a black liveryman holding a lantern and smiling broadly.

Taylor got out of the car and mounted broad steps to the

long verandah. The front door stood open above a floor of lacquered slate. At first, there was only silence, the call of a bird; then Officer Taylor heard someone crying.

A woman.

Inside.

Taylor's hand dropped to the butt of her weapon. She thumbed off the leather strap, stepped to the open door. She saw an ax on the floor by what remained of the piano. The top of it was splintered. Blows had shattered the keyboard and ivory teeth were strewn across the carpet. Everything else looked perfect.

Taylor keyed her radio, got dispatch. She gave her location and requested backup; then she drew her weapon, announced herself, and stepped over the threshold. She smelled liquor and saw open bottles on a coffee table. One of them was empty, the other halfway.

The crying came from someplace deeper in the house. Kitchen, maybe. Or a bedroom. Taylor stepped through the arched entry into the living room. Looking right, she saw a mirror on the sofa, rails of what looked like cocaine cut out in neat rows.

Wires were torn from the guts of the piano.

"Police," she called again. "I'm armed."

She found the woman in a short hall beyond the living room. She was young, maybe nineteen, with dark roots, bleached hair, and flawless skin. Her teeth were crooked but white, her hands rough and red. She sat on the floor, crying, and Taylor saw that her eyes were very blue. "He didn't do nothing. I'm okay." Her accent was from down east. Taylor had grown up poor in the sand hills and had known a dozen girls just like her, uneducated and pretty, desperate to find some better place.

"Can you stand?" Taylor held out a hand. The girl wore a

maid's uniform, shoulder torn on the right side, buttons burst on the blouse. One cheek glowed with a red heat, and she had angry finger marks on the soft part of her arm. "Are you alone?"

The girl didn't answer.

"Did Ken Holloway do this to you?"

She nodded. "He called me Katherine. That's not my name."

"What's your name?"

"Janee. With two E's."

"Okay, Janee. You're going to be okay, but I need you to tell me what happened here." Taylor looked at the ripped shirt, the sprung buttons. Her voice was kind. "Did he rape you?"

"No."

There was something in the way she said it. The hesitation. A slyness. "Do you have a relationship with Mr. Holloway?"

"You mean?"

Taylor said nothing, and Janee nodded. "Sometimes. He can be nice, you know. And he's, like, really rich."

"You had sex with him?"

She nodded, started crying again.

"And he struck you?"

"After," she said.

"Go on."

"He gives me nice things, sometimes; and he's got these real pretty words." She sniffed. "You know what I mean? Like a gentleman." She shook her head, wiped at an eye. "I shouldn't have told him that he called me somebody else's name. He said he didn't believe me, but I think he just didn't like me catching him like that. He didn't want me knowing."

"He called you Katherine. Did he use a last name?"

"Not that I heard. You saw the piano?"

381

"Yes."

"That's how mad he got. It's like that name just set him off. He said if I told anybody, I'd be next." She compressed her lips and bleached-blond hair fell over her eyes. "He gave me an iPod once."

"Janee . . ."

"He is a very bad man."

CHAPTER FORTY-NINE

Levi was burning. His momma's hair was on fire and the flames put hot claws in Levi's face as he ran for the door. It hurt, and he screamed as they crashed through the screen and fell off the porch, house coming down behind them, everything dark, and what wasn't dark, on fire. Levi thought maybe he was burning in hell. He knew he'd done something wrong, but that was later. Wasn't it? Not now, not with his momma burning, too. He was confused and he was scared.

Hot as hell was.

Big as forever was.

But this was the house burning, and Levi knew where he was, the only place he'd ever been. He'd spent his whole life there and never left. His momma said there was nothing out there but pain, no place for somebody like Levi. So he stayed. And that's where he was. He was home. He was burning in the yard . . .

. . . dying.

He opened his eyes to see if there was crows.

Sunlight in the barn.

"He's coming around." Johnny bent over Freemantle's face as the eyes flickered open. He saw confusion, fear. "It's okay," Johnny said. "I just need to get you in the truck. Can you get up?"

Freemantle blinked. There was mud ground into the crevasses

of his scarred face. He looked up at the rafters, then through the open door. "It's okay," Johnny said. He took Freemantle's good arm and tried to help him up.

The words bled into each other, made no sense, but the white boy had good eyes, dark and deep. Levi stared into those eyes, wondering at why they made him feel better. Like he'd seen them before, like he should trust them. He sat up, and the heat tunneled through him, the pain. He was still confused, still scared; then a tower of cool air spiraled down from some high, chill place, and he heard it again.

   The voice
   God's voice.
   So clean and strong he almost wept.

"Why is he smiling like that?" Freemantle's eyes were squeezed tight, his lips stretched so wide and tight it looked as if the cracked skin might begin to bleed. Jack stepped away.

"Maybe he likes gospel. Who knows? Let's just get him in the truck." Johnny helped him stand while Jack stayed clear. Johnny dropped the tailgate and Freemantle sat down, rolled backward. "All the way in," Johnny said.

"All the way in." It was a whisper, an echo.

"That smile's not right," Jack said.

Freemantle was on his back, knees bent, arms on his chest. The smile was wide and joyful. *Innocent.* The word sprang into Johnny's mind. *Pure.* "Just get in the truck," he said, and Jack got in. He closed the door and put his back against the handle, turned so he could watch Freemantle through the rear window of the cab. Johnny slid behind the wheel.

"His lips are moving," Jack said.

"What's he saying?"

Jack unlatched the rear window and slid it open. He turned down the radio and they could hear Freemantle's voice.

"No crows."

"Close the window," Johnny said, but they could still hear him.

"No crows."

CHAPTER FIFTY

Hunt was well north of town when Cross called. He answered on the second ring. "What have you got?"

There was a moment of silence on the phone, static, then Cross said, "You'd better come down here." Another pause, voices faint in the background.

"What is it?" Hunt asked.

"First body just came out of the ground."

"Not Alyssa." Hunt felt the blackness spread.

"Not Alyssa."

"Then—"

"It's Alyssa's father." A breath. "Johnny's father."

Hunt pulled to the side of the road. The tires dropped off the tarmac and the world tilted. "Are you sure?"

Cross said nothing. In the background, Hunt heard raised voices, shouting, then Cross, yelling as well. "No reporters, no reporters. Get him out of here. Now. Get him out."

"Cross?"

Cross came back on the line. "You heard that?"

"Yeah."

"You'd better get down here."

Hunt looked down the narrow road. Heat devils rose in the distance and he saw a battered truck turn onto the blacktop. It seemed to hold perfectly still, its lower half dissolved in the shimmer.

"Detective Hunt . . ."

Johnny's dad.

"Detective?"

"Lock it down," Hunt said. "I'm en route."

He turned back onto the road, wheel hard over. What he'd been told made no sense.

Spencer Merrimon was dead.

Katherine's husband.

Dead.

Hunt blinked in the sun. None of it made any sense, but then, suddenly, it did. Hunt understood, and he felt pity rise in his throat, sorrow and certainty. He shook his head, while behind him, asphalt faded to metal, to a bright silver haze where the distant truck seemed to float.

CHAPTER FIFTY-ONE

Freemantle was still talking, voice rising over the wind and the engine. The same words. Over and over. "This guy is freaking me out." Jack turned up the radio and started punching buttons. Every station he found was for gospel or full-time preaching. He turned the knob, muttering under his breath; and Johnny heard him say, ". . . shut up, shut up . . ." He said it mad, and he said it kind of scared. He fiddled with the tuner until he'd been from one end of the dial to the other. "Can't get shit out here." He turned off the radio, leaned back, and Johnny steered for the trail out. They followed it until it turned into a road, where Jack opened the gate, then closed it behind them. He kept an eye on Freemantle, but the big man had finally gone still and quiet, fingers curled. "He's out again."

Johnny looked back once, then put the truck in gear. They rolled onto slick blacktop, a snake of road with a single yellow stripe worn through to black. Ahead, a car was parked on the side of the road. It was almost lost in the heat, but Johnny saw it pull out, turn across the road and speed away. "Want me to drop you off somewhere?"

Jack looked tempted, so Johnny tried to ignore the way his friend's face twisted, the way his right hand beat a hard rhythm on the side of the door. Jack was scared. If he wanted out, he should get out; but when Jack finally spoke, it was a verbal shrug. "Still early," he said.

And that was that.

Jack was in.

They made their way back toward town, out of the emptiness, past the old mansions and the golf courses, then west to another lonely stretch of nothing that pushed against the back of Johnny's house. Johnny found the narrow gash in the long row of pines and turned back onto dirt. Jack opened another gate, closed it, and they drove into the abandoned tobacco farm. They passed through the thin row of trees and went left when the road split. It dipped once, then rose and cut back right, to where the tobacco barn sat in the scrub. Johnny rounded the bend and stopped the truck.

A single crow sat on the peak of the roof. It opened its beak and three more landed beside it. Johnny felt Jack tense beside him, saw his fingers touch the shirt where the silver cross lay against his skin. "Just relax." Jack leaned forward to stare up through the windshield. A fifth crow flapped onto the roof. "There's wild millet in the fields," Johnny said. "Blueberries, too. Lots of acorns. It doesn't mean anything."

"You've seen them like this before? Here? All still like that?"

Johnny studied the birds. He'd never seen crows at the barn before, not like this. They were so still, all of them, marble eyes fixed on the truck, feathers shining like black glass. "They're just birds," he said, and opened the door. He picked up a stone and skimmed it at the roof. It clattered a few feet from the birds. They stared for a few seconds more, and when he stooped for another stone they lifted as a group and dropped away into the distant trees. "See."

Jack climbed out. They lowered the tailgate and roused Freemantle enough to get him out of the truck and into the barn. It took awhile, but they got him stretched out on the floor. "He smells worse," Jack said.

"Fever's still climbing."

"Now what?"

They were standing outside, trees wind-tossed and green across the scrub, earth blackened where their fire had burned two nights before. Johnny pointed. "The house is past that big rock, between those trees. Hop a creek and you'll see it."

Freemantle's voice came from inside the barn. "Hop a creek and you'll see . . ."

The boys waited but Freemantle said nothing else. He lay still in the gloom of the barn. "Are you going to talk to your mom?"

Johnny looked in at Freemantle. "I can't think of anything else to do. Maybe she can talk to Detective Hunt. I don't know, man. If she's not there, I'll bring some clean water and food. Medicine if we have any. I just need a minute. One minute where he'll talk to me."

"That's no kind of plan, Johnny."

He shrugged. "If I can't make something happen soon, we'll call an ambulance, the cops, whatever."

Jack dug the toe of one sneaker into the still-damp earth. "What if he dies? That's heavy stuff, man."

Johnny stared into the gray interior, said nothing.

"What about me?" Jack said. "What do I do?"

"Somebody needs to stay here."

"I want to go with you."

"No."

"He's asleep anyway, Johnny. What if you get in trouble? There won't be anybody to help you."

Jack's words made sense, but Johnny knew, in truth, that his friend was scared. He pulled the gun out of the truck, held it out, and Jack took it. "Just stay out of his reach," Johnny said.

Jack stared into the barn and swallowed hard. "You owe

me," he said. "I want you to remember that." But Johnny was already walking. Jack watched him slip into the trees and fade, then he turned for the barn and willed himself to step inside.

Two minutes later, a lone crow settled on the roof.

Then another.

CHAPTER FIFTY-TWO

Hunt made it through the line of reporters without serious incident. Maybe it was something in his face. Maybe it was the wall of blue that stiffened to attention as he stormed past. One reporter had already slipped past the line, and that was a screwup. One more time, and somebody would be fired. No question. Hunt would see to it himself.

Little sun touched the forest floor, which remained spongy and damp. The air itself was a moist stew. Hunt pushed hard down the slope.

Stopping at the edge of the swale, he could feel the difference in the air. Finding an adult victim was unexpected, and no one knew what to make of it. Finding Johnny's father took things to the next level.

People were processing.

Hunt saw two medical examiners from the Chapel Hill office huddled over a fresh excavation halfway across the bowl. That would be the next body. He ignored them. To the right, a cluster of tense people stood beside a seven-foot camp table that canted slightly with the slope of the ground. Cross. The Chief. Trenton Moore, the Raven County medical examiner. All three stared at Hunt, waiting.

The body bag on the ground seemed longer than the others. More full.

Hunt walked over, stopped five feet from the bag, and squatted on his heels. He remembered Spencer Merrimon, the way he'd stayed strong for his wife, the way he tamped down the guilt and pretended that it wasn't killing him from the inside out. Seems like he'd always had a hand on his son's shoulder, a quiet word of thanks for the men working to bring his daughter home. Hunt had liked the man, maybe even respected him. "Is this him?"

Every eye turned to the bag. "We think so."

"How can you tell?"

"Over here," the Chief said.

Hunt stood and they all turned to the camp table. It was brushed metal, hinged in the middle. Gear cluttered the surface: laptops, a camera bag and tripod, a few notebooks, a box of latex gloves. A number of items were sealed in plastic evidence bags. The Chief pointed at a stained wallet. "This was in his pocket. It's nylon with a Velcro seal. That helped preserve the contents." Next to the wallet, the contents had been laid out, each in its own evidence bag. Driver's license. Credit cards. A few grungy bills, some receipts. A claim check for the cleaners. Some papers, folded at one time, but open now. Hunt saw a photo of Katherine and the kids. It, too, was stained, but the faces were recognizable. Johnny looked shy, but Katherine was beaming. So was Alyssa. "Christ," Hunt said.

"We'll have the medical examiner run dental records to confirm, but I don't see any reason to doubt that it's him."

"Doc?" Hunt looked at Trenton Moore.

"The body is male, age appropriate."

Hunt looked out at the remaining flags, the men stooped above the half-exhumed body of some unnamed soul. It was now very likely that one of these bodies was Alyssa Merrimon. He turned back to the table and examined the items from the wallet. He looked through the receipts—meaningless—then came to two pieces of paper that had been folded so many times the creases were worn through. The first was a child's drawing, stick figures of a man holding the hand of a child. "I Love my Daddy," was written in an awkward hand. The bottom corner read, "Alyssa, age six."

Hunt turned to the second page.

"Addresses," Cross said. "We'll check them when we get back to the station."

Hunt saw nine addresses. The handwriting was bad, but legible. There were no names, no phone numbers. Addresses. But Hunt felt the cold tingle in the back of his skull that told him he'd been right about Spencer Merrimon. Why his body was here. Why he died, if not exactly how. Hunt knew the addresses. He knew the names that went with them.

Registered sex offenders.

The bad ones.

Cross gestured at the body bag. He was unshaven, lips turned down. "I thought this Merrimon guy ran off."

"No." Hunt placed the page on the table.

"I thought the wife blamed him so bad he skipped town."

Hunt looked again across the field of shallow graves. He lifted the child's drawing. The crayon was red. Lopsided hearts hung in the open spaces. "No," he said again. "This man knocked on the wrong door." A perfect silence, Hunt's heart swelling with respect. "This man died looking for his daughter."

CHAPTER FIFTY-THREE

Johnny stepped into the woods and felt suddenly drained. The change happened in seconds. He was confident and focused, then Jack and the barn fell away, and he found himself hungry and tired, strangely disoriented. He walked a trail that turned in unexpected places, that seemed steep when it should be flat. It was the right trail, but looked wrong. Johnny felt hot, then cold. Tree branches scraped and the creek ran fast. He slipped twice in mud, then stooped at the edge of the water. He dipped his hands and held them, wet, to his face.

He felt better when he stood.

The house winked dirty paint beyond the trees.

Detective Hunt was halfway up the slope when his cell phone rang. It was Officer Taylor, who spoke as he hiked. She told him about Ken Holloway: the damage done to his piano, the physical abuse of his cleaning lady. "That's the piano Johnny hit with the rock, right?"

"Yes."

"Well, it's ruined now."

Hunt was breathing hard, the air close and damp, pressure on his lungs. "How about the cleaning lady? Is she severely injured?"

"No," Taylor said. "And it's a miracle. You should see this place."

"Bad?"

"The guy's off his rocker. Booze and coke, looks like. He called his cleaning lady Katherine."

"And?"

"That's not her name."

"Oh, crap."

"Exactly."

"Add an assault charge and get it on the wire, ASAP. Let's find him before he hurts somebody else. And do me a favor, call Katherine Merrimon and tell her to get out of the house. Tell her to drive to the station. I'll meet her there. Tell her I need to talk to her. Tell her it's important."

"That's the thing."

"What?"

"I already tried."

Hunt felt it coming.

"No answer at her house."

Johnny stepped out of the woods and onto the old piece of roofing tin that lay in the backyard. The metal was cooked under his feet, so hot he could feel it through the rubber soles of his shoes. He stepped off and the metal made a dull popping noise. Approaching the back of the house, he checked the windows. His room was empty, window locked. Same with his mother's room. It was dark, the bed a tangle of sheets. He saw the hallway through her open door, dim light, battered Sheetrock. He ducked around the corner, moved for the front.

Ken's Escalade was in the yard. Not in the driveway, but in the yard. He'd run over the line of stunted bushes and glanced off the yard's single tree. The front fender was folded, two feet of paint peeled from the side of the vehicle. The driver's door stood open; the right tire touched the bottom step of the porch.

Johnny put his hand on the hood. Still hot.

The house was shut tight, but he heard it plain enough: a scream.

His mother.

Johnny took the steps two at a time.

Jack had his small hand on the barrel, good one on the grip. He watched Freemantle, who stretched across the floor, shifting in his sleep, muttering under his breath as his chest rose and fell. He was a dark lump in the still, hot air.

A killer, afraid of crows.

A crazy man, talking in his sleep.

God knows.

Even asleep, he wouldn't stop saying it.

Jack pressed warm steel against his cheek. Where was Johnny? Why wasn't he back?

God knows.

He wouldn't stop saying it.

Johnny's hand found the knob and it twisted as the door was yanked open from the inside. The force was unexpected and immense. It pulled Johnny across the threshold and into the room. He saw his mother on the floor, hands pinned behind her back with twists of wire. She called his name, then Holloway caught him by the throat. He had a big hand, thick fingers. Johnny couldn't breathe. He couldn't speak.

Holloway kicked the door shut, then dragged Johnny across the room as he yanked curtains closed. Johnny pulled at the fingers. His face went hot, and pressure built in his eyes. His mother called his name again. Holloway lifted him off the ground and Johnny saw the hatred. "Got you now, you little shit."

The big hand drew back, rushed in, and Johnny's world blinked out. When his vision cleared, Holloway dropped him.

He rolled onto his chest, saw a slice of carpet, Holloway's perfectly shined shoes.

His mother screamed again.

Levi stood at the river's edge. His momma was fresh buried, the dirt of her grave still under his nails, and in the deep, calloused lines that cut the palms of his hands. He was soaked with sweat, hot from digging and grief, hot from the burns beneath the gauze on his face. He'd walked into town the day before and ordered the stone that would sit above her.

Creola Freemantle, it would read.

God Knows the Beauty of Her Soul.

Levi studied the dirt on his hands. It was God's dirt, black and rich. Hush Arbor dirt. Family dirt. He rubbed his fingers together, then stepped into the water. It rose cool to his knees, then to his chest.

"God knows," he said.

And the water bore him up.

Levi sat up in the barn. The gun was leveled at his face, and the boy behind it was scared. He looked familiar, but Levi wasn't seeing too good. The world was fuzzy, tilted. He saw white skin and wild hair. Eyes that jittered.

Levi didn't know where he was, but he felt the change like he knew it was coming. He felt the air pile up above him, the coolness of it pressing down. Then the voice filled him up. *One last thing*, it said; and Levi's teeth shone white in the gloom.

He stood, and the pain became a distant thing.

The pain became a memory.

Jack drove his feet against the floor, pushed himself back into the wall. The man's eyes held an insane light, and all Jack could think of were the two people he'd killed. Blood, like paint, Johnny had said.

Like paint.

398

Jack held the gun straight out and it shook. He couldn't help it. He was saying his own prayer: *Don't make me kill him, don't make me kill him . . .*

But Freemantle made no move to hurt him. "Past that big rock, between those trees." The words came thick and slow. "Hop a creek and you'll see it." He showed ivory eyes shot with red, then limped outside. He leaned back in the door, said one last thing to Jack, and then the door was empty.

For long seconds, Jack could not move, too stunned and afraid to even think straight. When he managed to step outside, it was in time to see Freemantle stop at the edge of the woods. Scarred and standing crooked, he wore no shoes, no shirt, and his muscles twitched and rolled under skin streaked with blood and filth. One hand was swollen near to ruin and six inches of black, jagged wood stuck out of the grasping wound in his side. But Freemantle seemed oblivious. He turned back and his head tilted, good eye up and staring. Jack followed his gaze and felt a door open to some cold place in his chest.

The sun burned high in a faultless sky.

The roof was black with crows.

His mother's voice still rang in Johnny's ears when the oiled leather arced in. He felt Holloway's foot in the small of his back, and then on his arm. Johnny curled into a ball, trying to protect himself, but Holloway kicked him again, and while he did, he was talking: "No one messes with Ken Holloway."

He grabbed Johnny by the hair.

"Don't go anywhere."

He pushed Johnny back down then disappeared into the hallway, into Johnny's room. There was a scraping sound, something heavy; and when he came back, he held the lead pipe that Johnny kept under his bed.

"You think I didn't know about this? This is my house." He

struck Johnny again, lead pipe on the meaty part of Johnny's leg. "My house," he said. "No one messes with me in my own fucking house."

Ken straightened and Johnny watched him. He crossed the room, lifted a roll of silver tape from the table and tore off a ten-inch stretch. He held Johnny's mother by the hair, and she fought as he slapped the tape over her mouth. "Should have done that a week ago," he said. Then he ignored her. The mirror was on the television. Ken picked up a rolled bill, pinched a nostril and snorted two lines off the mirror. When he turned, his eyes were huge and black.

"Where's your daddy, now?"

Holloway crossed the room, pipe up, and Johnny kicked him in the shin, then in the kneecap.

His mother thrashed as Ken hefted the pipe.

Johnny screamed.

And then the front door exploded. It slammed back, loose on its hinges, and Levi Freemantle filled the frame. Yellow eyes shot with red, breathing hard, his shoulders were so wide they touched wood on either side. He looked at the raised pipe, then stepped over the threshold. Holloway shrunk in his shadow, stepped backward, and his perfect shoe touched Johnny's ribs.

Freemantle moved into the room and the smell of him filled the air. There was no limp in his step, no hesitation. "The little ones are gifts," he said, and Holloway swung the pipe as the giant man came for him. But as tall as Ken stood, he was a child to Freemantle.

Just like a child.

Freemantle caught the pipe with one hand, twisted it away, and brought it from the hip in a backhand blow that drove eight pounds of lead into Holloway's throat. Holloway staggered once, then dropped to his knees in front of Johnny. His hands rose to his neck, and when he fell, their eyes were mere inches apart. Johnny watched him try to breathe, and knew what he was feeling. He saw the awareness rise, the certainty, and then the terror. Holloway clawed at his ruined throat. His heels drummed the wall, the floor, and then fell still. The last light was pulled from his eyes, and in its place rose a shadow, a flicker, a reflection of wings.

CHAPTER FIFTY-FOUR

Hunt braked the car, cut the wheel right and felt the end drift. The car was heavy, still going fast. It slid in gravel, then shuddered across washboard dirt. Hunt took in the Escalade with its crushed fender, the front door standing wide, the darkness beyond it. He racked the transmission into park and hit the yard at a dead run, weapon out and hot. Ten feet from the door, a hot wind touched his face. Shadows flitted across the ground.

Hunt broke the plane of the door and saw Katherine, bound on the floor. Silver tape covered her mouth, and she was sucking hard through her nose. Johnny lay on the ground, filthy, bleached of color. He was bleeding, too, bruised, and the look on his face was one of pure terror. Holloway was a sack of bones beside him, either dead or close to it. Freemantle stood above them, two feet of metal pipe in his hand. Torn and bloody and fierce, he looked like a desperate man, like a killer. For Hunt, the math was easy.

Lead pipe. Cinder block.

Same thing.

The gun tracked right.

"Don't," Johnny said.

But Hunt took the shot. He fired a single round that hit high and right. It was not a kill shot. Hunt wanted him down but alive.

The shot staggered Freemantle. It drove him back, but he

stayed up. Hunt stepped closer, weapon trained, but Freemantle made no aggressive move. A strange emotion crossed his face, confusion, then something like joy—sunlight, if such a thing were possible. His hand rose, fingers spread. He looked past Hunt, to the clear blue sky and the high yellow sun. He stood long enough to say a single word.

"Sofia."

Then he folded at the knees, dead before he hit the floor.

CHAPTER FIFTY-FIVE

When Hunt called it in, there was no way to keep it quiet. He needed cops, paramedics, the medical examiner. Word spread like a brush fire, and the reporters made a mass exodus from the road in front of the Jarvis site. An escaped convict was dead, so was the richest man in town. The bodies were in Johnny Merrimon's house.

Johnny Merrimon.

Again.

Hunt had to cordon off the street. He gave himself a quarter mile on each side of the house and put marked cars across the narrow road. He called in for barricades and had them erected, too. The day moved to midafternoon.

Hunt asked a few necessary questions, then gave Katherine and Johnny into the care of the paramedics. They were battered, both of them. Johnny could barely stand, but the paramedics thought they would be okay. In pain for a long time, but okay. Hunt kept his own feelings tamped down: his concern and relief, some stronger emotions that he was not prepared to deal with. He checked to make sure that the cordon was secure, then went back into the house.

Holloway was dead.

Freemantle, dead.

Hunt thought of Yoakum, and wanted to ask Johnny if Yoakum had been the man he'd seen at Jarvis's house. But he didn't have a photograph of Yoakum, and the kid was still in shock, so he left Johnny alone. He coordinated the photographers, the crime scene techs, and for the first time in his career, he felt overwhelmed. Ronda Jeffries, Clinton Rhodes, David Wilson. The children buried behind the Jarvis house. Jarvis himself. Meechum. Now Freemantle and Holloway. So much death, so many questions. When the Chief arrived, he stared first at Holloway, whose lips had pulled back beneath wide, glazed eyes, then at Freemantle, who, even in death, seemed massive and unstoppable.

"Another fatal shooting," the Chief said.

"I didn't hit him that hard. He shouldn't be dead."

"But he is."

"So fire me."

The Chief stood for a long minute. "One more dead convict."

"What about Holloway?"

The Chief stared at Holloway's swollen features. "He was beating the boy?"

"And the mother."

Sadness moved on the Chief's face, disappointment. "I think that maybe Yoakum was right."

"How's that?"

"Maybe darkness *is* a cancer of the human heart."

"Not always," Hunt said. "And not with everyone."

"Maybe you're right." The Chief turned away. "Or not."

An hour later, Hunt gave the news about Johnny's father. He told Katherine first, because he thought that was the right thing to do. She needed to get her head around the man's death in order to help her son do the same. She needed to be there for the boy. He told her in the yard, lost in the bustle of cops and paramedics. She took it well. No tears or wailing. A silence that lasted a full five minutes; then a question, her voice so weak he barely caught it.

"Was he wearing his wedding ring?"

Hunt didn't know. He called over the medical examiner and spoke quietly as Katherine watched her son, who was still being treated at the rear of an ambulance. When Hunt approached, she faced him again, and she was as thin as glass.

"Yes," Hunt said, and he watched her bend.

When Johnny was able, she and Hunt led him to the backyard, to a quiet place far from anyone's view. She sat beside him on the patchy grass and held his hand as Hunt told Johnny what they'd found in the woods behind the Jarvis house.

"He was looking for Alyssa," Hunt said, then paused, the moment full of meaning. "Just like you."

Johnny said nothing, those big eyes black and still.

"He was a brave man," Hunt said.

"And Jarvis killed him?"

"We think so." Hunt looked from mother to son. So alike. "If there's anything I can do . . ."

"Can you give us a minute?" Katherine asked.

"Of course," Hunt said, and left.

They watched him disappear around the house, and Katherine moved closer to her son. Johnny stared at a blank spot on the back of the house. She ran a hand through his filthy hair, and it took Johnny a minute to realize that she was crying. He thought he understood, but he was wrong.

"He didn't leave us," she whispered.

She swiped at her eyes, repeated herself, and then Johnny understood.

He didn't leave us.

Something vast and unspoken passed between them, and they shared that silent communion until footsteps stirred in the woods and Jack stepped off the trail. He was muddy, as if he'd fallen in the creek. He looked very small, and his eyes darted from the house to the sky before he saw them, sitting so still in the shade. He stumbled as he walked, then stopped five feet away. Johnny opened his mouth, but Jack raised a hand, then spread his palms.

"I know where she is," he said.

Nobody moved, and Jack swallowed hard.

"I know where she is."

CHAPTER FIFTY-SIX

Hunt was doubtful. He stared down, but Jack was resolute. "It was the last thing Freemantle said."

"Tell me again." Hunt crossed his arms. They were still in the backyard, out of sight near the woods. Katherine was in shock. Johnny's muscles were locked, his face flushed.

"He was asleep in the barn and then he woke up and went outside. I followed him." Jack looked at Johnny, then quickly looked away. "I followed him."

"But not to the house," Hunt said.

"I was scared." Jack said nothing of the birds. He did not mention the way they carpeted the roof of the barn, intent and unmoving. His fear of the crows was too much, too personal.

Hunt shook his head. "He could have been talking about anything."

Katherine held her son tight, but Johnny struggled. "He had her name tag when we found him. It was from the shirt she was wearing when she disappeared. Her name was on it."

"You've told me your story," Hunt said. "Right now, I'm talking to Jack." He gestured at the boy. "Did he mention Alyssa by name?"

"No."

"Tell me exactly what he said."

Jack looked from Hunt to Johnny, then back. He swallowed hard. "North Crozet Shaft. That's what he said."

"Word for word, Jack. That's how I want it."

Jack stammered once, then got it. "She's in the North Crozet Shaft."

"And you know for certain—"

"He was talking about Alyssa," Johnny interrupted. "We'd asked him about her before. That's what he meant. It has to be what he meant."

Hunt frowned. "You also said that he heard God's voice in his head. You see my problem."

"We have to try."

Hunt knew about the North Crozet Shaft. They all did. It was the last of the great gold mines, the richest ever worked in Raven County. Dug in the early 1800s by a Frenchman named Jean Crozet, it was a vertical shaft that plummeted seven hundred feet, straight down before branching out to follow the course of the vein. It was located in a barren patch of woods in a far northern part of the county. Hunt had toured the area once and remembered tall trees and granite outcrops, dynamite rooms built into the hillsides, and the shafts, lots of shafts. Of all the shafts—and there were dozens—North Crozet was the deepest and the most storied. In continuous operation for two decades, it killed four men and yielded the greatest fortune ever dug from North Carolina soil. Jean Crozet was a local legend. Streets were named for him, a wing of the library.

The whole area had once been open to the public as a historic site, but the state closed it down three years ago when shafts began collapsing and a geologist from Chapel Hill declared the entire area unsafe. North Crozet Shaft was not far from where they'd found David Wilson's body. From the shaft to the bridge was twelve minutes at high speed. Maybe fifteen. Hunt looked at the sky. The sun would be down in four hours. "It's late," he began.

But Katherine placed a hand on his arm. "Please."

Hunt hesitated.

"Please."

He looked away from the desperation in her eyes. He saw the medical examiner exit the house and said, "Wait here." He cornered Trenton Moore in a patch of sun at the side of the house. "David Wilson," he began. "You said he was a climber."

Moore squinted, shifting gears from one case to another. "Everything was consistent with that."

"Could he get the same physical characteristics from caving? The fingertips? The musculature?"

"Spelunking? Sure. A lot of climbers get into caving. Different world, different challenge." He shrugged. "Climbers go up, cavers go down. It's all climbing."

Hunt returned to the small, anxious group by the trees. He looked at the sky, then at his watch. Katherine, he could tell, was trying not to beg. Johnny looked like he might sprint for the woods if Hunt said no. "A quick look," he said. "That's all I can promise."

"What about me?" Jack asked.

"I've called your father. He's on his way here."

"I don't want to see my father."

"I don't blame you," Hunt said. "He's very angry. Your mother has been distraught."

"You don't understand." Jack tried again.

"I'll put you in a cruiser if I have to. Do I need to do that?"

Jack went from frightened to sullen. "No."

"Then stay."

He said it like he was talking to a dog.

Jack watched them go. Johnny looked back once and raised a hand. Jack did the same, and then Hunt put them in the back of his car. Hunt leaned in, said something, and Jack saw Johnny and his mother lie flat, probably to get past the reporters. He watched the car turn for the north barricade, saw them pass through and disappear. To the south, the second barricade opened and Jack's father drove through. The car moved with slow resolve and the sun was bright on its paint. Jack saw a hint of his father through the glass, then he slipped back into the woods and disappeared.

He knew what was coming and he couldn't handle it.

Not just now.

Not sober.

Johnny rode in the back with his mother. She kept her back straight and locked. Her hands were bloodless. Hunt drove north and slightly west. Cold air blasted from the vents and he watched Katherine's eyes when he could. There was hope there, but not much. Jack was wrong or he was not. Either way, the shaft was seven hundred feet straight down, its lower depths flooded with cold, black water.

Not much chance of a happy ending.

He slowed as they crossed the bridge where David Wilson had been killed. Johnny looked out the window, but no one else did. The river mirrored the high blue sky; the banks were muddy and lush. A mile more and the road began to rise. It curled away from the river, up into the low hills where fields fell away and trees thickened to uncompromising forest. There was not much pine in this part of the county. The forest was hardwood on rocky soil, empty and undeveloped. It's not that it wasn't pretty—it was—but the water table lay deep beneath the granite, and wells were expensive. Still, a few people lived here. They passed a handful of small houses set back in the woods, a trailer or two, but soon even those became sparse.

Hunt turned onto a narrow state road and crossed a single-lane bridge that spanned a small creek. Deeper into the forest, the sky diminished to a narrow strip. It was almost five. The sun would be down by eight.

"Almost there," he said.

Katherine squeezed her son.

They passed a dilapidated sign that read: RAVEN COUNTY MINES HISTORICAL SITE, TWO MILES. Someone had spray-painted the word "Closed" in white paint across the front of the sign. Bullet holes pocked the surface.

The road crossed another small bridge, then turned to dirt. On the right, a battered trailer sat on blocks under the trees. It was a single-wide, old, with a beater truck parked at the front door. A propane tank was hooked onto the front of the trailer. Lawn chairs sat on a flat place by the creek. A young-ish man leaned on the tailgate of the truck. In his twenties, unshaven, he was thin and burned by the sun. He held a can of beer in one hand; the bed of the truck was full of empties. Johnny raised a hand as they passed and the man raised his, too, squint-eyed but friendly. A young woman stepped onto the porch behind him. She was mean-faced and fat. Johnny raised his hand again, but she ignored it and stared after them until a bend in the road plucked her back into the woods.

"Some people don't like strangers," Hunt said. "And few people make it out this far. Don't worry about it."

A mile later, they hit the abandoned parking area. Weeds pushed through the gravel. There was a large map under a covered area and Johnny started toward it. "I know where the shaft is," Hunt said. "The main trail goes right to it."

They walked for ten minutes, slowly, then passed a series of warning signs before the ground simply opened up. The shaft was twelve feet across. Abandoned track stretched away into the woods. The rails were narrow gauge and rusted, overgrown.

They settled on rotting ties that still smelled of creosote and oil.

Johnny edged closer to the shaft. Sections of earth had collapsed at the rim. The ground was gravelly and loose underfoot.

"Don't."

He looked at his mother, leaned out. The air that struck his face was cool and damp. He saw the rock sides drop away into blackness. "We came here in school," he said. "There were ropes, then. To keep the kids back."

The posts were still there, set into concrete; but the ropes were gone, either stolen or rotted. He remembered the day. Overcast. Cool. Teachers made the kids hold hands and none of the girls wanted to be stuck holding Jack's. Johnny could see it. Kids leaning over the safety rope, waiting for the teacher to turn away, then tossing rocks in the pit.

Jack had been standing over there.

"Johnny." Her voice had an edge. She was wrapped into herself, worried.

Johnny stepped back and let his gaze wander to the place where Jack had stood, dejected. It was near the wood's edge, away from the other kids. He'd had his back to the class and he'd been staring at a small square of rusted iron secured with rivets to a slab of naked rock. Jack had been staring at the sign, pretending not to cry.

Hunt edged closer to the edge of the shaft and Johnny walked to the sign. It was original and dated back to the time the mine had been in operation. Letters were beaten into the metal. Jack had been tracing them with one of his small fingers. Johnny remembered how the finger had come back stained red with rust.

"I see pitons." Hunt leaned out, and Johnny realized that

413

he'd seen them, too: thirty feet down, metal still bright from the hammer blows. But the knowledge was distant, like Hunt's voice.

Johnny stared at the sign. He saw letters scored into the metal, rust, Jack's stunted finger, stained at the tip. He felt wind at his back. Hunt was on the phone.

"This is it," Johnny said, but no one heard him.

He stared at the sign and reached out a finger of his own. The letters marked the sign. The sign marked the shaft.

"She's here."

The name of the shaft was abbreviated, and Johnny traced the letters.

No. Croz.

His finger came back red.

No crows.

CHAPTER FIFTY-SEVEN

Hunt called in favors and kept it quiet. In less than an hour he had two off-duty firefighters in personal vehicles loaded with gear. Trenton Moore, too, rolled personal. Hunt hiked back to the lot and used bolt cutters from his trunk to cut the cable that blocked the trail. The first firefighter drove a dark blue Dodge Ram. He forced it up the trail, branches screeching on paint, then turned the truck around and backed almost to the lip of the shaft. The second one drove a Jeep. They were unloading rope when the medical examiner parked and got out of a station wagon lean enough to save its paint. Hunt looked at Katherine to see what effect the medical examiner's presence had on her, but she was beyond worry. She watched the big firefighters strap on web harnesses and snake thick coils of rope over the lip of the shaft. Then she sat down beside her son.

Hunt huddled with the firefighters next to the shaft. They were young men, and strong; but light was dying fast. "Down and out," Hunt said. "We don't know what this is, so no bullshit heroics."

The older firefighter was in his thirties. He clipped a final carabiner onto his harness. He wore a headlamp and carried a second light clipped to the harness. Their ropes were hitched to the back of the Dodge. He leaned on both to make sure they were secure. "A walk in the park, Detective."

"Shaft is seven hundred feet."

"Got it."

"Flooded at the bottom."

The fireman nodded. "A stroll."

Hunt stepped back, and then they were over, into the shaft. They called out to each other as they dropped, voices fading to hints, then gone. Hunt leaned out and watched the lights drop away. They lit the shaft in narrow arcs that constricted as the shaft swallowed them.

Hunt looked at Johnny. He was rocking where he sat. His eyes were glazed and his mother was crying. He watched them as the rope played out.

It didn't take long.

Hunt's radio crackled. He cranked down the volume and turned his back. "Go ahead."

"We've got something here."

It was the older fireman. Hunt looked once at Katherine. "Talk to me."

"Looks like a body."

Johnny watched a cloud as Hunt stood above them in the gathering gloom and talked of what the climbers had found. The cloud was orange on the bottom and shaped like a submarine. The orange faded to red. Wind pulled the cloud into something shapeless and flat.

"Johnny?"

That was Hunt, but Johnny couldn't look at him. He shook his head, and Hunt talked some more. Johnny watched the cloud twist. He heard something about the shaft having collapsed a hundred and twenty feet down, something about choke points and shifting rock. It was unstable. He got that. Johnny's head moved when Hunt spoke of a body that was wedged above the bottleneck. There was talk of bringing it up.

But it couldn't be Alyssa. It couldn't be like that, not like it was with his father. That's not how it was supposed to end.

Then Hunt said, "We can't make an identification yet."

That was good. That sounded hopeful.

But Johnny knew.

And so did his mother.

He looked away from the cloud and she squeezed his hand. Johnny stood. He watched the rope, and how weight came on it from some place deep in the ground. There was a winch on the truck, and it turned slowly with a small, electric-motor noise. Hunt tried to convince them to wait in his car, to let somebody take them home. His hand was shockingly warm on Johnny's arm; but Johnny refused to move. He listened to the slow grind of the winch; and that's what Hunt's voice sounded like, a whir, a hum. Johnny's mother must have heard it that way, too, because they were there when it happened.

Both of them.

Together.

The body came up as the last edge of sun dipped below the tallest tree. It was in a black vinyl bag that looked too empty to hold a human being. Hunt allowed them to come closer, but kept himself between them and the bag, even as it was loaded into the back of the station wagon. A small man with expressive eyes looked once their way, then shut the tailgate and started the engine to keep the inside cool.

Johnny felt dizzy and sick. Shadows stretched. His mother allowed Hunt to put her in another car and Johnny knew that she had nothing for him. She was struggling to breathe.

But not Johnny. Johnny was numb. He stared at the hole as the heavy rope went back into the shaft. It played out from the winch, and then it stopped. Hunt was still at the car with Johnny's mother when the bicycle came out. It was rusted and bent, but Johnny recognized it. It had yellow paint and a banana seat. If he looked closely, he would see that it had

three gears. But Johnny didn't need to look; he knew the
bike.

Jack's bike.

That he said was stolen.

CHAPTER FIFTY-EIGHT

Johnny's body shut down. His chest forgot to move and things went black at the edge of his vision. He stared at the bike and remembered all the times he'd seen Jack on it, how he bitched about the fact that it only had three gears, how he sat cockeyed to compensate for his small arm. He called it the piss bike, because of the color. But he'd loved it.

Hunt was huddled with the others by the cars. Nobody was looking, so Johnny touched the bike. It was small, yellow. He touched rust and cold metal, rubber tires cracked by rot.

The bike was real.

Johnny turned and threw up in the weeds.

All of this was real.

Hunt was listening to one of the firefighters. "The bike went in first and jammed in the bottleneck. Looks like the body went in after. Without the bike, it might have gone all the way down. Another six hundred feet, all that water." The fireman shook his head. "We'd have never found it."

"Is it Alyssa?" Hunt looked to the medical examiner.

"It's a girl," Moore said. "Approximately the right age. I'll check dental records tonight. First thing."

"You'll call when you know?"

"Yes."

Hunt nodded. He looked for Johnny, didn't see him, then did. He was on his knees in the brush.

"Oh, no."

Hunt got Johnny cleaned up and in the car. He sent the medical examiner away with the body and had the firefighters wrap the bike in a tarp and put it in Hunt's trunk. That's where it was now, a rattle when the car hit a rough spot, a question in the back of Hunt's mind. He shook his head as he drove.

"I shouldn't have let you come," he said, but no one answered. Hunt knew his reasons, and knew, still, that it was a mistake. He was too close. Emotionally engaged. His head moved again. "I shouldn't have let you come."

They were halfway back to town before Johnny was able to speak. He listened to the wind, to the tires on smooth pavement. "It's Jack's," he said.

Hunt turned as he drove. Johnny and Katherine were black figures in the back of his car. The road was empty. "What did you say, Johnny?"

Johnny looked out the window. A field stretched out beneath a high scatter of small, pale stars. The grass was unmoving and looked purple. Nothing made sense. "The bike is Jack's."

Hunt pulled the car to side of the road and stopped. He put the transmission in park and killed the engine. Johnny reached for the handle, but there was no handle. "Open the door," he said, then heaved again. But there was nothing left. He was empty, drained. Hunt got him out and walked him on the road's edge. "Breathe," Hunt said. "Just breathe."

After a minute, Johnny straightened.

"You're going to be okay," Hunt told him, and his voice was comforting. He walked Johnny down the road and back. He kept one hand on his arm, the other on his neck. "You're okay. Alright? You're okay."

Johnny was shaky, but he nodded. "I'm okay." They got back in the car and Hunt turned on the air for Johnny. Johnny put his face near the vent.

"Better?"

"Yes, sir."

"Tell me about the bike."

Johnny sat under the dome light and looked at the shadows that spilled off Hunt's face. The light was stark but small, the shadows hard-edged. "Jack had the bike forever. He got it old, used. It disappeared about the time Alyssa went missing. He said it was stolen. I didn't even think about it, the timing, I mean."

"And you're certain that this is Jack's bike?"

"Yes," Johnny said. "I am."

Hunt looked from Johnny to Katherine. "Jack's the one that saw Alyssa pulled into a van. He's the only witness to the abduction. Now, we have his bike . . ."

"What are you saying?" Katherine was stretched to the breaking point. Johnny touched her arm and felt heat.

"Maybe it was not an abduction."

Wind licked in the open window.

"Maybe Jack lied."

Hunt turned off the interior light and pulled back onto the road. He rolled his window up and it made the same electric-motor noise as the winch. When Hunt's phone rang, he stared for long seconds at the caller ID. His foot was steady on the gas. "It's Detective Cross," he said, and lowered the phone as his eyes rose to the rearview mirror. "It's Jack's father."

"What are you going to do?" Katherine asked.

The car ran smooth. "My job."

Hunt answered his phone. He listened for a few seconds. "No. I'm tying up some loose ends. Nothing important."

Johnny saw Hunt's eyes in the mirror. He was watching the road. Calm.

"No," Hunt said. "I don't have any information on that.

No. He was at the Merrimon house the last time I saw him."

A pause. Johnny heard Cross's voice through the phone. Indistinct. Another hum.

"Yes," Hunt said. "I will absolutely let you know." Hunt said goodbye and hung up the phone. Eyes in the mirror. Dash lights on the side of his face. He caught Johnny's eye. "He's looking for Jack," Hunt said. "It looks like your friend's gone missing."

Johnny's mom raised her head, put a hand on the seat. "What does this mean? I don't understand what this means?"

"I don't know yet, but I will."

She settled back and they rode in silence for a long time. Johnny tried to adjust to this new idea, the thought that somehow Jack had lied, that he knew something, anything. Johnny felt betrayed. He felt anger, and then doubt. No way, he thought. Jack had been squirrelly lately, freaked out by Freemantle and Johnny's recent behavior, freaked out by crows, for fuck's sake. But Jack was Jack. Jack was slicked hair and stolen cigarettes. He was Johnny's best friend, full of loyalty, hurts, and secret shames, but a friend who knew what it meant to be a friend. He'd helped Johnny look for Alyssa a hundred times. Ditched school. Snuck out late. This could not be right.

But the bike.

Jesus, the bike.

Johnny studied the side of Hunt's face. He was a good guy but he was a cop; and Johnny, too, knew what it meant to be a friend. So he said nothing about the tobacco barn or the truck parked in front of it. Johnny needed to talk to Jack first.

Hunt rolled into town, lights rising up on the roadside, stars fading out. Traffic thickened. "Our house is the other way," Johnny said.

"It's a crime scene. It's sealed."

The street widened out and Hunt turned onto the four-lane that bent around the edge of town. He pulled into the parking lot of a low-end chain motel and Johnny saw his mother's station wagon parked near the front. "I had it released from impound," Hunt said. "The keys are waiting at the front desk. The department's picking up the room." He steered for the portico and the glass doors. A red neon sign read VACANCY. "You'll have your house back in a few days."

"I don't want to go back there. Not even once. Not ever."

"We'll figure something out," Hunt said.

"What about Social Services?" Her voice was bleak.

Hunt put the car in park and turned off the engine. The red light was bright on the glass, and it was quiet in the car. Hunt turned in his seat, looked at Johnny's mother. "Let's worry about that tomorrow."

She nodded.

"Are you guys going to be okay?" Hunt looked from one face to another and Johnny felt a level of affection that surprised him. He didn't want Hunt to leave. He didn't want to be in a crap motel. He wanted to be home. Not Ken's house. Home. He wanted Hunt to say, one more time, that it would be alright.

"What happens now?" Johnny asked.

"I'm not sure yet. I'll come by tomorrow. I'll know more then."

"Okay." Johnny reached for the door.

Hunt stopped him. "I need the gun, Johnny."

"What gun?" It was instinct.

Hunt spoke softly. "Your uncle's gun. The one you took out of his truck. You don't have it with you or I'd have asked you sooner. It needs to be accounted for."

423

Johnny almost lied, but didn't. "Jack has the gun."

"Are you sure?"

"Yes."

"That's unfortunate."

"He won't do anything stupid."

Hunt nodded, but it was not a good nod. "Good night, Johnny. Good night, Katherine."

They got out of the car, alone in the neon.

CHAPTER FIFTY-NINE

The police station was close to empty when Hunt arrived. Night patrols were on the street. Office staff was at the minimum. The desk sergeant was an older man named Shields, a burnout and a short-timer. He didn't give Hunt the questions another sergeant might have, didn't care about the things that happened earlier in the day. Hunt asked for the phone logs and Shields handed them over.

Hunt spent thirty minutes with the logs but didn't find what he was looking for. He was at his desk, about to leave, when Yoakum walked in. He wore the same clothes and looked tired. "Look what the cat dragged in," Hunt said.

Yoakum sat opposite Hunt and popped the top on a can of Pepsi. "They dropped the assault charge."

"That's good."

"It was bullshit anyway."

"They searched your house," Hunt told him. "They brought in an entire team to do it. Six people, maybe more."

"Did they pick up after themselves?"

"One can only hope."

Yoakum shrugged. "Not much to see in my house."

Hunt thought of the day Yoakum had suffered: dragged out in cuffs, interrogated. His friend. A cop. "How was the rest of it?"

Yoakum sipped, took his time. "Raleigh's a daisy of a town."

"I should go there more often."

"Pretty girls."

"I bet."

"So." Yoakum looked around. "What did I miss?"

"Not much."

Yoakum saw the lie. "Really?"

"I think I know how your fingerprint ended up on a shell casing in David Wilson's car."

"You think?"

"Call it a theory."

"A theory would be timely."

"Yes."

"Are you messing with me?"

Hunt stood. "Let's take a ride."

Yoakum stood, too. "I get goose bumps when you say that."

Everything in the hotel room was limp: sheets, curtains, air pumping from the window unit. The rug was dark and patterned and smelled of other people. They'd checked in and said nothing to each other. There was too much, and not enough. She'd kissed him once on the forehead, then locked herself in the bathroom.

The shower was running.

Her car keys were on the table.

Johnny stood in the slash of red light that cut between the curtains. He stared at the keys and thought of Jack. He thought of the things they had shared, and he thought of Jack's bike. Cold metal and rust. Rubber rotted through.

Johnny looked outside. A half-moon hung in the clear night sky. The red light flickered. What would his father do if he was Johnny? How about Hunt?

What if they knew where to find Jack?

A friend.

A liar.

Johnny listened to the shower run. He wrote a note to his mother, then slipped through the door and locked it.

The car keys were heavy in his hand.

Hunt talked as he drove. Town fell behind them and the dark spread out as he steered for the mines. He told Yoakum everything and Yoakum took it in. What happened at Johnny's house. The body in the shaft. Jack's bike. All of it. Then he gave his theory. When he was finished, Yoakum said, "There are holes in what you're saying."

"Not many, and not for long."

"It's pure speculation."

"But easy to check." They crossed the same river, same bridge. "I'm tired of this."

Yoakum frowned. "Cross is a cop. I can't buy it."

Hunt drove in silence. "When David Wilson's body turned up, Cross is the one who pointed me at Levi Freemantle. He stood under that bridge with a map and showed me exactly what I needed to see. I went off on a wild goose chase for an escaped convict who had nothing to do with any of this."

"You sure Freemantle had nothing to do with it? He's the one that told Cross's kid where to find the body. He told Jack about the mine shaft."

Hunt looked sideways. "Did he? We don't know what happened between those two."

"So, Jack just knew?"

The tires hammered a rough spot on the pavement. "His bike," Hunt said. "I'm guessing he knew."

"But why would he tell? He's implicated himself."

Hunt had no answer.

"You think Cross killed David Wilson?" Yoakum asked. "You really believe that Cross ran him into the abutment?

Drove him off the bridge, then stood on his throat? That's hard-core stuff, Clyde, premeditated murder. Cross is not my favorite guy, but he's still a cop."

"Wilson had climbing gear and a dirt bike. I think he spent the day riding trails and exploring different mine sites. I think he saved the biggest, deepest shaft for last. I think he found Alyssa's body and finding it got him killed."

"It's thin, Clyde."

"Who found Wilson's Land Cruiser?"

"Cross."

"That's right. He said it was a drunk out shining deer. The drunk called it in from a pay phone and got Cross. No ID on the caller. Public phone. Convenient, don't you think?"

"Cops get lucky. That's what makes the job work half the time. I don't see you bitching when it's you that catches the break."

"Do you ever see Cross at the shooting range?"

"Of course."

"You ever fire your personal weapon at the range?"

"Oh, shit."

"Could he have picked up one of your casings?"

Yoakum had no easy response. He pictured how it was at the range: ear protectors, safety glasses, the narrow concentration, the target, and nothing else.

Hunt continued, voice sharp. "Word got out that I was looking for a cop. So Cross gave me a cop. He gave me David Wilson's car and a shell casing with a print on it. He gave me you."

Yoakum said nothing. Personal did that to him sometimes.

"We're close."

Yoakum stared out the window. "What do you know about these people we're going to see?"

Hunt turned right and the road shrank. Ahead was a sign, white spray paint and the word "Closed." "We drove past them on the way in, a man and a woman. He likes beer. She's ugly as stink. They live in a busted-up trailer near the entrance to the mines. One vehicle when I was here before. As far as I can tell, they're the only ones that live anywhere near the mine. Other than that," Hunt said, "I know nothing."

"Nothing?"

"Not even their names."

"Then why are we here?"

"Geography." Hunt crossed a narrow bridge over a small creek. "It's the only thing that makes sense." The road went to dirt. Small rocks clicked and banged on the undercarriage of the car. "Coming up," Hunt said.

"The Chief still has my weapon."

"Glove compartment."

Yoakum opened the glove compartment and retrieved Hunt's personal weapon. He racked the slide, checked the load. "Nice."

"Try not to kill anybody this time."

Hunt saw the old trailer, the pickup full of empty beer cans. Lights burned behind dirty windows. Inside the trailer, somebody moved. He killed the lights and coasted to a stop behind the truck. Keeping one eye on the trailer, he keyed in the license number on the truck. "Registered to Patricia Defries. Some misdemeanor convictions. Public urination. Drunk and disorderly."

"Lovely."

"Two felony counts."

"What kind?"

"Check kiting and fraud. One more felony and she goes down hard. Three strikes. That could give Cross leverage if he caught her doing something dirty."

"How do we play it?"

"Easy." Hunt opened his door. "We lie."

Yoakum tucked the gun away as they stepped onto the small porch. Through the window, they saw a long, low sofa, man on it, feet up. He looked the same to Hunt. Scrawny and unshaven. Dirty. He had a sunken chest and skinny legs, what could be the same beer can in his hand. The television put blue light on his face. The woman, too, was as he remembered. Short skirt. Mean face. From the way she was standing, she was angry about something. Hands on her hips. Mouth running. She stepped in front of the television and the man leaned left. "Domestic bliss," Yoakum said.

Hunt knocked on the door and the television winked out. He stepped back as the woman's heavy step put a vibration in the cheap structure. Her face filled the small window: brown teeth, bad skin.

"Be still, my heart," Yoakum whispered.

Hunt put his shield against the glass. Bolts dropped on the inside and the woman appeared behind the torn screen. "Hold it up again," she said.

Hunt held up the badge. "Detective Cross sent us."

The woman lit a cigarette, blew smoke. Her eyes ran over Hunt, then up Yoakum and back down. "What does he want now?"

"May we come in?"

She looked them over one more time, took another pull on the cigarette. "Wipe your feet."

There was no truck in front of the tobacco barn. No Jack. In the weak light from the car's one headlight, Johnny saw a single splash of color, his blue backpack. It was filthy, still stained at the bottom. Jack had placed it neatly in the center of the barn door. Johnny got out of the car, but left it running. The moon was giant and low and silver white. The air smelled of gasoline and burned oil.

Johnny picked up the bag, which felt empty. Opening it, he caught a whiff of dead bird. In the bottom was a note, written on the back of a receipt with Uncle Steve's name on it. The handwriting was Jack's.

Meet me at the place.

The past few years were full of places, but Johnny knew the one. It's where they went to drink beer and tell stories, the place they went to escape. It was the place that David Wilson died in the dust. The place this all began.

He turned in the scrub and the car bottomed out.

Johnny drove for the river.

He passed few cars. It was late. Large bugs clacked on the windshield and his vision blurred more than once. He was exhausted, stretched so thin that he almost missed the turn off the main road. The track was overgrown and rutted, weeds still bent from the cop cars that came for David Wilson. It dropped steeply toward the river, bridge rising on the left. Washouts twisted the wheel in Johnny's hand as the track fell away from the road. He saw the truck forty feet in, a ghost in the brush. The cab was dark and empty. Johnny turned off the car lights and got out. He walked past the truck and looked down on the river. Moonlight rose off the water and the rocks were slabs of silver gray. Blackness gathered beneath the bridge.

Johnny slid down the bank, hit a patch of sand, then walked out onto one of the broad flat rocks. Water moved, and something dark floated past. The willow was to his right, bridge to the left. He didn't see Jack.

"I'm over here, Johnny."

The voice drifted out from beneath the bridge. Jack's voice. Drunk sounding. Once under the bridge, Johnny could see him.

He sat at the edge of the water. One of the pilings came down from the bridge there; it had a narrow concrete shelf and Jack was sitting on it, feet trailing in the water. Johnny stopped twenty feet away. Jack was a blur, a hint of a face. He lifted a bottle and Johnny heard liquor gurgle. "Want some?"

"What the hell is going on, Jack?" Johnny wanted to stay calm, but he was losing it already. Alyssa was dead and Jack was drinking bourbon. Jack slid down off the concrete. He splashed out of shallow water, tripped once, and fell to a knee. "Come out here where I can see you." Johnny stepped out from under the bridge. Part of him wanted to talk. Part of him wanted to hit his only friend in the face.

"I'm sorry, man." His words were so sloppy Johnny could barely understand them. "Johnny, man." Jack stepped out into the moonlight. He was wearing the jacket he'd borrowed from Johnny. His pants were wet to the waist. He stumbled again and dropped the bottle. It smashed on the rocks and a liquor-smell rolled over the mud. Jack sat next to the broken bottle. "I'm so damn sorry."

"Sorry for what?" Johnny turned. "Tell me sorry for what?"

Jack shook his head, put his face in his hands. "Cowardice is a sin."

Johnny stared at his friend, whose voice came out part sob.

"Would you say good things about me if somebody asked?" Jack ran a forearm under his nose. "Just a what-if, Johnny. If somebody asked? Would you say I'm a good friend? I've tried, you know. All those nights out with you. All those nights looking. I watched your back because I knew you wouldn't stop. I tried to keep you away from the bad houses, the really bad ones. I'd have died if you got hurt. The guilt would have killed me, Johnny. It would have straight up killed me."

"What about the rest of the guilt, Jack? What about Alyssa? You knew where she was? All this time?"

"Lies and weakness. Those are sins, too."

"Jack."

"God forgives the little sins."

"All this time."

"I tried to keep you safe." Jack rocked on the stone. "She was dead." He shook his head. "She was already dead."

"What happened to my sister?" Johnny stood over Jack, hands fisted. He was losing it. He was going to lose it. "What happened, Jack?"

Jack pulled in a deep, rough breath, kept his eyes on the water. "I loaned her my bike. That's all I did. I was trying to help. You've got to believe that."

"Tell me the rest of it."

"We were at the library, a bunch of us. You remember that project we had to do?" Johnny said nothing, so Jack nodded. "We were in the same group, Alyssa and me. Volcanoes. We were doing a report on volcanoes. It was late, just dark, you know. Everybody said it was time to go." He trailed off for a second. "I loaned her my bike because your dad forgot to come and get her. He forgot and it was getting dark. Gerald had a new truck and was looking for every excuse to drive it, so I gave her my bike and called my brother for a ride. That's all I did, Johnny. Nothing bad should have happened, see? I was trying to be good. That counts, right? That counts."

Jack ground at his eyes. Small hand. Normal hand. Both of them balled and shaking. "He said he wanted to scare her."

"Who?"

"It was supposed to be a joke."

"Gerald?" Johnny asked.

"She was pedaling so hard."

433

"Oh, no."

"Right on the edge of the pavement." A pause. "He just wanted to scare her."

"What happened, Jack?"

"He was drinking."

Johnny grabbed Jack by the shirt. He pulled and it tore. "What the fuck happened?"

"She looked back, and I guess it was the headlights, the closeness. I don't know. She lost it. Went down. She went under the truck. Gerald freaked. He called my father." Jack was crying. "She was dead, Johnny."

"I don't understand."

"Dead and gone. I wanted to tell, but Gerald was already being scouted by the pros."

"What does that have to do with anything?"

"Dad said if word got out, he could kiss all that goodbye."

"You lied because of Gerald's baseball career." Johnny was yelling, Jack shaking his head. "Then what?" Johnny said. "What?"

"I wanted to tell."

"But you didn't."

Jack was crying softly now. "Johnny."

"All this time."

Jack stood and staggered. He put out a hand, but Johnny knocked it down. "I tried."

"How did you try?"

"You remember I told you that Gerald broke my arm?" Jack was shaking, begging with his eyes. "It was my dad, Johnny. I told him I was going to tell and he broke my arm. He broke my arm in four places. He held me on the ground and made me swear." Jack got a hand on Johnny's arm. "He made me swear."

"Because of Gerald's career?"

"It's all they talk about." Johnny stared. "Gerald and my dad."

Johnny felt his stomach clench. He bent at the waist and turned away. His hand found a branch and he leaned against it. "You said Levi Freemantle told you where she was."

"Another lie."

"Then why now, Jack? Why tell now?"

"Because Freemantle was sent here for a reason."

"What reason?"

Jack was terrified. "God knows."

No crows, Johnny thought. *God knows.*

"He kept saying it. Even in his sleep, he said it. No crows. God knows. You remember the name of the mine shaft? No Croz. I can't get it out of my head, Johnny. God knows, don't you see? God knows what I did." Jack broke off. "The last thing Freemantle said to me . . . the last thing he said . . . Oh, shit."

"What?"

Jack sat down on the stone. "God knows the beauty of her soul." Jack raised his small hand. "I'm going to burn in hell, Johnny." The hand came down, and Jack was begging. "If somebody asked, would you say something good?"

He was weeping.

"Johnny?"

Johnny turned and climbed up the bank. Jack's voice followed him, small, then smaller.

"Johnny?"

Nothing. Wind in the grass.

"Johnny?"

435

CHAPTER SIXTY

Hunt drove fast, blue lights hot behind the grille. Yoakum, beside him, was iron-faced. The dashboard clock read ten after one in the morning. Hunt had arranged an emergency meeting with the district attorney and the magistrate. It took an hour, but he had an arrest warrant in his coat pocket and two hand-picked uniforms rolling backup. Nobody else knew. Not the Chief. No other cops. They were running this thing dark, just in case Cross had friends who would go to the mat. "Five minutes," Hunt said.

For the third time, Yoakum checked the loads in his borrowed gun.

Hunt's phone rang. He glanced at caller ID then answered. The call was brief, and when it was over, he did not look at Yoakum. "Medical examiner," he said. "Dental records match. It's Alyssa."

Silence. Rubber on pavement.

"I'm sorry, Clyde."

"Four minutes."

Thirty seconds later, Hunt's phone rang again. He didn't recognize the number on ID, but he answered it, then listened. "Where are you, Johnny? Settle down. I'm here. No. No. Take your time."

Hunt listened for a full minute, saying nothing. When the kid was finished, the last piece clicked into place and Hunt had the picture. All of it. A perfect fit. "Okay, Johnny. I've got it and I

436

will handle it. No, I will handle it tonight. Right now. Where are you?" A pause. "No. I don't want you in the lobby. I want you in the room, now. I have it covered. We'll talk tomorrow."

He hung up again and Yoakum waited ten seconds. "What?"

Hunt gave it to him in short, hard sentences. The way Alyssa died. How she ended up in that shaft.

Yoakum had to chew on it for a minute. "She died in an accident?"

"Gerald was drunk. Cross hid the body to protect his son. He dumped her in that shaft. All alone." He sucked in a deep breath. "Jesus."

"You okay?"

"We bring Gerald in, too."

"We don't have a warrant for Gerald."

"Suspicion of manslaughter. It's enough to question him."

"That Johnny's a tough kid," Yoakum said.

"Yes."

"Cross is so going down."

"One minute."

Hunt turned into Cross's neighborhood.

Johnny opened the motel room with the key card. Two lamps burned. His mother sat on the edge of the nearest bed. She was drawn but clear-eyed.

"I couldn't call Hunt," she said, and stood. "He would never let me have you back."

Johnny stepped in and closed the door.

"You left me," she said, and Johnny saw how rigid she held herself.

"I will never do it again."

"How can I believe that?"

"I promise."

437

She crossed the room and put her arms around him. "Promise me again."

Johnny smelled soap and clean hair. "I promise."

She squeezed him hard, and when she stepped back, Johnny told her what he knew. It wasn't easy, and it took some time. Alyssa was dead, but it was an accident. He explained it twice, and the words rolled off her lips.

An accident.

They were quiet for a long time after that.

Quiet but together.

Hunt got the domestic disturbance call when they were two blocks out. "Be advised, neighbor reports a weapon at the scene."

"Shit."

Hunt hit the siren and the patrol car behind him did the same. Two quick turns and Cross's house was up on the right. Lights burned at the roofline, big spots on the corners, lights on poles by the sidewalk. The white truck was nose-first and crumpled against the side of the house. Grass was torn up behind it, shrubbery plowed flat. One taillight blinked on and off. Red. Red. Red. Detective Cross was in the yard; so was his wife and Gerald. Cross was yelling. His wife was on her knees, Bible in hand, clenched in prayer.

Jack had the pistol.

He was pointing it at his father.

Hunt and Yoakum came out of the car the same time as the uniformed officers. Weapons came out. "Control your fire," Hunt said. "I know the kid. I don't want him hurt."

The other cops heard him, but the guns stayed up. Hunt kept his own weapon in the holster. He eased onto the grass, hands out to his side. Jack was flushed and shaking. Tears stained his face. Cross was playing the stern father. "Jack, you give me that gun right now! Right this minute! I mean it!" Cross saw Hunt coming and held out one hand. "I've got this," he said. "It's under control." Back to his son. "Jack, you see this? Somebody called the police. It's time for this to end. Give me the gun."

Behind him, Jack's mother was rocking on her knees. Jack looked at her, and one hand found a silver cross that hung around his neck. Her voice rose and it was like she was speaking in tongues. "Don't, Momma." Jack's face twisted. "Just don't." He tore off the cross and flung it at her.

"Give me the gun, Jack."

Jack tore his gaze from his mother. His father was closer, now. Five feet. Four. "It's your fault." Jack's voice was a whisper.

"Son."

He stabbed the gun at his father. "I'm going to hell, and it's your fault."

Jack stepped closer as his mother wailed. Cross raised his hands. "Son . . ."

"God forgives the little sins."

Hunt saw the hammer move, but he was too far away. "No." He ran for Jack. The hammer rose and fell; Cross screamed as it dropped with a dry click. Jack pulled the trigger again, but nothing happened.

Hunt took the kid down.

The gun flew out of his hand and Cross reached for it. "Don't touch that," Hunt told him. He was flat on the grass, Jack pinned beneath him. "Don't touch it and don't move."

"What do you mean?"

"None of you move." Hunt hauled Jack to his feet and handed him over to Yoakum. "Gently," he said, and Yoakum led the boy away, crying and snot-faced.

"I want to talk to Johnny." Jack struggled at the door of the car. He thrashed and yelled, "I want to talk to Johnny." Yoakum's hand on the top of his head. "Johnny! I want to talk to Johnny!"

The door closed, cutting him off, and he beat his head four times against the glass. Hunt picked up the gun and cracked the cylinder. Empty. He put the gun in his coat pocket. Cross risked a step, hands out. "He's drunk. He has a problem. We're getting him help."

"You need to come with me," Hunt said. "To the station."

"He's my son, Hunt. I'm not going to press charges." Cross tried a weak smile.

Hunt remained expressionless, which took work. "You and Gerald," Hunt said, hand very near his holstered weapon. "My asking is a courtesy." He gestured to the neighboring yards, where several people stood and watched. Hunt stepped closer but did not lower his voice. "I have the story from Jack. What happened to Alyssa. Gerald's involvement. Everything." Hunt gave him one heartbeat. "We found her body a few hours ago."

Cross looked at his son, his still weeping wife.

"Let's do this right," Hunt said.

When Cross looked back, the mask dropped off. His face was pure calculation. "I don't know what you're talking about."

"David Wilson found Alyssa's body. At first, I thought he must have called the station and talked to you by pure accident, but there was no record in the phone logs, and nobody gets that lucky."

"You're wrong."

"Save it. I talked to Patricia Defries tonight. She told me everything." And she had. Cross had busted her on another check fraud scam. That would be her third felony, her third strike. If convicted, she'd pull twelve years, minimum. So Cross

440

had made it easy for her. He wanted to know if anybody came around the mines. Anybody. Any time. She said she didn't know why Cross cared about the mines, and Hunt believed her; not that he told her that. He liked her talking, liked her scared.

Hunt said, "I explained to her that check fraud is a much smaller charge than accessory to murder before the fact. I made her know that I was serious, and that she would go down with you. She talked and she'll testify. She'll tell how you showed up at the mines after she called, how five minutes later, Wilson tore past on his dirt bike with you right on his tail. She made note of the time. Johnny Merrimon saw Wilson come over the bridge railing fifteen minutes later."

"She's a crook and a drunk. No kind of witness."

Hunt made a show of looking at the line of cars in the driveway. "Where's your personal vehicle?" he asked. "Dodge Charger, right? How many body shops will I have to call before I find it? It won't be local, of course. But Wilmington maybe? Raleigh? One of the big cities, I should think. But we'll find it. Damage to the front fender. The paint will match what we found at the bridge."

"I want a lawyer."

Hunt motioned for the uniformed officers. "You're under arrest for the murder of David Wilson. You have the right to remain silent—"

"I know my rights."

"Anything you say can and will be used against you."

"Wait a minute. Wait a minute." Cross licked his lips. "I need to talk to you. Just to you. Just for a second." Hunt hesitated. "You want to do the right thing, right? That's what you're all about, right? God damn Boy Scout." Hunt held up a hand and the uniforms backed off. "You should think about what you're doing. You should think real hard."

"I don't need to think. I have a warrant."

Cross leaned in. His eyes flashed at the uniforms over Hunt's shoulder and his whisper put hot breath in the air. "Your son was in the car, too."

Hunt stepped away. "He was not."

"He was in the front seat when Alyssa went under the tires."

"I don't believe you."

"How's he been the past year? Your boy? Normal? Same kid you had a year ago? Oh, let me guess. Sullen? Edgy? Gone dark on you, has he? Do the right thing, Hunt. Nothing more important than a man's family. That's what it's all about."

Hunt looked around the yard. Jack was a red splotch in the back of a cop car. Gerald was on the verge of tears. Cross's wife had her eyes closed as she rocked and begged and wailed. "I don't think your family is doing too well, Cross."

"He's your only child, right?"

Hunt held his gaze for three seconds.

"Do the right thing," Cross said.

Hunt stepped back and motioned to the uniformed officers. "You have the right to an attorney."

The cuffs came out.

Cross fought, and then went down, screaming. He lost his slippers as they dragged him to the car.

It was close to six when Hunt left the police station. Cross refused to talk, but the words spilled out of Gerald like a tide. It was guilt. Pure and simple.

The boy was eaten up.

The sun made a dim blush when the streets rose up, but Hunt's house was still in a pocket of dark. He let himself in and stood quietly in the kitchen. The refrigerator hummed. A garage door opened somewhere down the street.

Hunt put his gun on the counter, his badge. The stairs sighed

442

under his feet and he felt warm air when he opened the door to his son's room. The boy was a tangle of blankets, blond hair, and lost innocence.

The past.

So many good things.

Hunt pulled a chair next to the bed and sat. He pressed fingertips against his eyes and saw the same crazy sparks. This did not have to be an ending. There was power in choice. Hunt believed that. It was never too late to do the right thing.

His lips moved in silence.

Never too late.

Hunt watched his son sleep, and his lips moved again.

Repeating it.

A prayer of his own.

It took Allen twenty minutes to wake up, and they were the longest twenty minutes of Hunt's life. Twice he rose, but twice he stayed, until light, pale and pink, touched his son on the face. His eyes were very innocent when they opened. "Hey, Dad. What's going on?" He scrubbed at his face and sat up against the pillows.

"You know I love you, right?"

"Yeah. Sure. What—"

"If you were ever in trouble, I'd do everything in my power to help you. You know that, too. No matter how bad things are, I'm your dad. I'll help you. You know that, don't you, Allen?"

"Sure. Of course."

Hunt kept himself still. "Are you in trouble, son?"

"What? No."

Hunt leaned in. "Is there anything you need to tell me? Anything at all. I'm on your side. You and me. Okay?"

"No, Dad. Nothing. What's going on?"

Hunt was dying on the inside. He put a hand on his son's

443

arm. "I'm going to lie down for a while." He stood, looked down. "It's a big day, Allen."

"What do you mean?"

Hunt stopped in the door. "I'll be awake if you need me."

Hunt crossed the hall and stretched out on his own bed. For a moment, the room spun, but he fought it.

The knock came sooner than he'd dared to hope.

CHAPTER SIXTY-ONE

Johnny slept for seven hours, woke briefly to eat, then went back down. He heard his mother, once, talking to Hunt, but it felt like a dream. He heard angry voices and the sound of something breaking. There was talk of Alyssa and of Hunt's son.

"I don't know what to say, Katherine."

That was Hunt.

A long silence. "I need to take a walk."

"Katherine . . ."

"Will you stay with Johnny?"

The door closed and Johnny woke. It was not a dream. Hunt stood at the window watching her walk away. Johnny sat up and the dream came back to him. "Was Allen really in the car with Gerald?"

"You heard?"

"Is it true?"

"Allen wasn't driving."

"But he knew what happened and didn't tell."

"Gerald's dad was a cop and Allen was scared, but I can't make excuses for him, Johnny. He was wrong." A pause. "He turned himself in voluntarily. He's in custody. He'll be punished. So will Jack."

"Punished, how?"

"It's up to the juvenile courts. They may go away for a while."

"Prison?"

"It's not like that."

Johnny got out of bed. "I'm going to take a shower," he said.

"Okay, Johnny."

The water was weak but hot. Johnny washed twice, then studied the stitches in his chest. The skin was red and puckered; the scars would last forever. He combed his hair with his mother's comb. Hunt was still in the room when Johnny came out.

"Better?" Hunt asked.

"She's still gone?"

"She's trying to decide if she hates me."

Johnny nodded. It was a very grown-up thing for Hunt to say. "May I ask you a question?"

"Yes."

They sat side by side on the edge of the bed. Johnny's fingers were shriveled from the long shower. His palms peeled where a blister had burst. "Jack believes that some things happen for a reason."

"Are you asking about Alyssa?"

Johnny wasn't sure he could say what he meant, so he shrugged. He felt Hunt tense, then relax, like he'd made a decision.

"We found seven bodies buried in the woods behind Jarvis's house. Children. Did you know that?"

"Mom told me."

Hunt hesitated again, then pulled a photograph from his coat pocket. It was Meechum's autopsy photo. It showed him from the chest up, undressed on a metal table. "Is this the man you saw with Jarvis?"

His face had hollowed out in death and he had no color at all, but Johnny recognized him. He nodded.

446

"Why did you think he was a cop?"

"He carried handcuffs and a pistol on his belt. That's what cops do."

Hunt put the photo away. "He was a security guard at the mall. He and Jarvis served together in Vietnam. Both got dishonorable discharges at the same time. There were rumors—"

"What kind of rumors?"

"Bad ones."

Johnny shrugged. He'd heard the stories anyway.

"They were bad men, Johnny. They did bad things for evil reasons and they would have kept on doing them if you hadn't come along when you did."

"I didn't save Tiffany. I told you that."

Hunt stared through the window. "If Jarvis had not been busy with you on the street, Tiffany would not have made it past the house. He'd have caught her and he'd have killed her. She'd be in the woods with the rest of them. Jarvis and Meechum would have kept on killing. Maybe they'd have killed a few more. Maybe they'd have killed a lot more. What I do know is that they were stopped because you were on that street when you were."

Johnny felt Hunt's eyes on the top of his head, but he could not look up.

"You would not have been on the street if Alyssa hadn't died." Hunt laid a hand on Johnny's shoulder. "Maybe that's the reason, Johnny. Maybe, Alyssa had to die so other kids would not."

"Jack thought Freemantle came because God sent him."

"Jack has problems no kid should have."

"He thought God sent crows to scare him, and sent Freemantle to make him face the truth of what he'd done."

"I know nothing about that, Johnny."

"The last time I prayed, I asked God for three things. I asked him for an end of pills, and for my family to come home. Those things have happened."

"That's two things."

Johnny looked up, and his face was marble. "I prayed for Ken Holloway to die. I prayed for him to die a slow and terrible death." He paused, dark eyes shining. "I prayed for him to die in fear."

Hunt opened his mouth, but Johnny spoke before he could say anything. He pictured Ken Holloway's eyes as the light died in them. He saw the crow shadows rise, the flicker of dark. "Levi Freemantle gave that to me," Johnny said. "I think *that's* why God sent him."

Hunt had a late meeting with his son's lawyer, then found himself parked in front of the jail, a blunt, graceless building that filled a full city block not far from the courthouse. Allen was in there, somewhere. He'd handled it well, Hunt thought; tears as he told his father—regret and shame and guilt—then courage as they'd gone to the police station together. Hunt's last memory was of his son's face as a steel door swung shut between them.

He turned off the engine and walked to the jail's main entrance. He checked his weapon and was buzzed in. He knew the guards, and the guards knew him. He got a pat on the back, a few sympathetic nods, at least one cold stare. "I need to see him."

The guard behind the desk was square and soft-spoken. "You know I can't do that."

Hunt knew it. "Can you give him a message?"

"Sure."

"Will you tell him that I'm here?"

The guard leaned back. "I'll make sure he gets the message."

448

"Tell him now," Hunt said. "Not that I *was* here. Tell him that I *am* here."

"It's that important?"

"There's a difference," Hunt said. "I'll wait."

When Hunt left the jail, he sat on a bench two blocks away. The sky was high and starless. Home was a shell. After a few minutes, his phone rang. It was Trenton Moore. "Did I wake you?" he asked.

"Not much chance of that."

A pause. "I heard about your son. I'm sorry."

"Thanks, Doc. I appreciate that. Are you calling for some other reason?"

"As a matter of fact, I am." He cleared his throat and seemed strangely reluctant. "Umm. Do you have a minute?"

The medical examiner worked out of the hospital basement. Hunt had never liked going there, especially at night. Lighting was sparse in the long hall in. The concrete seemed to sweat. Hunt passed the viewing room, the refrigerator banks, the quiet rooms, and the silent dead. Dr. Moore was in his office, dictating, when Hunt tapped on the door frame. Moore looked up, and excitement kindled in his eyes. "Come in, come in." He put down the Dictaphone and reached for a coffeepot on the credenza behind him. "Coffee?"

"Sure. Black. Thanks."

He poured coffee into short Styrofoam cups, handed one to Hunt. "First of all," Moore said, "I should give you these." He pulled a plastic evidence bag from a drawer and tossed it on the desk. It landed heavily and metal gleamed.

Hunt picked it up and saw that it was sealed and dated, signed by the medical examiner. He rolled the bag on his palm and counted six bullets with stainless casings and divots in the tips. "Let me guess, .32 caliber hollow points?"

"From Mr. Freemantle's right front pocket. Other than his clothing, that's the only property he had on his person at the time of death."

"Well, that answers a question."

"Which is?"

"Why a certain ex-cop is still breathing, and more important, maybe, why his thirteen-year-old kid's not charged with murder." Hunt slipped the evidence bag into his coat pocket. "Thanks."

"Don't mention it." They sipped coffee and the silence spooled out. "Speaking of questions." Moore rolled forward in his chair. He was small and compressed, so full of energy he could barely sit still. "There are very few mysteries in what I do, Detective. Unanswered questions? Yes, all the time. But no mysteries. The human body, alas, is a very predictable instrument. Follow the damage and it leads you places, leads you to conclusions, determinations of cause and effect." The energy flared again in Moore's eyes, the excitement. "Do you have any idea how many autopsies I've performed?"

"No."

"Neither do I, but it's a lot. Hundreds. More, maybe. I really should count them up some day."

Hunt sipped his coffee. Normally, he'd be irritated, but he had nowhere to go.

Moore drummed fingers on the desk, eyes alight, skin flushed. "Do you believe in mysteries, Detective?" Hunt opened his mouth but Moore waved him off. "Not the kind of mysteries that you deal with every day." He leaned over the desk and cupped his hands as if holding a small world between them. "Big mysteries, Detective. Real ones. Large ones."

"I'm not sure I understand."

"I'd like to show you something." Moore lifted a file folder and rose. He crossed the room and flipped a switch on the X-ray viewer. Light flickered, then steadied. "Beyond a small note in the report, I debated sharing this." A nervous laugh. "I have my reputation to think about." Moore took an X-ray from the folder and snapped it into the viewer. Hunt recognized the structure of a human torso. Bones that seemed to glow. Amorphous hints of organs. "Levi Freemantle," Moore said. "Adult male. Forty-three years of age. Heavy musculature. Massive infection. Borderline malnutrition. See this?" He touched the image. "This is where you shot him. Bullet entered here. Fractured scapula at the exit wound. See?"

"I didn't mean to kill him."

"You didn't kill him."

"What do you mean?"

Moore ignored the question. "This." He traced a rough white line with his smallest finger. "This is a tree branch, a hardwood of some sort. Oak, maple. Not my area. The subject impaled himself somehow. The limb was brittle, not rotten. Jagged. See these sharp edges. Here and here. It's hard to tell from this image, but it's about twice the diameter of your index finger. Maybe a thumb and a half. It entered here, just below the lowest rib on the right side, then angled in such a way that it pierced the liver through and through. It did damage to multiple organs and tore a three-centimeter perforation in the large intestine."

"I don't understand."

"This is massive trauma, Detective."

"Okay."

Moore stepped away, then back. He raised both hands and Hunt sensed his frustration. "This—" He moved his hands over the X-ray, then stopped. "This is a fatal injury. Without immediate surgery, this is fatal. He should have been dead days before you shot him." Moore raised his hands again. "I can't explain it."

A cool finger touched Hunt between the shoulder blades. The hospital pressed down. He pictured Moore's eager eyes, his questions about large mysteries. "Are you saying it's a miracle?"

Moore looked at the X-ray, and the light put a cold white sheen on his face. He laid three fingers on the line of jagged wood that pierced Freemantle's side. "I'm saying that I can't explain it."

CHAPTER SIXTY-TWO

Social Services came for Johnny the next day. He held his mother's hand as two case officers stood by the car's open door. Heat rolled off the parking lot. Cars flew by on the four-lane. "You're hurting my fingers," Johnny whispered.

His mother loosened her grip and spoke to Hunt. "Is there no other way?"

Hunt was equally subdued. "With all that's happened. The violence. The media. They have no choice." He stooped and looked Johnny in the eye. "It's just for a while. I'll speak on your mother's behalf. We'll make this right."

"Promise?"

"Yes."

Johnny looked at the car and one of the ladies offered a smile. He gave his mother a hug. "I'll be okay," he said. "It'll be like doing time."

He got in the car. And that's how it was for the next month. Like doing time. The family they gave him to was kind but detached. They treated him like a hard word might break him, yet conspired to act as if nothing unusual had happened. They were unfailingly polite; but he caught them at night, watching the news reports, reading the papers. They'd shake their heads and ask each other: "What does something like that do to a boy?" Johnny thought they probably slept with their door locked. He thought of the looks they would give if, just once, late at night, he rattled the knob.

The court ordered Johnny to see a psychologist, and so he did, but the guy was an idiot. Johnny told him what he needed to hear. He described made-up dreams of domestic boredom and claimed to sleep through the night. He swore that he no longer believed in the power of things unseen, not totems or magic or dark birds that steal the souls of the dead. He had no desire to shoot anyone, no desire to harm himself or others. He expressed honest emotion about the deaths of his father and sister. That was grief, pure gut-wrenching loss. He loved his mother. That, too, was truth. Johnny watched the shrink nod and make notes. Then he didn't have to go anymore.

Just like that.

They let Johnny see his mother once a week for supervised visitation. They'd go to the park, sit in the shade. Each week, she brought Jack's letters. He wrote at least one a day, sometimes more. He never discussed how bad it was in the place they'd sent him. Never about his hours, his days. Jack talked most of regret and shame and of how Johnny was the only good thing in his life. He talked of things they'd done together, plans they'd made for the future. And he begged to be forgiven. That's how he ended all of his letters.

Johnny, please.

Tell me we're friends.

Johnny read every letter, but never responded. They filled a shoe box under the bed at his foster house.

"You should write him back," his mother told him once.

"After what happened? After what he did?"

"He's your best friend. His father broke his arm. Think about that."

Johnny shook his head. "There were a million times he could have told me. A million ways."

"He's young, Johnny. You're both so very young."

Johnny stared at the court-appointed monitor while the idea rolled in his mind. "Did you forgive Detective Hunt's son?"

She followed Johnny's gaze. The monitor sat at a nearby picnic table. She was hot in a blue suit too heavy for the season. "Hunt's son?" she asked, voice distant. "He seems very young, too."

"Are you seeing Detective Hunt?"

"Your father's funeral is tomorrow, Johnny. How could I be seeing anyone?"

"It would be okay, I think."

His mother squeezed his arm and stood. "It's time." The court monitor was approaching. "You have the suit?" she asked. "The tie?"

"Yes."

"Do you like them?"

"Yes."

They had a few seconds left. The next time they were together, it would be to bury the ones they loved most. The monitor stopped a few feet away. She gestured at her watch, and her face reflected something like regret.

Johnny's mother turned away, eyes bright. "I'll pick you up early."

Johnny took her hand and squeezed. "I'll be ready."

The funeral was a double service. Father and daughter, side by side. Hunt called in favors and had the cemetery cordoned off to protect the family from the idle curious, the press. The priest was not the same fat, red-faced priest that Johnny remembered in such poor light. This was a young man, thin and serious, a blade of a priest in white, flashing robes. He spoke of choice and the power of God's love.

Power.

He made the word sing, so that Johnny nodded when he said it.

455

The *power* of God's love.

Johnny nodded but kept his eyes on the coffins and on the high blue sky.

The high, empty sky.

Three weeks after the funeral, Katherine stood in the yard of a well-maintained two-bedroom house. It had a covered front porch, two bathrooms, and the largest, greenest yard she could find. The kitchen was newly remodeled. Down the street was the house that Johnny had lived in all of his life, minus the last year or so. She'd hoped to buy that one, but the life insurance from her late husband had to last until she figured what to do with her life. How to make a living for her and her son.

She stared down the street, then let it go. This place had a tree house, a creek that ran through the backyard.

It would be enough.

When Hunt came out of the house, his shirt was wet with sweat. A tuft of fiberglass insulation sprouted from the back of his head. He turned and looked back at the house. "It's solid," he said. "It's nice."

"You think Johnny will like it?"

"I think so. Yes."

Katherine dipped her head. "Johnny comes home tomorrow. We'll need some time, you know. Just the two of us. Time to find some kind of rhythm."

"Of course."

"But in a month or so, I thought maybe you might come over for dinner."

"That would be nice, too."

Katherine nodded, nervous and scared and uncertain. She turned and looked at the house. "It really is okay, isn't it?"

Hunt kept his eyes on her face. "It's perfect."

EPILOGUE

Summer heat was a fading memory when Johnny and his mother drove to Hush Arbor. It was Saturday, late afternoon. The trees towered over the car as she drove. Ahead, sunlight pushed through, and they could see granite posts and blackberry brambles. "I can't believe you came out here like you did."

"Chill, Mom."

"Anything could happen way out here."

Johnny pointed. "The cemetery is that way." She drove as far as she could, then they got out. Johnny led her through the cut in the trees. "Detective Hunt says he was buried here last week. Some friend of his mother paid for it." They walked farther. The paint on the fence was still white. The grass was long and gone to seed. "I should come out and mow sometime."

"Please, don't," she said, but Johnny was already thinking about it.

They walked to where Levi Freemantle was buried. The earth was freshly turned. His daughter was beside him, and she, too, had a new stone. "Sofia," Johnny said. "That was her name." They looked at Freemantle's headstone. It gave the dates of his birth and death. The inscription was simple.

Levi Freemantle
Last Child of Isaac

"I counted headstones," Johnny said. "The night I spent out here. There are three for those who were hanged." Johnny pointed to the small, rough stones at the base of the giant oak. "And forty-three descendants of Isaac Freemantle. Forty-five, now." They looked across the rows of weathered stone. "If Isaac had been killed, hung like the others, then none of them would have lived or died."

"Your great-great-grandfather was an exceptional man." A pause. "So was your dad." Johnny nodded, unable to speak. She went on, "Ken Holloway was as bad, that day, as I'd ever seen him." She rubbed at her wrists, where scars still showed the deep bite of piano wire. "We might have died without Levi Freemantle."

Silence. Sunlight on new-cut marble.

"He told me life is a circle."

His mother looked at the trees, the rows of stone. She put an arm around Johnny's shoulders.

"Maybe it is."

That night, Johnny wrote to Jack. He told him everything that had happened in the months that he'd been gone. It took ten pages to do it. He addressed it to Jack Cross, My Friend.

Read the opening chapter of
John Hart's acclaimed first novel

THE KING OF LIES

'*Presumed Innocent* meets *Fatal Attraction* . . . Hart's
prose is like Raymond Chandler's, angular and hard'
Entertainment Weekly

Jackson Workman Pickens – 'Work' to his friends – an
unambitious lawyer in a small southern town, has some
serious baggage. His mother died a year ago from a 'fall' down
the family's colonial staircase, and his father, Ezra, has been
missing ever since. Work is left to deal with his psychologically
damaged sister, his father's legal caseload and his own
rocky marriage.

Power and greed bring many enemies, especially for a man
as cruel as Ezra Pickens, so when his body turns up pretty much
everyone in town is a suspect – but only one man is charged
with the murder. With time, his wife and public opinion against
him, Work embarks on his toughest case yet: proving his own
innocence. His investigation uncovers a web of intrigue he could
never have imagined, and he soon realizes that no one is above
suspicion – even those he loves most.

'Akin to the close-range gut-roiling atmosphere
summoned by the legal thrillers of Scott Turow'
New York Times

Available in paperback from John Murray

CHAPTER ONE

I've heard it said that jail stinks of despair. What a load. If jail stinks of any emotion, it's fear: fear of the guards, fear of being beaten or gang-raped, fear of being forgotten by those who once loved you and may or may not anymore. But mostly, I think, it's fear of time and of those dark things that dwell in the unexplored corners of the mind. Doing time, they call it—what a joke. I've been around long enough to know the reality: It's the time that does you.

For some time, I'd been bathed in that jailhouse perfume, sitting knee-to-knee with a client who'd just gotten life without parole. The trial had damned him, as I'd told him it would. The state's evidence was overwhelming, and the jury had zero sympathy for a three-time loser who had shot his brother during an argument about who'd get control of the remote. Twelve of his supposed peers, and not one cared that he'd been drinking, that he was cracked to the gills, or that he didn't mean to do it. No one cared that his brother was an ass and a felon in his own right, not the jury and least of all me. All I wanted was to explain his appeal rights, answer any legal questions, and get the hell out. My fee application to the state of North Carolina would wait until the morning.

On most days I was ambivalent, at best, about my chosen profession, but on days like this I hated being a lawyer; that hatred ran so deep that I feared something must be wrong with me. I hid it as others would a perversion. And this day was worse than most. Maybe it was the case or the client or the emotional aftermath of one more needless tragedy. I'd been in that room a hundred times, but for some reason it felt different this time. The walls seemed to shift and I felt a momentary disorientation. I tried to shake it off, cleared my throat, and stood. We'd had bad facts, but the decision to go to trial had not been mine to make. When he'd stumbled from the trailer, bloody and weeping, he'd had the gun in one hand, the remote control in the other. It was broad daylight and he was out-of-his-head drunk. The neighbor looked out the window when my client started screaming. He saw the blood, the gun, and called the cops. No lawyer could have won the trial—I'd told him as much. I could have had him out in ten, but he refused to take the plea arrangement I'd negotiated. He wouldn't even talk about it.

The guilt may have been too much, or perhaps some part of him needed the punishment. Whatever the case, it was over now.

He finally tore his gaze from the jail-issue flip-flops that had known a thousand feet before his and forced his eyes to mine. Wet nostrils shone in the hard light, and his red eyes jittered, terrified of whatever they saw in that jigsaw mind of his. He'd pulled the trigger, and that brutal truth had finally taken root. The trail had wound its way across his face as we'd talked for the past few hours. His denials had sputtered to a halt, and I'd watched, untouchable, as hope shriveled and died. I'd seen it all before.

A sopping wet cough, his right forearm smearing mucus across his cheek. "So that's it, then?" he asked.

I didn't bother to answer. He was already nodding to himself and I could see his thoughts as if written in the dank air that hung between us: life without parole and him not yet

461

twenty-three. It generally took days for this brutal truth to bore through the bullshit tough-guy act that every dumb-ass killer carried into this place like some kind of sick birthright. Maybe this joker was smarter than I'd given him credit for. In the brief time since the judge handed down his sentence, he'd grown the lifer stare. Fifty, maybe sixty years behind the same redbrick walls. No chance of parole. Not twenty years, not thirty or even forty, but life, in caps. It would kill me, and that is God's own truth.

A glance at my watch told me I'd been in there for almost two hours, which was my limit. I knew from experience that the smell had by now permeated my clothes, and I could see the dampness where his hands had pawed at my jacket. He saw the watch come up and he lowered his eyes. His words evaporated in the still air, leaving a vacuum that my body settled into as I stood. I didn't reach to shake his hand and he didn't reach for mine, but I noticed a new palsy in his fingers.

He was old before his time, all but broken at twenty-three, and what might have been sympathy wormed into a heart I'd thought forever beyond such things. He started to cry, and his tears fell to the filthy floor. He was a killer, no question, but he was going to hell on earth first thing the next morning. Almost against my will, I reached out and put a hand on his shoulder. He didn't look up, but he said that he was sorry, and I knew that this time he truly was. I was his last touch with the real world, the one with trees. All else had been pared away by the razor-sharp reality of his sentence. His shoulders began to heave beneath my hand, and I felt a nothingness so great, it almost had physical weight. That's where I was when they came to tell me that my father's body had finally been found. The irony was not lost on me.

The bailiff who escorted me out of the Rowan County Jail

and to the office of the district attorney was a tall, wide-boned man with gray bristles where most of us have hair. He didn't bother to make small talk as we wound through the halls packed with courthouse penitents, and I didn't push it. I'd never been much of a talker.

The district attorney was a short, disarmingly round man who could turn off his eye's natural twinkle at will; it was an amazing thing to watch. To some, he was a politician, open and warm. To others, he was the cold, lifeless instrument of his office. For a few of us behind the curtain, he was a regular guy; we knew him and liked him. He'd taken two bullets for his country, yet he never looked down on people like myself, what my father had often called "the soft underbelly of a warless generation." He respected my father, but he liked me as a person, and I'd never been sure why. Maybe because I didn't shout the innocence of my guilty clients the way most defense lawyers did. Or maybe because of my sister, but that was a whole different story.

"Work," he said as I entered the room, not bothering to get up. "I'm damn sorry about this. Ezra was a great lawyer."

The only son of Ezra Pickens, I was known to a few as Jackson Workman Pickens. Everybody else liked to call me "Work," which was humorous I guess.

"Douglas." I nodded, turning at the sound of the office door closing behind me as the bailiff left. "Where'd you find him?" I asked.

Douglas tucked a pen into his shirt pocket and took the twinkle from his eye. "This is unusual, Work, so don't look for any special treatment. You're here because I thought you should hear it from me before the story breaks." He paused, looked out the window. "I thought maybe you could tell Jean."

"What does my sister have to do with this?" I asked, aware

463

that my voice sounded loud in the cramped, cluttered space. His eyes swiveled onto me and for a moment we were strangers.

"I don't want her to read about it in the papers. Do you?" His voice had chilled; the moment had not played well. "This is a courtesy call, Work. I can't go beyond the fact that we've found his body."

"It's been eighteen months since he disappeared, Douglas, a long damn time with nothing but questions, whispers, and the looks that people give when they think you can't tell. Do you have any idea how hard this has been?"

"I'm not unsympathetic, Work, but it doesn't change anything. We haven't even finished working the crime scene. I can't discuss the case with a member of the defense bar. You know how bad that would look."

"Come on, Douglas. This is my father, not some nameless drug dealer." He was clearly unmoved. "For God's sake, you've known me my whole life."

It was true—he had known me since I was a kid—but if there was any cause for sentiment, it failed to reach the surface of his lightless eyes. I sat down and rubbed a palm across my face, smelling the jailhouse stink that lingered there and wondering if he smelled it, too.

"We can do the rounds," I continued in a softer tone, "but you know that telling me is the right thing."

"We're calling it murder, Work, and it's going to be the biggest story to hit this county in a decade. That puts me in a tough spot. It'll be a media frenzy."

"I need to know, Douglas. This has hit Jean the hardest. She's not been the same since that night—you've seen it. If I'm going to tell her about our father's death, I'll need to give her some details; she'll want them. Hell, she'll need them. But most of all, I need to know how bad it is. I'll need to prepare her. Like you said, she shouldn't read it in the paper." I paused, took in a breath, and focused. I needed to visit the crime scene, and for that I needed his agreement. "Jean needs to be handled just right."

He steepled his fingers under his chin, as I'd seen him do a thousand times, but Jean was my trump, and he knew it. My sister had shared a special friendship with the DA's daughter. They'd grown up together, best friends, and Jean was in the same car when a drunk driver crossed the centerline and hit them head-on. Jean suffered a mild concussion; his daughter was nearly decapitated. It was one of those things, they said, and it could just as easily have been the other way around. Jean sang at her funeral, and the sight of her could pull tears from Douglas's eyes even now. She'd grown up under his roof and, apart from myself, I doubted that any one person felt her pain the way Douglas did.

The silence stretched out, and I knew that my arrow had slipped through this one small chink in his armor. I pressed on before he could think too much.

"It's been a long time. Are you sure it's him?"

"It's Ezra. The coroner is on-scene now and he'll make the official call, but I've spoken with Detective Mills and she assures me that it's him."

"I want to see where it happened."

That stopped him, caught him with his mouth open. I watched as he closed it.

"Once the scene is cleared—"

"Now, Douglas. Please."

Maybe it was something in my face, or maybe it was a lifetime of knowing me and ten years of liking me. Maybe it was Jean after all. Whatever the reason, I beat the odds.

"Five minutes," he said. "And you don't leave Detective Mills's side."

Mills met me in the parking lot of the abandoned mall where the body had been found, and she was not pleased. She radiated pissed-off from the bottom of her expensive shoes to the top of her mannish haircut. She had a pointed face, which emphasized her look of natural suspicion; because of this, it was impossible for anyone to find her beautiful, but she had a good figure. She was in her midthirties—about my age—yet lived alone and always had. Contrary to speculation around the lawyers' lounge, she wasn't gay. She just hated lawyers, which made her okay in my book.

"You must have kissed the DA's ass to get this, Work. I can't even believe I've agreed to it." Mills stood only five five or so but seemed taller. What she lacked in physical strength, she made up for in smarts. I'd seen her shred more than one of my colleagues who had presumed to challenge her on cross.

"I told him I won't leave your side, and I won't. I just need to see. That's all."

She studied me in the gray afternoon light and her animosity seemed to drain away. The sight of a softening expression in a face rigorously trained against such things was vaguely repellant, yet I appreciated it nonetheless.

"Stay behind me and touch nothing. I mean it, Work. Not one damn thing."

She began a purposeful stride across the cracked, weed-filled parking lot, and for a moment I was unable to follow. My eyes moved over the mall, the parking lot, and then found the creek. It was a dirty creek, choked with litter and red clay; it flowed into a concrete tunnel that ran underneath the parking lot. I could still remember the stink of it, the chemical reek of gasoline and mud. For an instant, I forgot why I'd come.

466

It could have happened yesterday, I thought.

I heard Mills call my name and I tore my eyes away from that dark place and the childhood it had come to represent. I was thirty-five now and here for a very different reason. I walked away from it, walked to Mills, and together we approached what had once been the Towne Mall. Even in its prime, it had been ugly, a prefab strip mall sandwiched between the interstate and a power-transfer station that chewed at the sky with towers and high-tension lines. Built in the late sixties, it had struggled for years with imminent closure. Only a third of the stores had had tenants as of a year ago, and the last one had fled with winter. Now the place crawled with bulldozers, wrecking balls, and itinerant workers, one of whom, according to Mills, had located the body in a storage closet at the back of one of the stores.

I wanted the details and she gave them to me in short, bitten sentences that the warm spring breeze could not soften.

"At first all he saw were ribs, and he thought they were dog bones." She threw me a glance. "Not bones that a dog would eat, but a dog skeleton."

I nodded foolishly, as if we weren't talking about my father. To my right, a hydraulic jackhammer gnawed concrete. To my left, the land rose to the heart of downtown Salisbury; the buildings there seemed to gleam, as if made of gold, and in a sense they were. Salisbury was a rich town, with a lot of old money and a fair amount of new. But in places, the beauty was thin as paint and could barely hide the cracks; for there was poverty here, too, although many pretended there was not.

Mills lifted the yellow crime-scene tape and ushered me underneath. We entered the mall through what used to be a double door, now a ragged mouth with crushed cinder-block teeth. We moved past boarded-up storefronts to the last in the

467

row. The door was open beneath a sign that read NATURE'S OWN: PETS AND EXOTICA. Nothing more exotic than rats had been behind those plywood sheets for years—rats and the decaying corpse of Ezra Pickens, my father.

The power was off, but the crime-scene unit had set up portable spotlights. I recognized the coroner, whose pinched face I would forever remember from the night my mother died. He refused to meet my eyes, which was unsurprising. There had been many difficult questions that night. From the rest, I got a few polite nods, but most of the cops, I could tell, weren't happy to see me. Nevertheless, they moved aside as Mills guided me through the dusty store to the closet at the back. My gut told me that they moved out of respect for Mills and my father more than they did for any grief they might imagine me to feel.

And just like that, there he was, ribs gleaming palely through a long rip in a shirt that I had forgotten but now remembered quite well. He looked something like a broken crucifix, with one arm outflung and his legs folded together. Most of his face lay hidden beneath what looked to be a candy striper's shirt still on its hanger, but I saw a porcelain stretch of jawbone and remembered whiskers there, pale and wet under a streetlamp on the last night I saw him alive.

I felt eyes upon me, and they pulled me away. I looked at the gathering of eager cops; some were merely curious, while others, I knew, sought their own secret satisfaction. They all wanted to see it, my face, a defense attorney's face, here in this musty place where murder was more than a case file, where the victim was flesh and blood, the smell that of family gone to dust.

I felt their eyes. I knew what they wanted, and so I turned to look again upon the almost empty clothes, the flash of bone so pale and curving. But I would give them nothing, and my body did not betray me, for which I was grateful. For what I felt was the return of a long-quiescent rage, and the certain conviction that this was the most human my father had ever appeared to me.

Read more ...

John Hart

DOWN RIVER

Winner of the 2008 Edgar Best Novel Award

Going back is never easy . . .

Adam Chase spent years in New York, trying to forget. Until a phone call from his best friend summoned him home. Within hours of returning, Adam is beaten up, accosted and has to face the hostility of old friends, enemies and the woman he cannot forget.

And then people start turning up dead. For a man only just acquitted of murder, Adam's homecoming does not go well. As the past threatens to overshadow the present, only he can clear his name . . .

'Grisham style intrigue and Turow style brooding' *New York Times*

'Hart's fast-driven narrative is exciting' *Sunday Telegraph*

'A beautifully written drama' *Literary Review*

'Atmospheric' *The Times*

'Explores betrayal and forgiveness in indelible prose' *Observer*

'Hart's prose is like Raymond Chandler's, angular and hard' *Entertainment Weekly*